A Passing Storm

B G Lawson

To Matthew.
with fondest wishes

Bernard.

Good luck pal.

Published by YouWriteOn.com, 2010

A CIP catalogue record for this title is available from the British
Library.

For Jane, who asks for so little and gives so much.

My thanks to my editor and proofreader: Lauren Saunders

Also for the cover design: Steven Paull

Part One

Chapter 1

1916

For her second interview Elizabeth wore a thin cotton dress, cream stockings and plain cream leather shoes. Her boater sat squarely above her silky, copper hair, which shimmered in the light from the window each time she moved her head.

Around her in the waiting room, other young ladies sat the latest fashion; layers of silk or Egyptian linen, buttoned boots and gloved hands clutching parasols, each glittering in her grandmother's jewels. The earlier disapproving glances thrown at Elizabeth's simple attire were now looks of envy, as these young ladies paid for their vanity in the heat of the room. It was September and the early morning haze gave ample warning that the day would be hot; now all but a few delicately dabbed her forehead, or subtly ran a handkerchief across her top lip.

Nervous fidgeting stopped when the door opened. 'Please pay attention,' a woman dressed in khaki said. 'The names I shall call out will remain seated. The rest may leave. Thank you all for coming.' Elizabeth suppressed a smile when her name was called.

'Congratulations to each of you for reaching this stage,' the woman said to the eight young ladies left in the room. 'However, we only have six places available for this intake, so I'm afraid two of you will be disappointed. The commandant will make the final decision, so make an impression, remain sharp. If you wish to stretch your legs for five minutes, do so. Miss Abraham,' she said, looking for a raised hand, 'the commandant will see you first.' The woman left the room, followed by one of the candidates, an elegant young woman dressed in white, Irish linen.

'Phew,' said one of the applicants, turning to Elizabeth, 'what a strain and it's so hot. I don't know whether I can stick it.' Elizabeth gave the girl a sympathetic smile. 'I do hope they accept me,' the girl whispered, 'it will make my mother so proud me serving the flag.'

'I shouldn't tell the commandant that.'

The girl's face coloured. 'Wouldn't your mother be proud?'

'She doesn't know I'm here.'

Elizabeth returned to her book. She glanced up when the door opened. The young lady in white linen rejoined them. Elizabeth's eyes followed her to her seat. When they had first assembled the previous day, their eyes had met, yet not a muscle had moved in the other's face in response to Elizabeth's smile.

A few moments later the door opened again. 'Right Miss Abraham, let's be having you. Miss Hodges, you'll follow.'

For the next hour and a half the room began to empty. It was a voice speaking her name that lifted Elizabeth's eyes from her book to the only other person left in the room with her. It was the girl in white linen. 'I asked if your name is Turner.'

'Yes it is.'

'My name is Fitzclarence. So, you're the blue stocking,' she said with a purr. Isabella Fitzclarence seemed to relish the blush that coloured Elizabeth's cheeks and nodded towards Voltaire on her lap. 'That's not exactly a Penny Dreadful. Translation, is it?'

'No,' Elizabeth said, slipping the book into her bag. 'One would lose the heartbeat of the writer in translation.'

'I don't know anything about that. I'm not an Oxford grad.'

'How do you know so much about me?'

'I was round the back having a gasper. They were arguing about you in there before the others began to go in. Heard them through the open window as a matter of fact.'

'Arguing?'

'Yes arguing, about you. Good sign though, don't you think?'

'No! It suggests a difference of opinion,' Elizabeth said screwing up her face. Her eyes lifted to Isabella. 'Do you always eavesdrop on other people's conversations, Miss Fitzclarence?'

Isabella's face brightened. 'Oh yes, often. Don't you?'

Elizabeth followed the young woman's well-tutored steps round the room and felt a critical gaze from her as she passed. Isabella stopped at the photographs on the wall. She studied the First Aid Nursing Yeomanry personnel standing by their ambulances in a foot of snow, heavily wrapped in sheepskin coats, then, after a minute, she turned to Elizabeth. 'You've lost someone, haven't you? I see it in your eyes. Is that why you've applied?' Isabella watched Elizabeth lower her head as if about to pray. 'Two of them in there think you're too young, too bookish. How old are you?'

Elizabeth's voice was a whisper. 'Twenty.'

'Did you let them know that?'

'Yes.'

'You could have fibbed, old thing. They're strict about age.'

Elizabeth winced at the upper-class accent. 'I'm still on the short list.' Although Elizabeth never mixed socially with toffs, there was something about Isabella that was different from those she had met at Oxford. 'Are they taking you on?'

'Didn't hang around for that. Look, I'm sorry if I hit a nerve. I've lost somebody too. Brother, Ypres; absolutely destroyed my parents. I bet every girl in this room has a similar story.'

The door opened. 'Lady Isabella.'

Isabella turned to Elizabeth and said, 'I'll wait for you, old thing. I've nothing better to do.'

Elizabeth could no longer concentrate on her book. Her eyes found the large clock on the wall. Isabella seemed to be taking longer than the others. She began to pace the room, her mind racing. Perhaps she should have lied about her age during her first interview, as she had about her marital status. Elizabeth took hold of the ring that hung on a thin gold chain round her neck under her dress. She had removed it from her finger and dropped her married title to save painful questions, but she was not prepared to give up Robert's name; it was all she had left of him. She jumped when the door opened.

'I need another gasper.'

Elizabeth watched Isabella light a cigarette and deeply inhale. 'Well?'

Isabella nodded. 'Beware, the commandant's a cow.'

'Congratulations,' Elizabeth smiled. 'Lady Isabella—'

'Isabella.'

'Isabella... can we drop the *old thing* bit? I'm Elizabeth... Bess if you prefer.'

Isabella inhaled and blew the smoke in the air. 'Quite right... you're rather too beautiful to be anything else. You've to go straight through... last door on the right. See you later then, Elizabeth.'

*

Elizabeth took a seat facing the two women who had interviewed her the previous day. The commandant sat between them, shuffling a few papers. Eyes that were reddened with fatigue, lifted. 'I left you until last Turner, because I'm not sure about you, so I am prepared to hear what you have to say. Tell me, why should I take you?'

'I have a duty to this country as well as any man, Commandant. Kitchener's pointing finger was aimed at all who saw it, women as well as men, and if it wasn't, then it should have been—'

'Hear hear!' cried one of the other two women.

7

'–men to fight, yes of course, but women can drive ambulances.'

'Quite right,' said the commandant, with a glance at her exuberant colleague, 'but driving ambulances full of badly injured men close to the line is not girl-guide's adventure weekend, Miss Turner. It's tough out there. I want women who will not faint at the sight of blood.' She looked into Elizabeth's eyes. 'Apart from your age, what are you...' she said, turning a page in Elizabeth's file, '...twenty and an undergraduate? Well, Flanders is no university campus, Miss Turner. It's very dangerous and you will have to get your hands dirty.'

'I'm not afraid of that,' Elizabeth said. 'Yes, I'm only twenty, but if you'll forgive me for saying so Commandant, there are younger men than I in Flanders who are recipients of the Victoria Cross. I insist you consider me on my ability, what I can offer you, rather than reject me based on my age.'

The Commandant sat upright in her seat, her eyes blinking rapidly. 'Good Lord, you should curb your tongue, young lady. I haven't quite reached the rejection stage... but another outburst such as that and I shall.' The commandant's sharp frozen features faced Elizabeth's tight-lipped expression. 'Very well then Miss Turner, what can you offer me?'

'I speak fluent French. I can drive and I know first aid. I have much to offer you.'

The commandant's features thawed a little. 'Umm, why didn't you tell my colleagues that yesterday?'

Elizabeth shrugged. 'I had no idea how competitive it was.'

'How long did you live in France, Miss Turner?'

'I lived with my aunt and uncle in Amiens for three years. Then I went to the Sorbonne for eighteen months before I went up to Oxford.'

'I see...' the commandant said, looking at her two colleagues. 'It would have been helpful if you had written this down when you applied, Miss Turner. There's little point in being modest during competition.' After a moment's silence, that seemed an age to Elizabeth, the commandant's eyes lifted. 'You're not concerned about interrupting your studies to join the Corps?'

'This is more important than French literature.'

'Indeed it is, Miss Turner.' The commandant said nodding and glanced at both her colleagues who also nodded. Her eyes returned to Elizabeth's solemn features. 'Despite your age I'm going to take you, Miss Turner. You have spunk, I like that, and as you intimated, your ability to speak French will be useful to us working with the French. The probation period is four months, after that you will join your unit.'

'Thank you, Commandant.'

'The hours will be long, you'll need a strong stomach and it can be very dangerous. You will not receive any pay for your work. We in the First Aid Nursing Yeomanry do it for King and Country and you will settle your own mess bills. There is a ten and sixpence fee for joining and a further four and sixpence for your identity disks. This must be paid on the day of your arrival for training. You will receive an allowance towards your uniform. It's all here, just read it, along with the address where you can have it tailored,' she said, handing Elizabeth a sheet of paper. 'I suggest you go there today if it's to be ready before you report for duty. Any questions? Good, I think we have covered everything. Oh yes, you will need to fill out this form and hand it in to the clerk,' she said, sliding it towards Elizabeth. 'Next of kin, blood group, religion, that sort of thing.' The commandant's stern face then broke into a smile. 'Welcome to the Corps, Turner.'

Elizabeth shook the hand of each woman with a sudden feeling of excitement. She went to the clerk's office and filled in her form naming her father-in-law as her next of kin and giving his London home as her contact address. It was consistent with her story as a single woman rather than a widow. It would also be better that he should break any bad news to her mother, rather than for her to experience again the cold, heartless news in a telegram.

'Do you know where Savile Row is?' Elizabeth asked Isabella as they left the building.

'That can wait. I'm in the chair for lunch. Do you live in town?'

'Digs in Oxford, but I'm staying with my parents-in-l ...' Elizabeth suddenly stopped and imitated a cough. 'My parents in London.'

'We could have dinner together, too. I'm staying at Claridges.'

'Yes, if you allow me to pay.'

'Certainly not. It was my suggestion.'

'Then I insist on paying for lunch.'

'Done,' Isabella said slipping her arm through Elizabeth's. 'I think we're going to be friends.'

Elizabeth glanced at Isabella's happy features and felt a sudden surge of excitement knotting her stomach for the adventure ahead. It gave her hope that after losing her husband, father and brother in the opening attack on the Somme, the candle that once burned bright within her soul may ignite and burn again.

9

Chapter **2**

Eighteen months later.

Twenty ambulances moved in a sluggish line along a narrow road.
They were passing too close to the front line to use headlights. The
drivers relied on what light there was from the moon as the convoy
negotiated great waterlogged shell holes. The shape of the line had
changed after the last attack and now the road could be seen by a
distant German observation post. Although they had only made this
trip a few times and there were some landmarks to help the lead driver,
there was no reason why the convoy should have taken a wrong turn,
but in war, when reason sleeps, monstrous tragedies emerge from the
darkness.

The long line of vehicles eventually came to a halt. At the rear of
the column, Elizabeth yawned and rested her head on the steering
wheel. Waking with a start she cursed herself, removed her leather
gloves and blew into her hands, rubbing them together then tucking
them under her armpits, but still her fingertips stung with cold. A
pitiful voice came from the back of her ambulance. 'Morphine...'

'Shhh, not so loud,' she whispered to the men in the back. 'We'll be
there shortly.'

'Why have we stopped?' said another.

'Quiet! You'll wake Fritz. I'll go and find out.'

Elizabeth stepped down from her vehicle and screwed up her toes a
couple of times before making her way towards the front of the
convoy. From the back of each ambulance she passed, she could hear
the groans of pain as the morphine began to wear off. When she
reached the ambulance with number 12 at its rear, she walked to the
front of it and tapped the driver on her boot.

'What's the holdup, Cathy?'

Elizabeth met Catherine's smile as her friend unwound the scarf
from her face. 'Taken a wrong turn,' Catherine whispered, her face
momentarily lost in vapour. 'If we carry on down this road I'm sure
we'll end up on the Hun's front lawn. Is Bella leading?'

Elizabeth smiled. 'Don't be horrible. Bella knows the way.'

'Stop chatting and get back to your vehicle, Turner,' the
commandant snapped in a whisper as she strode towards the lead
ambulance. 'You two aren't in Paris yet.'

The two friends looked at each other and grinned then poked their tongues out at the disappearing figure of authority. The following morning they would begin their annual leave. They had gone to Paris together the previous year; five days of uninterrupted sleep, good food, wine, and more sleep. Before the commandant had walked another ten paces, a flare rose up from the German line somewhere to the right of them and broke into white, soft, downward dilating radiance, lighting up Dante's landscape in a greenish haze and exposing the stationary row of twenty vehicles on the horizon. The flare's sudden appearance stunned Elizabeth and, while other drivers were beginning to turn their vehicles, she stood watching the light as it burned itself out.

'Christ!' Catherine gasped when another flare followed the first. 'Don't just stand there Bess, move yourself!'

The roar of engines almost muffled Catherine's frenzied cry as vehicles began to accelerate away, because, in the far distance, light from German guns now ran and trembled, flashed and quivered before them. The first two shells rushed overhead with a noise of engines blowing off steam in Cannon Street station, exploding fifty yards wide of the convoy.

Elizabeth rushed towards her ambulance, while ahead huge flames leapt up like gigantic red seas beating against a breakwater. Another explosion followed and another which caused her body to tremble with fear. Ahead, she saw an orange ball of flame and black smoke that was once an ambulance full of wounded men. Everything suddenly became a blur over which she had no control. She watched another ambulance roll off the road, falling on its side in flames. As her vehicle reached it, she slowed and glanced at the lifeless body at the wheel, it was the new girl, Helen. The concussion from another explosion caught Elizabeth's breath, which burned her lungs as the heat from the blast hit, shredding the flimsy canvas covering the back of the vehicle. She felt the vehicle jump as if it had sped over a humped bridge. The howls that were coming from the back stopped. Tears filled Elizabeth's eyes because she knew only death would stop their pain.

Elizabeth screamed a curse at the German gunners. This was all too easy for them; they would have long had the road's coordinates mapped out. Further along the road, she slowed and drew alongside another burning ambulance. She retched at the smell of burning flesh as men trapped in the back by their wounds were unable to escape the flames. A woman's voice called out. Elizabeth saw the driver's raised arm move. Trisha's leg had been severed from just below the knee; the flesh around the shattered tibia hung ragged, with blood running onto the booted foot lying close to the accelerator pedal. Elizabeth had only seconds to get her colleague out otherwise she would not be able to get close enough to save her friend. She pulled her free then removed her scarf and used it as a tourniquet. 'Stay awake, Trish,' was all she could say to her friend. 'Shout and scream, just stay awake.'

*

When Elizabeth drove through the gates of the hospital, she heard men shouting orders. Some of the girls were bent double beside their vehicles vomiting the fear from their bodies. Medics were already unloading the casualties from the ambulances that had made it there. After giving Trisha morphine, two orderlies took her away on a stretcher.

None of Elizabeth's casualties had survived the journey. She saw Isabella across the yard talking to a medic. Elizabeth's eyes swiftly searched for Catherine, her stomach feeling hollow with worry for her friend. The commandant approached and placed an unfamiliar friendly hand on her shoulder.

'We lost four of our girls,' she said in an unsteady voice. 'It would have been five if it were not for you. Patricia Williams has just told me what you did. Well done, Elizabeth. Well done indeed.'

'Will she live?'

'They've taken her to the operating theatre now, but yes, the doctor thinks so.'

'Have you seen Catherine?'

'She's coming now,' she said as she left striding across the yard.

Elizabeth turned and a light went on in her heart when she saw Catherine running towards her with outstretched arms. The two young women squeezed their bodies together. 'Bess,' Catherine whispered kissing her, 'if anything had happened to you...' Then Catherine saw the great dents in the metalwork of Elizabeth's ambulance, its tattered canvas flapping in the wind. 'Oh God, just look at your old bus. How on earth did you get through that?' There was no answer. Catherine pulled Elizabeth closer and kissed her again. 'Your cheeks feel like ice.' She removed the cashmere from around her neck and wrapped it around Elizabeth's. The whistle blew the signal to prepare to move.

Elizabeth held on tighter to Catherine, finding the warmth of her neck with her cold lips. 'I love you Cathy,' Elizabeth whispered.

'Break it up, you two.' It was Isabella; her eyes had a vacant look. 'It's you and me for the cemetery, Bess,' she said and then leaned across and kissed Elizabeth's head. 'Heard what you did to save Trisha, you crazy fool.'

'Save Trish...' Catherine looked puzzled. 'I thought Trisha was... I saw her ambulance take a hit.'

'She's all right,' Isabella said, 'thanks this blue stocking of ours.'

'You pulled her out of that inferno?' Catherine gasped. 'Bess, don't take risks like that—'

'Get ready to leave with the rest of us, Catherine,' the commandant said as she approached. 'Elizabeth and you Bella get going. Drive back carefully.'

'Yes, Commandant.'

'Why don't you have your fellows transferred to my bus,' Elizabeth said to Isabella when the commandant left them. 'It's pointless us both losing sleep.'

'Really? Thanks, Bess. My nerves are shattered.'

Catherine gasped. 'Elizabeth can't drive back alone in that. Just look at it.'

'It drives well enough,' Elizabeth said, giving Catherine an affectionate smile.

Catherine glared at Isabella. 'Get the orderlies to load your boys into my bus. I'll go with Bess.'

'No,' Isabella sighed. 'I'll go,' then she walked to her ambulance and crank started the engine. The whistle blew again.

'You'd better leave Cathy, before the commandant throws a paddy. I'll be all right.'

'I'll wait up.'

'No, don't. Get some sleep.'

'Paris tomorrow...'

Elizabeth looked at her watch. 'Today...' she said, showing Catherine the time. They walked to Catherine's ambulance arm in arm.

Catherine crank started the engine then climbed up behind the wheel. 'Bess,' she said, looking down into Elizabeth's eyes, 'I love you too.' Then she blew a kiss as the vehicle moved. Elizabeth followed it with her eyes until it was out of sight. The cashmere around her neck felt soft and warm, and when she lifted it above her nose she inhaled her friend's perfume.

*

As the two ambulances approached the cemetery, two soldiers, too old for the front line, stared at Elizabeth's damaged vehicle. They muttered obscenities. 'Sorry Miss, but it ain't right,' said one, who was a little unsteady in speech as well as gait. 'It just ain't right.' He reached inside his tunic pocket and handed Elizabeth a flask after she jumped from her vehicle. 'Take a swig. It'll warm you up.'

The other patted her shoulder. 'Nay, lass. The Hun shouldn't have done that.'

Elizabeth moved to the back of her vehicle and looked inside. She was not prepared for what she saw. She knew a man is just as dead by one means as by another; but it is infinitely more horrible and revolting to see a man shattered and eviscerated than to see him shot cleanly through the heart, and she vomited.

'Leave this to us, lass. This is no job for a gentlewoman.'

Elizabeth stood with Isabella, unable to watch as men, limbs and torsos were removed. After her ambulance was cleared, one of the men threw buckets of disinfected water inside while the other swept it out, then they went to Bella's ambulance. The last body to be lifted out was a young lieutenant. Elizabeth turned and caught sight of the soldier's face. 'Wait!' she called and went over to them. She looked into the dead man's opaque eyes, no longer the twinkling blue she remembered flirting with her. She stood motionless for a moment then ran the back of her fingers across his young, cold cheek.

'You know him, Miss?'

She nodded. His smile, when he had asked her out, reminded her of her late husband Robert. She had told him that rules did not allow her to dine alone with a man, she would have to bring a chaperone, so he had suggested he brought a friend along to make it four. Isabella and Catherine were on duty so she had asked Kate to join her. At the restaurant they had talked and laughed, four young people relaxing and enjoying life.

'We must go,' Jack had said at last. 'I have to check the men's kit before we move up the line.' Elizabeth imagined that the year before his mother would have checked his before he returned to school. The other two had walked on ahead at a lazy pace. Elizabeth and Jack had followed in silence as if they had exhausted all conversation over dinner, their step slowing when they neared the billets. He took her hand. Elizabeth caught his eye and smiled. He had suddenly pressed his lips to hers in an awkward kiss. 'Please,' he said, running his hand over her breasts. 'Please...' He attempted to kiss her again.

She pulled away. 'No! Don't do that.'

'I don't want to... I don't want to die and never...'

Elizabeth met frightened, wet eyes. 'You poor boy,' she whispered, her irritation changing to sudden despair for him. She ran the palm of her hand over his cheek and kissed his lips. 'You poor, poor boy.' He was so young. They were all young, Britain's bright youth decaying in Flanders. He lifted her skirt and tugged at her knickers. 'No, please, not that.'

'Yes...'

'No, let me...' She brazenly ran her hand over the front of his trousers, as she imagined a whore might do. It was something one of the girls had said appeased a man's passion. 'There's no need to be afraid,' she whispered, when he had stopped struggling with her. She kissed his cheek as if she were comforting a child. It was over quickly. He stepped away from her and turned his back while he tidied himself.

'I'm sorry,' he whispered.

They walked on in silence no longer holding hands. When they reached the gate they said goodnight with a handshake, because Kate and Jack's friend were waiting. As the two young women walked towards their billet, Kate asked if he had tried anything on.

'No. We talked. He's afraid of going up the line.'

'Who wouldn't be...?'

Later, in bed, Elizabeth thought about what she had done. She was surprised by it; she had slept with women but her only other experience with a man had been with her late husband Robert. They had consummated their marriage after a quick civil ceremony in London. It hurt and she didn't enjoy it. After they left the hotel he had caught a train for Folkestone then a boat for France. A week later he was dead. He had now been dead for almost as long as she had known him alive. Was doing what she had done for Jack proof that she had stopped loving Robert? Did she ever love him? She turned and looked at Catherine sleeping in the bed beside hers. A tender smile crept to Elizabeth's lips. She reached across and touched Catherine's flesh with her fingertips, close to the swell of her breasts. In that single touch she felt more excitement than she had that night in Jack's arms. One of the other girls began snoring. Another turned in her bed. Elizabeth pulled the blanket over her head and closed her eyes. Jack would be leaving for the front line about now. Although it gave her no pleasure doing what she had done for him, she did not regret it. She hoped she had made him happy. In the distance, the odd chatter of machine gun fire disturbed the peace of the night.

*

Isabella placed a comforting arm round Elizabeth's shoulder. 'Let's go, Bess. We've got a long drive and you're off to Paris, you lucky devil.'

The two young women watched as the men lay Jack down with the others. Groundsheets were thrown over them. The two old soldiers, it seemed, had seen too many dead to worry about sentimentality. Jack would be buried later that morning with the others when the padre arrived.

Chapter 3

Buckingham, England.

A thick carpet of bluebells rippling in a light breeze and glistening with dancing, silver sunlight, spread through some woodland to a lake by Brooke Farm. Deciduous trees were already in leaf and red horse chestnuts blushed with pink blossom, not quite in bloom. Beyond in the meadow there were sheep and cattle. Some fields had low green barley and others were under the plough. Brooke Farm had emerged from winter into a spring patchwork quilt of scented colour. Away from the lake on higher ground, close to a cluster of outbuildings with ruddy tiled roofs and tawny brick walls stood a Georgian house, which seemed to have grown out of the landscape, like the trees around it. It was large and majestic; the symbol of power, the home of one man and his staff.

From one of the bedroom windows, Christina Brennan observed the tranquil, dewy world of the English countryside. She stood listening to the lowing protests of some dairy cattle calling their calves as one of the men moved them from the barn into a field, and she imagined the scene had not changed for centuries. Christina had become part of that scene since moving into the house which could just be seen from the road that left Buckingham, travelling south towards Winslow.

Twenty-three months had passed since her husband and son had been killed on the Somme, twenty-one months since her daughter Elizabeth had left the safety of Oxford's cloisters to join the uncertain world of the First Aid Nursing Yeomanry, now serving overseas in France. Each week a letter arrived. They were mostly scrawled words to say all was well, occasionally, a more detailed, neater, more orderly text described what she and her friends had done on their off duty day in Amiens. Names such as Isabella, Catherine, Trisha and Kate were now as familiar to the Brennan household as girls from the town that had gone to school with her daughters. There was never any mention of the fighting Christina had read about in the newspapers, or of the slaughter she had heard about from angry, drunken soldiers home on leave.

She moved to the mantelpiece where there were a number of photographs of her family and took hold of the family picture. It was taken just before Elizabeth went up to Oxford. Christina was sitting in the front row with her husband, their twin daughters, Jane and Stephanie, either side of them; behind, their three eldest children, William in the middle, Elizabeth with her serious expression to his left and Louisa to his right. Now her husband and son were dead. Louisa had married a soldier and moved to Sussex, and Elizabeth was in France. Her family had been broken by war.

The ache in her heart returned when she met the eyes of her dead son, now another child was in France. She picked up a picture that Elizabeth had sent to her from Paris the previous year, during the late spring of 1917. She was arm in arm with her friend Catherine. Written in ink on the bottom right of the picture was, *Paris 1917, with Cathy*; in the background was the Eiffel Tower. Elizabeth's bright eyes shone into the lens of the camera. They seemed almost golden as they took in the light under her long, dark lashes, while Catherine's gaze fell upon Elizabeth's happy features. Catherine appeared rather grand. It was as though she preferred to pose in profile, exhibiting her long neck and fine jaw-line below a perfectly shaped nose. Catherine, Christina noted, was very beautiful.

'Bess…' she whispered, 'I know you suffered most with Robert lost too, but why did you have to run away like that?'

She glanced at her watch. There were ten minutes to go before the sound of the breakfast gong would reverberate round the house. The cook always produced a good breakfast. Christina replaced the photograph on the mantelpiece and removed a box of letters from the trunk by her bed. She sat in the armchair close to the window and selected the first, which had been written in September 1916. The number one circled in red ink showed it to be the very first of many letters Elizabeth had sent after joining the Corps.

Dearest Mamma,
I hope you have forgiven me for leaving Oxford. What I am doing now is far more important in the short term. My tutor said my eighteen months at the Sorbonne will count towards my degree, so I've only two terms left to complete my degree when all this is over, so you see, I haven't 'ruined my chances' of a good education, as you argued.
Let me explain to you what life is like here.
There are forty of us in training, broken into two squads. In my squad they are mostly toffs; however, they seem very nice and despite our different backgrounds, we all seem to get along, with one exception perhaps, the girl who shares my room. Trust my

18

luck. Her name is Catherine Neale. She is stunningly beautiful. In the first hours of being here all the men tripped over themselves to catch a glimpse of her. She strikes me as someone with a sublime lack of awareness of the ordinary human condition and wafts with an air of superiority typical of the upper classes. The rooms were already allocated, otherwise I would have asked to share with Isabella, or Bella, as she now prefers to be called. However, I am determined to get along with Catherine. I think she has probably never met anyone of my class and maybe doesn't know how to speak to me, which would give the impression of being standoffish. We'll see.

Now I must try to sleep. Tomorrow we have lessons on the internal combustion engine that drives the ambulances. They are Ford Model T's, which are American. Catherine is worried about her nails. Wish me lots of luck.

Love and regards to you all.

Bess.

PS. Please remember I am addressed as MISS Turner (NOT Mrs), as if Turner is my maiden name, so when you write please remember that.

Christina returned the letter to the envelope then took another from a different pile, which was the first she had received from Belgium, four months later.

Bonjour Mamma,

Well, here I am in Belgium. I am sorry I cannot tell you exactly where I am, censorship and all that. We are a long way from the fighting although we can hear the guns when the wind blows from that direction. It sounds rather like a passing storm echoing round the Aylesbury Vale.

You asked me for my advice regarding the secretarial and housekeeping position Mr Wilding has offered you at Brooke Farm. I think you would be wise to accept it. The money is very good and it will prevent you from digging into what Papa has left you. It will also offer a new start for you and the twins in what sounds like a very beautiful home. To think, Jane and Stephanie will each have their own room. It will make them feel rather grand, I'm sure.

Back to Belgium.

The landscape is flat, rather like Norfolk, but not as pretty. I am the unit's interpreter. Papa would have been so proud of me. How I love and miss him! Rumour has it we may soon be attached to the British army. I do hope so. Being with one's own people is quite natural and the British soldier is rather special; coarse although very polite, always complaining, very amusing – and we are their womenfolk, which makes us special to them.

Catherine is with me. I was dreading she would be sent to another unit serving in France, but we are together. I adore her. Against all odds, we have become the best of friends. Who would have thought it, a toff such as Cathy making friends with me? We have this pact. We may discuss anything other than our backgrounds, which probably means her family are stinking rich or something like that. It was her idea, but I'm happy to go along with it. Neither must disclose a thing about our lives in England, absolutely nothing. When the war ends, we will reveal everything. I know it is silly, but it is fun to be a little secretive sometimes.

Catherine and I are going to spend our first leave in Paris. Bella would have come too, but she has been transferred to another unit for six months. She's livid. I will miss her, but she'll be back soon enough.

We now have to attend a lecture on the dos and don'ts of a young lady abroad on active service. Catherine says it will probably be, if you DO have sex DON'T get pregnant. A few months ago that would have shocked me, but little shocks me now.

Love to all.

Bess.

Christina frowned. She was concerned that this Catherine girl might be a bad influence on Elizabeth. 'There's no excuse for such language,' she had told her blushing twin daughters over supper when reading the letter out to them, 'however grand this girl may be, it's no way for a young lady to behave.'

At the sound of the breakfast gong, Christina placed the letters back in the box and left her room to join the others at the table.

*

Tim Wilding never began breakfast until all were seated. The twins had not yet arrived. After greeting Christina his eyes lowered to his newspaper and returned to the report he was reading of the German offensive on the Somme.

'I'm sorry Mr Wilding. I'll go and hurry them up.'

'Please, sit down Mrs Brennan. They're helping out in the yard.'

'They are keeping you waiting.'

'They'll be here shortly.' He smiled. 'I've grown rather fond of your girls, Mrs Brennan. They are keen to learn about farming.'

Tim Wilding was thirty when his late wife died with the baby she was trying to bring into the world, twenty years ago. For years he told himself he was no longer interested in a wife and sons, until Christina Brennan walked into his home. She came to be interviewed for the position of secretary and housekeeper after his previous secretary retired. Tim suggested Christina moved into the house with her daughters. The girls could occupy two rooms on the second floor, while Christina would have a rather nice room on the first. As the weeks passed, he invited them all to eat at the table with him rather than in the kitchen with the other staff. Christina's presence and the sweet nature of her daughters gave him a warm feeling of family, something he realized he had missed and should now like to have. He began to consider Christina as a wife. She was only in her early forties, still handsome and young enough to give him a son.

Christina flashed a glance at him when he lowered his eyes. She had often felt them on her when he thought it was safe to look. Once in the drawing room when he stretched across her to reach for something, she was troubled by his physical proximity for days. It shocked her, because she had only ever known one man and thought herself incapable of ever having another. But two years had passed since her husband had been killed and more since she had felt the comfort of him in her bed. When Christina looked up she met Tim's intense eyes. She quickly lowered hers as he cleared his throat.

'Any... any letters from Elizabeth?'

'Not for four weeks. It's unlike her.'

'How long's she been overseas, Mrs Brennan?'

'Sixteen months with just one break, when she went to Paris with her friend last year, although they do have a day off each week. Elizabeth said in her last letter that she's going to Paris again with her friend, Catherine. She should have been and returned by now... not even a postcard. I really thought she would come home to meet you, Mr Wilding.'

'Why should she want to meet an old man like me?'

His laughter brightened her eyes. 'You're not old Mr Wilding, far from it.' She caught his smile before her eyes lowered to the table. 'You've been very kind to us. That's why she ought to meet you.'

He gave a dismissive flick of the fingers. 'So, she's not written for four weeks.'

'She's having too much of a good time to think of her family.'

'Oh let her have some fun, Mrs Brennan. The poor girl has suffered enough losing her husband, father and−'

'We've all suffered, Mr Wilding.'

'Yes, yes I know,' he said placing a hand over hers.

It was warm and strangely comforting. She let it linger there before slowly withdrawing her hand to brush some hair from her eyes. 'I don't know about this Catherine friend of hers. She's the girl I was talking to you about. I'm not sure that she is a good influence on Elizabeth.'

'The beautiful one in the photograph you showed me?'

'I think my Elizabeth is just as beautiful; perhaps not in such a sophisticated way as her friend, but still rather lovely.'

'She certainly is, Mrs Brennan. You have some fine-looking girls.'

Tim Wilding noticed a little pink rise to Christina's cheeks. Now, without the distraction of his newspaper, he began to drum on the table with his fingertips, while Christina's attention focussed on the dining room door, then on her watch and finally back to Tim Wilding where she offered him a shy smile.

'Stop fretting, Mrs Brennan. They'll be here shortly.' He drummed some more. 'Does Elizabeth speak French?'

'Fluently.' Christina explained that her previous neighbour was from Picardy where the war was now being fought. 'They were always speaking French together. Then when she was sixteen she went to live in Amiens with my sister.'

'Your sister lives in France?'

'She married a Frenchman. Dominique. He's a lawyer. They're now living in Lyon.'

'What about the twins and Louisa... do they speak it?'

'Not very well. Elizabeth is the clever one. She takes after her father.'

The twins suddenly entered the dining room and met their mother's disapproving eyes. 'I'm sorry we are late, Mr Wilding. We had to wash.'

'Of course you did, girls. Have some breakfast... you've earned it.'

Cook entered pushing a trolley. The smell of bacon filled the room when she removed the cloche covers.

'Any mail Mamma?' Jane asked as she helped herself to some scrambled egg.

'No. Bess is probably having too much fun in Paris to think of us.'

'I doubt it! One of the men has just told me the Germans have

22

launched their offensive. They've overrun our positions–'

'Who's been filling your pretty little head with that nonsense?' Tim said. 'I was reading that our lads have got them on the run.'

'That's not what the men are saying.'

'I don't think you should talk to the men.'

'It's been four weeks and not a word from my sister, Mr Wilding. I have this awful feeling something has happened to her.'

'Elizabeth won't be anywhere near the fighting dear, so don't worry about her.'

'How can you say that, Mamma? Ambulances are used to pick up the wounded. Hasn't she ever told you what's going on over there?'

'She never writes about the war, you know that.'

'Because she's protecting you from the truth of it.' Jane jumped up from her chair and excused herself from the table before Christina had time to protest. When she returned, she handed her mother an envelope. 'Read it, Mamma. See exactly what a lovely a time Bess is having. Look at the date. That was four months ago. I expect nothing has changed.'

November 1917.
My dearest Jane,
The battle for Passchendaele Ridge is now over at an unimaginable cost of life yet the guns do not stop. I cannot imagine life without the hideous sound of death ringing in my ears, the smell of it in my nostrils, the sight of it - God - the sight of it. This miserable creature is condemned to see it awake or in sleep for the rest of her wretched life. Even Dante in a depressed state of mind would not have condemned the most evil sinner to spend just five minutes in such purgatory. I HATE GENERALS - they are the Devil's lieutenants who have turned Flanders into Golgotha. How can I ever settle back into student life after this? I am a different person, no longer one of you, but one of us. We are always tired. Sleep is our greatest and only luxury. Was it only four months since my leave in Paris? Five glorious days away from an existence here we call life. Five days of hot baths, good food and wine, and sleep, wonderful sleep. Five days with my dearest Catherine.
Please say nothing to Mamma. We women should be cheery and remain silent, but how will the truth about this place be known if nothing is ever said? The newspapers talk of victories. They lie. There are no victories, only death.
Tomorrow we leave Belgium and return to France. Catherine has been there for the past two weeks, with the advance party,

preparing for our arrival. I never thought I could miss someone so much; I long to see her beautiful face break into a smile. She looked so tired when I kissed her goodbye thirteen long days ago - even my adorable Aphrodite is looking mortal. All the men at the camp ask after her. It does little for one's own ego. What must they feel in the presence of such beauty? Yet men find it difficult to look Catherine in the eye, as if she were the gorgon Medusa. Surely, it is worth the risk. Most of them will die anyway. Tomorrow I shall be with her. Tomorrow I shall be happy again...

Christina looked up from the page and said, 'All this talk of Catherine and not a mention of how we are. She could have finished at Oxford by now.' She handed the letter to Tim. 'What do you think, Mr Wilding?'

Jane's eyes widened. Her voice lowered. 'Mamma... that letter is private... to me.'

Tim handed it back to Jane without looking at it. Jane gave her mother a cold stare. 'Bess wouldn't write those things to me unless she was really unhappy.'

'I'm sure she'll be all right,' Tim said, his face breaking into a smile. 'You would have heard by now if there was anything wrong.'

Jane watched him squeeze her mother's hand and was shocked to see her meet his eyes and smile at him in a way she could only describe as flirtatious.

Chapter 4

Christina watched the car disappear along the driveway and gave it a final wave as it turned the corner out of sight. She went back into the house, climbed the stairs and hesitated at the bottom of the next flight, which led to her daughters' rooms. She was unsure whether she should just leave them to their grief or go and comfort them. They had each other to hold as they always had since their birth, but Christina had no one. It was only when she sat on her bed that she began to shed tears for the first time since Mrs Turner had given her the news, one mother to another, while George Turner paced the courtyard outside. They didn't stay long, only long enough to help cushion the initial pain.

It was dark when Tim returned from London. As the taxi drove through the gate he saw the house in darkness. Susan wasn't there to greet him because it was her day off; cook would no doubt be in her room with a half bottle of whisky. The twins, he gathered, must be out with their young men, but where was Christina? He poured himself a whisky, added a touch of water and sat in his favourite armchair by a dying fire. With an unsettled mind he was not enjoying the drink, so he left it and climbed the stairs to an early bed. As he passed Christina's room he saw a soft light under her door. He walked to his room, then back again, hesitated then returned to his room. Five minutes later with more confidence and determination, he knocked on Christina's door.

'Mrs Brennan, is everything all right?' After a little silence he asked again. There was a tearful reply. 'Whatever is the matter?' he asked, his hand gripping the handle and twisting it. With a tentative step he entered her room. She was sitting up in her bed red-eyed, her dark, loose hair over her shoulders. Elizabeth's letters were strewn all round the quilted bedcover. 'What's the matter, Christina?' he repeated. Tim had never addressed her that way before. He sat on her bed and listened to her news and when finished, her head fell on his broad shoulders and she began shedding tears again. 'I'll fetch you a brandy. It'll help you sleep.'

'No…' she said looking into his eyes, 'don't leave me. Please, don't go.'

*

The following morning, Christina was uncertain how Tim would receive her at breakfast. When she entered the room he stood and went to her as if the coil of a spring had sprung. He clasped both her hands in his. 'I meant what I said,' he assured her. 'It wasn't just… I've thought about it for some time.'

'It wouldn't be right just now, with Elizabeth—'

'We must bring her back. Yes, I'll pay for them to bring her home.'

'They've already buried her.'

His chin lowered to his chest. He pulled her to him and felt her head settle lightly on his shoulder. 'I'm so sorry, I'm thinking of myself,' and then he stepped back from her. 'Forgive me.'

She took his hand and looked up into his eyes. 'Tim... do you really want me?'

'Yes!' he gasped, his ruddy features lighting up. 'Surely you can see that.'

A little happiness covered her face. 'Then yes. I'll tell the twins when the time is right.'

As he embraced her, Christina thought of Elizabeth who had adored her father. No man could ever take his place. She had been spared that, at least.

*

Neither of the twins came down to breakfast that morning and at lunch a tray was taken to their rooms. Tim was busy with the vet most of the day and dinner that evening was a subdued affair. Later, after the twins retired to their rooms, Christina went for a walk in the grounds with Tim. It was the first time they had walked anywhere together.

'I've only a brother. He's married, but he doesn't have any children. Phillip's not interested in farming,' he said. 'He's a London doctor, a psychiatrist they call him. He's a nice chap, you'll like him. I was going to leave the farm to Luke, their son, but he was...' he swiped at a weed with his stick, '...Ypres, 1915. I'd like to think we'll have a son and pass it on to him.'

Christina blushed. 'I would like another son.'

It was a clear night with a slight breeze which carried with it the scent from a line of yews. Tim's large, rough hand clasped hers. They stared across at the distant farmhouse where the dim lights shone yellow behind the drawn curtains. How strange life is, Christina thought. It was the death of her husband that had brought her to Brooke Farm and now the death of her daughter that would make her mistress of it.

'You've made me very happy, Christina,' Tim said, 'and you'll want for nothing.'

'It's not being there to see my children buried that hurts me most,' she suddenly said. 'How can I believe they're gone? One moment you have them then the next a telegram tells you otherwise. No funeral service, no prayers, no grave to visit... nothing.'

'Why didn't the War Office send the telegram to you?'

'Bess put them down as her next of kin. She didn't want to let them know she was a widow when she joined.'

'Surely it would have been easier to join in her maiden name.'

Christina shook her head. 'No, she wouldn't deny Robert his name. That's all she had of him, she told me. I understood.'

Tim nodded. 'After the war Christina, we'll go then, put flowers on William and Elizabeth's graves. They'll not be forgotten. We'll say a prayer for them together.'

Christina pressed his hand to her mouth. 'You're a good man, Tim.'

*

The following week after the breakfast gong sounded, Jane appeared holding a large brown envelope. Her mother, she had noticed, now sat close to Tim at the table in the place once occupied by Stephanie. Jane sensed something had changed between her mother and Tim, that there was definitely something going on between them. She had noticed the looks, lingering and engaging, his eyes following Christina out of a room and the look of pleasure on his face when she returned. Her mother was entitled to some happiness, Jane knew, but Elizabeth would hardly be cold in her grave. It was indecent of her mother to court one while grieving for another.

'This has been forwarded on for you, Mamma,' Jane said, handing Christina the envelope and kissing her cheek. Jane turned to Tim and offered him one of her sweet smiles. 'Good morning, Mr Wilding.'

'Good morning, Stephanie.'

'I'm Jane.'

'Jane...yes, yes, of course you're Jane.'

The twins were identical in looks down to a small mole below the throat, which could be clearly seen when the top button of any blouse was undone. Had Tim known the girls better, he would have seen the difference between them by their manner. Jane was tolerant of other's faults. Stephanie was not. When Jane spoke, she smiled very charmingly, shyly and openly, and she raised her eyes upwards in an engagingly severe way. Stephanie found it difficult to meet the other's eyes. Jane was confident in all she said and did. Stephanie constantly blushed and caught her breath. She was flirtatious when talking to men, and to Christina's irritation, wet her lips with her tongue, which made them shine.

'Are you going to join us?' Tim asked.

'Thank you. I have no appetite, Mr Wilding. Will you please excuse me?'

'You run along. If you'd like anything later, I'll have Susan bring it up to you on a tray.'

When Jane left the room Christina opened the bundle. 'This is from Mrs Turner,' she said, removing the contents. She opened one of the three letters. 'It's from Elizabeth's commandant. I'll read it to you:

I am writing to offer you my deepest sympathy for the loss of your daughter, Elizabeth. You will have been told she was lost on March 21st. What you would not have been told is how. She was returning from a military cemetery when the Germans began their offensive. She was, alas, in the wrong place at the wrong time, but she was not alone. Her friend and colleague Isabella Fitzclarence was lost to us too. We shall miss them both. Elizabeth was an extremely courageous girl and we are all humbled by and very proud of her. On the way to the hospital, German gunners shelled the convoy. It was a traumatic experience for us, but while some drivers passed a friend in desperate need of help, Elizabeth stopped her ambulance in the middle of the most appalling bombardment and risked her life to save a colleague. The young lady in question survived the ordeal and is now in England with her family. Elizabeth was different from the others - quiet, intelligent, always willing to help. I never saw her boastful, bitter or spiteful. Your daughter is a great loss to us. She always busied herself doing something - generally for others. Her quiet inner strength and unflappable manner, sometimes under the most trying circumstances, saw many of us through difficult times. We all recognized her physical loveliness, but her real beauty came from within. The Belgian government has already recognized Elizabeth's work by awarding her the Croix de Guerre with Bronze Star. I have recommended her for a decoration from our own people.

With this letter I have enclosed another that was sent to Elizabeth, which she never received and one she never sent. Her personal affects have been boxed up and dispatched to you in a separate parcel. Once again I offer you my condolences and may perpetual light shine over Elizabeth resting in everlasting peace.'

Christina folded the letter and replaced it in the envelope. 'I remember when Elizabeth took a similar letter round to Mrs Turner when Robert was killed. We've all suffered so much in this war.'

Tim's only response was to clutch her hand. She opened the second letter, which was addressed to Elizabeth. Four £5 notes fell to the ground. 'Good heavens, all this money,' Christina gasped.

Tim took the letter as Christina retrieved the fallen notes. 'It's from Mrs Williams, whoever she is. Shall I read it to you?' Christina met his eye and nodded.

Dear Miss Turner,
My daughter Patricia told me how you saved her life at great risk to your own and these words I write can never express the gratitude and debt I owe you. Although she has lost her leg, Patricia is safe and away from that dreadful war. The good news is that her fiancé still plans to marry her when she leaves hospital. He is a decent chap and we are so proud to welcome him into our family. Miss Turner, we beg you to come and visit us when the war is over, and stay with us for a few days, or when you are next on leave if you could spend the time away from your family, because my husband and I should love to meet you and thank you personally. I know Patricia would love to see you again. She has always spoken so highly of you, how sensible and level-headed you are compared to so many of the others. Please do not be offended, but my husband has enclosed £20 for you to spend on a good dinner and Champagne with Patricia's friends and colleagues to celebrate our daughter's return to us. God bless you and keep you safe and well.
Yours sincerely, Mrs G. H. Williams.

'You must be very proud of her,' Tim said, replacing the letter in the envelope.

Christina took it from him. 'If Bess couldn't find the time to visit us then I doubt if she would have gone to Lancashire. I'll return the money and let her know that God didn't keep Bess safe and well.'

'It does no good to be bitter towards our maker, Christina. I look to Him to give me a good harvest,' Tim said, placing a comforting hand on her shoulder. 'There's one more letter here. Are you going to open it?'

'It's Elizabeth's handwriting. It will be the letter we all waited for. I'll read it later.' She gave Tim an affectionate smile and said, 'Bess and I fought like cats and dogs, but I did love her. I should have told her that in my letters, but I never did, and now it's too late...'

*

On a warm afternoon in May, Christina stood beside her new husband outside the church of St Peter and St Paul in Buckingham. To her left, the twins with their eldest sister Louisa, smiling with the hope of happiness for their mother. To the right, the groom's brother and his wife, Dr and Mrs Phillip Wilding, beaming with undisguised pleasure by the groom's side. Later, Mrs Christina Wilding returned to Brooke Farm with her three girls and her new family.

The following day before leaving for Sussex, where Tim and Christina had planned to spend a week's honeymoon in Brighton, Christina sat looking around the library of the farmhouse. She knew Elizabeth would have loved the room. There was a piano in the corner and several shelves of books around the walls. They all looked as though they had been bought for show rather than to read. Their hardback covers were spotless and the pages lightly stuck together as though they had just been removed from the press, unlike those in her late husband's study where the books looked exhausted and in need of a rest.

After kissing her twin daughters goodbye, Christina climbed into the waiting cab and sat between her husband and Louisa who took her mother's hand.

*

The week passed quickly and on their return, as the taxi entered the gates to the farm, the twins were running up the driveway to meet it. From inside the vehicle, Christina laughed. 'Ah bless them. Look at those girls; they just can't wait to welcome us home again.'

'Mamma, Mamma,' Jane said breathlessly. 'Mrs Turner telephoned yesterday. It's Bess. She's alive, Mamma... alive. The Red Cross says she's a prisoner-of-war in Germany.'

Christina's eyes stared. 'Why did they tell us she was dead? Why be so cruel?'

'Rejoice, Christina,' Tim said, passing her a handkerchief. 'Mistakes, no matter how terrible, happen in war. I'm sure an explanation will follow.'

It didn't.

*

In the second week of November 1918 the guns stopped. Now the bells could ring and go on ringing, announcing what all British people desired to hear - the war was over. There was wild rejoicing and crowds went crazy with delight. Yet behind these loud peals of joy, there was the toll of spectral bells for those who would return no more.

Christina received news from Mrs Turner that Elizabeth had returned to England on a Red Cross ship and was now in a military hospital for rest and precautionary check-ups after her captivity. Christina held her swollen, pregnant belly thinking how much easier it all would have been had she been able to write and tell Elizabeth that she had remarried and was expecting a child in March.

The twins and their mother travelled up to London the following day. They followed a nurse along the bare white shining walls of antiseptic corridors. They passed other nurses, hurriedly ferrying hideously mutilated patients in wheelchairs through doors, hiding them from the incredulous eyes of the visiting public. Thus it was in this environment that Christina saw something of the war that she had only read about in the newspapers.

The severity of the regime seemed everywhere, from the layout of the wards to the long stiffly starched aprons of the staff that crackled when they walked, to impatient, overworked doctors, who poked and prodded like inspectors at a meat market, long accepting how badly the meat had been butchered, tired with the vast quantities of produce they had to examine.

'There is no ward in the hospital specifically for women, so Miss Turner has a single room normally reserved for senior officers,' the nurse said in a disapproving tone. 'Well, here we are. I shall leave you with her.'

Before Christina was a white painted door, a simple wooden barrier that now separated mother from daughter as time had previously done. It might have been made of stone, iron, or cold steel - a drawbridge between past and present, but now it was going to be lowered and bring them together again. Christina felt the child in her body move, as if it too was nervous meeting Elizabeth.

When she opened the door, a ghostly face turned towards her and produced a weak smile. It disappeared when Elizabeth's eyes recognized her mother's pregnant condition. Christina stopped in her tracks and gasped at the sight of Elizabeth's appearance. She felt anger. It was the anger of a trusting mother who had left her child in the care of others and returned to find her trust betrayed. Elizabeth's eyes, which had once danced with inquisitive brightness, were now heavy and vacant in their darkened sockets. Her sallow face peered through strands of unkempt hair which hung on a thinner frame than

31

the one Christina remembered leaving the market town of Buckingham two years before.

While Christina and Stephanie tried desperately to adjust to the sight of Elizabeth, Jane let out a cry. She ran towards her sister's bed. The two locked themselves in a tangle of arms and wept, while Stephanie and her mother stood frozen at her bedside, finding what comfort they could in each other's hand.

Two days later, another visitor arrived at Elizabeth's bedside - a senior member of the First Aid Nursing Yeomanry. She had brought with her a uniform. Above the left breast pocket were sewn two ribbons, one was the Military Medal of thin red, white and blue stripes, another, the familiar red with five green strips of the Croix de Guerre on which was sewn a small bronze star. The uniform, Elizabeth was told, had been paid for by the Corps and was for her to wear when going to Buckingham Palace to collect her Military Medal from the King.

'We are so proud of you, Miss Turner...' her visitor sang, 'so very, very proud.'

Elizabeth looked up at the woman but said nothing.

'Your country is not the only one to honour you; gallant Belgium has too. This ribbon...' she said, enthusiastically pointing to the Croix de Guerre, 'is from the Belgians. It has a Bronze Star with it, do you see?'

'I've seen the medal before... on dead Belgian soldiers. Their country was very, very proud of them too.'

'But yours is for all those Belgian soldiers whose lives you saved. The Belgian ambassador will present you with it after you receive the Military Medal from the King. So hurry and get well Miss Turner, the King awaits you.'

Elizabeth looked into the eyes of the woman bedside her and saw them brimming with sickly pride. 'How is Patricia Williams?'

'She's well and married now, thanks to you; such an unselfish act of heroism. When we heard what you had done some of us wept, quite unashamedly, believe me, Miss Turner.'

The woman looked into Elizabeth's eyes and felt the sudden awkwardness of one who had not been there. One who had waved banners and shouted hurrahs for those who had returned; one who spoke in metaphors for those who did not. The woman held Elizabeth's hand and soft words were whispered. Yet, no matter how comforting her words were meant to be, nothing could wipe the memory of Isabella slumped over the steering wheel of her ambulance with half her head blown away.

'I expect you cannot wait to return home Miss Turner and be with your family? Everything will soon be back to normal, you'll see.'

'Normal? How can things ever be normal again?'

'Miss Turner...'

'It's *Mrs* Turner... not Miss!'

The woman's eyes quickly flicked over the papers in her hand. 'I'm so sorry. The records state that you are... unmarried.'

Elizabeth gave the woman beside her a cold stare. 'I am. My husband is dead but his name isn't. That's something the generals couldn't kill.'

The woman looked into Elizabeth's unhappy eyes and stood to leave. 'You're tired. I'll leave you. If there's anything I can do for you, please do say... anything?'

'Yes, there is. Will you try to locate a member of the Corps for me? Her name is Catherine Neale. We served together.'

'Of course I shall try and locate her. It shouldn't be difficult. Now try to rest.'

'Thank you. Would you also give me Isabella Fitzclarence's address? I should like to write to her parents... explain.'

'You must rest and grow strong again. Remember, you are due at the Palace in two weeks,' the woman smiled, tapping Elizabeth's hand. 'I shall return tomorrow with Lady Isabella's address and hopefully, news of Miss Neale too.'

Chapter 5

When Elizabeth was dressed in her uniform and due to leave the hospital, she waited in her room for Dr Wilding to arrive. It had been arranged that she would stay at his home for a few days before her return to Buckingham with her mother, something she was trying to delay for as long as possible. She was not looking forward to meeting the man who had stepped into her dead father's shoes.

Elizabeth just wanted to be left alone, away from sympathetic eyes and jovial well-wishers. There was only one visitor she wanted to see... Catherine; but she was now lost to her. Her visitor returned with Isabella's address and explained that Catherine had joined the FANY using a false name and address and her whereabouts were therefore unknown.

'There is little hope of finding her, Mrs Turner,' the woman said. 'I'm sure you can see the difficulty. If she gave a false address, then she would have given a false name too. It's not uncommon, alas.'

*

'Elizabeth,' Dr Wilding said. 'You're looking better today.'

He had a friendly smile and a soft voice. Elizabeth's eyes rose to his. 'Good morning, Doctor.'

'Phillip,' he said. 'I'm your uncle not your doctor, so we can forget the formalities.' He closed the door and beckoned Elizabeth to sit, while he explained how she would be in his care for a few days. 'My wife Melanie is looking forward to meeting you. I'm sure you two will get along splendidly.' They chatted for a few minutes and when Elizabeth stood, Phillip Wilding took her small suitcase. 'Let's go, then. We'll be home in time for lunch.'

Elizabeth opened the door to leave her room but was impeded by a convoy of wheelchairs passing along the corridor. In a low whisper, Dr Wilding explained to her the men were released from German military hospitals and had arrived in England earlier that morning. The wheelchairs slowed and came to a halt. Dr Wilding saw Elizabeth's face show irritation at the delay. He knew she wanted to get away from those that reminded her of the war and her captivity.

'Patience, Elizabeth. It will only be a short delay.'

Elizabeth looked down and met the gaze of a soldier looking up at her from a wheelchair. She disliked soldier's eyes; they had either the look of lust or death in them. She wanted to escape. Escape the hospital, escape the world, but where could she run to? There would always be eyes on her.

She returned the soldier's gaze and met his blue eyes which were the same colour as Catherine's. With some relief, she saw no lust, no life; they were dead like the countless blank eyes she had seen on the Somme and in Ypres, ready to be tied in sheets before being laid out in the long deep trenches. She used to look into their faces with macabre fascination trying to imagine their last thoughts, thoughts that had left such strange expressions at the moment of death. The memory of it haunted her now. Yet then, in Flanders, until Catherine had found her and led her away, she often looked into dead men's eyes and wondered if Robert or her father had time to think of her, before their eyes were left staring into a fierce July sun.

She saw the soldier's eyes fall on the medal ribbons above the swell of her breast then move back to her face. His lips moved without any sound and he nodded, as if to acknowledge that he knew that she had been there, that she was part of the brotherhood of the damned who would relive the war in their sleep. The wheelchairs moveed forward. She did not see him glance back at her; she had already lifted her eyes to the ceiling, as if to escape every set of eyes that now tormented her as they passed. When the last of the wheelchairs disappeared, she made her way to the reception hall and hurriedly left the building.

'You'll soon adjust, Elizabeth,' Dr Wilding said softly, stepping aside as an ambulance pulled up beside them. Instinctively Elizabeth cast a critical eye across it, as if inspecting the vehicle; this ambulance and its driver had never driven along those long muddy roads in Flanders. They were both clean and shining; no mud, no blood, fit for early morning inspection parade. The young driver, sweet-smelling with shining, youthful eyes that had not seen death, looked down from the wheel at Elizabeth then at the medal ribbons.

'Gosh! You're Elizabeth Turner, aren't you? Your picture is on the wall in our mess.' The young woman's face glowed. 'I say, wait 'till the other girls hear that I've met you,' she said, removing her leather gantlet and thrusting out her hand. 'Nora Hanley-Brown.'

Elizabeth looked at the small soft hand whose nails were manicured and clean, then up at the pretty rose-pink face. She saw a little of Catherine in her eyes and had a sudden urge to embrace the young woman and kiss her soft, childlike lips. Instead, she turned from her and quickly hurried away.

Chapter 6

In an office attached to the ward where the returning prisoners-of-war were taken, a doctor began to read the medical notes of a new patient, the young man that had stopped in front of Elizabeth. He closed the file and looked up at Sister Ross, 'What's Corporal Walder doing here, Sister? His wounds are healed.'

'I believe his wife is coming for him today, Major Andrews.'

'Splendid, I'll discharge him. Tell her she can take him home.' He looked up into her ice blue eyes and smiled. 'Thank you Sister.'

Corporal Walder opened his eyes after a few hours sleep. What he saw and smelt was little different from the German hospital he had left a few days before. He turned and met the inane grin of the patient in the bed beside his.

'Welcome 'ome chum, me name's Fred Jacks but you can call me Jacko, everyone does.' The soldier wheezed and beat his chest. 'Got a whiff of gas at Loos. Not Jerry's, ours. Bleeding typical eh? Me lungs ain't never been the same since.' After another wheezing fit, Jacko's comic face turned to one of priestly concern. 'POW long were yer son?' When he received no answer he nodded understandingly, 'Yea, well, at least you were out of it.'

Corporal Walder gazed into the eyes of the soldier before him. The wounds he saw seemed to improve rather than disfigure the round rubbery visage. Great black bushy eyebrows arched above close-set enquiring eyes. The broken squashed nose seemed to have melted into his face above an enormous handlebar moustache which hung below his fat round lips. The mouth might have been impossible to see had it not been hanging open, showing only gums, the teeth having long been extracted. The mouth had a habit of hanging open after asking a question, as though speaking the words caused the jaw great fatigue. The old soldier's leg was set in plaster, supported by ropes hanging from a frame above the bed. The stiff limb pointed towards the ceiling like a Howitzer, the very weapon he had been loading when a German shell demolished it along with most of its crew. Jacko's right arm was heavily bandaged and set at an angle; his head was covered in gauze giving him an oriental appearance.

Jacko saw the strange expression on his neighbour's face, which caused his mouth to close and his face to shrink, prune-like, into a thousand creases as it screwed into a wide grin. 'I know what yer thinking, me old son. I look a mess, dun I? Well, I suppose I do, but me mates never made it so I'm the lucky one. I bought this lot a week before the armistice. Just my luck eh?' Jacko said, smiling at his own misfortune. 'I went through the whole bleeding war without a scratch, apart from the whiff of gas, and then copped this lot in the last week. Bleeding typical... still, I made it back ter Blighty.'

Jacko looked at his companion who had remained quiet throughout his tale of woe and asked where he had 'copped it'. The only visible sign of injury was a scar running down the soldier's left cheek.

'What's yer name, chum?' Jacko had seen shellshock before. He had dished it out for four years and he guessed there were several young German soldiers in similar hospitals suffering similar pain. 'Well, it's over now, thank Christ. I'm done with soldiering so now I can get back to me garden.'

Jacko looked at the man in the opposite bed. He glanced up at the ceiling with an exasperated gesture and returned his gaze to his silent companion. He offered another sympathetic smile which quickly disappeared when the doors swung open and the figure of Sister Ross entered the room. She marched between the rows of beds giving each nurse she passed a cold stare.

'Corporal Walder,' she said. 'We're discharging you. Your wife will be arriving at 1500 to take you home. Your travel documents are being prepared and will be ready for you by the time she arrives.' She observed no reaction at the news. 'I'm aware you have not seen her for some considerable time, but that is no excuse for... for any conduct unbecoming a military ward. I will not tolerate it, do you understand?'

'You mean he can't give 'is missus a kiss, Sister?'

'Quiet Bombardier Jacks, I was not addressing you... and wipe that stupid grin from your face. Now, Corporal Walder, this is a military hospital not a bordello—'

'Land fit for heroes, my bleeding foot.'

'I shall not warn you again, Bombardier. You will be put on report.' Red faced, she turned back to Corporal Walder and said, 'Have I made myself clear? Very well,' then she left the ward snapping at one of the nurses to get on with her work.

'Cow,' Jacko said. 'Yer know what she needs if anyone is man enough to try it.' He turned once again to his neighbour and smiled. 'So you can't speak then, me old son. Never mind, yer missus will do the talking for you. I ain't never met a woman who can keep her gob

shut for five minutes. Still, yer'll get yer leg over tonight, lucky
bleeder.'

A gruff laugh from the bed opposite followed his remark. With a
final patient smile at his neighbour, Jacko winked at the soldier who
had laughed, painfully moved into a more comfortable position and
closed his eyes.

Corporal Walder could not remember a wife in his life, or children,
or a home, anything. He closed his eyes feeling tired again, and
wanted to sleep. Slowly he began to drift into another world with
distant gunfire from machine guns. A face emerged from the smoke
and din of battle; a tired, pretty face with melancholy eyes. She wore
khaki, with two gallantry medal ribbons sewn above the breast pocket
and a military hat on her head which covered most of her hair, but it
did not hide those sad grey eyes, eyes that looked like stars as a mist
draws across them.

*

When the clock in Sister Ross' office struck three she heard a
knock at her door.

'Come.' When a woman entered, Sister Ross saw she was at least in
her forties and dressed in the clothes that betrayed her class. 'How
may I help you?'

'I'm Mrs Walder.'

'Corporal Walder's mother?'

'No! His wife.'

Sister Ross' eyes narrowed. 'Mrs Ramsay Walder?'

'That's right.'

'Come in, Mrs Walder. Please shut the door.'

'Is my husband all right? The letter told me nothing other than he
was here. Is he badly hurt?'

Sister Ross recognized the anxiety in Mrs Walder's voice. She had
heard it in all the others - the fear of what she would discover; hideous
wounds, lost limbs, broken spirits and the inability to work - poverty.
This woman was no different from any other she had met in the past
four years; women from different parts of the King's realm descending
upon her with soft, frightened voices, pathetic eyes and the same list of
questions.

'Come, come, Mrs Walder, he is perfectly well. Here, these are his
personal effects. They arrived this morning. You can give them to
him.'

'What's wrong with him? Because he hasn't written I wondered if, if he had lost a limb, his arm. So many men have.'

'Mrs Walder, although the German artillery almost killed him, their doctors saved his life, certainly his leg, many British surgeons would have amputated it. He is quite well, I assure you.' Sister Ross saw the woman's eyes brighten at the news. 'Now, follow me to the ward. You may sit with him while the doctor finalizes his discharge.' She paused at the door. 'Now I expect you to behave in the proper manner and curb any instinct for affectionate greetings. A brief embrace and kiss on the cheek is acceptable, nothing more. The ward is full of men who have been denied women's company for some time. I expect you understand what I mean, Mrs Walder.'

'Yes, Sister.'

'There is one thing more, not serious but you should know before you see him. There is no physical reason for him not speaking… that is, his larynx has not been damaged, but he has a loss of voice, and he suffers with amnesia… loss of memory. The doctors are confident they will return once he settles down in his natural environment. Shock, you see… does funny things to one.'

Mrs Walder remained silent. It was all too much for her to comprehend and she felt too intimidated by Sister Ross to question her further. With her husband's personal effects clutched to her breast, she followed Sister Ross into the ward between the rows of beds. She was painfully conscious of the eyes upon her, assessing her the way men do when they look at a woman. It was as though she walked the gauntlet of unforgiving eyes, punishing her lack of beauty, condemning her loss of youth and shape. The more critical their gaze the less steady her gait, until she almost collapsed with nerves upon the bed at which Sister Ross stopped.

'Look who has come to take you home, Corporal Walder.'

Because it was a minor distraction from the monotony and discomfort of daily life, the other patients watched the reunion with casual interest. Jacko's grin disappeared as his eyes settled on Mrs Walder at close quarters. He glanced towards his new friend with surprise, his jaw hanging lower than usual. 'Is this yer missus, me old mate?'

'Thank you Bombardier Jacks. That will do,' Sister Ross said noticing a strained look on Mrs Walder's features.

'This man's not my husband.'

The eyes round the ward lit up. Those who could sit sat up. Jacko sensed drama. Sister Ross said nothing. She had long considered it an unlikely match.

The tears welled in Mrs Walder's eyes as she shed her questions one after the other. 'Where's my husband? He's dead, isn't he? Why won't you tell me where he is?'

'Come to my office, Mrs Walder. There'll be an explanation for it, I'm sure. He's probably in another ward. It happens sometimes. We'll sort this out.'

As the two women left the ward, the chatter of patients sounded like a class of schoolboys after the master had left the room. Jacko leaned towards his new friend and tapped the side of his nose. 'You got out of bloody jail there, me old son.'

The young man looked unmoved by it all, unconcerned at the chatter around him.

'Stroll on, what a turn-up eh... I bet yer bleeding glad about that? I know I would be, and I've had some rough ones in me time, I can tell yer,' Jacko laughed. 'Talk about a scarecrow. I'd rather roll over and open my eyes to a bleeding firing squad than meet that face first thing in the morning, straight up I would.'

Many round the ward laughed and those who didn't were beyond being amused by it anyway. Jacko winked at the men in the beds opposite then laid his head down on his pillow, a smile spreading his lips.

*

In his office, Major Andrews fidgeted as he sat listening to Mrs Walder's sobbing. He wanted to get home and this business could delay his departure. He glanced at his pocket watch for the umpteenth time, snapping it closed, a habit Sister Ross had observed when he was fast losing patience. Uncharacteristically, she placed a comforting arm round Mrs Walder's shoulder and suggested they looked into her husband's personal effects, which had accompanied his medical records from Germany. The seal was broken and the contents spilled out onto Major Andrews' desk. A photograph was passed around showing the likeness of Mrs Walder sitting with a baby on her lap, a small child on the knee of his father wearing the uniform of the Grenadier Guards, and four progressively older children round them. The soldier was definitely not the young man they had just left. The pay-book was in the name of Corporal Walder and the letter to him was written in Mrs Walder's hand.

'These are his things,' Mrs Walder said, 'but where is he?'

Sister Ross looked towards Major Andrews for an inspired answer;

when she saw none coming she collected the things together and replaced them in the brown envelope.

'The young man in the ward arrived here with identity discs round his neck saying he is Corporal Walder. We can do no more other than search the wards for your husband, Mrs Walder. He has to be here somewhere.'

Resigned that he would no longer have time to return home to see his daughter off at Victoria station, Major Andrew removed his spectacles and rubbed his eyes. 'So who the devil is that fellow we have in your ward, Sister?'

Chapter 7

Dr Phillip Wilding, a psychiatrist, or the trick-cyclist as the soldiers called him, was weary after a long war. It had begun to show in his face; thin lines, dark shadows and tired eyes. He sighed, removed his spectacles and glanced up from his notes regarding his latest patient as the taxicab drew up outside his home. He thought of another tortured mind, Elizabeth, his niece by marriage. Dr Wilding stepped from the cab and entered his Kensington home to the sound of laughter filtering from the drawing room. It comforted him as he unbuckled his Sam Browne belt and straightened his tie in front of the hall mirror.

'Hello my love,' said his wife when he entered the room. 'You have timed your arrival impeccably as usual,' and began pouring him a glass of sherry.

He pressed his lips lightly onto her raised cheek. The act of affection was then repeated on the cheek of his sister-in-law. 'How are you Christina? You look radiant.'

'I feel it,' she said, placing a hand on her swollen belly and glancing tenderly into her husband's proud, smiling features.

'And where's Elizabeth?'

'She's packing. I'll go and fetch her.'

'Packing! Where is she going?'

'She heard from her tutor this morning. She's going back to Oxford.'

'Umm,' Phillip stroked his moustache while he considered the wisdom of her decision. 'It can't hurt, divert her mind. We'll see.'

'You look tired, Phillip dear,' said his wife, handing him his drink. 'How is everything with your wounded soldiers?'

He sat and in his mind saw broken young men, silently staring through crazed eyes, others flinching, all mentally disturbed. 'How some will cope after what they have been through, I shall never know.' He took a sip of sherry. 'I have rather a sad case now,' and proceeded to tell them about his latest patient. 'He's suffering from amnesia; his past life is a complete blank. To add to his problems, and ours, he and we have no idea who the poor fellow is. When he was taken prisoner, the German Red Cross took him to be someone else because he had another man's ID tags and papers.'

'How come?'

Dr Wilding shrugged. 'I can only think someone thought he was dead and switched them. It happens. We don't know because he cannot speak, mutism we call it. Although his larynx hasn't been damaged he is unable to utter a sound. Classic symptom of shock.'

'What will you do?'

He shrugged. 'Mutism and speech disorders are the most common form of war neurosis. Although he was admitted as Corporal Walder, we know that is no longer true. I think this young man was an officer and that is probably why his ID was stolen, to make life easier for the real Corporal Walder if he was made a prisoner-of-war.'

'What makes you think this fellow was an officer?' Tim asked.

'The most severe cases of shellshock occur in officers who have made a name for themselves as daredevils. These men were ashamed by their overwhelming fear and performed daredevil acts to show their men that they were not afraid. Mutism, for example, is four times higher among officers than among other ranks. Their positions required them to continually repress their emotions in order to set an example to their men.'

'That's dreadful.' said Phillip's wife.

'There's more. On top of all that, this chap has nightmares, insomnia, heart palpitations, dizziness, depression and disorientation - again, symptoms more common among officers.'

'Will he ever recover?'

'Oh yes, I'm sure of it, given time. Physically he's fit and would normally receive outpatient treatment. The wounds he received are healed. The Germans did a good job there... saved his leg for sure, although he will never walk as he could. He refuses to use a stick.' Phillip sighed. 'We can't keep him but have nowhere to send him. Hospitals are busy places, particularly now with this flu pandemic. They are dropping like flies.' Tim Wilding finished his sherry and stood. He walked across the room holding the small of his aching back with one hand as he stretched with the other and then refilled his glass. 'Anyone else?'

'What will you do with him?'

Phillip shrugged. 'His voice may return next week, next year, who knows. When it does I'm certain his memory will return with it and he'll make his way home. That will be a shock to his family because they would have been informed that he was missing, presumed killed. Meanwhile, we can't just throw him out on the streets.'

'I see no reason why he cannot come to the farm with us,' Christina said. 'At least until he remembers who he is, then he can return home to his family.'

'Come to the farm, my dear!' Tim exclaimed. 'What use will he be?'

'What use? We can give him a home, Timothy Wilding. The poor lad has suffered. You could give him a job if he wishes to earn himself some money. I'm sure we can find something to occupy him. Matthew is getting on in years. He could do with some help with the sheep. Phillip's young man doesn't need a voice for that.'

'A shepherd, but he's a gentleman,' Tim mocked.

'Where's your charity, Timothy?' Christina gasped. 'You are in a position to help him. You must! Who else will?'

Tim Wilding looked at his wife and smiled. If that is what she wanted then he would agree to it. He expressed these sentiments and delighted in her reaction.

'That is very kind of you, Timothy,' his brother added. 'I shall put it to the authorities. If they agree to discharge him, then he is all yours.'

*

While a young man's immediate future was being settled downstairs, Elizabeth's was already settled. Her tutor had agreed she could return immediately. The following morning couldn't come soon enough. She found her mother's pregnant state repulsive and wanted to be as far away from it as possible. Her thoughts were interrupted by a tap on her door followed by her mother entering the room.

'We'll be eating in twenty minutes, Bess.'

'I'm not hungry,' she said, glancing at her mother's swollen belly.

Christina felt her daughter's critical eyes burning into her womb and placed her hand there as if to protect it. She sat on the bed beside her. 'We're hoping for a boy.'

'I don't wish to talk about it.'

'He's a good man–'

'And expedient too. He's already begun replacing the country's lost youth.'

'I know you miss your father–'

'Please, Mamma, leave Papa out of this.'

'He would have been so proud of you. If he was here now–'

'If he were here now I would curse him to his face. Curse him for leaving us, for getting himself killed and taking William with him.' While her mother sat open-mouthed, Elizabeth took a deep breath and squeezed her eyes shut. 'His stupid patriotic sense of honour cost his family dear, and for what?'

'I thought you loved your father.'

'I adored him,' she said louder than she intended, 'which makes it worse. It's because I loved him so much I hate what he did. Now look at you, just look at you.' Elizabeth pushed past her mother and went to the window. Christina went to her and placed a hand on her shoulder which Elizabeth shrugged off and then moved to the other side of the room.

'What have I ever done to hurt you?' Christina said softly. 'Why are you being so cruel to me?'

'Cruel? You have no idea what cruelty is, Mamma.'

'Did anything happen to you over there? If... if you were badly treated tell me, it helps to speak of it.'

'I've nothing to say.'

Elizabeth sat silently on the bed beside her suitcase and slowly began to fold a dress.

'Have you heard from that girl you served with? The one you were fond of... Catherine.'

'Fond...' Elizabeth's face crumbled, tears began to well in her eyes. 'I've no idea where she is and if Catherine thought there was the smallest chance that I was alive she would have tried to find me. I know that.'

'Don't upset yourself, Bess.'

'I'm sorry, Mamma. I cry a lot these days. I don't know why. I'm not as strong as I was.'

Christina handed her a handkerchief. 'Well it's all over now. I should just put it behind you.'

Elizabeth gasped. 'All over! Like a cricket match. Let's get back for tea. What Catherine and I went through together has bonded us for life. How can I ever forget that? I don't even know if she has survived the war and if she did, is she now a victim of this flu?'

'What flu?'

'I cannot believe you don't know this. After millions died in the war millions more are dying of this flu. No one is safe and people say there's a God...'

'Don't blaspheme, dear. Remember your grandfather was a bishop.' Christina took her daughter's hand and squeezed it. 'Please come and join us downstairs. It seems rude to stay in your room. Your aunt and uncle have been very kind to you.'

'Yes, they have.'

'Thank you, dear. Will you do something else for me? Give your stepfather a smile. He senses you don't like him.'

When Elizabeth entered the dining room, she was met with silent, understanding and sympathetic eyes. Since she was a child she hated being the centre of attention and she did not want it now. She sat with her head lowered and after a minute when her eyes rose and met Tim's for a brief second, however hard she tried she could not return his smile. Elizabeth apologized and left the room.

Christina closed her eyes and tightened her lips. 'I'm so sorry Phillip; after all you've done for her. I'll go and speak with her.'

'Leave her, Christina. It's going to take time.'

*

A week later at Brooke Farm, Tim relaxed in the sitting room talking with his brother Phillip, while Christina welcomed Phillip's soldier to her home. She paused and looked into his eyes seeing that same desolate look she had witnessed in Elizabeth. She was certain she was doing the right thing, helping this young man, while so many others were turning their backs on the returning troops, as if a gulf had risen between those who had served in the war and those who hadn't.

'Dr Wilding tells me you have chosen to call yourself David Shepherd, because you have come here to help look after the sheep.' Christina smiled. 'Very appropriate… the shepherd boy who killed Goliath. I'm pleased to see you have a sense of humour, Mr Shepherd. Well, there has been enough killing, I'm sure.' She stopped talking when she noticed that his eyes were no longer on her, but on a photograph of Elizabeth. 'That is a photograph of my second daughter. She lost her husband on the Somme, like so many young wives. She then served with the FANY... in Flanders.'

David was certain it was the same girl he had briefly stopped beside in hospital. How could he ever forget those eyes?

When Christina saw his eyes still fixed on the photograph, she said in a more stern voice, 'Elizabeth is up at Oxford. I have twin daughters who live here at the farm. None of my daughters are available to you or any other man on this farm. I hope I make myself clear, Shepherd.'

He turned and answered her with a nod of his head.

When Tim Wilding walked into the room he said, 'Phillip's leaving, my dear.' His eyes then focussed on David. He looked him up and down as if he were a heifer he was considering buying. 'Well, Shepherd, allow me to welcome you to Brooke Farm. My foreman, Mr

Wilson, is outside. He will take you to your cottage and explain your duties. You can have a couple of days to settle in. There's no pressure on you. Take your time.' He shook his head as he watched David leave, dragging his lame leg slowly behind him.

Christina turned to the photograph of Elizabeth. She had received a letter from her that morning saying she wasn't coming home for the Christmas holiday. Christina regarded it a deliberate rejection of Tim and a snub to her.

Chapter **8**

After Elizabeth completed her degree, she immediately began a teaching job at the small junior school in Buckingham. The headmaster of her school, who had taught Elizabeth when she was a girl, could not believe his luck; he had an Oxford graduate who would normally have been snapped up by much grander schools than his.

Elizabeth found a small cottage to rent in a village north of the town. When her mother discovered this, she was furious. Tim had offered her a home at the farmhouse. Elizabeth had deliberately snubbed them again. All Elizabeth wanted was to be left alone.

*

One Friday evening after she had completed marking schoolwork, Elizabeth looked out of the cottage window across the fields, where the shadows began to lengthen. She decided to go for a ride on her bicycle. She made her way down the hill towards Buckingham and when she reached the Old Gaol, she swung right through the town towards the road that led to Winslow. She had a sudden urge to see Brooke Farm, although at a distance, in the hope of bumping into one or both of her sisters. Although she had spoken to Jane, she hadn't seen her mother since she was presented with her medal by the King.

All communication between Elizabeth and her mother had ceased. They were just not getting on, so it was easier, Elizabeth thought, just to avoid each other. Her mother thought so too. If her daughter could not accept that she had begun a new life with another man, then there was little she could do about it.

Elizabeth left her bicycle against a tree and crossed a field towards what looked like a small copse, which she knew from Jane's description eventually led to the farmhouse. She reached the wood and discovered it was not a coppice, but trees surrounding a huge lake, where the golden light of the evening sun flickered on the surface. The lake was separated from the farm buildings by another huge field where hundreds of sheep grazed. To the east, on higher ground, she saw a group of three labourer's cottages and imagined how cold they would be in winter exposed to the wind lashing across the high open ground.

Close to the water's edge, there was an area of tangled growth where reeds grew, and where she could see everything without being seen herself. She sat and listened to the different songs of birds around her. Among those sounds, Elizabeth heard the cluttering of two wood pigeons escaping the trees and she watched them fly off in an arch towards the shelter of the woodland opposite. A figure emerged and slowly approached the water's edge. She tensed at the sight of a man. Elizabeth had lost her trust in men since her captivity and no longer felt comfortable in their company. At night in her cottage, she would lock her bedroom door, even though she lived alone. Fat round faces with pig eyes and leering lips smiled at her in her sleep, which caused her to wake suddenly in fear of more abuse; now alone in an isolated spot, she felt vulnerable and frightened again.

She watched him cautiously move towards the bank and awkwardly lower himself to the ground. Her irritation turned to sympathy. It was not so long ago she had offered her shoulder to so many wounded soldiers; held their hand and written their letters, suggesting to them what a sweetheart might like to hear.

In the fading light, she saw him staring towards a gap in the trees to a field where her stepfather's sheep were grazing. Her eyes strained to focus on his face, but he was sitting too far away to be recognized. He opened a book and began to read. Afraid to disturb him, she remained where she sat and closed her eyes. A crane overhead let out a loud cry as it flew in to land on the other side of the lake, which woke Elizabeth from her thoughts. The stranger had left without her seeing him go.

After that, whenever the weather allowed her to do so she would go to the lake, finding comfort sitting by the water's edge, while reading a book or marking homework. One evening, the stranger appeared again. He approached the bank with the same awkward, slow step. He lowered himself to the ground and stared at the passing swans with their growing cygnets. In his hand, the book he had brought to read remained unopened. For forty minutes he didn't move a muscle. Periodically, Elizabeth's eyes rose towards him. When the lack of light began to tire her eyes, she closed her book and saw that he was gone. She rose and slowly made her way home too.

*

One warm evening, shortly after Elizabeth returned home from school, Jane was waiting for her. She kissed her sister's cheek. 'Hello Jane. Have you been waiting long?'

'Bess, what have you done to your hair?'

'As you can see, I've cut it.'

'You look like a boy.'

Elizabeth glanced down at her breasts. 'Strange looking boy, don't you think?'

When they were inside the house, Jane said, 'Why won't you go and see Mamma's baby?'

'Is your presence here a friendly one, Jane?'

'Of course it is.'

'Did Mamma send you?'

'No, she's as stubborn as you. For heaven's sake Bess, you haven't seen her once since we went to Buckingham Palace. It's not like you to treat her like that.'

'Tea?'

'It hurts me to see you no longer love Mamma!'

Elizabeth banged her fist on the table which made Jane jump. 'Do not question my love for Mamma!'

'Then why are you avoiding her?'

'I'm not good around babies.'

'It's natural for Mamma to want a child with the man she now loves.'

'And was her child conceived out of love, or an expedient way of catching a wealthy man?'

'What are you talking about?'

'I've heard the gossip, Jane. It's all around town.'

'What is?'

'Just work it out for yourself.'

Elizabeth went into the kitchen and poured water into the kettle. She slammed it onto the stove. When Jane appeared, she saw her sister leaning against the wall. Jane went and embraced her. Elizabeth responded, desperate for the close contact of someone she trusted and loved. Jane sensed it was best to just hold her and let the tears flow. When at last they parted, Elizabeth kissed Jane's cheek and went to the boiling kettle.

'I cry a lot,' Elizabeth said, pouring the water into a teapot. 'I used to be so strong. Others in France relied on me for strength. I gave it willingly. Now I seem to have none left for myself.'

'Who cares what people say about Mamma? They're jealous, that's all.'

'You're very sweet, Jane.'

'She knows you're avoiding her, Bess. Please come and see her.'

'I can't go there, Jane. I cannot bear to see Mamma with that man.'

'He's our stepfather and has been very kind to us. He was very upset when we were informed you'd been killed.'

'I wish I had been; I'd be with Papa—'

'How dare you say that!' Jane snapped. 'How dare you! You will never know what we suffered when we thought you were dead.'

Elizabeth quietly left the kitchen. Jane followed two minutes later and placed a cup of tea on the table. The silence between them lengthened. Eventually, Jane said, 'I'm sorry I shouted.'

Elizabeth sipped the hot tea and stared into her teacup. She looked up into her sister's red eyes. 'You've been crying.'

'I hate to see you like this.'

'Forgive me Jane,' Elizabeth said, reaching for her hand. 'You're the last person in this world I want to hurt. Tell Mamma I hope that she will come and call on me here... alone. Tell her that.'

'Of course I will. They're going to London tomorrow to show Harry off to Aunt Melanie and Uncle Phillip. They'll be away for two days. I might be out for the evening, but come over anyway and see Stephie. I know she would love you to visit her. Surprise her, please... for me.'

*

The next evening after supper, Elizabeth cycled towards Brooke Farm. The front door was unlocked so she entered. When walking into the drawing room, Stephanie moved guiltily from a young man's embrace. Removing a wayward lock of hair from her eyes she smiled then began to giggle. 'Bess! What have you done to your hair?'

Elizabeth glared at the young man at Stephanie's side. He did not rise from his seat immediately - a point of some delicacy restrained him. Elizabeth recognized it and she said through gritted teeth, 'If you will excuse me, I should like a private word with my sister.' A protesting Stephanie followed Elizabeth to the living room. 'Why are you alone in the house with that man, Stephanie?'

'I'm not alone... Susan and cook are here, at least in their rooms.'

'Who on earth is Susan?'

'She's the maid. What harm is there in seeing a chap alone? We were only kissing. I'm perfectly safe.'

'Men are not to be trusted.'

'I trust John. I... I love him.'

'Love... you will do well to remember that love and trust are vulnerable twins in the company of lust.' Elizabeth sighed with frustration at her sister's sudden laughter. 'It's far from amusing and may I suggest you button up your blouse. His fingerprints are all over it.'

Stephanie's hand jumped to the buttons on her blouse. 'Hark at you! Jibber, jibber, just like a monkey.'

'Apes jibber, you stupid girl, monkeys chatter.' Seeing that she had upset Stephanie, Elizabeth reached out to her. 'I'm sorry, Stephie. You're not stupid. Please forgive me. I don't know what's wrong with me. First I upset Jane and now you.'

'We were kissing, Bess... that's all.' When Stephanie met her sister's eyes she looked to the ground. 'All right, he went a step further, but I let him. He wasn't taking advantage of me. It's a strain not to. You must have felt that with Robert.'

'I just don't want you getting into trouble or hurt.' Elizabeth leaned forward and kissed her sister's cheek. 'I shall only worry.'

'You should worry about yourself, Bess. It would do you good if you found a boyfriend instead of hanging around with Katie Crenshaw. I've seen you go to her lodgings.'

'Katie is my friend.'

'She's weird.'

'No she's not. I've liked Katie since we were at junior school together.'

Stephanie looked into Elizabeth's eyes as if searching into her soul. 'You know she's never been out with a fellow. During the war it was rumoured she was living with another woman in Winslow.'

Elizabeth laughed. 'I shared lodgings with another woman in Oxford; does that make me strange too?'

'Why don't you come here to live? It's not right you living on your own when your family lives just a few miles away.'

'I'm perfectly happy being on my own and living alone.'

'But why? Half the fellows I know swoon at the sight of you.'

'Only half?'

Stephanie laughed, which lightened the mood. 'There's a dance at the young farmer's club tomorrow. Jane and I are going. Why don't you come with us? We could have some fun. Please say you will.'

'No, I don't think so... thank you. I have lots of marking to do.'

'There you go again. You're just like him,' Stephanie said, pointing out of the window at a distant figure. 'He's always on his own, but then I'm not surprised. He's always shaking and throwing fits at the slightest noise around him.'

It was the stranger who came to the lake. He seemed to be heading that way now. Elizabeth watched his proud manner and slow progress and felt an inner desperation for him. 'Who is that man, Stephie?'

'He's Mamma's wounded soldier, as she calls him. He's got this horrible scar down his face. It gives me the creeps and he can't speak, nor does he know who he is or where he's from. He's pathetic. No one bothers with him, but then how can anyone possibly have a conversation with a mute? Mamma brought him here to help the shepherd. You know Mamma and her good little deeds.' Stephanie began to giggle. 'He was useless, because he kept having funny turns and the sheep would run wild. I remember Gabriel Oat's sheep doing that in *Far From the Madding Crowd.*'

'It's Gabriel Oak not Oat, and it was his dog not the shepherd at fault. So don't put the blame on that poor fellow. Show some charity, Stephanie.'

'Yes, all right, Miss Clever Clogs. I think he ought to be in a madhouse.'

'It's shellshock, poor chap.'

'He calls himself David Shepherd, which isn't his real name. He doesn't know that. Now he looks after Mamma's garden I suppose he ought to be called David Gardener.'

'Don't be cruel, Stephie. He has obviously suffered a great deal.'

'I should stay far away from him. Mamma has told us to stay away from him, as if I want anything to do with him anyway.'

'Stephie darling, will you do me a favour and not tell Mamma I was here. I came to see you, only you. I'll leave you with lover boy. Remember what I said about love and trust.'

After Elizabeth left the farmhouse, she cycled home determined to speak to David Shepherd when she next saw him. Although she did not like to be alone with men, David Shepherd was broken, not whole; she liked that. Broken men didn't hurt her. She helped them into her ambulance and took them somewhere to be mended. She felt safe with broken men. The next time she saw him she would speak to him - one broken person comforting another.

*

A week later, during a fine, crisp evening, Elizabeth saw David making his way slowly through the trees down towards the lake. She rose and went to him. At the sound of a breaking twig he looked up and saw her approaching. He removed his cap. Elizabeth saw the scar running down his cheek and felt she had seen him somewhere before, but couldn't place where that may have been.

'I'm sorry to disturb you. I believe you're Mr Shepherd,' she smiled. 'I'm Mrs Turner, one of Mrs Brennan's… I mean Mrs Wilding's daughters. I have twin sisters who live at the farmhouse. I expect you've met them?'

David's gaze became so intense Elizabeth began to feel uncomfortable, yet she sensed that he seemed to know her too, which made her certain that she had met him before. 'I feel I have met you before, Mr Shepherd,' she said. 'Perhaps it was in France or Belgium. I... I was over there,' she said almost in apology. 'I've certainly seen you here before, a few times in fact… always alone. I came over to say you're not alone, Mr Shepherd. If you ever feel the need to talk…' Elizabeth met his eyes and coloured a little. 'I'm sorry… I mean, if you ever feel the need to be with someone, simply to feel the comfort of someone's presence. You see, I shared a little of it too. Not as you did, but a little… enough to know just how you must have suffered.' She looked up at him and offered a shy smile. 'I'm sorry. I talk too much.' She fidgeted. His eyes still bore into hers. Now she spoke to the ground. 'Unfortunately, we now seem to be an embarrassment to those who were not in Flanders. Them and us, I believe is the expression. It seems a sin for a young man to be in a wheelchair...' In the silence that followed, she suddenly remembered where she had seen him. It was one of those dazzling coincidences that logicians loathe and poets love. 'I remember now, you were arriving with other prisoners-of-war the day I left the Royal Herbert. Of course you won't remember me, but I clearly remember you... in a wheelchair...'

He took her outstretched hand. It felt soft and warm in his. When she felt the pressure of his fingers tighten around hers she quickly withdrew it and felt guilty for doing so in such an unfriendly manner.

'I'm pleased to meet you again, Mr Shepherd. You're looking so much better than when I first saw you. I expect it's all this fresh, country air.' She became aware that she was smiling at him and blushed. An awkward silence developed between them. Elizabeth fidgeted again.

David could see she was nervous and feeling uncomfortable. He stepped back from her. His movement made her eyes rise to his. 'I'm sorry. I expect you would like to read your book. I'll leave you in peace.'

*

A few days later, Elizabeth arrived at the lake after David. He jumped when she greeted him. Then she saw him relax and his eyes soften.

54

'I've brought you a book of Shakespeare's sonnets to read. I understand you like poetry. My sister Jane told me she saw you reading Shelley. I'm rather fond of him myself.'

He accepted the book and gestured for her to sit. Elizabeth knew a milestone had suddenly been reached between them. If she sat with him now she could never sit away from him again without it appearing rude.

'I really ought to go. It looks as if it might rain.' For a moment she battled with herself then with a smile, she sat. 'Perhaps I can stay for a while. Would you like me to read to you?'

He handed her the book. As she read, he concentrated on her voice rather than Shakespeare's words; a clear, even voice with no hint of the Buckingham dialect he had now grown to recognize. A faint breeze caught her hair sending some loose copper strands dancing, as if flames spitting from a log fire. He wanted to reach out to them, but her hand rose in an unconscious movement and tucked them behind her ear. He closed his eyes and heard Shakespeare's words begin to filter through Elizabeth's soft voice. When she closed the book and handed it back to him, he saw her eyes deliberately settle on the scar running down his cheek. David was surprised that she did not turn from him as others always did. She undid the first button of her blouse at the collar and showed him a dark, blue scar, on the part of her neck that met her shoulder. 'I too have a calling card from Fritz,' she said smiling shyly.

He noted her smile; when she relaxed it was quite dazzling, lighting up the whole of her face. She was very attractive, he thought, yet she seemed quite unaffected by it.

'You're the only person I've ever willingly shown that to. Not that I find it ugly, but no one has a right to see it unless they themselves... if you follow. ' Elizabeth pulled at some grass. There was no sound as they sat together, other than the wind rustling through the leaves of the trees. Even the birds were silent as if exhausted by singing all day. 'I received that wound when my ambulance was hit. It killed the girl with me. I was taken prisoner by the Germans.' She pulled a little more grass. 'I've never spoken about it to anyone. Maybe it's good to do so.' She looked at him and smiled. 'Do you think I look like a boy?' she suddenly asked.

David's shoulders shook briefly and when she saw it, she laughed too. He shook his head. She saw there was nothing sexual in his gaze when he looked up at her and smiled.

'Everyone else seems to think so.'

They sat in silence again and watched the swans give a cursory glance as they swam by. 'I'm going away tomorrow for two weeks, to visit my sister Louisa in Sussex.'

His eyes found hers.

'I have neglected my family too long. My sister Louisa has just had a baby. It's becoming a habit in my family.' She stood and shrugged her shoulders. 'Well... goodbye.'

David stood and watched her leave. He willed her to turn and wave or just turn, give him one last look with those magnificent grey eyes. He saw her stop when she reached the clearing and wave, then she was gone. His breath filled his lungs. He was worth a final look.

Alone with his thoughts, he pondered on what he had heard the men on the farm say of her, fragments of praise emerging from coarse remarks, all out of earshot of Jacob Wilson, the farm's foreman, who boasted he would have her one day. She was not for Jacob Wilson, they all knew. 'Some rich chap will have her,' one said and they would all nod and agree, then speculate whom the fellow might be.

David picked up a twig and scratched at the hard ground, then stood and slowly limped away.

*

Jane joined Elizabeth for supper that evening. After, they cycled back to the farm because Tim and Christina were out having dinner with some friends. They left the bicycles by one of the barns and then went for a walk along the bank of the lake.

'I used to take a walk at this time with Catherine, before the hospital run.'

Jane looked her sister in the eye. 'In your letters to me you said you loved her. Was that the same sisterly love you have for me?'

'Is there any other love one woman has for another?'

'Bess, you know there is. We've both read Sappho.'

'Jane, it's easy to become close to one's own sex in war,' Elizabeth said with a shrug. 'I saw love between men, the love that Saint John spoke of when he said, "Greater love hath no man than this..." many of them did lay their life down for a friend.'

Jane smiled at her sister. 'One day you'll find her, I'm sure.'

'Maybe I'll bump into her in Sussex.'

'To think Bess, we're now aunts. Aunt Jane. It sounds rather grand. Would you like to marry again... have children?'

Elizabeth shrugged. 'I have no wish to play the courting game.'

'Game?'

'Attraction, pursuit, capture, intimacy... familiarity, boredom, rows... then all the bother of disentangling oneself.'

'My word Bess, such melancholy. You've only courted once, with Robert.'

'Robert has been dead for three years.'

'So there have been others?'

'I've had my affairs.'

Jane suddenly stopped at the very spot where Elizabeth had sat talking with David earlier and she said, 'Here's another in the making. Someone has scratched out your name.'

Chapter 9

Elizabeth felt sudden happiness as she stepped off the train at Petworth station. Smoke belched from the train as it laboured up the hill, its driver pulling the cord that sent out a loud whistle whose purpose could be for no other reason than to attract the attention of someone. When the smoke cleared, it revealed Elizabeth alone on the platform. She looked around for Louisa. Only an elderly porter could be seen cleaning the waiting room windows.

'Excuse me, how do I get to Burton Park?'

'Left out the station and keep walking for a mile or so,' he said. 'If you reach the Cricketers, you've passed it.'

Louisa's house was a pretty place with a garden blooming with summer flowers. Flushed from her walk, Elizabeth knocked. She heard her sister's voice through an open window. 'Bess, if that's you come in.'

The younger sister followed her elder sister's voice to the sitting room and found her feeding her baby. She kissed her sister whose face radiated healthy contentment.

'God, what have you done to your hair? You look like–'

'A boy, I've heard it all before.'

'I hate it. Why did you cut it that short?'

'I... oh, it doesn't matter.'

'You're quite mad, Bess. Why do such a thing?'

Elizabeth's shoulders dropped as she sighed. 'If you really must know Lou, men stare. Their eyes are always on me. I don't like it.'

Louisa's jaw dropped. 'I've never heard of such a thing. Of course men look at you. They always have Bess. You're a beautiful woman. Just look at your face, your figure. I still haven't forgiven our Lord for giving it to you and not to me.'

'I thought you were going to meet me at the station.'

'Don't change the subject, Bess.' Louisa sighed and shook her head. Her younger sister was a puzzle to her. 'What has happened to you to dislike men's eyes?'

'I've always hated them staring at me. Let me look at my nephew.' Elizabeth's smile broadened as she took the baby's tiny hand. 'He's so sweet. Look at his tiny fingers and little nails, so perfectly formed. You must be so happy.'

'Yes, now that he has arrived. I won't describe what I suffered bringing this little chap into the world, so unless you enjoy pain, don't have children,' Louisa replied, secretly feeling happy that she had achieved something her younger sister had not. 'Nothing's private. The way one is poked and prodded, all one's bits on display and, of course, pregnancy will destroy that lovely figure of yours. I mean, look at my breasts,' she said displaying them 'I look like a cow.'

Elizabeth turned and walked to the window. She had been impregnated by one of her guards, which of the two she didn't know. Had she not spat in the fat guard's face, he would not have beaten her, which caused her to miscarry. Had she not miscarried, her baby would have been nine months older than her nephew was now.

'Mamma tells me you've been quite beastly to her,' Louisa said, wiping her breast. She looked up at her sister as she fastened the buttons of her blouse. 'You can't be bothered to walk a couple of miles to see Harry yet you will travel all this way to see Danny.'

'It's you I've come to see. Daniel is a bonus.'

'Harry is your brother. Remember that.'

'My half brother - and if I had any doubts about my shortcomings then I can always rely on you to be the most helpful of my sisters.'

'Are you going to be beastly to me?'

'As you always were to me when we were younger?'

During the silence that followed, Elizabeth spotted a squirrel that had seen Louisa's cat crouching by the hedge. She followed its rapid ascent up the great towering oak which cast shadows across the lawn. Unconcerned, or too unfit for the chase, Kaiser Bill sat and began to lick his paw. 'Lou, I hope we can enjoy each other's company without fighting for once.' Elizabeth said at last.

'Come on Danny boy, let's hear that burp,' Louisa whispered rubbing her baby's back. When he obliged her, she looked back up at Elizabeth. 'I've been looking forward to seeing you. I haven't many friends here, only Bertie's colleagues and they're all so tediously boring.'

'Did you know that Stephanie has just become engaged?'

'Yes. He'll be henpecked the day the honeymoon ends.'

Elizabeth laughed. 'He already is. Jane is still waiting for her bloke to pop the question. She adores him. I hope he doesn't break her heart.'

'Honestly Bess, you have always been far too protective towards Jane. She can look after herself. What about you?'

59

'What about me?'

'You know very well. Have you got anybody?'

'I'll make some tea.'

'Oh, I see. It's like that is it? Shut up Louisa and mind your own business.'

'There isn't anyone.'

'Come on young man, bed for you.' Louisa disappeared with Daniel into the next room. When she returned she said, 'Has there been anyone since Robert?'

'You've always taken too much of an unhealthy interest in my sex life, Lou.'

'I want to know what my gorgeous sister gets up to.'

Elizabeth smiled. 'There's nothing to tell you.'

'Considering your good looks I always thought you diffident with men. It surprised me when you got married.'

'Why?'

'You hardly knew him. I always thought he was a little effeminate.'

'Like Bertie, you mean.'

Louisa laughed. 'He's man enough. At least we didn't have an epistolary courtship.'

'One can learn a lot about another through letters.'

'But one cannot kiss, touch, fondle and thrill' Louisa said, planting a kiss on her sister's cheek. 'We had sex before we were married,' she whispered. 'Bertie was all hands. At least I felt wanted. Did you ever have it off with Robert before you became Mrs Turner?'

'No.'

'I really ought to ask if you actually did it with him at all. I mean, he left for France pretty sharpish after the wedding.'

'There was time enough.'

Louisa glanced at Elizabeth as she went to the kitchen to fill a kettle. 'You know, sister dear, at one time, I thought you preferred girls.'

From the kitchen Louisa was spared Elizabeth's blushes. 'What gave you that idea?'

'The way you used to look at Katie Crenshaw.'

'It was a schoolgirl crush. That's all. She's very pretty.'

'You're the beauty now.'

'For heaven's sake Lou, will you please stop going on about that.'

'Stephie tells me you still see her and that she has cut her hair short too. You know the rumours about her I presume?'

'Gossip, you mean. Katie is a friend, I am allowed girl friends aren't I?'

'Yes, but girls your age usually have a fellow in the background, don't they? You don't.'

*

As the clock struck six, Louisa's husband arrived home. After the greetings were over and a glass of sherry taken, they all sat down to eat. Elizabeth glanced at her brother-in-law, unable to see what attracted her elder sister to him. Compared to Louisa who had a strong personality, Bertie was weak. Perhaps that's what she liked about him, she was able to dominate him as she had always bullied her three sisters. Bertie was also a fussy man, slight of frame and tall of stature, boring with little imagination. He found himself in France during the war, but did not fight because his eyesight was poor and therefore was restricted to office work at General Headquarters, rather than be trusted with a weapon, whatever calibre it was. When the war ended he wore the same medals the fighting men did, returned to his old job at the bank and was welcomed home a hero.

'Would you care for some more wine, Bess? Having also served in France, I expect you have acquired a taste for it like me,' Bertie said, pouring a little into her glass.

'Bess lived in France before the war, Bertie dear.'

'Of course, I forgot.' After swallowing the last of the steak and kidney pudding Elizabeth had cooked, he wiped his mouth. 'Delicious. Apart from being an academic you're a good cook too. France, I expect.'

'Steak and kidney pudding is an English dish, Bertie. It was our mother who taught us to cook,' Louisa said again.

'Yes, I'm sorry.' Bertie said. 'You're an excellent cook yourself, my dear.' Then to Elizabeth he changed the subject, 'We were lucky to get this house. Sir Edward, who owns this estate, and a very important customer at the bank I might add, wanted to let the property to someone who had been over there. He thought it only right having served in France himself. So, it was offered to me... us.'

Elizabeth felt sudden irritation that Bertie should steal the laurels of fighting men and said, 'Perhaps word had reached him that you were a wounded war hero Bertie, poisoned by licking the lead from your pencil.'

Louisa burst out laughing, which made Bertie wriggle uncomfortably in his seat. 'I know you're being sarcastic Bess, but we all did our bit. Artillery does not discriminate between fighting men and clerks. We were all in danger.'

'I'm sorry Bertie. That was unfair.' Elizabeth said, 'Tell me about the grounds here. I expect they're lovely.'

'I imagine they are,' Bertie said, still sulking from Elizabeth's rebuke. 'We have Sir Edward's permission to walk them, but we never do.'

Elizabeth looked up in surprise. 'Why ever not?'

'Because it would seem as if we are taking advantage of his generosity.'

'I should like to see the grounds,' Elizabeth said to Bertie's obvious dismay.

'They're beautiful,' Louisa said, 'and there's a lake with swans and—'

'How do you know this, Louisa?'

'I go for walks. I've even been for a walk with Lady Hannah.'

'You went for a walk with *Lady Hannah*?' Bertie gasped, his eyes suddenly resembling a lobster's. 'Louisa, my dear, we are their tenants. Good heavens! Lady Hannah is the daughter of an earl... she was being polite. Whatever were you thinking?'

'She was very friendly.'

'Louisa, those people do not make friends with the likes of us. I think it is ill-advised to socialize with your betters. It will give you delusions of grandeur.'

The sisters looked at each other and burst into laughter. When Elizabeth stood and collected the dirty plates, she bent and kissed Bertie on the top of his thinning hair. 'You're very funny, Bertie. I can see what attracted my sister to you.'

He looked up at Louisa his cheeks filling with blood.

In the kitchen, Elizabeth spooned some trifle into some pudding dishes. Louisa entered saying that Bertie was sulking. She pressed into her sister from behind, placing her cheek to Elizabeth's cheek, gripping her round her midriff in an act of affection. Catherine used to do it to Elizabeth in France and whisper, 'I love you, Bess.' Elizabeth closed her eyes and imagined Louisa's arms were Catherine's arms, and a tear crept to the corner of her eye.

'Are you crying, Bess?'

'I was thinking what I had lost and how happy you are, with your baby, Bertie...'

'I'm happy you're here, really,' Louisa said. 'Sometimes I feel quite depressed being out here on my own.'

'I should love it here. I like to be alone.'

'I know. Jane wrote to me. She's quite worried about you.'

'Perhaps she thinks I isolate myself too much. Maybe I do.'

'Poor Bess,' Louisa teased, running her fingertip down the length of her sister's nose, 'such a pretty face and all that brain yet you hide away so no one may share them.'

'I have a friend whose company I enjoy.'

'A male friend?'

'Yes.'

'I thought you didn't have anyone.'

'It's not that sort of friendship and he certainly has no sexual interest in me.'

'I don't believe that for a moment. Other than a homosexual, there isn't a man alive who wouldn't want you in his bed.'

'He doesn't. It's very refreshing. We sit by the lake and I read to him.'

'Christ... another Robert.'

'He's not! He suffered a lot in the war. Often, we just sit in silence. We find comfort in each other's company.'

'Sounds like a heap of fun.'

'I like him because I feel safe in his company. He doesn't look at me with lustful eyes the way other men do.'

'Bess, honestly! It's what makes the world go round. Not all men have lurid thoughts... Bess darling, you're trembling. What's the matter?'

'Why don't we take Danny for a stroll in the grounds tomorrow?'

'Bess, did anything happen to you in Germany?'

'Nothing happened.' Elizabeth glanced at her sister. 'Shall we go and see the grounds then?'

'Yes, let's do that. I shouldn't think there would be any lustful eyes there,' Louisa said with another furtive look at her sister, 'although we might bump into Sir Edward. Now *he* is what I call a dish,' which brought a smile to Elizabeth's lips.

It was then, when Elizabeth moved and with her the collar of her blouse, Louisa saw the deep blue scar on her sister's neck. 'What's that?'

Elizabeth's hand went to it, covering the scar. 'Nothing.'

'Let me see it.'

Louisa held her sister and pulled her blouse to the side to inspect the scar more closely. 'What happened?'

'I was struck by some shrapnel the day of my capture.'

Louisa bent and kissed it, as if it might disappear. 'My God... another inch and...' She ran her finger along the length of it. In a brighter voice she said, 'I like it. It's blemished you and makes you less perfect.' Louisa straightened Elizabeth's collar and they returned to the dining room where Bertie was flicking though a newly-published book. Louisa took it from him. 'Not at the dinner table please, Bertie.'

'I bought it today. It's about my regiment. The battles they fought.'

'*They* fought, not *you*, and don't you go telling anybody you did,' Louisa said. 'Bess was in the thick of it and got two medals for being brave so don't start playing the hero and giving us any more of your war stories. She's even got a scar where she was wounded−'

'Please Lou. There's no need to tell Bertie that.'

Bertie fidgeted and loosened his collar. 'I know Elizabeth was brave. I've always been very proud of Bess, particularly being thrown into a German prison too.'

'It was a hospital,' Elizabeth said, 'not a prison.'

'Did you ever attempt to escape?'

'I really don't want to talk about it, Lou. I'd rather hear about your aristocratic neighbours. They seem far more interesting than my captivity.'

'Why don't you ever discuss the time you were a prisoner?'

'Because there is nothing to discuss.'

'I'm sure Elizabeth would rather forget about the war, my dear.'

'You talked enough about it on your return, husband dear,' Louisa cried, glaring at him. 'Bored me solid with it. Now I should like to hear what my sister did.'

'I think you may have had a little too much wine, dear.'

Elizabeth closed her eyes, dreading Louisa's reply. There was silence. When she opened her eyes again, Bertie was cowing under the weight of Louisa's glaring eyes. They turned to her sister. 'I have not drunk too much wine. I simply asked to hear about your captivity.'

'There really is nothing to say, Lou. I worked with a girl called Sylvie, a French prisoner. We slaved all day in the laundry room and were locked in our rooms at night. We weren't allowed to talk to each other because the guards could not understand French and they thought we might be plotting to escape.'

'You must have talked sometimes.'

'Of course we did, always in whispers when the guard wasn't paying attention or if he was in a drunken sleep.'

'Sleep! If he slept then surely you could have just walked out of the place.'

Elizabeth sighed impatiently. 'Sylvie's family lived in the occupied sector. The Germans threatened to shoot them if either of us tried to escape. It was a threat I took seriously. I couldn't compromise their safety, that's why I made no attempt. Now please, let's change the subject.'

Elizabeth glanced at Louisa who returned a quizzical gaze. To Elizabeth's relief, Louisa leant back in her chair as Bertie changed the subject, discussing his new responsibilities at the bank. As much as she tried to prevent it, Elizabeth's mind returned to the basement of the German hospital. She remembered the first time it happened, during the changeover of duties. One of the guards burst into her room. He was overweight and useless to any fighting unit. He stank of alcohol and became violent with drunken anger when she hit him. He beat her then began to unfasten the buttons of his trousers while the other guard waited his turn.

'Bess, you're shaking. Something happened to you, didn't it?' Louisa said firmly. 'Bess, snap out of it! What did those Germans do to you? Tell me. What did they do?'

Elizabeth looked up into her sister's face. 'Just give it a rest Louisa, and shut up.' She fled from the table into the garden. She could hear her sister and Bertie arguing then the baby started to cry. Why did she always end up annoying her family? She heard Kaiser Bill meow and felt him curl against her leg. Elizabeth picked him up and rubbed her cheek against his soft coat. 'Have you come to comfort me, Kaiser Bill?' She whispered and stroked him under the chin when he began to purr.

*

After a late breakfast, the sisters left the house and pushed the baby in his pram down a narrow road lined with rhododendron bushes until it emerged into vast lawns and the smell of summer's dry heat. Elizabeth looked across the landscape illuminated by patterns of light dazzling through the trees. Ahead of them was the great Portland stone house appearing solid and magnificent in the distance. At the first floor level, above what seemed a rather silly narrow door, four Ionic columns below a large ornate balustrade, dominated the front of the building. There were several huge Georgian windows to light what

Elizabeth imagined to be vast rooms with high ceilings. The face of the building was covered in a huge wisteria; the last of its summer flowers hanging as if rotting bunches of grapes. Beyond the tennis courts the orderly structure of the gardens was in complete contrast to the wilfulness and wildness of nature where the South Downs reached high into the sky.

They saw a figure approaching them. Elizabeth gathered Louisa was not happy to see him by the sound of her sigh. When the man arrived at their side, he nodded at Louisa whose lips tightened in a smile that did not reach her eyes. However, the man's eyes narrowed in what seemed to be recognition when they focused on Elizabeth.

'Ladies,' he said, with a slight bow of the head.

'This is my sister Elizabeth Brennan, Mr Jenkins.'

Jenkins lifted his hat, nodded, and walked on.

'Why did you tell him my name was Brennan?'

'You are a Brennan. Robert's dead, darling. You were only married to him for a few days and you were only with him as his wife for a few hours. You're not a Turner.'

'That's my late husband's name and I choose to keep it. Please remember that in future.'

'God, you're touchy this morning.'

'Who was that man?'

'Lady Hannah's butler... a stuck up nobody. He looked as if he recognized you.'

'I don't know him.'

'I heard you tossing and turning in bed, last night. Did you have problems sleeping?'

'A strange bed,' Elizabeth lied. 'What's that little building over there?'

'A Norman church. I think it was built sometime around 1070. You ought to go and look at it while you're here. It's very pretty. Inside there's a painting on the wall of a girl hanging upside down. She's a redhead. It was probably you in a previous life.' Louisa looked at Elizabeth and smiled. 'Rumour has it that her ghost, the *White Lady*, walks the halls of the Manor. Do you believe in ghosts?'

Elizabeth did not answer. She saw plenty of them every night in her sleep. As the sisters passed the rose garden, the scent lingered and sweetened the air they breathed. They stopped to admire them. There was sudden excitement in Louisa's voice when she saw a horseman approaching them at a canter.

'It's Sir Edward Wyatt.'

The horse slowed and a slight tug at the rein brought the animal to an obedient halt. It snorted its protest and was pacified by a few affectionate taps on his large muscular neck. 'Good morning, Mrs Simpson. Enjoying a stroll I see? It's certainly the weather for it.' Sir Edward spoke to one sister yet his eyes dwelt on the other.

'Good morning, Sir Edward. May I introduce you to my sister? She's staying with me for a couple of weeks. Thought I'd show her your lovely grounds.'

'Good morning,' he said looking down into Elizabeth's eyes. 'Have we ever met somewhere before?'

'That's very unlikely,' Elizabeth said turning from his eyes.

'Forgive me,' he replied, startled by her cold manner. 'Mrs Simpson, I hope you will be coming to the fete on the fourteenth.'

'Yes, Sir Edward. I'm looking forward to it.'

'And will we have the pleasure of seeing you there too–'

'No. I shall be returning home before then.'

'To an impatient husband, I expect.'

'My husband is dead. He was killed by incompetent, upper-class generals and their staff,' Elizabeth replied, causing Louisa to burn bright red.

Sir Edward bid them good day, dug his spurs into the horse and cantered away in the direction of the church.

'Did you have to be so rude? Christ Elizabeth, I have to live here.'

'All that rot about seeing me before somewhere…'

'Well his butler seemed to recognize you too so he may have done. God, he was only being friendly.'

'You were practically throwing yourself at him.'

'I was flattered by his attention, although you had most of it. What's wrong with you, Bess? Why are you like this? You're not the sister I knew before you went to Flanders. You've changed so much. Something happened to you in that hospital didn't it?'

Elizabeth held her head in her hands to block out her sister's voice. A dark cloud began to envelop her as Louisa kept throwing questions at her and demanding answers. She needed to escape, to be in the light before she confessed what she had suffered at the hands of her guards - the awful shame and humiliation of those months. She needed to be free of them, to escape their eyes, their hands… their lust.

'Bess! Don't be silly. I'm sorry, come back. *Bess…*'

Louisa watched Elizabeth run away and head towards her home.

She went to follow but stopped when she saw another horse and rider approaching her at a trot.

'Good morning, Mrs Simpson,' the rider said, watching Elizabeth disappearing down the road. 'Who's that boy and what's his hurry?'

'It's my sister, Lady Hannah.'

'Your sister! Is everything all right?'

'I've upset her…' Louisa's voice trailed away as she watched Elizabeth disappear from her sight. 'We were discussing the war. She suffered so much…'

Lady Hannah's voice became cold. 'The war was responsible for a great deal of suffering, Mrs Simpson. Have you seen Sir Edward?'

'He headed towards the church.'

'Thank you, Mrs Simpson. Good day,' she said, leaving Louisa standing watching the disappearing horse and its rider.

When Louisa arrived home there was a note on the kitchen table.

> Dearest Lou,
> I have embarrassed you and I am sorry. Please try to find it in your heart to forgive me. I have left for London. My parents-in-law have a house there so I can be alone for a while. Please do not tell Jane - she will only worry. Why do we always fight? I was so looking forward to seeing you after so long. I do love you Lou and I value your friendship, truly, but I need to be alone. I am happiest when I am alone. That way I cannot offend anyone.

Louisa folded the notepaper and placed it in her pocket, looking towards the far end of her garden where Kaiser Bill was tossing a mouse in the air. When she heard her baby cry she rested her head against a pane of glass, closed her eyes and placed her hands over her ears.

Chapter 10

The heat of summer slowly cooled into autumn's season of grey mists and mellow fruitfulness. David and Elizabeth now regularly met by the lake. At first, they mostly sat in silence, but it was precisely in the fact of their silence, and their sitting together, that a trusting closeness reigned. Elizabeth's softly-spoken voice gradually began to outgrow the silences between them. Her habit was to read poetry because the poets reached the souls within them both, filling the silences that followed with the lingering pleasure of their words.

David began to prepare questions on pieces of paper which he would produce during their time together. Sometimes when he smiled, his eyes would shine and his face light up giving Elizabeth so much pleasure to see it. She longed to hear him speak, to make a sound, however small or trivial it might be. Once, when silence seemed more appropriate than words, they heard the distant town hall clock strike. After the final chime, Elizabeth said: 'The curfew tolls the knell of parting day, / the lowing herd wind slowly o'er the lea. / The ploughman homeward plods his weary way, / and leaves the world to darkness and to me.' She fidgeted awkwardly at an intrusive memory and turned to him. 'There was a church in Germany close to the hospital in which I… I worked. Often I would hear its clock strike out the time. Thomas Gray's words would come to me and remind me of home.'

David took out his pen and some paper and wrote - *Now fades the glimmering landscape on the sight, / and all the air a solemn stillness holds.*

She read the following line to the Elegy and felt consumed by sudden emotion. David, she knew, was considered by most as a mute fool, yet she knew he was far from that. When her chin began to quiver, fingers with the softest of touches curled round hers. Elizabeth gripped his hand as she looked up into his desperately sad eyes.

'I'm sorry, what right have I to feel… when you have suffered so much yourself?'

Reluctant to remove his hand from hers, he wrote – *Tell me what makes you so unhappy.*

She shook her head and jumped up, running from the spot with him struggling to rise to his feet. When she was out of sight, Elizabeth leaned against a tree to allow her lungs to calm and with her handkerchief, wiped her eyes. She looked at the line of poetry he had written and read it again. How sweet those words would have sounded coming from his lips. She raised her eyes at the sight of an approaching figure and saw Jane.

'Bess, what's the matter? Please don't cry. Just tell me what's upset you.'

Elizabeth said nothing. She hung onto her sister and wept for a lost generation.

*

After supper, before the light began to fade, Elizabeth went for a walk with Jane. The sisters walked arm in arm until they reached the other end of the lake where the golden brown leaves of the lime trees were already beginning to fall in heaps. In the distance, they saw a figure limping towards the cottages on the higher ground.

Jane looked into her sister's eyes and spoke. 'It was he who wrote your name in the ground that time, wasn't it? You like him, don't you?' and when Elizabeth nodded Jane said, 'Bess do be careful. It's very isolated there and we know very little about him.'

'I'm perfectly safe!'

'Bess, I'm only thinking of you.'

'Forgive me,' Elizabeth said taking Jane's hand. 'I didn't mean to snap. I'm on edge. It's that time of the month. Please don't say anything about us to Mamma. She will only nag about me keeping the *wrong* company.'

'Bess, you still haven't seen Mamma. You promised you would go. Have you any idea how she feels about that?'

'I asked you to tell her that I would be happy to see her… but not there… with him.'

'She's as stubborn as you. Mamma will not come to you because she feels you have cut her out of your life and therefore it is up to you to make amends.'

Jane noticed Elizabeth was not listening. Her eyes were following the proud limping figure in the distance and when he disappeared her head seemed to bow sadly.

'Bess,' Jane said softly, 'are you in love with him?'

Elizabeth didn't answer.

*

When they next met, David studied Elizabeth's features as her face turned towards the lake, the sun illuminating a strand of saliva

70

stretching between her parted lips. The sight of it awakened in him that sense of a sheer physical hunger. Suddenly, as if Elizabeth had emerged from the shadows, he was seeing her sexually it seemed, for the first time. Until now, he had looked at her with distant pleasure, as if in an art gallery studying a painting, admiring its beauty yet never thinking of possessing it. Now his eyes followed the line of her throat to the swell of her breasts, lingering there as he watched them rise and fall with her breathing. He found his own breath thicken in his throat. She brought her knees up to her chin and wrapped her arms around her legs. Her eyes fixed ahead, her face filled with the trouble and the perplexity of her thoughts as she stared across the lake. The thin cotton dress she wore clung tighter to her body.

'Would you consider accompanying me to a concert?' she said suddenly turning to him. A flush of pink rushed to her cheeks when she met the full force of his gaze. She quickly turned from him as if she had witnessed something she should not have done. It was desire for her, she had seen it, recognized it, since she was sixteen.

David cursed himself. Had he given away his thoughts in one unguarded moment? Had she spotted it in his eyes? For a moment there was silence between them. The only sounds were leaves rustling in a light breeze. To David's relief Elizabeth spoke.

'I've been given two tickets,' she said without facing him. 'It's all Beethoven; his sixth symphony, the Moonlight Sonata…'

Trapped in his silence, David was overjoyed. This lovely woman was happy to be seen in public with him, he who people avoided; the weird cripple, the stupid mute, scar face. He had heard the names whispered behind his back; men he worked with imitating his limp and the stifled, sniggering laughter from those who watched.

He looked into her expectant eyes, shining with health, but not with happiness, those cold, grey eyes as he once heard her mother describe them, but he had felt the warmth of them settle on him as he felt it now. He thought her quite beautiful, like Waterhouse's *Lady of Shalott* with the lake glistening in the background and the pink still warming her cheeks. He smiled and nodded at her offer.

She gave a shy smile in return. 'It's this Saturday. I could borrow my father-in-law's car and we could drive down to Oxford in style,' she said. Then her smile broadened. 'We could be swells for a day.'

She stood and stretched her arms. 'This ground is hard,' she said, then sat down again, a fraction closer than before, David considered, close enough that he could smell her fragrance. It was unbearably

71

exciting on his senses. He silently took in long deep breaths through his nose. 'It begins at seven,' she continued, 'but if you wish, we could go in the afternoon when you have finished work. I know a very nice teashop where we can have tea. I first went there with my father, then when I was an undergraduate. I could show you Somerville College...' David listened watching the movement of her lips. They moved into a smile. 'It's my treat, as my dearest friend Cathy used to say.'

Looking up, she saw he was no longer facing her but staring across the lake, silently cursing his sudden desire for her. He knew their friendship was based on a platonic understanding. She had never once encouraged him to think she was sexually interested in him. She had only seen him as a sister looks upon a loving brother. He knew he may lose her if she discovered that his friendship had turned to lust. He could not chance that. She was all he had in the world. David felt a sudden overwhelming loathing of himself - he had debased her, reduced her to a sexual object with one sudden rush of blood.

When Elizabeth saw the sudden change in him, her smile lost its light and became a frozen shadow of itself. Of course, he would have little money, she thought. Her hand reached out and rested lightly on his arm. 'David… if I have offended you by offering to pay, I'm sorry. I meant well.'

David tried not to show the pain of her touch as it burned into his flesh. He had to move from her before he grabbed the hand on his arm and forced it to his lips. He rose and began to walk. She instinctively stood and followed him. A thrush in the foliage above them launched casually into song as his eyes met hers. Elizabeth felt a sudden flush of happiness. In all the months they had known each other it was the first time they had walked anywhere together. As they strolled in silence along the path that led to the wood, a dead sparrow caught David's eye. He lowered himself awkwardly and took it in his hand, stroking its limp neck as if willing it to live and sing again.

Elizabeth glanced into his face and saw a sadness that made her want to reach out and hold him. She was reminded of so many young men whose hands she had held before they died. David then clawed out a shallow grave and buried the lifeless body into the damp earth. When he stood she moved closer to him and watched him write something. *Saturday then.*

'Shall I pick you up at your home, say two o'clock?'

He wrote some more. *Outside the railway station… 1430hrs.*

'1430 hours. Yes *sir*,' she said saluting him.

Instinctively, he returned Elizabeth's salute. She laughed as if he were joining in with her game. David did not hear her laugh or see her smiling face. He found he was looking beyond her eyes into a moment of his lost past. He was dressed in uniform wearing the rank of a captain. Men were marching towards him. He heard the bark of a company sergeant-major's orders. 'Eyes... right!' Young men's eyes turned and faced him as they marched past. He casually returned the company sergeant-major's salute. The following week his battalion would leave England for France. They were ready for war.

'David, sit down for a moment. Relax... it will pass.' She gently stroked his head and whispered in his ear. 'I'm sorry. My salute reminded you of the war. Forgive me.'

But David was too deeply involved with fighting his battle on the Somme to feel her soft lips press against his burning cheek.

Chapter 11

When Elizabeth looked out of her bedroom window it was
threatening rain. Later, when she met David outside Buckingham
railway station, the dark clouds had thinned to grey. By the time they
reached Oxford, the sun was shining brightly.

Elizabeth parked the car on a road close to the river and found the
teahouse she had often visited with her father when she was a girl and
later as an undergraduate. The room was filled with the aroma of
freshly ground coffee. She suddenly went into a dream that featured
her father. Her heart began to ache as it always did when she thought
of him, the way he was taken from her without any chance to say
goodbye. She forced the image of her father's face from her mind and
looked at the profile of another.

David was looking out of the window, his attention fixed on a white
horse. When he turned and faced her she raised her cup to her lips,
which hid all but her large grey eyes, below the fringe of her copper
hair. Her eyes were now fixed on his. He passed her a note. She
glanced at the words he had written enquiring whether she ever saw
any of her friends from the war because she had never spoken of them.

'I have no idea where any of them are,' she replied and briefly told
David how she missed two friends in particular. 'Bella was killed and
Cathy... dearest Cathy... I have no idea where she is.'

David passed her another slip of paper asking why Mrs Willows,
his neighbour, referred to her as, *young Paddy*.

This brought a smile to Elizabeth's lips. 'Mrs Willows is Irish. I
was born on St Patrick's Day...' As she spoke, her hand rested on the
table within easy reach of his as if she were inviting him to take it. His
eyes lowered to the slim fingers and the neatly trimmed nails. He
noticed the thin golden band on her finger. Did she wear it still as a
memory to the husband she had lost or as a warning to others that she
was not available? He removed his hand from the table and tried to
remember his family. Faces came to him, lingered and left, leaving
him confused and angry.

'Well lookie here, if it ain't the lovely Lizzie Turner. How's the
tennis Liz, still as rusty as ever?'

Elizabeth looked up at the tall, slim woman who was elegantly
dressed and rather beautiful. 'Hello Emma. You're back then.'

'Hey, I love the hair. You look like a cute little boy.'

Elizabeth glanced towards David who met her eyes with a smile. 'Good to see you, Emma. I hope you are well.'

'Likewise.' Emma's eyes moved from Elizabeth towards David when he stood. 'Is this your brother?'

'You know very well my brother was killed in the war. This is a friend, Mr David Shepherd.' Elizabeth turned to David and said, 'Miss Emma Morrison. We sometimes played tennis together when we were undergraduates.'

'We played a lot together,' she said without acknowledging David, who now excused himself with a nod of the head as he moved from their company to outside the cafe. 'What's wrong with the guy?'

'Physically or because he left us?'

'That scar on his face. He looks as if he's just dripped from Mary Shelley's pen.'

'He was badly cut up in the war... he left us because he's a gentleman and thinks we may like to talk alone.'

'Sleeping with him?'

'No.'

Emma's eyes lit up. 'Anyone?'

'No.'

'Where are you these days?'

'Buckingham. You wouldn't know it.'

'I'm at the same lodgings if you're ever this way again.'

Elizabeth met Emma's eyes and they held, but not in the same way as they used to. 'I don't play that game these days.'

'Shame, you were good at it, Liz. So you've changed teams?'

Elizabeth glanced at David whom she could see outside smoking a cigarette. She smiled and then shrugged. 'What brought you back?'

'A PhD. It was either Oxford or Yale. With my mother on my doorstep, I thought I'd come back here; much more fun and this place holds all those lovely memories of us,' Emma said slowly, 'playing tennis.'

'Who's your friend stretching her neck?'

'Her, she's cute, but not as good in the sack as you honey. Well, must dash as you guys say. Good to see you looking as beautiful as ever Liz, even with that crazy haircut.'

Emma winked and left the cafe with her friend turning to have a last look at Elizabeth.

When David returned, she smiled at him and shrugged her

shoulders. 'Sorry about that, that was Emma... American... from New England, Connecticut, Hartford to be precise... the home of Mark Twain I believe...'

Her tea was now cold and she pushed it aside. Elizabeth knew she was rambling, her mind was running loose; not so much because of seeing Emma again, for she knew she no longer held those feelings for her, but because she realised how much she liked David. Her eyes found his and he returned her smile. She felt in her stomach a flicker of desire. It was something she had never felt for a man before, even for Robert whom she married.

After leaving the teahouse, they strolled towards the river. Elizabeth sat on a bench in the shade and watched David slowly drag his leg to the water's edge where some boys were preparing to launch a toy yacht. She observed a particular air about him she had never seen before. He seemed to have an inbred dignity that is acquired by a man only through long acquaintance with the higher strata of society. It made her wonder about his background and his friends. She watched him standing close by the fathers gathered round the boys playing. He was doing nothing other than standing, smoking a cigarette, yet he looked so different from the other men; a gentleman, and so handsome in his dark blue suit, which Elizabeth felt certain was new.

When he returned she suggested that they walked a while and adjusted her pace to his. They passed couple after couple arm in arm, strolling slowly as lovers do in the afternoon sun. Elizabeth clasped her hands behind her back and walked with him in silence, slowly following the bend in the river.

*

At six-thirty, in the claustrophobic atmosphere of an old Territorial Army drill hall that had been hurriedly converted into a concert hall for the evening, David and Elizabeth took their seats. Elizabeth recognized two of her mother's more obnoxious and socially pretentious friends sitting four rows in front of her. As if by sixth sense one of the women turned and saw Elizabeth. Her eyes remained cold even though her mouth imitated a smile. When it dawned on her that Elizabeth's companion was Christina Wilding's gardener, the smile disappeared. Elizabeth ignored the two women now engaged in exuberant whispering and backward glances, which stopped only as the audience began to applaud the appearance of the orchestra's leader followed seconds later by the conductor.

After the music was a few bars into the recapitulation of the first movement of Beethoven's sixth symphony, David closed his eyes as if in sleep. A sudden light flashed in his head leaving an image of himself dressed in khaki. His eyes sprang open as if he had suddenly woken from a bad dream. He glanced at Elizabeth, who had sunk into the transcendental world of Beethoven's countryside. He tried to concentrate on the music but now he heard screams of shells and men, the zip and crack of bullets and the sound of the dying calling out for their mothers. He trembled when he heard a voice call out for his. David opened his eyes again. He swallowed and straightened himself in his seat.

As the music moved from the first movement into the delicious melody of the second, he tried hard to concentrate his mind on Elizabeth. He wanted her, but what could he possibly offer her? He had nothing, not even his own name to give her. He sensed that she trusted him, but he dared not hope that she had any feelings for him. She was definitely more relaxed in his company since her return from Sussex; he could see that. He had long decided that if she wanted him, she would let him know; he would be patient and see how their relationship developed, although, other than smiles and warm looks, he had never seen anything to show she was prepared to extend their friendship further. Had the war made him blind and insensitive to signs of affection? Did all that death, destruction and misery kill something in him too?

The music seemed to recede as the image he now saw of himself was back in the trenches looking tired and concerned. He was facing the ruins of a small French hamlet set low in the Ancre valley, where the road once ran from Albert to Bapaume. The name Ovillers La Boisselle meant little to him other than it was his part of the line that stretched for twenty-six miles. His immediate concern was for a patrol he had sent out earlier to inspect the German wire in front of his company. They had still not returned. He moved along the trench speaking with his lieutenants, until the light shimmering on the horizon began to thicken into dawn and made it dangerous from sniper fire.

His soldiers respected him, he knew. He had earned their respect. Under the brims of their helmets he could see living eyes moving relentlessly in blank faces. He passed his men, walking-stick in hand, as the dumb-coloured shadows shuffled aside to let him pass. He returned to a hole dug into the side of the trench that was his quarters and placed his walking-stick on the table. He had taken that stick to

Mons then Ypres in 1914, then onto Loos where he received his first wound, and then onto the second battle of Ypres in 1915 where he picked up another wound that took him home for six wonderful weeks. Then early in 1916, he was transferred to Kitchener's new army and given command of a company. Now he was on the Somme, still with his trusty walking-stick, waiting for another battle to begin. Would they both get through this one together, he wondered? He lay on the bed and closed his eyes, but could not sleep. His mind reached back into those past battles, groping among obscure and broken memories, for it seemed to him now that for the greater part of the time he had been stunned and blinded, and that what he had seen he had seen in sudden, vivid flashes, instantaneously. Again he felt the tension of waiting that became impatience, for now fear and responsibility lay heavy on his mind. Now he just wanted to get on and be done with it.

He sat up on his bed knowing he must write a final letter to his sister and enclose another to be given to their parents if the worst should happen - and in the pit of his stomach, he sensed the worst. He sealed the envelope then opened the last bottle of champagne from the Fortnum & Mason hamper his mother had sent out to him. As he poured himself a glass, the officer he had sent out to inspect the enemy wire fell breathless into his quarters. The lieutenant's erstwhile boyish complexion was now an ashen grey mask, which greeted him with tired, dark and frightened eyes.

'What delayed you, Johnson?'

The young man was shaking as he tried to uncork a bottle of whisky. 'I've just lost four of the patrol… Leonard, Bates, Kelly and Corporal Paling. One of our shells dropped short, killed by our own artillery. Matthews has got a Blighty, lucky devil. He's with the MO now.'

'And the wire?'

'Wire! What about my men?' Johnson cried, unable to meet his Company Commander's concerned eyes. 'Kelly has just become a father. His poor wife... child...'

'I'm sorry about your fellows, but I need to report to the Colonel. A great many more of us will die today and if that wire is still uncut...' he couldn't finish the sentence. It was too awful to contemplate. He watched Johnson still trying to uncork the bottle. 'Would you like a glass of this? It's not chilled alas, but it's still very good.'

Johnson looked up into his Company Commander's eyes. 'How can you be so damn calm about all this?'

'Calm!' he snapped. 'Inside I feel sick. Now tell me about the wire, damn you.'

'It's uncut, Sir. After a week of pounding from our artillery, it's still intact.' The young lieutenant's hand shook as he eventually removed the cork from the bottle. His bloodshot eyes found his captain's face. 'Bastards! They promised it would be cut.'

'Surely you do not believe anything the brass hats say?' His voice was calm again. He scribbled out a note and called out to the runner. 'Take this message to Colonel Harrison. And hurry, we haven't much time. Listen Johnson,' he said when the runner left, 'I've put you up for the Military Cross. You've done more than your share and deserve it.'

'I say, Mother will be proud,' he said sarcastically then took a swig of whisky and poured another. 'I'm sorry I shouted.'

'There is worse news, I'm afraid. We attack this morning at seven-thirty.'

'Daylight!' The word seemed to choke from his mouth. 'They must be mad! We'll be slaughtered.'

'Let's hope Fritz keeps his head down long enough for us to get across.'

'We'll never get through that wire, let alone cross three hundred yards of open ground. My God, they've done for us.'

'Try not to show your concern in front of the men, there's a good fellow. We must set an example to them and not let them down.' He was surprised how calmly he spoke the words, because his chest felt so heavy he could hardly breathe. He knew that with the wire uncut his company would be massacred trying to find a way through it, that's if they were still alive to reach it. He looked at his lieutenant - not quite a boy and not yet a man, dressed in a man's uniform. Johnson was only eighteen. He was four years older. They were all young men destined never to grow old. He took another mouthful of champagne after toasting Haig, Rawlinson and their staff, because in a few hours, a disaster of their making was about to unfold.

'Sir, if I don't return after the show, will you go and see my mother? Would you do that for me? It's important, you see. She respects you, trusts you... knows your family,' he laughed at his impertinence. 'Not socially of course, but... anyway, she is thrilled to think that you of all people are my company commander. She tells everyone. She's a frightful snob I'm afraid, but I do love her and I'm very afraid for her. I'm all she has since she lost my two brothers at

Ypres.'

'You'll be all right, old chap. I've informed the others that if I go down you are to take command of the company. Thatcher will be your second-in-command.'

Johnson was momentarily stunned. It had never occurred to him that his captain might be killed and how calmly he discussed it. His gaze fell to the medal ribbons on his company commander's tunic, ribbons that showed he had been through all this before and with valour. The lieutenant's young sallow face looked up in admiration. 'What's it like, Sir, going over the top?' When Johnson observed the expression in his captain's eyes, it made the blood in his veins run cold.

Without David realizing it, the symphony had slipped into the third movement. He did not hear the oboe dancing above the deep bass of the bassoon or the clarinet playfully frolicking before a horn joined the fun. His mind was on the coming storm. Not Beethoven's storm of the fourth movement where nature would unleash its full fury through the orchestra, but another storm, man's storm, which nature could never match. Already he could hear the ear-splitting, monotonous labour of the guns.

The morning of July first was bright. It was going to be hot. At seven o'clock, thirty minutes before zero hour, each man smoked a great deal and tried to talk above the intense sound of shells roaring like steam trains overhead. He looked about at his men. Their nervous grins warped their faces, showing their teeth as a dog might. Men may conceal their emotion easily enough, but it is far more difficult to hide the fact that they are concealing it. They avoided the other's eye fearing the other would discover what he himself felt - nerve-ends raw and aching, and vomit, which refused to erupt from tight empty stomachs, plagued every man. He ordered his Company Sergeant-Major to issue a double ration of rum to the men. Now the rum warmed and soothed those nerve-ends. Some began to joke, it seemed easier to laugh. Others just sat about and waited with pondering brows, lost in their own deep thoughts. Hand grenades were being primed, magazines filled with rounds, bayonets polished and sharpened.

He looked at his watch – just minutes to go. Now the air above him was a canopy of shrieking shells, the noise increasing as the time approached zero hour. He strove to overcome the knotted feeling in his stomach and prevent the saliva in his mouth from making him sick. Ladders were being placed against the parapet ready to climb from deep trenches. He had words with each platoon commander as he passed them. The soldiers stared at him with tired, trusting eyes. The burden of weight they carried bent them forward as if old men. It was an order from the staff to carry it all. Well damn the staff; they no longer mattered. Now captains were in command, not generals.

'Sergeant-Major! Tell the men to get rid of all their equipment. I only want them to carry their weapons and ammunition.'

Someone shouted three cheers for the captain. They all cheered. Men from other companies along the line heard the cheer. They had no idea why, but it made them feel better and they cheered too.

Three minutes to go. The noise of the guns increased in ferocity. Nothing, no matter how hard it was to imagine, would ever be as noisy as this again. His body shook from the air about him, hot and broken, pushing him along the trench as if a drunkard. With less than thirty seconds before zero hour they watched him climb the ladder and stand alone, leaning with one hand on his walking-stick, looking through his binoculars towards the enemy lines as if he were watching the line-up at Ascot.

'Mad bastard,' someone shouted. 'He'll do for us.'

'Shut your fucking mouth, Burrows,' cried the Sergeant-Major, 'or I'll do for you.'

But it will not be he that does for them, the generals have already seen to that, yet Burrows was right, he was mad - now was the time to be mad, he needed his men to see he was not afraid so they would follow him to their deaths.

An eerie silence rang across no man's land when the guns stopped. A bird began to sing. He blew hard into the whistle in his hand. All along the line whistles began to blow. Thousands of men climbed from the trenches and lined up as if on parade. They slowly began to walk as ordered towards the German wire - no talking, eyes front, slope arms. This was madness. He ordered his men to run forward, to give them a chance before the machine guns were sighted, but the German machine gun crews had already left their deep dugouts and were beginning to fire their weapons. Bullets swished, cracked and spat up the earth around him. Above, artillery shells exploded with great crumps, casting their deadly shrapnel and jagged fragments down to earth, tearing through rough khaki and soft flesh. The massacre of Kitchener's army had begun.

From the rostrum, the conductor's baton moved swiftly through the Presto at the end of the third movement as the music raced towards the storm of the fourth. The menacing sound of the cellos and basses gave warning of the forthcoming tempest. Quietly at first, then it began its long formidable crescendo. The reed and brass burst into a sustained fortissimo with the timpanist laying into his instrument with such a ferocious roll the sound crashed through the concert hall. The whole audience jumped from the sudden shock of it. From the stage, the timpani and brass created booming thunder. Strings created howling winds that blew great blasts of angry noise through the hall.

David gripped his seat. When it seemed there was no ending to Beethoven's storm, fortissimo gradually became piano and piano, pianissimo. The winds calmed and the melancholy notes of the oboe heralded the passing storm - then a flute imitated a bird flying up into a clear blue sky.

As the audience relaxed, the French horn followed the clarinet into the fifth and last movement, yet the storm continued to rage in David's head. The vastness of the hall seemed to close in on him and filled him with terror. He was back, caught in a shell-hole with every German gun concentrated on him. Shell after shell crashed about him, each trying to claim what life was left in his torn and broken body.

Elizabeth became aware of David's torment when she turned and saw him shaking and clutching his head. He began to slide between the seats for protection, knocking against a middle-aged man sitting beside him. The man cursed between clenched teeth. People looked on in confusion, others told him to leave. More heads began to turn.

'What's the damn fool playing at?' hissed the middle-aged man. 'The lout is drunk. Get him out of here.'

All who observed the growing commotion heard the word *drunk* and glared at Elizabeth with disgust in their eyes. David tried to bury himself deeper into the shell-hole between the seats. He reached up to embrace anyone who would help him. A face appeared above him with tearful eyes full of concern. He reached for her. She disappeared and was replaced by another two, masculine and angry.

David felt himself being pulled to his feet and dragged from his shell-hole. He could hear music flowing above his head. The Germans were killing his men to the accompaniment of Beethoven. Confused and shocked faces watched him being dragged away. He could hear the woman with tearful eyes begging the two men to be careful with him. When they passed though some double doors he was thrown onto the street.

Elizabeth clenched her fists in rage. 'You great bully,' she shouted and punched one of the men fully on his nose. He yelped - the other slapped her hard, sending her crashing to the ground holding her stinging cheek.

'Cow,' he said and left them both lying on the pavement.

Elizabeth went to David who was still shaking, his lips moving silently calling for his mother. Elizabeth held him. She laid his head to her breast. 'There, my love, it's all right. Mamma has you. Mamma has you.'

Chapter 12

When Elizabeth woke the following morning, the memory of David's suffering immediately filled her mind. Her thoughts were interrupted by a sudden knock at her door. She ignored it. There was another knock, louder, more determined. She looked out of her bedroom window and saw her twin sisters looking up at her. When she let them in Stephanie pushed passed Elizabeth with a look of disapproval written across her face.

'You look disappointed, Bess. Were you expecting someone else?'

'No, but if I had been it would be none of your business, Stephanie Brennan.'

'Your cheek is bruised. Has someone hit you?' Jane said kissing it.

Elizabeth's hand moved quickly to her face. 'Does it show?'

'Yes, it does,' Stephanie said, hanging her hat on the hat stand. 'Did that cripple do that?'

'Stephanie, his name is David. He became lame in the line of duty, something your fiancé managed to escape.'

'So... David is it? You've lowered your sights since the war. I mean, walking out with Mamma's gardener in Oxford.'

'Who told you that we were in Oxford?'

'It was Mrs Walker,' said Jane, pulling a face at her twin. 'She couldn't wait to pay Mamma a visit last night. I heard her say she saw you at a concert and David was thrown out because he was drunk. Luckily, our stepfather was out so he doesn't know about this. Mamma, of course, is hopping mad.'

Elizabeth gasped. 'How dare she say such a thing? He was suffering from shellshock. You'd think there would have been men there who would have recognized that, but not one single person took pity on him. The attendants treated him abominably.'

'Jacob Wilson would be terribly upset if he knew you were out with *David*,' Stephanie mocked. 'He's always had a fancy for you, Bess... forever asking after you.'

'Then that great oaf mustn't know about this, Stephie,' Jane said. 'You must keep your mouth shut if you can manage it.'

'Hark at you.'

'Stephie,' Elizabeth said taking her hand. 'You'll be doing me a great disservice if you mention this to Jacob Wilson. He's spiteful enough to make trouble out of it for David.'

'What trouble?'

'Jacob has asked me out many times and I've refused him. He is a fool and always was.'

'Bess, be careful.' Jane said. 'Our stepfather once warned us if we ever associated with any man on the farm he would get rid of him. We would then be responsible for him losing his job and that means his home too if he lives in a tied-cottage.'

'I don't live with our stepfather so he can mind his own business.'

'But you are still his stepdaughter and David is completely dependent upon him for work and a home.' Jane took her hand. 'It's only Mamma that's keeping him in a job. Heaven knows what she will do now. She thinks that you went out with him just to embarrass her.'

'Embarrass her! I think Mamma has risen above herself since she married that man.'

'You're not bringing him to my wedding. I'll not be shown up,' Stephanie added.

'One more remark like that, Stephanie Brennan, and I'll slap you.'

Stephanie saw Elizabeth's eyes narrow when they caught hers. 'God, I can't believe it,' she said. 'You actually have feelings for him.'

Elizabeth ignored her and turned back to Jane. 'Surely Mamma wouldn't have him thrown out. She brought him here. She knows David has nowhere else to go.'

'In the end she'll support her husband.'

'He would get rid of him just to spite you, Bess,' Stephanie said with less venom in her voice. 'He knows that you don't like him because he married Mamma.'

'What rot!' Elizabeth exclaimed. 'I've never heard anything so ridiculous.'

'You *don't* like him Bess, be honest. That's why you don't go round to see Mamma. You resent him being our Papa, don't you?'

Jane looked across to her twin. 'Stephanie, if you carry on it will be me who will slap you.' She then turned to Elizabeth. 'Just be careful, Bess. If our stepfather knows you are seeing David he will get rid of him. He feels that he has taken him on unnecessarily and wants his cottage for one of the other men who will soon be getting married.'

'I'm not seeing him, not really. We only went to a concert. Until then we were having such a wonderful day together. For the first time in ages I was happy. I was really happy.'

*

85

The following Tuesday, Elizabeth went into the town centre to do some shopping. It was market day and the town was crowded with people who had flocked in from the surrounding villages. She suddenly caught a glimpse of David leaving the barber shop and turning in the direction of the sheep-pens opposite the Old Gaol. She followed his progress through the crowd and thought he looked like fine porcelain that had been dropped, shattered and stuck back together again. If one ignored the cracks and chips, its original beauty was still evident; the shape of his head, the fine line of his jaw, the thick dark brown hair and sapphire blue eyes. These were the few bright features darkened by the melancholy expression and the unhurried step of a stiff crippled leg dragging behind him, because of his inability to lift and bend it at the knee. He was often seen in the town on market days with only his shadow as company. His head was always held high, yet people would turn from him rather than look him in the eye. His gaze never turned left or right in recognition of a friendly face - he knew no face he could call a friend. Few wished to bother him and he troubled no one. David was a newcomer among generations of country folk - an outsider to them and a stranger to himself.

A lump filled her throat as she watched his broken body dragging its way across the road with two boys trailing in his shadow imitating his limp. She wondered why people were so cruel to those less fortunate than themselves. She went to follow him but suddenly saw her mother walking towards her.

'Hello Mamma.'

'My God, your hair! Whatever processed you to do that?' Christina said gasping. 'You've ruined it.'

'I like it.'

'You're quite mad Elizabeth, quite mad. Is that a bruise on your cheek?'

'I fell.'

'Quite mad.' Christina's eyes moved to the large grey eyes of her daughter. 'Nine months… nine months you have stayed away. Is that the way to treat your mother?'

'I invited you to visit me. You never bothered.'

'So I must run after you. Have you any idea how much you have upset me? What have I done to deserve being completely ignored for all this time by my daughter?'

'I was going to come and see you this evening, truly,' she said, her eyes following David's slow progress through the crowded street.

86

Christina turned in the direction of Elizabeth's gaze and saw David before he disappeared round the corner. 'Let's have some tea at the bakery. I'd like a word with you.'

'Mamma, do you mind if we leave it for another time?' she said glancing at her watch. 'I have a great deal of work to mark before I resume my class.'

'You have all night for that.'

'I haven't, Mamma. It's for lessons this afternoon.'

'Then I will see you at the bakery after school. You had better be there Madam, or I promise you there will be trouble for a certain person we both know.'

Elizabeth glared at her mother. 'I'll be there.'

*

Amid the clatter of cutlery and the drone of indistinguishable conversation, Christina watched her daughter manoeuvre round tables towards her. It pained her to think she was wasting her time on a man who had no hope of offering her any future. 'You're late.'

'I'm sorry, Mamma.'

'I'll come straight to the point Elizabeth…'

'There is no need Mamma, I know what you have to say.'

'So it's true then? You've descended to the level of a gardener!'

'He is what you made him.'

'Elizabeth, we've been estranged long enough so I do not intend to fight with you, but I cannot be witness to what you are doing.' Christina glanced round the room and then back to Elizabeth. 'He's hardly what you might call, *a catch*. He doesn't even know who he is let alone where he's from. He might be anybody.'

'I know he's a gentleman. You too must realize that.'

'The whole thing is ludicrous.'

'What's ludicrous about having a friend?'

Christina leaned forward and whispered, 'Are you carrying on with him?'

'Carrying on?'

'You know exactly what I mean.'

'He hardly knows I exist.'

Christina's shoulders relaxed but her eyes narrowed. 'I know you're unhappy about losing Robert, but remember, I lost a husband and a son.'

'Which meant I lost a father and a brother... and you've now replaced them both.' Elizabeth watched her mother's face crumble.

'I'm sorry, Mamma. I didn't mean that.'

'Your father and brother are still in my heart Bess, but life goes on. You would do well to remember that.'

'Then please don't take it out on David.'

Christina searched through her bag for her handkerchief. She snapped the bag closed and met her daughter's stubborn gaze. 'Your stepfather won't like you mixing with−'

'Your *husband* should mind his own business,' Elizabeth said firmly.

'Keep your voice down! There is no need for the whole tearoom to hear what you have to say. Just show him a little respect, Madam.' She could not meet her daughter's eye. Instead, with a strained smile, she nodded respectfully at someone passing her table that she knew. 'He cares what happens to you although I don't know why. You have always resented him.' Their eyes met. 'Oh yes you have Elizabeth, so don't deny it. I loved your father, but he was taken from me along with William. Life goes on. I am trying to get through it as best I can.'

Elizabeth watched her mother dab her eye with her handkerchief. She reached for her mother's hand. Christina withdrew it.

'Heaven knows what you two have in common, I mean, you have an education from the Sorbonne and Oxford... he can't even speak a word.'

'He speaks more to me in his silence than half the men in this town do with their useless chatter.'

'What does that suppose to mean? I'm really at a loss to understand you, Bess. What man would be interested in you now with hair like that?'

'Oh, I don't know, Mamma... although I remember overhearing soldiers in France say... "You don't look at the mantelpiece when stoking the fire," so there's still hope.'

'Stop talking in riddles and listen to me, girl. It's time you found a proper young man and settled down, had children. You're not getting any younger.'

Elizabeth smiled for the first time. 'Mamma, I'm only twenty-three.'

'I was married at eighteen and expecting William at nineteen. Just look how all the men admired you when you walked in here. You could have any of them, even with that dreadful hairstyle.'

'What's wrong with short hair?'

'You look like a boy... There, I've said it. I didn't want to, but now

I have.'

Elizabeth couldn't be bothered to comment. She looked round the room and caught a young woman's eye. They exchanged smiles.

Christina's eyes darted in that direction. 'Isn't that Katie Crenshaw?'

'You know it is.'

'I really don't like the way she has always looked at you. It's unnatural.'

Christina smiled at the waitress when she arrived. 'A pot of tea please. Would you like some cake, Bess?'

'No, thank you.'

'Just a pot of tea, thank you.' When the waitress left, Christina said, 'You're heading along the same road as that Crenshaw girl.'

'And what road is that, Mamma?'

'You've been seen out with her... going to her home. What does that look like? You'll be stained with the same reputation she has. People will think you're like that.'

'Like what?'

'Unnatural, that's like what.'

'She used to stay overnight with us, Mamma.' Elizabeth leaned towards her mother and whispered. 'You put her into my bed, remember?'

Christina crimsoned. 'You were young girls... friends...'

'We were fifteen and yes, very good friends.'

'I know you're trying to shock me Bess, but it won't work. Why can't you just be like the daughters of my friends? They're all married and have children.'

'I've been married. Can't you accept that I may never want to marry again... that I may not want children?'

'Don't be so silly. It's natural for a woman to want children. Anyway, how can you call what you had a marriage, be honest, how can you? The moment he put the ring on your finger he left for France.'

'We found time to consummate it, so it's legal—'

'I don't want to hear about your intimate life, Bess. It's not the sort of thing one talks about to her mother,' Christina said, her eyes moving round the room. 'I would have felt the back of my mother's hand if I had spoken to her the way you speak to me.'

Elizabeth fell into sudden silence. She picked up the teapot and began to pour the tea, remembering the back of her guard's hand before he raped her. Then he would leave her in tears in the awful knowledge that it would all begin again the next morning. No one listened to her complaints; they were not interested in her, because on the floors above lay desperately sick and dying soldiers, young lives destroyed by Elizabeth's countrymen.

'Elizabeth! What on earth is the matter with you?' Christina cried irritably. 'For heaven's sake girl, stop shaking! Put the pot down girl, you're spilling it everywhere.'

Chapter 13

As autumn crept into winter, the milky morning mists turned into frosts, which changed golden brown leaves into a darker hue. They dropped in heaps, carpeting the area around the great skeletons of trees until great onslaughts of wind caught them and scattered them across the streets as if tossed confetti.

It was through this that Elizabeth strolled towards her in-laws' house. She was in deep thought, wondering if her father-in-law had any vacancies at his London chambers for clerks. It was obvious to her that David had received a good education. If he found another job with better pay he could rent a house, be away from the farm and her stepfather's threats. It annoyed her that Tim Wilding could throw David out of his home for nothing more than seeing one of his stepdaughters. She frowned as her mind raced in thought. He had no right to dictate how she ran her life. She knew however, she would have to tread carefully at present, for David's sake.

Three hours later, Elizabeth kissed her mother-in-law goodnight and went to the sitting room to join her father-in-law George, for whom she had deep affection.

'Have a nightcap before you leave, Elizabeth.'

'Yes, I will. Thank you.'

George poured two drinks from a decanter of port. He handed Elizabeth one of them. 'It is lovely to see you again, Elizabeth. We so seldom see anything of you now we're spending more time in the London house. You must come up and stay the weekend. See a show, do things that young people do. Start to live your life as Robert would have wanted you to. Why don't you come for dinner next week? Bring someone. Do you have a young man?'

'Sort of.'

'Surely you do or you don't.' George kissed the soft mass of Elizabeth's copper, slightly dishevelled hair. 'I see you're beginning to grow it again... I'm glad.' He smiled and tapped her hand. 'Henrietta would like to see you find someone. Settle down. She's dying you know. The doctors can only give her medicine to make her comfortable. God bless her. When she goes I shall only have you.' He kissed Elizabeth's head again. 'We know Robert's death drove you to the Western Front, the unhappiness that has since caused you. It would

91

be a great joy to see you remarry, have children. I should like to think Henrietta might be alive to see that.'

He sipped his drink and smiled affectionately then tapped her hand again and went to the other side of the room. From a silver box sitting by a picture of Robert he removed a cigar and lit it.

'I'd like you to meet David, Papa.'

'Do you have feelings for him, Elizabeth?'

'Yes... I do.'

'Then bring him to dinner. I'll blow the dust from one of my bottles in the cellar,' he said, looking up at the photograph of his son. It was almost an act of apology to him. Elizabeth, he knew, had moved on.

'I will. Thank you.'

'Elizabeth, I bumped into your mother. Naturally you were the subject of our conversation. She is worried about you. Says you never visit her... because of your stepfather. Is that right?'

'I had tea with my mother yesterday.'

'I'm pleased to hear it. Look Elizabeth, Wilding is not a bad fellow. You should give him a chance. He was there for your Mamma in her moment of crisis, when she thought she had lost you. It was a very trying period for us all. She loves you very much. We all do. Every one of us needs love; your mother found it with your stepfather. Surely you cannot deny her that?'

Elizabeth shook her head and looked to the ground knowing how unfair she had been to Tim Wilding. 'I've been beastly to that man.'

'I know how much you loved your father and no one could replace him. Let him rest in peace knowing his widow is being cared for.'

Elizabeth's eyes suddenly began to sting. 'You're always so sensible, like my Papa. I know I can always depend on you as I could him.' Her eyes were wet, but her mouth stretched in a smile. 'I do love you.'

'And we love you, Elizabeth. You're the daughter we always wanted and never had until Robert brought you home.' Elizabeth put her face in her hands and her shoulders shook. 'Come, come now Elizabeth, please don't... none of that, my dear, none of that. Your father's death was a tragedy. He should never have gone,' George said softly.

George Turner drew on his cigar and exhaled the smoke, which hung in the air. Elizabeth was filled with affection for him and went and embraced him. Over his shoulder she glanced at the photograph on the mantelpiece of Robert, young and proud, dressed in his uniform.

The day it was taken they had become engaged. They had toasted their future with champagne, unknowing that Robert had only three months of life left to him.

'What does David do?'

'He is my mother's gardener.'

George felt Elizabeth's eyes burn into him, looking for the slightest sign of disapproval. He smiled. 'I'm sure I shall like him.'

He saw Elizabeth's smile light up the dim, smoky drawing room. George returned it. He glanced towards the picture of his son again, his heart heavy in his breast for all that Robert had lost from life.

*

The following evening as the shadows lengthened across the pale, yellow waning light that filled the landscape, Elizabeth cycled towards David's cottage. Leaning her bicycle against the fence, she walked to his front door, noticing a curtain move at the window next door but one. Elizabeth straightened some strands of her hair that were dancing in the breeze then tapped lightly on David's door. There was no answer. She glanced at her watch. He should be home by now she thought, and knocked a little louder. Stepping back, she looked up towards the open bedroom window. There was no movement. She turned the doorknob and gently pushed the door open. It creaked as she edged her way in, calling out with each step she took.

The house was small, ideal for one person, two at the most. It wasn't many years ago eight would have occupied it. Inside, a fire burned in the grate, its dying yellow flame gasping for breath. She raked it a little and placed another log on top. The fire cracked, spat and burst into life. For a second she saw Bella's ambulance on fire and the same question came to her mind. 'Why you Bella, and not me?' Elizabeth caught sight of her reflection in a mirror and ran her fingers through her growing hair. She studied her features; her large eyes, full lips and high cheekbones. She had always regarded her good looks a curse rather than a blessing. Men's eyes, as well as women's were always on her. She remembered when Katie Crenshaw slept over the second time. When heer father said it was time for bed, it was the look Katie gave Elizabeth that sent an inexplicable frisson down her back. She sensed something was going to happen between them. It had been on Elizabeth's mind since the first time they slept together, when they whispered in the dark telling each other their secrets, until Elizabeth's father knocked on the door and told them to go to sleep. Katie had leant over and kissed her goodnight on the lips. It had felt strangely exciting. This time Elizabeth was first in bed. Katie washed herself from the bowl of water in the corner of the room. Katie turned the light out and the rustle of her underclothes could be heard in the dark. She lay on her back too. Neither spoke. They listened to each other's breathing. It seemed a lifetime before Elizabeth heard Katie swallow and reach for her hand. Their fingers entwined. In silence they faced each other. They were sixteen. Three years later when Robert asked her to marry him she agreed, because she thought she was in love with him and he was leaving to fight in the war. When she met Catherine, Elizabeth realized her feelings for Robert had been a meeting of intellectual minds, friendship rather than sexual love. The deep, passionate love she had once for Catherine, she now felt for David. She had never felt it for any other man before.

Elizabeth sighed. She ran her hand through her hair again. Her fingers removed a wayward lock from her eyes. It was something Cathy always did when they were together. '*Bess darling, I love your hair, but you really must do something with it. It has a mind all of its own. It really has.*'

'I love him, Cathy,' Elizabeth whispered. 'I never thought I would feel anything for a man again, but I can… I do.'

She sat down at the table looking at David's open notebook. A fountain pen rested across the first line of writing. She carefully moved it a little with her fingertip so she could make out a little of what David had written: *She looked as if the dawn, her flaming hair the sky.*

Was she the subject of this verse? Elizabeth wondered. Feeling suddenly happy, her mood lightened. Looking around, it occurred to her there were no photographs anywhere, not one. She would give him one of her, dressed in her FANY uniform to remind him of their first meeting. They could go to the photographers and have one taken together - place it on his mantelpiece, and so Elizabeth's mind raced until a sudden dark cloud of doubt cast its shadow across that flickering light of happiness. Recently, he had begun to sit further from her by the lake when she would have welcomed him sitting closer. He showed no interest in her as a woman. He never flirted with her, never held her eye and never found an excuse to touch her other than by an innocent action. Elizabeth suddenly felt irritation. He was so aloof, so controlled. In France, soldiers flirted with her all the time. If she had wanted to, she could have had any of them, but she didn't want any of them. Yet now, she wanted this man. If David wanted her, she would let him have her, she would welcome it, but he would have to make the first move, she would never encourage it.

She moved to the kitchen which was very small; just a stove, a small table with a washing bowl and a larder. There was no sink. No running water. That came from a shared well outside. The walls were damp. The window frame was riddled with rot and a metal bathtub was propped up in the corner. She opened the larder door and saw little to eat. In the corner of the cupboard, on a stone shelf behind a plate of bread and cheese, was a small cup. In it were curled a couple of notes. One was a pound, the other, ten shillings; there were some coins - two half-crowns and four florins, a total of two pounds, three shillings. It was probably all the savings he had in the world. He wouldn't be paid much, she knew. Her mother was mean. She always had been; it was the result of bringing up five children. Elizabeth dug into her purse and found a pound note. She placed it into his cup along with a half-crown and a florin. It was not very subtle she knew; he probably could account for every penny he had. She left the kitchen and closed the door.

When she sat again, she noticed an old tennis racket leaning against the wall in the corner of the room. It needed to be re-stringed. Elizabeth wondered why he had it. David couldn't play tennis with his lame leg. Had he bought it to remind him of a game he once played; could he remember that? Elizabeth suddenly imagined him in white, running for the ball, hitting it from the middle of his racket. Who was his opponent? A friend? A lover? A wife? *A wife!* It was a thought that had never occurred to her before. He may be married. A frisson shot through her body. She sank her face into her hands. She knew so little about him yet she was prepared to give him everything of herself.

The house was shrouded in eerie silence, the only sound came from the wind outside. After a few minutes she cautiously began to climb the narrow staircase, calling out his name. She pushed the bedroom door open. A single bed stood in the corner, close to an open window. A pillow lay crumpled at an angle to the head rail. She wondered if he had slept badly. When her mind was active, no matter how tired she felt, she couldn't sleep. The men with grey faces marched past her bed, each looking down at her. *Remember me, you held my hand? Remember me, you stroked my brow? Remember me, you shed that tear? Remember me? Remember me?* Elizabeth squeezed her eyes closed. Yes! Yes! She had not forgotten.

She lay on his bed and closed her eyes. It was uncomfortable. The mattress needed replacing. Elizabeth tried to imagine David lying beside her, kissing her, caressing her body, running his hands over her breasts, between her legs. She sat up with a start when the fat face of her guard appeared in her mind. She could never enjoy sex with David while the two guards were in her head. She would always be reminded of her rapists. Elizabeth let out a long sigh. She was woken from her thoughts by a voice from outside.

'You've got a visitor, Mr Shepherd. A woman...'

When the front door opened he saw Elizabeth standing near the fire, her face flushed, rubbing her hands as though she were warming them. David was dressed in his working clothes; cheap, dirty material tied in the middle with a thick leather belt. His boots, caked in mud, were fastened with string, the leather laces having long broken. He removed his cap. His dark hair spilt across his forehead. A hand instinctively moved to brush it away from his eyes.

'Hello,' she said. 'The door was open. I hope you didn't mind me waiting. I've put a log on the fire.'

At first she saw that David seemed stunned by her presence, and then he smiled. He seemed pleased to see her. She was happy. Did it show? The doubts disappeared.

'We seem to have missed each other since the concert,' she said changing her weight from one foot to the other as if she were a coy schoolgirl in the presence of a prefect, on whom she had a great crush. She watched him remove his muddy boots then he offered her a seat. Sitting opposite her, he ripped off the page with the poem, screwed it into a ball and threw it into the fire as if what he had written meant nothing to him. Elizabeth watched the paper burst into flame. He wrote something and passed the notebook over to her. *Because I do not know your address, I could not write and thank you for your kindness.*

She took his pen and wrote her address down for him. 'There, now you can call on me. I… I'd like that. Perhaps you will let me cook something for you. I'm told I do a fantastic steak and kidney pudding.'

She watched David imitate splashing water over his face pointing upwards to his bedroom without acknowledging her offer. Had he just rejected her? Her eyes never left him, yet he would not fix his on her. When he rose to his feet, she watched him climb the stairs one at a time because he could not bend his left knee. She heard water being poured into a metal bowl from the jug she remembered seeing standing on the small table close to the door. She heard him splashing water liberally, washing his face, his body. The sound of the towel rubbing against his skin seemed to echo though the room. She swallowed, closed her eyes and tried to imagine that she was now drying his body, feeling the warmth of his skin. Floorboards creaked as he crossed the room. She heard the rustle of clothes, a moment's silence, then his door opened and he returned downstairs clean and tidy, his hair wet, combed back and parted, a collarless white shirt and brown corduroy trousers with a thick leather belt round his waist.

David smiled as he passed her, imitating drinking tea. He placed the kettle on the stove, feeling her eyes watching his every movement. When he looked across at her, their eyes met and held. He saw her smile. He turned from her. David wondered if the rumours about Jacob Wilson and Elizabeth were true. He had heard the men talk of an understanding between them. Recently David had noticed how friendly Mr Wilding was with his foreman; laughing, slapping his back, inviting him into the house for a drink when his day was done. David glanced towards her again. She was still watching him and wondered if it was only pity Elizabeth felt for him, just another stretcher case being removed from the back of her ambulance; another wounded soldier's hand to hold.

*

Elizabeth was lost in thought as she cycled home. During their tea, she had invited David to dinner at her father-in-law's house. At first, he seemed reluctant to accept. Was she forcing herself on him? Did he have someone else? No - she would know about it. Buckingham was too small to hide any clandestine courtship, and Stephanie would be the first to rush and tell her if he did. As she left the lane she passed Jacob Wilson lumbering up the hill. He called out to her, but she rode by, as if she did not hear or see him.

Jacob wiped his mouth on his sleeve and returned the cap to his hip flask. He was sure she had deliberately ignored his call; she would have seen him, the light was not good, but it was not dark.

'I'll have you yet,' he spluttered, then took another swig from his flask. He continued to climb the hill, glancing towards the distant cottages. He stopped and reached for the support of a tree to prevent himself from swaying like wheat in the wind. 'Now what would she be doing over there?' he whispered, looking through the slits of his eyes. He remembered old Mrs Willows and considered Elizabeth must have been visiting her mother's old friend. He stumbled on. Why did Elizabeth refuse his attentions? There was so much he could offer her. He knew Mr Wilding disliked his stepdaughters associating with the men, yet he felt sure Mr Wilding had been encouraging him to begin a liaison with her. *"What that girl needs Jacob, is a man,"* the farmer had said, looking him in the eye. Jacob Wilson considered himself to be that man. He took another swig from his flask, cursed when it was empty and began to sing as he neared his home.

*

At the weekend Elizabeth took David to dinner at her in-laws' home. When the evening was over, George and Henrietta Turner stood at the door and waved them off.

'What do you think?'

'Elizabeth is in love with him,' Henrietta said. 'She couldn't take her eyes off him.'

'But he hardly gave her a second glance.'

'He's probably shy, poor lamb. He can't express himself and meeting us for the first time must have been a bit of an ordeal for him. His manners are impeccable though, which tells a lot about a fellow. He'll be from a good family, mark my words.'

'I just don't want to see Elizabeth hurt.'

'George Turner, Elizabeth can look after herself.'

'This will end in tears. I can see it. At least he appreciated the wine. That tells you a lot about a chap too, I suppose.'

*

When Elizabeth pulled up outside David's cottage, he seemed determined to be away from her, hurriedly climbing from the car with a polite smile and a slight bow. When he reached his front door he disappeared inside without looking back. On the seat where he had been sitting, there was an envelope with Elizabeth's name written on it. It was David's writing. For a moment she stared at it, nervous of what it contained. She suddenly grabbed it and tore it open. Inside there was money, the very note and coins she had left him. The message was short. *Thank you. It was a very generous thought, although quite unnecessary.* She looked up towards his house wondering if she was making a fool of herself. 'He doesn't want me,' she whispered. 'I fall for a man who doesn't want me.' She put her face in her hands and began to weep.

From the darkness of his sitting room window, David looked towards the stationary car. He could not see Elizabeth, but the memory of her eyes tormented him. *Why doesn't she leave? Go, otherwise I will lose my self-control and go to you.* He knew he had to risk everything and go to her, but as he opened the front door the car's engine roared into life and the vehicle began to move away.

98

Chapter **14**

As Tim Wilding talked to his foreman, he noticed a cobweb above the bookshelf close to one of the windows. His eyes began searching the room for others. Jacob's eyes however, had a habit of drifting towards the group of photographs on a table by the piano. He sighed. The sound of it seemed to bring Tim's inspection of the room to an end.

'What on earth are you sighing at, man?'

'Nothing Mr Wilding, Sir.'

'So, this fellow Shepherd. He's been here for almost a year now. Is there anything else we can find him to do other than my wife's flower gardens?'

Jacob looked up at his late father's old friend and said, 'There's that barn that needs sorting, or we could have him help repair some of the fencing.'

'No, no. Mrs Wilding won't have him doing any of that work. He's her good deed, her wounded soldier, although she seems to be going cold on him recently. Perhaps the novelty has worn off. Is he capable of doing other work?'

'I don't know. He's done a good job on that garden, I have to say that,' Jacob replied grudgingly. 'He's transformed that area completely.'

Jacob felt uncomfortable in David's presence. The wounds David had were a constant reminder to him that he had not fought on the Western Front. Indeed, he had not fought anywhere. It was his Achilles heel. During the war Jacob had worn the King's uniform, he even went to Palestine, but he never once heard a shot crack over his head. The nearest he ever got to the enemy was guarding a few frail, scruffy Turks who had deserted from their units.

'I haven't seen him have any of his turns recently,' Jacob said. 'I don't know about after work, we never see him. He never mixes. There's something arrogant about the fellow, something I can't quite lay my finger on, as if he thinks he's better than the rest of us.'

'My brother says he's a gentleman,' Tim said grunting. 'You'd think that after a year he would have recovered his voice and memory. Terrible thing that war. There're limbless young men in the street, begging. I always give them a penny. No, it was a terrible thing.' Tim sighed as if the breath leaving his body was an end of the subject.

'That's a good picture, that, Mr Wilding,' Jacob said, his eyes wandering towards the photograph again. 'Miss Elizabeth looks grand in her uniform.'

'So she is the cause of all these sighs. Well, it will do you no good Jacob, believe me. Yes, she's a fine looking woman, I wouldn't argue with that, but what lad would put up with her cold manner? No wonder she only has female friends.' He frowned as he remembered how unfriendly she had been towards him when she met him in London. 'She cut me dead, in my brother's house. Cut me dead! There's no love in her. I see it in her eyes. No warmth. Eyes like ice. You know she hasn't bothered to come and see my Harry? Not once I tell you, her own brother, unfeeling girl.'

'As you once said, she needs someone to sort her out, Mr Wilding.'

'Did I? Umm you could well be right. Do you know Jacob, after nine months without sight or word, her mother finally gets to see her by bumping into her in the street. What sort of daughter would treat her mother like that? She didn't even tell her when she had graduated from Oxford. We only found out she worked at the junior school by accident.'

'I saw her the other night, coming from Farm Cottages on her bike−'

'Isn't that where Shepherd lives?'

'It is, Mr Wilding. I called out to her but she ignored me.'

Tim looked thoughtful for a moment. 'You don't think Shepherd...'

Jacob laughed. 'Not for a moment, Sir. I reckon she'd been visiting Mrs Willows.'

'Oh yes, Mrs Willows. So she will visit an unrelated old woman, but not her own family. What's wrong with that girl? She is so unlike her mother. Mrs Wilding's a wonderful woman, full of warmth. Bagged a son with the first shot I fired.' He looked pleased with himself as his eyes feel on the photograph of his wife holding young Harry. Then he glanced at the one of Elizabeth in her FANY uniform at Buckingham Palace. 'If I was to be charitable Jacob, I'd say it's not all Elizabeth's fault. She should not have gone off to that war. Had she been a daughter of mine I would not have allowed it. It has obviously affected her deeply. Just like that Shepherd fellow. Mind you lad,' Tim cried wagging a finger at Jacob who was suddenly full of attention, 'I will say this, I was the proudest man in the kingdom when I saw the King pin that medal on Elizabeth's chest. By heavens, I grew a few

100

inches that day. "That's my daughter," I said to a newspaper man and he took a picture of me.' Tim smiled to himself then glanced towards the big man opposite. 'You never actually saw combat, did you Jacob?'

Jacob coloured and lowered his head.

'Well it's all over now. Thank God it's now all in the past. Now then, where were we? Shepherd... so, the fellow doesn't fit in. In fairness Jacob, have any of you made the effort with him?'

'None of us really know him, Mr Wilding. I mean you can't talk to him, can you? Have a conversation like. He just won't mix with the rest of us. As you know, we all go to the *Horse and Groom* for a couple of drinks after we've been paid. It's always good to socialize after a hard week. It makes the lads feel part of a team, particularly with me being there with them.'

'You're a good lad, Jacob. I used to have one or two there with your father, God rest his soul.'

'So you did, Sir. Well, I always invite Shepherd,' he lied, 'yet he's never once joined us. Tonight we're celebrating young Tom Hollis' engagement to Bert Fairbrother's eldest. As soon as they find a home, they'll wed. We're all going, except Shepherd. I made a special point in mentioning it to him, but still he refuses to join us,' he lied again.

'He's a strange one, no mistaking. Just like Elizabeth. Between you and me Jacob, I'd like to be shot of him, but Mrs Wilding won't have it. There's something about him that makes me feel awkward. I don't know what. I took him on to please my wife so you must make an effort with him. Just leave him to his damn garden.'

The door suddenly opened. Christina entered the room with Elizabeth. Tim coloured. Jacob fidgeted awkwardly. Elizabeth made a point of avoiding Jacob's eye.

'Look who has come to visit us, my dear.'

'Good Lord, Elizabeth! Well, well, well,' Tim said, struggling to his feet. 'We were talking about you a moment ago, weren't we Jacob?'

Elizabeth forced a smile, remembering the promise to her father-in-law to make an effort to be friendly, but did not approach to kiss him.

'What have you done with your hair, Miss Elizabeth?'

Elizabeth closed her eyes. The exhalation of breath was quite audible. 'Are you going to suggest I look like a boy, Mr Wilson?'

'No! I meant...'

'Well, well, well,' Tim said again, watching the colour rise in

Jacob's cheeks, which gave the big man the appearance of a William Holman Hunt rustic. Tim suddenly felt uneasy in Elizabeth's company. 'Fancy that,' he said. 'Take a seat. You'll stay for supper with us?'

'Thank you, but—'

'No buts Elizabeth,' her mother interrupted. 'You'll stay. We need to mend fences.'

From her peripheral vision, Elizabeth could feel Jacob Wilson tormenting her with his eyes, the way her German guard leered at her after he had raped her, reminding her with his sickly grin that he had had her and would have her again. As her breasts began to rise and fall, she felt Jacob's eyes feast in their movement. Elizabeth held back the urge to strike out at him; instead, she turned and gave him a cold stare. Her withering look might have diminished any man, but it seemed to have the opposite effect on Jacob Wilson, as if he delighted in her discomfort. He smiled and made no attempt to avert his gaze. She jumped up from her seat and asked for a drink.

'Yes, yes of course. I'm sorry, I should have offered,' Tim said, wanting to please her. He turned to his wife. 'Would you care for a glass of your usual sherry, my dear?'

'No thank you,' Christina replied noticing Elizabeth's discomfort and imagining it to be because of Tim.

'I should like a whisky, if you have any,' Elizabeth said walking to the window.

'You shouldn't drink that stuff, Bess. It will spoil your complexion.'

'In France it helped us cope, Mamma.'

'Another beer, Jacob?'

'I'd better not, thank you Mr Wilding, Sir.'

Elizabeth's breathing became irregular when Tim invited Jacob to join them to eat. Instant relief enveloped her when Jacob reminded Tim that he was expected at the pub with the rest of the men. Reluctantly, she sat again. She could hear Jacob's breathing and was again reminded of her Teutonic tormentors. She jumped to her feet and went back to the window, putting the glass to her mouth not realizing it was already empty.

'For heaven's sake Bess, what's got into you?' Christina cried. 'You're like a Jack-in-the-box. Why do you keep looking through that window? Are you expecting someone?'

Elizabeth longed to see David. He never seemed to be home when she called, nor had he been to the lake since they had had dinner at her parents-in-law. He was avoiding her, she knew. 'Your garden is looking very nice, Mamma.'

'So you've taken a sudden interest in my garden.'

'Jacob and I were just talking about the fellow who does your Mamma's garden, Elizabeth. Perhaps we should have called him what young Stephanie suggested, Gardener, not Shepherd.'

Tim laughed. Elizabeth closed her eyes when Jacob joined in.

'I don't suppose you've met him,' Tim continued. 'I have to say he makes me feel uneasy.'

'That's no reason to mock him.'

Christina caught her daughter's eye as she moved uneasily in her seat. 'I think I will have that drink,' Christina said to Tim, and rose to pour a sherry.

Tim was still smarting over Elizabeth's rebuke and asked his wife to pour him another. 'Your mother is Shepherd's guardian angel, aren't you my dear? What would he have done if you hadn't taken him under your wing, I wonder?'

'As Elizabeth said, the garden is looking lovely but nobody is indispensable. There are lots of men looking for work,' Christina said, handing her husband his drink. Her remark was addressed to Tim, but Elizabeth knew it was meant for her and her eyes lifted towards her mother who felt defiance in her daughter's gaze.

'Right then, Jacob,' said Tim. 'I think we are through with our business. No doubt you'd like to get along and have your drink with the men.'

Jacob swallowed the last of his beer, his eyes lingering in Elizabeth's direction. He bid her goodnight. Elizabeth ignored him.

'Bess, Jacob said goodnight.'

'I heard, Mamma. But don't let's delay him further. I'm sure he will have a pint or two already drawn and waiting for him.'

When the door closed behind him, Christina turned to her daughter. 'You were rude to Jacob, Bess. A little politeness wouldn't have gone amiss.'

'Even so, Jacob couldn't take his eyes off your picture Elizabeth, and they fairly popped out of his head when you walked in here,' Tim said laughing. 'I think he's soft on you.'

When her mother laughed, Elizabeth felt her skin burn.

'Have you noticed the way he looks at you, Bess?'

'Mamma, I'm old enough to be aware of men's eyes. I even know how to interpret their gaze, or in Jacob Wilson's case, his leer.'

'That's not a nice thing to say.'

'I like Jacob,' Tim said, 'known him since he was a babe. His father was one of my oldest friends. Poor chap fell on bad times. It killed him.' Tim knew how difficult it would be to run the farm without Jacob. He discovered that during the war when Jacob was away. Marriage to Elizabeth could be the answer. He would encourage it. It would make her mother happy to see the girl settled, and it would bring Jacob into the family, making sure the farm remained in safe hands until his son could take over. He liked the idea of it. 'Jacob would make a fine husband for some lass, wouldn't you agree, my dear? He's a hard worker, sticks at it. Good qualities in a man. Wouldn't you say so?'

'I would. What do you think, Bess?'

'Stop it! Both of you! You must sense how I loathe the man.'

Great cavities appeared in the faces of Tim and Christina as they were stunned into silence. Elizabeth rose and poured herself another drink. Tim coughed and commented about an imminent storm, then began to discuss the New Year's Eve party he was going to give to celebrate the new decade.

'I hope you will join us, Elizabeth. Everyone will be here. No expense spared. We are going to see this terrible decade out in style. I believe 1920 promises to be a great new start for the family, what with the twins getting married.'

'Instead of wasting money on senseless parties, why don't you spend it on improving some of the homes in which your tenants live?'

'And what would you know about that, Elizabeth?' Tim said coldly.

'I have been in Mrs Willows' home,' Elizabeth replied catching her mother's eye. 'It's damp and in need of repair.'

'Look Elizabeth, it's the party we're discussing, not your social conscience. Come if you wish. All your family will be here. I'm sure it will do you good to get out. There'll be lots of nice young men to dance with.'

'That's a relief, I thought you had me lined up for Jacob Wilson.'

'Jacob is a good lad, Elizabeth. I couldn't do without him.'

'Louisa, Bertie and little Danny will be here, Bess. It's a time for families to be together.'

'You're right, Mamma,' Elizabeth suddenly said, 'but supposing I had no family... that I was alone.'

'What are you saying?' Tim laughed. 'You do have a family, one who loves you. There's no reason to be alone on New Year's Eve, especially this one... a new decade, a new start.'

'Quite right,' Elizabeth said smiling brightly at Tim who flushed at seeing it. 'Jane tells me she knows someone who has no family and will be all alone over the holiday. As I've no one to bring, I think it would be an act of Christian kindness if I invited him to this party of yours.'

Christina glared at her daughter.

'Do I know this person?' Tim said cheerfully.

'Yes. I believe he is this fellow you were discussing, Mamma's gardener.'

Tim's nose screwed up as if he had smelt something distasteful. 'Shepherd! No, no.'

'I understand he's a gentleman under your care, rather than a labouring man.'

'I pay him.'

'Is your veterinary surgeon coming?'

'Yes, and his wife.'

'Don't you pay *him*?'

'Stop trying to be clever, Bess.' Christina's eyes narrowed as her lips tightened. 'Just drop it. He is not coming to this party.'

'Why? Is he socially unacceptable to your grand friends?'

'Because he is an employee,' Christina snapped.

'I seem to remember you were once in Mr Wilding's employ yourself, Mamma.'

Christina turned vermilion. Tim choked on his drink. 'I think you should apologize to your mother, Elizabeth.'

'If I am wrong or misunderstood your position in this house then I'm sorry, Mamma. But I hope you see the weakness in your argument.'

Tim began to explain his reasons for not inviting any of the men and that he had intended to organize a separate party for them and their families in one of the public houses in town. His voice was softer now and he chose his words carefully. He did not want to give Elizabeth any opportunity to turn the argument in her favour. As he spoke, a distant rumble of thunder caught Elizabeth's attention. She rose and walked to the window. Through the dark grey landscape tossed by the wind and darkened by rain, her eyes were drawn towards David's cottage. It could not be seen from the farmhouse, but she knew where to direct her gaze. It lay two miles to the east, behind a small copse on high ground where the wind whipped across the valley. She could not get him out of her mind. She ached with worry that he did not want to see her again.

'So you see,' Tim continued. 'If I invite… Elizabeth… for God sake Christina, she hasn't been listening to a word I've said. She's in one of her dreams again.'

'Elizabeth!' Her mother snapped. 'Stop daydreaming and listen when you're being spoken to. You've had too much of that whisky.'

'I'm sorry, what were you saying?' Elizabeth said, returning to her seat.

Tim found her eye but could not hold it, so he turned towards his wife. 'If I invite Shepherd, then I shall have to invite all the men.'

'But it will not be *you* inviting him, do you see? It will be me.'

'That's not the point. I'm not having you in this house with one of the men.'

'It was *the men* who died for this country while you grew fat on the war.'

'Elizabeth!' gasped her mother.

'The money I made then gives them a living now, including this Shepherd fellow,' Tim said, showing his teeth as he spoke. 'I think it's as good a time as any to say this Elizabeth, as I told Stephanie and Jane. I will not have any of those uncouth louts anywhere near you. Do you understand? Your circumstances have changed. You're now above their station.'

Elizabeth's eyes rose towards Tim. 'How dare you say such a thing−?'

'Now, now, Bess,' Christina began to fidget. 'Calm down.'

Elizabeth threw her mother a contemptuous look then her eyes turned to Tim. 'My circumstances have *never* changed. My grandfather was a bishop. My father was a professional man. I was married to an officer in the British Army, a professional man's son and I am a graduate of the Sorbonne and Oxford Universities. Nothing has changed in my social standing. It would only diminish if I were to move into this house.'

'That's enough, Bess−'

'If you are so keen for me not to mix with the men, why are you trying to pair me with Jacob Wilson?'

Tim threw his hands in the air. 'Jacob is from a *good* family. His father was my friend.'

'Oh! Jacob Wilson is a gentleman! To think I mistook him for an uncouth lout.'

'God give me strength!' Tim exclaimed. 'You would try the patience of a saint.'

'Calm down. Both of you calm down,' Christina said, her eyes welling with tears. She went to Tim placing an arm on his shoulder. 'Just hold your tongue, Elizabeth.'

'Now look what you've done. You've upset your mother. I won't have it. What's wrong with you, girl?'

'I simply suggested a kindness to a lonely man.'

'What's he to you?' His eyes suddenly narrowed. 'I hope there is nothing going on between you two. You were seen cycling away from Farm Cottages and don't deny it.'

'I don't. I was visiting Mrs Willows,' Elizabeth said, glancing at her mother, 'so the next time Jacob Wilson wishes to tell tales, tell him to get his facts right.'

'That's what he said, if you must know.' Tim reached for his drink. 'Listen Elizabeth, I know Shepherd has suffered, that's why you're taking pity on him now, but he is not coming to my party with you, or anyone else. Do you hear me girl?'

Elizabeth rose and went back to the window. 'I'm sorry,' she said softly. 'I should not have come here. I meant to build bridges and instead I've upset you both. Forgive me. I shall leave.'

'Please sit down Elizabeth,' Tim sighed, suddenly calming. 'There's a storm about to break, you'll be caught in it.'

As he spoke, another distant rumble of thunder sounded across the Aylesbury Vale. Elizabeth poured some more whisky into her glass and walked back to the window. The storm reminded her of the constant artillery duels over the Ypres Salient during the third battle at Passchendaele Ridge, gunfire flashing and quivering with light that was tremulant on the horizon before flitting into the darkness, to rise again with luminous wings that filled the whole sky with light. Now the distant rumble rolled towards them, with cracks and explosions. Elizabeth imagined unseen angry dragons stalking the skies, ponderously approaching the farmhouse, just as the German barrage did that had killed Isabella.

'Elizabeth! Will you come away from that window?' Christina cried.

As her mother spoke, Elizabeth caught sight of a ghostly figure outside when a flash of lightning briefly illuminated the courtyard. 'I think there's someone outside, Mamma.'

107

A frantic knock at the front door followed. Susan entered the room. 'Excuse me Mr Wilding, Shepherd's here. He's soaking wet. I think he's going to have one of his turns. I've let him shelter in the hall if that's all right.'

'What's he want?'

'Timothy!'

Tim glanced at his wife and then looked towards Elizabeth knowing she would go for his jugular if he turned David away. 'Show him in here, Susan. Let him warm himself by the fire.'

'Yes, Mr Wilding.'

David limped in - his wild staring eyes unable to focus. Elizabeth's heart jumped as she observed him unseen from the shadows of the room.

'Just look at you. You're soaking wet! What were you doing out in such weather?' Christina said with a genuine look of concern. 'Susan, go and fetch a towel. Hurry girl or he'll catch his death.'

'Susan's right. He's going to have another of his turns,' Tim sighed impatiently. 'Come on lad, pull yourself together. It's just a little thunder.'

'Oh leave him!' Elizabeth cried. 'Can't you see he is suffering from shellshock?'

Her voice was lost as thunder split and cracked, which shook the building, the sound ricocheting across the flat pasturelands, leaving a rumbling echo in its wake. David brought his arms over his head as if to protect it from falling shrapnel. Another deafening explosion followed. He fell to the floor. He was back in his nightmare. Elizabeth was back in hers and did not see David fall.

Her parents stared in horror at David thrashing about as if having a fit, holding his shattered leg, trying to seek shelter under the table. The farmer and his wife could do nothing but stand with open mouths and wide, disbelieving eyes.

Elizabeth looked up and when she saw David, the shelling suddenly stopped, only the thunder remained. She ran to him, knelt beside his shaking body and put her finger in his mouth to release his tongue while her mother and stepfather looked on. 'Leave us,' Elizabeth said with some authority. 'I know how to deal with this.'

'Yes, leave it to Elizabeth. She has experience of these things,' Tim said pushing his protesting wife from the room.

Elizabeth switched off the light and returned to him. 'Hush, it's all right, my love. It will be over in a moment. Stick it a little longer,' she whispered. David continued to struggle. She took hold of him, pressed him to her body to prevent him struggling further. When at last he calmed, she held his limp frame to her. His lips were moving... *help me*.

She couldn't remember how many times she had heard those words from young men when holding their hand, until it slackened in hers. Each death killed a little more of her. Each death reminded her of her mother-in-law's face as she listened to the news that her only child was never going to return home.

David's eyes fell on the front of Elizabeth's dress, which had been pulled open in the struggle to calm him. He reached out and took a breast in his hand and gently ran a thumb over her nipple. When their eyes met, the two of them came together with deep, frenzied kisses. She fell back on the rug lifting her bottom when she felt him pulling at her knickers, gasping at the suddenness of him filling her. Pinned to the floor, Elizabeth turned her head and concentrated on the dancing flames of the fire as logs began to spit and crackle. Anything to keep the memories of her guards away. She began to think of Catherine and something began to stir inside her. No! It was David she wanted. She whispered his name and enveloped him tighter in her arms, surrendering herself to him completely. There were no soft caresses, whispered words or an experienced lover's finesse, only a mad urgency to finish what they had begun. She lifted her knees when David began to move faster and felt his hot, broken breath burn her cheek as he emptied himself into her body.

'Stay inside me,' she whispered. 'Don't leave me yet,' and for a moment they lay motionless, locked together. It was only when he did move from her that her mind became alive to the danger of her mother so close along the hall. She wiped herself with her knickers and quickly threw them into the fierce flames of the fire as the door to the room opened.

'Why on earth is this light out?' Christina demanded when she entered the room, her eyes catching Elizabeth's hand moving quickly to the bodice of her unbuttoned dress. Christina glared at her daughter and then at David. 'I suggest you return home immediately, young man. I'll talk to you in the morning.'

'I'll see you home, David.'

'I'm sure Shepherd can manage, Elizabeth,' her mother said sharply.

Elizabeth clenched her fists and tightened her lips. Before she had a chance to speak, David held up his hand. He turned, nodded his thanks to Christina whose eyes avoided his. Elizabeth went to the door, straining to catch the last glimpse of his dark, disappearing frame. When he was gone, Elizabeth turned with blazing eyes sharply towards her mother. 'Will you allow me to live my life as I see fit, Mamma?'

When Elizabeth's hand dropped from the front of her dress it fell open at the bodice exposing her nakedness beneath. The slap from her mother that followed cracked hard across her face.

'Slut! You filthy slut! Look at you. What would your dear father think of you now, his sweet, precious girl… a labouring man's whore?'

'The sweet, precious girl my father knew died in France,' Elizabeth replied, holding her stinging cheek. 'The one you see before you now is struggling to live again.' She took her coat from the peg and faced her mother, and in a calm voice said, 'If you ever raise a hand to me again Mamma, or try to do anything that may harm David, you will never see me again…*never*!'

Christina put her face into her hands and wept as the door slammed behind her daughter.

Chapter 15

When Elizabeth opened her eyes, she was unsure at first where she was. Glancing down at the floor from the bed, she saw her clothes scattered where she had hurriedly thrown them from her body the night before. David had long since left for work. After washing herself, making the bed and tidying the room, she left the house into a chilling wind to collect her bicycle. It was gone. Mrs Willows appeared at her front door shaking a duster. The ageing features of her old family friend screwed prune-like into a smile. 'Hello, my duck.'

'Oh! Mrs Willows! Good morning. Are you well? I—'

'Good Lord, what have you done to your lovely hair, young Paddy Brennan?'

'Please Mrs Willows. I've been driven insane by that question. How are you?'

'Oh, you know. Come in, young Paddy. I'll put the kettle on; this wind is killing my bones.' She shuffled inside with Elizabeth reluctantly following her. 'Mrs Sharp next door said she saw you the other day visiting Mr David. You should watch yourself, my duck. She's a bit of a chatterbox is that one.'

'He'd been taken ill at a concert. I went to see if he was feeling better.'

'You being a nurse in the war, I expect.'

'I drove an ambulance, Mrs Willows. I was not a nurse.'

'The paper said you were a nurse in a German hospital, showing compassion to the enemy as if they were our own wounded boys.'

Elizabeth laughed and was amazed that she did so. 'Mrs Willows, I worked in the basement of the hospital, in the laundry room to be precise. Sometimes I had to clean lavatories and scrub floors, depending on the mood of my guard. I had no freedom, nor did I ever see a wounded German soldier, only their blood soaked sheets and bandages.' Elizabeth was incredulous at the ease with which she talked of her erstwhile tormentors, yet in the last thirty seconds of conversation she had said more to Mrs Willows about her captivity than to any other living person. She suddenly felt elated. A corner to her recovery had truly been turned. She smiled brightly at her elderly friend's indignant expression, which made her wrinkled, pendulous jowls hang like a bloodhound. Elizabeth tried to imagine Mrs Willows as a young woman. It was difficult to tell whether she had once been pretty.

'How can you smile at a memory like that, Paddy Brennan? Those horrible people treating you like that, you, a young lady.'

'It wasn't so bad,' she lied.

'Dear me, it's been such a long time since I've seen you. You know, you look the spitting image of your Grandmamma. I said to your Papa, God rest his soul, you would be his mother's image. A fine looking woman if ever I saw one. Has your Mr David left for work?'

'So you think he's *my* Mr David?'

'He's a lovely lad; a proper gentleman. Nothing's too much trouble for him, with his bad leg and all.'

Mrs Willows suddenly leaned closer to Elizabeth as though she were about to disclose her greatest secret. 'He's in torment though,' she whispered. 'It fair breaks my heart to hear him tossing and turning in his bed at night. If he could scream, I think he would.'

Elizabeth blushed. 'You can hear him in his room, Mrs Willows?'

Mrs Willows coloured too. 'I'll make that tea.'

Elizabeth avoided Mrs Willows' eye and grew crimson in the certain knowledge that she knew she had spent the night with David. Mrs Willows recognized Elizabeth's discomfort and squeezed her hand.

'Paddy dear, you need someone to love after what you have lost and Mr David is a fine lad. I'm just a silly old woman. Take no notice of me.'

Elizabeth kissed the old woman's cheek. 'I have to go, Mrs Willows. I'm travelling to London this morning with Jane and Stephanie. We're going to do some early Christmas shopping.'

'Come and see me again, and don't make it so long next time.'

'I seem to have lost my bicycle.'

'I put it round the back. I didn't want any nosey parker knowing your business,' she said, tilting her head towards Mrs Sharp's house next door. 'Her husband works for your stepfather and is friends with that lout Jacob Wilson.'

*

Elizabeth wore a bright smile as she made her way along the lane that would take her towards the farmhouse. Unknown to her, the progress she made from the cottage was under the gaze of another some distance away. Jacob Wilson turned his horse and headed for the other end of the lane along which Elizabeth now cycled.

As she rounded the bend, she saw Jacob ahead of her inspecting his horse's shoe. She groaned at the sight of him. 'Excuse me Mr Wilson, I should like to pass.'

'Oh! Good morning, Miss Elizabeth,' he said, touching his cap and acting as if it were a chance meeting. 'What are you doing around these parts this time of the morning?'

'That's my business, Mr Wilson. Will you please move. I really am in a hurry.'

'Just a second, Miss Elizabeth. Lady has picked up a stone... there, that's got it,' he said, slapping the horse's rump. 'I think I should walk her for a bit. Give her a rest.'

'I expect she will be grateful for that,' Elizabeth said, dismounting her bicycle, but still she could not find a way past the horse.

'If you are going to the farmhouse, then perhaps you will allow me to walk with you. There is something I wish to talk to you about.'

'I thought we were done with talking, Mr Wilson,' Elizabeth said impatiently. 'I'm in a hurry and as you say, you must rest your horse.'

'Surely you can walk a little?'

'No—'

'It's about the New Year party your stepfather is giving,' he stammered, his rehearsed conversation abandoning him fast. 'I've been invited to go and wondered if you would care to accompany me as my guest.'

'You're the guest, Mr Wilson. I am a member of the family giving the party. Anyway, I'm not going.'

'Mr Wilding said it would be all right—'

'What would be all right?'

'To take you.'

'Mr Wilding has no say in the matter,' Elizabeth snapped. 'Why do you persist in pursuing my company when I have made it quite clear to you that I do not want it? I do not like you, Mr Wilson. I thought I had made that quite clear.'

Jacob's great thick neck coloured as the blood rose to his face. 'Aren't I good enough for you? Is that what it is? You prefer to be the whore to some crippled mute.'

The slap across his face shocked him. He recovered quickly, grabbing hold of her, all sense and reasoning gone. 'You've been asking for this, you stuck-up bitch,' he said forcing his mouth onto hers. She pushed at him but could not budge from his embrace. He covered her mouth with a large, rough hand when she began to scream

113

at him. Now she could hardly breathe. The more she fought him the quicker her strength began to desert her. His hand left her mouth and began to search inside her clothing as she choked for breath. The round naked flesh of her breast filled his hand. Elizabeth's body went limp in his arms.

'Yes, that's right,' he whispered. 'Just relax, you'll enjoy it.'

Elizabeth's mind raced. Jacob's blood was up and this was an isolated spot, far from where people normally walked. His hand left her breast and went up her dress. He discovered she wasn't wearing any knickers, because she had burned them the evening before. He attempted to lower her to the ground, assuring her that they would not be disturbed. Once on the ground, Elizabeth knew she would not be able to escape him. 'All right,' she said breathlessly, 'but not on the ground, it's damp. If you want it then do it against the tree.'

Jacob looked at her suspiciously. 'You'll not try to escape if I let go of you?'

'Just get on with it.'

He let go of her and began grappling with the large, leather belt around his waist. His trousers fell exposing his swollen flesh. 'I knew this day would come,' he said in a triumphant boast. 'I knew it.'

Jacob stepped closer. As he lifted up her dress, her right knee came up into his groin with such force it almost lifted him off his feet. The big man doubled up and wheezed in pain. In Jacob's face she saw the fat round features of her German guard and kicked him again sending the big man to his knees as a great cry left his lips. Finally, a clenched fist caught him hard on the nose. She yelped and shook her hand as the power of the blow knocked him backwards. It split his nose and filled it with blood. With his trousers round his ankles he found it difficult to climb to his feet.

She stood above him breathing heavily, her teeth resembling a snarling dog. 'If you ever lay a hand on me again I will stick a knife into you.' She wiped her mouth with the sleeve of her coat and spat the taste of him on the ground. 'I loathe you. I hate the very sight of you. You make my flesh *crawl*. Now is that clear enough, you great oaf?'

The venom in her voice hurt him mentally as her knee and fist had done so physically. Jacob felt as if his heart had been submerged into a pool of frozen water. Avoiding her crazed eyes, he slowly pulled his trousers up, stood, and then painfully mounted his horse. He wiped the blood from his nose with the back of his hand and inspected it.

'Will you tell Mr Wilding about this?'

'You'd lose everything, wouldn't you? If I ever hear a word that you're taking your spite out on David Shepherd I'll let my mother know and that will finish you, Jacob Wilson. Now get out of here.'

He said nothing as he dug in his spurs and cantered away.

Elizabeth began to shake. Only moments ago she had been happy. She had given herself freely to the man she loved, which had helped exorcise the memories of her past. Now another man had tried to take her against her will. She was determined not to allow this incident to upset her. She began to make herself look decent, but her fingers found difficulty in buttoning up the front of her dress.

When she reached the farmhouse, she was almost pulled into the sitting room by her sister Jane, who whispered a quick warning. 'Go home. I'll meet you there. Mamma's livid. She knows you spent the night with David.'

'How—'

The door burst open. Christina stormed into the room, her intense glare focussing on Elizabeth. 'Be off with you, Jane. I want to speak with your sister alone.'

When Jane left the room, Elizabeth turned from her mother and looked though the window. 'Don't turn your back on me, girl. Look at me!'

Elizabeth faced her mother and calmly said, 'There's no need to shout, Mamma.'

'You stayed the night with him, didn't you?'

'Yes, I did.'

'You brazen hussy!' Christina screamed and raised a hand, but Elizabeth was ready for her, quickly stepping away from her mother's reach.

'I warned you never to raise a hand to me again, Mamma. Don't squander what love I have for you by hitting me again.'

'I'll not have you bring shame on this house, my girl. If you see that man again I'll let your stepfather know, so I will. He'll have him whipped and thrown out into the gutter where he belongs. Do you hear me?'

'Yes Mamma, I hear you. You'll have him whipped and thrown into the gutter where he belongs. I shall then pick him up out of the gutter and take him home to live with me, whatever shame or scandal it might bring upon your house.'

'Live with you!' Christina fell into a chair hardly able to breathe. 'Merciful heavens! What has become of you, child?'

'That, Mamma, is where you are sadly mistaken. I am no longer a child.'

*

Three weeks later, during the last day of the decade, there was a knock at Elizabeth's front door. When the front door opened Elizabeth met her mother's eyes.

'I've come over to see you as you couldn't be bothered to come over on Christmas day. The whole family were there except you, Elizabeth. Is that the way it will be in future?'

'I was with my in-laws in London.'

'Rather than with your family.'

'They are my family. I'm all the Turners have.'

'Are you going to invite me in or are we going to debate this in the street?' Elizabeth stepped aside and allowed her mother to brush past her into the sitting room, her eyes taking in everything as she removed her hat and coat. 'So, after what, almost a year, I finally get to see inside my daughter's home.'

'Would you like some tea?'

'No thank you. I've come here to have a serious talk with you.' Christina lowered herself onto the sofa and looked intensely at her daughter. 'Why, Bess? Why are we fighting like this? Do you hate me so much?'

'Mamma, please! I have only ever loved you—'

'You have a strange way of showing it. Is it your stepfather you hate?'

'No. He's good to you and the twins. I respect him for that.'

Christina's eyes travelled around the room during their silence. She shook her head. 'There's not a sign of Christmas here.'

'There was no sign of it on the battlefield, either. I do not believe in God.'

'That, my girl, is blasphemous. I'll remind you that your grandfather was a clergyman and you were brought up in the church.' Christina's breathing quickened as her eyes met her daughter's. 'I brought you up to be a decent girl and it upsets me to see how you have turned out.'

Elizabeth lowered her eyes as her mother's voice echoed round the room. 'And how have I turned out, Mamma?'

'You, of all my girls. I wish I had never brought Shepherd here. He's the cause of our troubles. He only remains because I have said nothing to your stepfather.'

116

'He remains because you cannot bear to face the alternative.'

'That's right. I have to live here. You are a schoolmistress in this town. Spending the night with an unmarried man, the humiliation of it... what will the parents of your pupils think?'

'They will think the worst. It wouldn't be Christian to do otherwise.'

Christina jumped up from her seat and walked across the room. 'You're too clever for your own good, Elizabeth.'

'Mamma, if I'm branded a harlot it doesn't mean a jot to me. Most women in this town dislike me because they see their husbands eyeing me. I never encourage it, but I see it all the time. Most men are like dogs, whatever bitch−'

'Yes! I understand your meaning; there's no need for graphics.' Christina sat again and took her daughter's hand. 'I only want to see you happy, settled, with a family. You've had some wonderful chances since the war. Look at young Doctor Lawson. He asked you out a couple of times and you refused him. Now he's married to that awful Campbell girl.'

'Dr Lawrence wasn't my type,' Elizabeth said as she left the room. 'I'm going to make some tea.'

'Bess, I know it can't be easy for you after what you've been through−'

'You haven't the faintest idea what I went through, yet you boast to your friends what a brick I am. "My Bess was over there doing her bit for the Flag. Got the MM, don't you know; even the Belgians gave her a medal... so brave, so patriotic". I've been told this. It's embarrassing. Next time you have one of your little soirées with the town's gossips and the subject arises, tell them that I could hardly sleep with fear... fear of throwing up when I saw the state of the men's wounds as I helped them into my ambulance; fear of how many would be dead before I got them to a hospital. Fear for my friends' safety, that these memories will never leave me as long as I live−'

'Snap out of it, Elizabeth,' Christina cried. 'Stop feeling sorry of yourself. I'm sick and tired of it−'

Both women became silent. Elizabeth returned to the kitchen overwhelmed with emotion. A few minutes later Christina followed.

'Look Bess dear, listen to me, I don't want to argue. It upsets me to know you had a bad time of it, but life goes on... you have to put the past behind you.'

Elizabeth looked at her mother with incredulous eyes. 'Put the war behind me. Yes Mamma, I'll start today. Nothing ever happened. It was all an illusion.'

'That's right dear, look to the future. Now, I have something to put to you,' Christina said, following Elizabeth out of the kitchen. 'Why don't you stand still for a moment? Sit down, please. That's better. Now, your stepfather would like to retire so we can do some travelling, go to Paris as you did. With that in mind, there is only one man he considers capable of running the farm.'

Elizabeth sighed, rose from her chair and walked across the room. She leaned against a chair staring at a photograph of Catherine while her mother droned on. *Darling Cathy, are you going through all this too?*

'Elizabeth! You haven't heard a word I've said, have you?'

'Mamma, I'll say it for the very last time. I do not want Jacob Wilson. Now let us drop this subject.'

'What do you want, then?'

'To live the way I want. Not how you want.'

'With him, I suppose.'

'If I didn't have David, the alternative would crucify you.'

'Don't talk in riddles to me, young lady. Just think of Mr and Mrs Turner. What about them?'

Elizabeth sat down and put her face into her hands. 'I hope they will understand.'

'Of all my children... I don't know what to say.'

'Then say nothing, Mamma. It will save both of us heartache.' Elizabeth looked into her mother's face and remembered when she was a small girl how she had loved the sight of that face. Now, something was lost between them. Something was missing that used to be there. 'I do love you Mamma, please believe that.'

'Then perhaps you might show it in a little consideration for my feelings. We'll discuss this another time, when you have come to your senses,' Christina said standing. 'Will you be coming to the party tonight?'

'May I bring David?'

'No! I will protect him, but I will not encourage your relationship with him.'

That evening, when the family and their friends filled the farmhouse eating and drinking, preparing for the arrival of the New Year, Elizabeth was absent. As the first bell of the distant town hall clock struck midnight, brilliant colours burst into the sky welcoming the beginning of the third decade of the new century. Elizabeth did not see the fireworks, or hear the bell toll midnight. She slept. David was awake beside her. He shuddered at the colours lighting up the sky. In his mind he saw the Very lights illuminating the dark nights on the Western Front, the rockets calling for artillery support, the inevitable carnage that would follow. He rested his head beside Elizabeth, wanting to hear her breathing, but as the fireworks continued to burst, all he could hear was the chattering machine guns and the cries from dying men.

Chapter 16

On the morning of the third day of January, 1920, Elizabeth finished packing for her annual trip to Ireland, which left her two hours before she needed to catch the train for the first part of the long journey to Stranraer, then across to Larne where her aunt would be waiting to meet her. But first she wanted to see David to say goodbye. When she arrived outside the little row of cottages, each with their neatly trimmed front garden covered in a thin, white shroud of snow, Mrs Willows appeared from David's front door wrapped in a large shawl, holding a broom in one hand and a small duster in the other.

'Hello, young Paddy,' she said. 'Come to visit the sick and wounded?'

'Is David unwell?'

'Got a fever, a touch of flu, I think. There's a bit of it going around. Not as bad as that lot in 1918, I'm happy to say. Hurry in, Paddy love, otherwise you'll be laid up in bed too.' The old woman followed Elizabeth into the cottage and then called up to David. 'You have a visitor, Mr David, she's coming up.'

'Thank you for looking after him, Mrs Willows,' said Elizabeth softly. 'I'll see you before I go.'

'I'll be at my place. I'll finish in here when you've gone.'

Elizabeth removed her woollen hat and climbed the stairs, brushing a lock of her growing hair from her eyes before walking into his room and kissing him. 'Hello, I've brought you some books. I thought you might be in need of them.' She flashed a smile at him. David loved that smile. It lit up her face and made him ache with desire for her. 'I'm going to Ireland to visit my aunt and cousins. I shall be gone for two weeks. I wish you could come too. You would love my aunt. She is such a lovely person, typically Irish, all heart and hospitality.' David watched her remove her hat, gloves and scarf. Her hair shone in the sunlight spilling through the window. 'I have resigned from teaching,' she casually said unbuttoning her coat. 'I shall not be returning to school next term. I'll explain after my holiday. All you must worry about is getting better.'

Elizabeth came over to him and pressed her lips on the top of his head as a mother might kiss her child. He pulled her to him and tried to kiss her. She recovered from his sudden embrace and looked him in the eyes. 'You are not well enough for that Mister, and alas, I haven't the time.' She placed her hand on his forehead. It was hot and lined with a fine film of perspiration. 'Poor darling, you're not very well, are you?' She rose from his bed and went to the bowl of water returning with a damp flannel. 'Is there anything you want before I leave?' she said laying it across his brow.

David looked into her face. She looked radiantly happy. He knew his time on the farm was limited. Jane had already warned him to be careful and now Stephanie, who had always been aloof, had come to him in the friendliest of manners advising him to watch his back.

'Try to sleep, David. I'll read to you.'

She began to read to him, her soft voice filling every cell of his body as he fought against the awful weight of fatigue. Elizabeth looked up and saw that he was asleep. She studied his features, the colour of his hair, the shape of his mouth, the line of his jaw. Her eyes sparkled with love for him. He was gone from her until her return from Ireland. Gathering her clothes, she blew him a kiss and left the room.

'Are you sure you can cope, Mrs Willows? He has a high temperature, poor love. I'll cancel my trip if—'

'You get yourself going. Your aunt will be very disappointed if you cancel now. You're the only one of her brother's children who bothers to visit her. Now off you go. Give her my love. I'll look after Mr David, don't you fret about that.'

Elizabeth bent and kissed the old woman's head. 'I shall feel a lot happier knowing that, Mrs Willows.'

In a rush of emotion that had been denied her for more years than she could remember, Mrs Willows threw herself into Elizabeth's arms and kissed her hard on the cheek. 'He's like a son to me. The child I never had,' she cried. 'Take good care of yourself on that journey, young Paddy Brennan.'

'It's Elizabeth Turner now, Mrs Willows. Young Paddy Brennan has grown into a woman.'

'Yes, she has and a very beautiful one too, my duck.'

*

Because of bad weather, Elizabeth's return to England was delayed a week. When she finally arrived back in Buckingham, she went to her in-laws' home and was disappointed to hear that the house into which she was due to move was still not ready.

'It will be finished in another week, Elizabeth,' George said tapping her hand. 'The bad weather put them behind. Tomorrow afternoon,

121

Henrietta and I are returning to London. We shall stay there for the rest of the winter so you can stay here for as long as you wish. Remember, my dear, this is your home too.'

'I will. Thank you.'

Henrietta looked at the warm colouring of her daughter-in-law's cheeks, like the bloom on a ripe peach; the gentle shape of her mouth, the grey eyes under the richness of her copper hair. She was like one of the women in Botticelli's Primavera, beautiful, with contentment that she was with child.

'You look radiant, Elizabeth,' her mother-in-law smiled. 'Almost as if you were—'

'Pregnant... I am,' Elizabeth said.

George suddenly choked on his cigar, which rendered him incapable of protesting.

Henrietta took Elizabeth in her arms. 'If it's a boy will you name him Robert?'

Henrietta Turner no longer worried about gossip or morals. She was dying. Elizabeth's baby was something she should like to see before she departed this world.

'Yes, I will.' Elizabeth looked towards her father-in-law. 'Forgive me if I have embarrassed you, Papa. I know you're shocked, but I am thrilled to be having this child.'

'Oh bother with all that,' his wife quickly said. 'I presume David is the father?'

'Of course. I'm off to tell him now. I'm going to ask him to marry me.'

'Elizabeth!' George gasped. 'You cannot do that.'

'He cannot ask me, Papa.'

'Then do it quickly,' Henrietta said, 'before it shows. People can be so cruel.'

George looked at his wife in astonishment. Inside he felt empty, still unsure about Elizabeth's relationship with a man who had no social standing, yet Elizabeth's happiness could not raise any anger in him. He took her in his arms and kissed her.

*

Elizabeth drove her in-laws to the station and after a porter unloaded their luggage, she kissed them goodbye and excitedly turned towards David's house. During the journey there, she began thinking of the consequences of being pregnant. Her mother would probably disown her. David would certainly be thrown out of his cottage and off

122

the farm within the hour. Although her parents-in-law didn't seem to mind, they might be saved from the inevitable gossip because they would be in London. Elizabeth knew she would certainly be labelled a tart, but none of it mattered. She had more than enough money with the allowance she was given from her late husband's estate, so she didn't need to work and they could live in George's home until theirs was ready. Yes, she thought, the new house would be theirs, not hers, or perhaps she should let it and move away altogether, start afresh, somewhere where they were not known.

These thoughts disappeared when she rounded the bend and climbed the hill. From a distance, she noticed that Mrs Willows' house was in darkness and wondered if she was with David whose lights lit up the front lawn. She pulled up alongside the row of cottages hurrying to the front door. It was locked. She knocked and waited before hearing a young woman's voice call out. When the door opened, Elizabeth faced a plain-looking girl whose face was known to her.

'Rosie Fairbrother! What are you doing here?'

'It's Rosie Hollis, now Miss Elizabeth.' The girl's heavy Buckingham accent hung in Elizabeth's ear as she tried to make sense of this. 'Tom and me was married two weeks ago. Mr Wilson were our best man. He got us this house.'

'But... this is Mr Shepherd's house.'

'Not any more. He's gone.'

Elizabeth suddenly felt sick. 'Gone! Gone where?'

'Don't know. All I do know is he's gone. Left Buckingham... Tom may know; he works on the farm.' She stood back to allow Elizabeth to pass. 'Why don't you come in and sit down, you've come all over queer. I'll put the kettle on and make you a nice cup of tea.'

Elizabeth followed the young woman into the room and glanced around, taking in all the alien sights of other people's things. Her eyes closed, praying the shock would not cause a miscarriage. The thought of losing David's baby brought her close to tears.

'Thank you for the offer of tea Rosie, but I really must go next door and see Mrs Willows.'

The young girl's face reddened. 'You haven't heard then?'

'Heard what? I've been away.'

'The old lady's dead.'

'Dead!' Elizabeth gasped, steadying herself against a chair. 'When? How?'

'She were old,' Rosie said with a shrug. 'She died a couple of days after we moved in here. We'd like to swap cottages. Do you think we would be able to, Miss Elizabeth? Next door being in the middle would be away from the wind. It really blows across…'

Rosie's voice trailed away as Elizabeth's eyes filled to the brim with tears. This was her mother's doing, she knew. How wicked! She had waited for her to be out of the way and then thrown David out and caused the death of old Mrs Willows. Elizabeth began to sob uncontrollably. Rosie's frightened eyes filled with relief as the front door opened and the figure of her husband loomed large at the entrance. He saw Elizabeth's bent, shaking body sitting on his sofa, her head in her hands. He glanced down at his wife who grabbed his arm and pulled him into the little kitchen.

'She came looking for the fellow who lived here and then, well, I told her about the old dear next door. What shall we do?'

'Hush, my duck. She obviously had no idea about old Mrs Willows and it's come as a shock.'

'Do you think that crippled bloke and her were carrying on?'

'You be quiet, girl. It doesn't do to poke our noses into other people's business.'

*

When Elizabeth entered the farmhouse, Jane was descending the stairs. Her smile collapsed when she saw her sister's red eyes.

'Jane, where is he?'

'I don't know. I've been away and had no idea he was gone until—'

Elizabeth did not wait for Jane to finish what she was saying. She burst into the drawing room, where the sound of her mother's laughter suddenly diminished to a low, embarrassed cough. 'Bess, you're back at last. I expect the bad weather delayed your crossing?'

'Where's David?'

'He… he left,' her mother said avoiding her eye. 'He decided to go, that's all. We have no hold on him, you must know that.'

'You're lying. Where on earth would he go?'

'Please do not be rude to your mother, Elizabeth.'

She threw her stepfather a scornful look.

'Don't you dare look at your stepfather like that,' Christina cried. 'If you cannot show some respect then—'

'Then what, Mamma? Will you have me thrown out too?'

'Elizabeth,' said her stepfather, 'the man came to your mother with a note, a damned note I tell you, asking for your hand in marriage.

How ludicrous, a man like that wanting to marry a girl like you. Who does he think he is?'

'He's the father of the child I'm expecting,' she snapped.

Only the echo of Elizabeth's voice could be heard resonating around the walls of the room. Tim turned bright red, Christina ghostly white; she looked visibly sick as she sank into a chair. 'No! Please no. Tell me it's not true.'

Tim stood, his fists clenched. 'Did the cad take advantage of you?'

'Mamma,' Elizabeth said, ignoring her stepfather, 'tell me where David has gone… please?'

'You stupid, thoughtless girl! I know important people in this town. They will talk.'

'Do you think that this family has never been the subject of gossip before? The very people you entertain in this house have been talking behind your back for years. All you are to them is a jumped-up housekeeper who found her way into her employer's bed—'

'Get out of this house,' Tim roared, his face now vermilion. 'I'll have no labouring man's whore or his bastard under my roof. Get out! Get out and don't come back.'

Elizabeth was momentarily speechless. When she did find her voice, she was amazed how calm it was. 'Have no worries, Mamma. No one will know about this child. There's nothing to keep me here now so I shall leave this town and save you further gossip from your friends.'

'Calm down, both of you.' Christina cried. 'Timothy, give Elizabeth the letter.'

'Letter! David left me a letter?'

'Yes, he did. Go and fetch it, Timothy.'

No longer the raging bull, Tim closed his eyes and placed his face in his hands, struggling to admit to an act of great folly he had committed in a hot flush of temper.

'Well?' Elizabeth cried. 'Where is it?'

'I… I burnt it,' he whispered.

His wife gasped. Elizabeth turned white.

'You burnt it?' The action of speaking the words seemed to sap the strength from Elizabeth's body. The whole room began to close in on her. She sank to her knees on the very spot where she had first made love to David, where she may have conceived his child. Her hand went to it as if to protect the foetus from those who might want to take it from her and leave her with nothing of the man she loved. She looked up at Tim through watery eyes. If ever he had wanted to hurt her, he had done so now.

'Tell me you read it before you burnt it. Tell me you know where I can find him.' Her stomach felt hollow when she saw Tim slowly shake his head. 'How could you? How could you destroy what happiness I had?'

Her mother was shaken by the misery in her daughter's voice and went to her but was shrugged away. Elizabeth rose quietly and left the room. When she reached the front door, Jane and Stephanie appeared. They had heard everything. Jane's cheeks were hot and wet with tears. She pushed past her twin and embraced her elder sister, begging her not to leave. Elizabeth looked into the great, wide eyes of both sisters. The twins were identical in features yet, although they carried the same elements, they were as different as ice is from water and water is from steam.

'I'll write.'

The door opened and Elizabeth was gone. At the window in the sitting room, Christina watched her daughter race towards the car. She had not believed for one moment that Elizabeth might leave Buckingham, but now, as the half-bent figure of her daughter disappeared into the vehicle without so much as a glance back at the farmhouse, she had the awful premonition that she may never see her again. She stretched out her hand towards the disappearing vehicle as the sound of her daughter's name left her lips in a strangled cry.

Part Two

Chapter **1**

Amiens, France. Nearly three years later.

Catherine Davina Roberta Brennan was two when Elizabeth received a letter from her mother. She had dark curls, cupid lips and a smile that shone from her light blue eyes. She also had a little patch of brown skin on the bicep of her left arm just as her father had, as if it was his brand so no other man could claim her as his.

The letter was the first communication between them since Elizabeth had left Buckingham, almost three years ago. A lump filled her throat when she recognized the small neat handwriting on the envelope. Something must be wrong, she thought, Jane would never break a confidence and give her address to their mother unless it was serious. She looked out of the window, across the square and saw Sylvie and her husband leaving the charcuterie holding Catherine's hands as they crossed the road. It brought a smile to her lips, which weakened as she ripped open the envelope.

My Dearest Elizabeth,
I have discovered where you are through Jane. Please do not be cross with her; she gave me your address because something terrible has happened. Your stepfather is dead. He was thrown from his horse and his neck was broken. The funeral is tomorrow. By the time you read these words he will be buried, gone from my life - and yours. You have no idea of the strength he gave me when I thought you had been killed in 1918. I loved him, differently from your father, but he made me happy. It is possible to find love when another dies. You will learn that one day, although of course, you already have.
How you have broken my heart. You have deprived me of the first two years of my little Catherine's life for something that was beyond my power to prevent.
When David came to see us with his proposal, Tim would not listen to reason. In the end, he convinced me that it was for your own good that David should go. It upset me so much to see you in such distress. How could I know you were pregnant or how much you really loved David? Now Catherine has lost her father, something I sincerely regret. Can you ever find it in your heart to

127

forgive me? If you can, please come home, on my knees I beg you, please come back to me.
Kiss Catherine and tell her it is from her Grandmamma who cannot wait to see her.
Your ever loving, Mamma.

*

Elizabeth took hold of Sylvie and pressed her to her body when the final call to board the train for Paris echoed round Amiens station. 'How can I ever repay you for what you've done for me?'

'How can you say such a thing? Be strong like you were against those pigs. David has gone from you, oui, but he left you little Catherine, his precious gift. Now you must look for another man, have more babies. Be happy again.' Sylvie kissed Elizabeth and smiled. 'Now go before I make a fool of myself.'

Elizabeth boarded the train with Catherine and went to an open window. A tear shone from Sylvie's eye. She wiped it, smiled, blew out her cheeks and shrugged in that French way. Elizabeth fought the emotion welling up inside her.

'Write to me and come back soon, Elizabeth.'

'Goodbye, Sylvie. Give a kiss to Maurice. I'll always love you both.'

But a blast from the train's whistle denied Sylvie hearing the last words, only seeing them form on Elizabeth's lips. Sylvie blew a kiss and smiled. It was an affectionate smile, which broke Elizabeth's resolve to be strong.

When Sylvie's waving hand disappeared into the distance, Elizabeth wiped her eyes and took her seat. She looked into the little oval face staring up at her. Delicately, she brushed the dark curls from Catherine's eyes. How like her father she looked.

'Nous allons en Angleterre, cherie.'

At Calais, as the boat drifted away from the quay, Elizabeth watched the desolate, deep, dark water, gliding wider between her and what she now realized with piercing anguish was a country she would dearly miss. The small town of Albert where she had spent many months during the war was only twenty miles from Sylvie's home in Amiens, yet Elizabeth had returned there just once, on her father's birthday in the seventh month of her pregnancy. The town was still being cleared of war damage. Rebuilding was everywhere. Her taxi left Albert travelling north through Aveluy, which had been razed to the ground. She passed another village, Authuille, which had met a similar fate then onto Thiepval, another destroyed village, where she began her search for the cemetery in which her father and brother were buried. She found it by the side of a small muddy track beneath a sunny sky softened by nebulous clouds. Among endless rows of assorted wooden crosses, she stood with a stabbing pain in her chest before two of them, both bearing the name that once was hers. At that moment, Elizabeth decided to revert to her maiden name. She held her swollen belly and whispered to her father's remains that another generation would be born carrying his genes and with it, his name. An hour later, she left his graveside and never returned. The sight of those two crosses among so many depressed her too much.

Leaning on the rail of the boat holding Catherine's hand, she watched the dark, jagged coastline begin to flatten into the horizon. When it was gone, she took Catherine in from a chilling wind. The little girl looked around at other passengers who were speaking a language that she did not understand.

*

From the drawing room window at Brooke Farm, Louisa observed a taxi driving up the narrow lane which led to the house. When it stopped she gasped as Elizabeth stepped out of it and rushed from the house to meet her sister, calling out to her mother that Elizabeth was home.

Christina's breathing became uneven and heavy in her lungs. She hurried to the front door, her eyes jumping around in their sockets with indecision between settling on her daughter or her grandchild. Mother and daughter's eyes met. The embrace that followed almost squeezed the breath from them both. When Christina opened her watery eyes they gradually focussed on a blurred little angelic face staring up at her.

'Oh my little baby! My little Catherine. She's beautiful. Look at those eyes,' she cried leaving Elizabeth and taking her granddaughter from Louisa's hand.

Catherine's big blue eyes widened as the strange woman picked her up. In a panic, she stretched out towards her mother and started to cry, asking in French for her mother to take her. Christina and Louisa looked at one another in such disbelief it made Elizabeth laugh. She doesn't understand English, Mamma.'

'Can't understand English? What are you saying?' Christina said in disbelief.

Catherine's crying stopped the moment Elizabeth took her and pressed her soft lips to the little girl's cheek. 'She'll soon pick it up.

Children learn quickly. Naturally Catherine has only heard French. France is where she was born. It's the only home she's known.'

'I cannot believe you ignored our language,'

'I want French in her head. It may be useful to her one day as it was with me.'

'I'm glad to see you've grown your hair, Bess. It's beautiful. I'm surprised Catherine hasn't got your colour.'

'She's the image of her father.'

'Come my little pet,' Christina said, 'let your Grandmamma give you a big kiss.' Elizabeth stroked her daughter's cheek with the back of her fingers as Catherine looked into her grandmother's face. 'I've missed you, Bess. We have so much to talk about. All I know about the past three years is what you've allowed Jane to tell me.'

'You look even more beautiful than when I last saw you,' Louisa said, placing an arm around her younger sister. 'I bet you sent those Frenchmen wild with desire for you.'

'How are the twins, Mamma?'

'Stephanie is expecting another. I expect they will rush over here now you are back. You only just caught Louisa. She is returning home tomorrow,' Christina said, kissing the top of her granddaughter's head. 'You'll meet your other two aunts and little cousins, Catherine, my little pet.'

'Where's Harry?'

Elizabeth's question momentarily stunned Christina because she had never enquired after him before. 'He's taking a nap. I'm sure Catherine and he will be good company for each other.'

Elizabeth looked into her mother's face and thought she was suddenly looking older. Was it because she was grieving for a second husband, or was it fatigue? Or, Elizabeth wondered, was it because *she* had caused her mother so much worry? 'Yes,' Elizabeth said, taking her mother's hand. 'I'm sure they will.'

*

That evening, Elizabeth and Louisa walked through the grounds, avoiding the lake. Elizabeth was not ready for that yet. She felt the wound had healed but the scar it left was still tender and could be reopened at the slightest knock. The lake was special. It needed more time before she could be where she fell in love with the father of her child.

'Bess,' Louisa suddenly said, as if reading her sister's mind, 'have you ever heard from Catherine's father?'

130

Love, Elizabeth knew, was an iniquitous, fickle emotion, but when it is snatched away as if death had taken it, then life itself seemed lost. 'I miss him so much.'

Louisa observed the expression on Elizabeth's face and said, 'You can't still love him surely, after what he has done to you?'

'What has he done to me?'

'He ran off leaving you pregnant and unmarried. You know people will talk.'

'Catherine has changed my life. I adore her and I really don't care what people say about me as long as it isn't against David.'

'What? After putting you in the family way and leaving you, you're defending him?'

'I know in my heart he wouldn't have left had he known I was pregnant.'

'Oh yea...'

'Lou, I don't blame David. I threw myself at him. It works both ways, you know.'

Louisa laughed. 'You old tart. Has there been anyone since... in France?'

Elizabeth's mind returned to a pavement table in the Parisian sunshine, a year after Catherine's birth. She saw herself drinking coffee, watching a young man across the boulevard trying to procure the services of a prostitute. The woman rejected him. An argument followed, until her pimp appeared, slapping her for her trouble before pulling her away. When he crossed the road and sat at a table close to her, Elizabeth looked into his disfigured face, which made her heart go out to him. She imagined him desperately alone in the world as David had been. The young man might have been handsome once, but he had been made ugly by war. She could see the expressions on people's faces tortured him. His head remained lowered as he sat drinking his wine, afraid to raise it and sicken anyone glancing his way. She felt his desperation. He felt her gaze. Their eyes met, his vivid brown, quite beautiful in the background of his twisted flesh; hers, light grey, large, alive in her lovely face. Emotions fused into an understanding between them. She placed some money on her table and left. He followed seconds later from his. They found a quiet alley. He ran his hands over her breasts then lifted her dress. It was quick and without love.

After, Elizabeth's fingers toured the contours of his disfigured jaw and the smooth shiny scars on his face. She hoped she had given him the will to live.

'Why?' he asked.

'There will be someone out there for you. You must believe that.'

Within the hour she was on a train back to Amiens and never saw him again.

'There *was* someone,' Louisa said breaking the silence. 'You're thinking of him now, aren't you? I've heard Frenchmen are rather dishy. To think, at one time you wouldn't look at a man.'

Elizabeth smiled at her sister's enlivened face. 'David cured me of that. I began to realize men are not all the same.'

'Bess darling,' Louisa said, suddenly kissing her cheek. 'Tell me to shut up if you will, but when you were a prisoner−'

Elizabeth's eyes found her sister's. 'I had a bad time, the worst a woman could have. I don't want to talk about it.' She felt Louisa's arms encircle her body and embrace her.

'Why didn't you share that burden?'

'I was ashamed.'

Louisa took her hand. 'I had an affair with a fellow in the village. It didn't last. He dumped me. He was married too.'

'Why are you telling me this?'

'To let you know we all have our secrets... our shame.'

'Are you ashamed?'

'Yes, because I know I will probably do it again someday. Bertie is not Mr Wonderful, but he loves me. I should appreciate that, but a woman has her needs and that is where we fall down as a couple. I'm weak I suppose, or grateful that another man found me attractive. You wouldn't understand that. I've seen the way men drool over you.'

'Good looks bring their own problems, Lou. Does Sir Edward still say hello to you or did I ruin that for you?'

'I could have killed you, Bess,' Louisa smiled, 'although, oddly enough, he does ask after you when I bump into him. He's a proper gent.'

'Poor Sir Edward,' Elizabeth laughed. 'I've changed a lot since I last visited you. I even think I could handle your *Sir Edward* and Lady whatever her name is.'

'Lady Hannah. She's beautiful. God, it's so unfair. You and she get all the looks and what do I get? Bertie...' Both the sisters burst into laughter. 'Why don't you come and stay with me for a couple of weeks. Make up for last time. You'll meet Lady Hannah. For a toff, she's nice, stuck up, of course, but nice.'

'Toffs are generally full of their own self importance, although I knew many in the FANY. A different type of toff, I suppose. One, Isabella, was killed before my eyes.'

'Don't talk about it, Bess. You'll upset yourself again. Did you name Catherine after that friend of yours?'

Elizabeth's smile shone in the fading light. 'Yes, I did. You know it's strange, but when I look at my little Catherine I can see Cathy in her eyes.'

'Bess, did you... you and Cathy, did you have feelings for each other?'

'I loved her Lou.'

'The way you loved David?'

Elizabeth smiled when his face entered her mind. 'It was like loving the same person.'

Louisa glanced at her sister and gave a little shake of her head when she saw the expression on Elizabeth's face. 'So when will you come to Sussex?'

'Not yet. I must spend some time with Mamma. Let her get to know Catherine.'

'Yes, all right. Perhaps you'll have a new chap by then so you can bring him along too. Separate rooms, of course.'

Elizabeth smiled and took her sister's arm. They walked along the lane watching the great spherical orange globe slowly sink into the horizon. By the time they reached the house, long indigo shadows lay dark upon the fields and the silver moon hung as if a Chinese lantern in the pale green sky.

Chapter 2

Buckingham, England.

Jacob Wilson left the farm the day Elizabeth returned. Stephanie's husband was employed to manage it until a replacement was found. Elizabeth now threw herself into the dual roles of writer and mother. She had long decided to write a fictional account of a First Aid Nursing Yeomanry ambulance driver at war, based on her own experiences. She bought a mare, named her *Cathy* and learnt to ride. Early risers would often see a horse and rider briefly pause in the valley looking up to a group of terraced cottages on the high ground, then canter away in the direction of the lake.

The gossip regarding Elizabeth's return with a child, but no husband, was something with which Christina had to live and ignore. She was never happier than when she was running around looking after both Harry and Catherine, while Elizabeth was in her study writing. They had replaced the void in her life that Tim's death had left. What made Christina happiest of all was seeing the change in Elizabeth. Little Catherine had brought the light back into her daughter's eyes. She often watched them walking hand in hand across the fields, stopping to inspect something that Mother Nature had left since their previous visit to that spot; or to see a little raised arm pointing to the sky following the flight of a bird. Elizabeth would crouch beside her daughter following the direction of the pointed finger, then little arms would invariably encircle Elizabeth's neck and stay locked in that position.

Unfortunately, Henrietta Turner never lived to see Catherine. Now Elizabeth spent a great deal of her spare time with George Turner, whose affection for Catherine strengthened the rumours about the child's father. When George wasn't taking Elizabeth to concerts, the theatre or the ballet in London, as he used to take his wife, he would occasionally entertain small groups of ex-servicemen and their wives, or girlfriends, at his home in Buckingham. Elizabeth would always be there by his side. At one such party, she was unavoidably detained and arrived after most of the guests. When she entered the room, young men's heads turned, one in particular. It belonged to a schoolmaster, John Graves. He followed Elizabeth's progress round the room, flitting in and out of easy conversation with various people she knew. Her good looks and bright smile immediately struck him. He also noticed how affectionately she hung onto George Turner's arm, as if his presence was a warning to the various young single men gathered around her to keep their distance. Every time she laughed, George Turner's face brightened as he gazed affectionately into his daughter-in-law's eyes. He adored her, it was obvious and John Graves could well understand why.

John was a handsome man and he knew it. As with most single men of his generation who had fought in the war, it was time to rebuild his life and make up for lost years. John built his through women. Since his arrival in Buckingham he had known a number. His relationships never lasted very long once he had slept with them. To him it was a battle won, often too easily and there were many others to fight. Each woman was just another face, just as those who had replaced the dead in his platoon, until they themselves were replaced. Names were soon forgotten - nothing was permanent in life, John had discovered. There was little point in forming relationships, or becoming too involved.

Until Elizabeth arrived, he had been amusing himself with a married woman, whose eye he had caught from a safe position across the room. He liked having other men's wives - the happier the marriage, the greater the challenge and the sweeter the conquest. He glanced back at the woman who was chatting to her friend. She gave him a smile. He almost yawned. From experience, he knew she was halfway to his bed.

'Too late old girl,' he whispered to himself and looked back at Elizabeth across the room. 'I now have a far more attractive fish to hook.'

The woman watched him turn from her and direct his gaze towards her host's daughter-in-law. She waited for his eyes to return, when they did not, she burned with indignation. She had been rejected in favour of a tart with a bastard child.

'Who's the beauty?' John casually asked a colleague standing with him.

'The erstwhile Mrs Elizabeth Turner,' he replied, 'now Miss Elizabeth Brennan. A metamorphosis I find rather puzzling, Graves old chap.'

'Why?'

'She may look the model for Botticelli's *Venus*, with her flaming hair and virginal looks, but she disappeared to Froggy land and returned *avec une fille de père inconnu*. I first met her through Robert,

135

her late husband, an old school chum of mine. Met her again in Belgium. She was very chummy with an absolute dish, though alas, an ice maiden.'

'Try anything?'

'Not with the lovely Elizabeth, she hadn't been long widowed, but I did have a go at her friend. Didn't get anywhere with her. A bit stuck up. Then I bumped into Elizabeth in London. She was over for her mother-in-law's funeral. We went out to dinner together.'

'And?'

'Not a chance. She was eight months pregnant.'

'Who's the father of *la petite fille*?'

'Some say our genial host, although I do not believe it for a moment. Others say a farmhand from her late stepfather's farm.'

John Graves faced his friend. 'A labouring man! You have to be joking.'

'I do not jest, old chap. They say the cad stuck her in the family way then did a bunk. By all accounts he was knocked about a bit during the war. Hard to imagine what she saw in him.'

'Likes a wounded hero, perhaps?'

'Bit of one herself. You won't get a better looker than Elizabeth Brennan around here… although her twin sisters aren't bad, I suppose. Married, of course, not that that bothers you.'

'Brennan, where have I heard that name before?'

'Daniel Brennan, MA. The school's late Classics master. His name is on the *Roll of Honour* in the assembly hall. You have his old job, and that little beauty is his second daughter. Brennan bought it on the first day of the Somme, along with his son, son-in-law and half the bloody new army.'

John went silent for a moment. He remembered the carnage and hopelessness of that morning. 'I was in that show.'

'Is that where you got your gong?'

'Yes.'

'And the bar?'

'Third Ypres. Another cock-up.' John looked over towards Elizabeth as she turned. Their eyes met, he smiled; she turned her head and ignored it.

'I say, you were snubbed there, old boy.'

'Early days yet. Just casting a line. What was Gallipoli like?'

'What do you think, stuck on a cliff for eight months while Johnny Turk used us for target practice? The place became lousy with flies.

Swarms of the little sods.'

'Clouds, old chap.'

'Clouds?'

'The proper term... a cloud of flies.'

'Don't be such an intellectual snob. One can also use swarm.'

Elizabeth had noticed John Graves the moment she entered the room with her father-in-law, although she tried not to show it. He was irritatingly handsome and she guessed he was full of reptilian charm. His eyes spent an eternity following her around the room while he was talking to Roger Macdonald. She wondered if John was playing a game with her - a game of cat and mouse. More like rat and mouse, she thought to herself - but he is rather a handsome rat. She looked his way and again met his eyes.

John understood women and their body language. That last look from Elizabeth was very encouraging. He combed the hair from his eyes with his fingers and straightened his tie. 'Let me refill your glass old man, then you can tell me all about her. I want to know everything.'

When Roger finished his story, he swallowed the last of his drink and said, 'Of course, the papers were full of it, "The local heroine shaking hands with the King". I like Elizabeth, despite the gossip. She has pluck.'

'I think I will go and introduce myself.'

'You won't get anywhere with her. The Virgin Mary, that one.'

'What about her child? An immaculate conception?'

'Well, if it were old boy, then for once in my life I should love to have played God.'

When John appeared at his side, George Turner introduced him to Elizabeth then left them alone to talk. Elizabeth saw in John's eyes the confidence of a man who had known many women. She had met many men like him in France after they had drunk a half bottle of wine. Their charm was wasted on her and at Oxford; again they were wasting their time. She was sleeping with Emma and had no interest in men. Now things were different. She had known a man's love and liked it. Although Elizabeth found John attractive, she intended to give him a hard time, because she sensed he had made a wager with Roger Macdonald that he could get a date with her. But John surprised her. There were no uneasy silences between them. He spoke little and listened a lot, a skill she knew from experience, few men have mastered.

'I have two tickets for the theatre,' he said before he left. 'They're for Saturday. Would you care to join me? We could have dinner after.'

Elizabeth smiled. 'Did your first date throw you over?'

'Actually, I was going with Roger, but he can no longer make Saturday.'

'And will you win your wager if I accept?'

'There is no wager, Elizabeth,' he said calmly. 'We were talking about you, yes, because Roger knows you and I should like to know you. I've invited you out because I am single and so are you, I believe. It's quite a natural thing to do I should have thought, but if you do not wish to go with me then you may have the tickets and do with them as you please.'

Elizabeth looked into his eyes and felt that she may have misjudged him, so she accepted his invitation.

*

Although friends were eager to warn Elizabeth of John's reputation, he behaved as a perfect gentleman the evening they went to the theatre, as he did the following week when they went to a concert then a third time out to dinner, after which, Elizabeth was happy for John to kiss her goodnight. It was outside the front door, late at night with the moon low in the sky which sent a silver glow through the courtyard. The kiss was becoming very passionate. He found his way into her clothing squeezing her breast. Her compliance made him more adventurous, moving his hand down between her slightly parted legs. She removed it and breathlessly whispered goodnight and slipped inside the house. With her back pressed against the front door, she heard his footsteps disappearing up the path. She closed her eyes and let out a long sigh. It had been a long time since she had done that and knew her body ached for more.

When John next arrived to see Elizabeth, Christina invited him in and entertained him until her daughter appeared holding Catherine's hand. She introduced one to the other. Elizabeth watched John closely as he crouched and chatted to Catherine in French and some English.

Christina caught her daughter's eye. Elizabeth smiled. In that moment, Christina wondered whether Elizabeth intended to develop the relationship.

*

'It's a beautiful house Elizabeth, and your little Catherine is lovely,' John said as the cab turned out of the gate. 'She has inherited her mother's beauty.'

'Actually, she looks very much like her father. Same eyes, hair, smile.'

John gave her a furtive glance. 'I hear he was knocked about a bit on the Somme?'

'Yes, he was.'

So it was the farmhand. 'I believe your father was a schoolmaster at—'

'Yes, he was. You have his old job.'

John felt a raw nerve had been touched. 'You were at Oxford—'

'Yes, I was and you ask too many questions, John.'

'Isn't that the art of conversation? One of us asks a question, the other answers it.'

'You could make it sound less like an interrogation.'

'Since we have known each other, you have hardly spoken a word about yourself, as if you want to keep your life a secret.'

'A secret! Any gossip in Buckingham will tell you what you wish to know. Anyway,' she continued, 'I did keep my life a secret once and have regretted it ever since.' Elizabeth told John about Catherine and how they had never discussed their lives or background, and because of it, they had lost touch.

'If you were reported dead then your friend will not be trying to look for you. Or, she may have been posted elsewhere before the news that you survived filtered down to your unit. It's a difficult one.'

'Or she didn't survive the war herself.'

'I don't want to think about that.'

*

Seconds after the conductor brought the baton down on the final piece in the concert; Elizabeth leapt from her seat and fled from the hall with John running after her. 'What has got into you, Elizabeth?' he said in the street. 'It was a misprint in the programme, that's all.'

'They should have said something.'

'What's wrong with Beethoven's *Sixth* anyway? You went prepared to sit through his Third. Honestly, getting up and rushing out like that. It was embarrassing.'

'I'm sorry,' she said and kissed his lips as a mother would kiss her child. John was not satisfied with that so he pulled her into the shadows of a shop doorway and kissed her more passionately. He took her hand and placed it at the front of his trousers and held it there so she could feel his growing flesh. Elizabeth pulled away.

'What's wrong with you? We've been seeing each other for weeks.'

'I'm not ready for that.'

'When then? I'm not made of stone.'

'When I'm ready. Be patient, John.' They left the doorway and made their way towards the restaurant. 'Thank you for taking me this evening,' she said at last. 'I enjoyed the other music and thought the soloist played Mozart's horn concerto beautifully.' She held his arm a little tighter and began humming the tune as they walked. A policeman strolled by and touched his helmet in a salute.

Elizabeth flashed a smile. The policeman stopped in the shop doorway they had just left and watched Elizabeth's long legs carry her lazily along the road then he turned and saluted another concert reveller leaving early, humming the same Mozart tune.

During their meal, John looked into Elizabeth's grey eyes and smiled. 'Tell me about your time in the jolly old snob Corps.'

'Why do you call it that?'

His boyish grin gave him a youthful look. 'Because your Corps was full of upper crust young ladies.'

'Then I managed to squeeze in through the servant's quarters. Socially I was without standing. The others considered me odd because I enjoyed reading French literature rather than discussing men and fashion. My friends Catherine and Isabella were toffs, I suppose. Dearest Bella... and Kate, whom I liked very much, were killed.'

'I lost friends... too many...' his voice trembled a little and trailed away.

Elizabeth looked hard at him. She had never seen him like this. He straightened himself in his seat, smiling, his cheeks a little pink. John rarely mentioned the war to her, as if it had never happened. For a second, he had shown emotion, genuine emotion, which made Elizabeth wonder what terrible memories he had locked away. She found that she wanted to talk about the war. To do so would keep alive the memory of the dead. John had been out there and would understand.

'It is sometimes good to talk and remember lost friends,' Elizabeth said, taking his hand. 'We must never forget them.'

'Why did you volunteer?'

'I had some absurd idea that I could help.'

'Would you do it again?'

Elizabeth remembered the screams coming from the back of her ambulance. 'I couldn't go through that again.'

'What did you do to be awarded your gongs?'

140

'Heavens, you must be the only person in Buckingham who doesn't know. The paper was full of it. Mostly rot - journalistic licence I think one might call it. Anyway, my spies tell me that you have the Military Cross and a bar to it.'

'And what else have your spies told you about me?'

'That you are not to be trusted; that you sleep with women then leave them. Do you intend to do that to me?'

He was taken aback by her reply, yet certain that she was unaware of his current liaison with a young widow in Winslow. There were lots of keen young widows looking for a husband. Mostly they had children and were easy prey. Elizabeth was an exception, but she was worth the wait.

'I can't say I'm proud of my past Elizabeth, but that was my past. We change, especially when we have a lot to lose if we don't.'

'We?'

'Me.'

He saw her eyes brighten and knew he had said the right thing. He thought he may dump the widow and stick with Elizabeth. 'Why did you run out of the concert hall like that?'

'Because someone I loved suffered an attack of shellshock during Beethoven's Sixth. I have never liked it since.'

'Catherine's father?' He watched her nod. 'Will you tell me about him?'

'No.' Elizabeth took a sip of wine. 'Not a soul wanted to know him when he lived here and no one shall know anything of him now he has gone. It broke my heart when I discovered he had left. That was nearly five years ago, now I know I must move on and make a new life for myself and Catherine.'

John smiled. 'Are you eyeing me up for the job?'

She returned his smile. 'Don't flatter yourself, Mr Graves. Shall we go? The last train leaves at ten.'

On the way back to the railway station, helped by the wine she had drunk, Elizabeth's mood lifted. She laughed at John's stories about happier times before the war at his seaside home in Kent. She had enjoyed her evening and said so.

'You look so beautiful when you smile,' he said, taking her arm.

She said nothing. She never did when he paid her a compliment, as if it embarrassed her to hear it. He watched her gaze up to the dark dome of the sky studded with pinpricks of light in the familiar patterns of their youth. The brightness of a moon that was almost full made her face glow. Her lips spread into a smile, but not for John; she was in her other world, which did not include him. He would not enquire where she was, only enjoy her presence and admire her profile.

'Tonight's moon reminds me of a Shelley poem that Robert, my late husband, read to me on one of the rare occasions we were together. *The cold chaste moon, the queen of heaven's bright isles, who makes all beautiful on which she smiles…*'

'Shelley could have written that for you, Elizabeth,' John said, taking her hand.

She turned and smiled at him but said nothing. When they arrived at the station, they were alone. They found the shadows of the platform and began to kiss each other. John ran his hands over her breasts and the rounded cheeks of her bottom, squeezing the solid flesh that filled his hands. As he did so, he felt her groin move into him.

'I want you,' he whispered.

She pulled away from him. 'The train's coming.'

It arrived at the platform and clanged to a halt screeching and belching steam. Carriage doors slammed and a tired-looking guard cried out the name of the station for the benefit of those who were half asleep and to remind himself that he would also soon be home. John followed Elizabeth into the single carriage vacated by an elderly couple. She took her seat by the window and John sat beside her. They were alone. He found her hand. She squeezed it affectionately. The guard shouted his final warning. The high-pitched shrill of his whistle pierced John's ears it was so close. Slowly the train moved out of the station to the sound of the labouring grunts of the engine.

The whistle disturbed John. It reminded him of his own whistle that had sent so many good men over the top to their deaths on the Somme, and then through the quagmire of Passchendaele. Young officers all along the line emptied their lungs into these metal objects. The sound of a triumphant roar followed from a hundred thousand souls as men climbed out of their trenches into the uncertainty of no man's land, silhouetted against the pale background of the sky. He remembered the sound of machine guns, the cries of dying men and the dead he passed looking as if sacks dropped from a wagon, their hideous faces staring up unseeing at the changing sky. He knew nothing in the world is more still than the dead, men emptied of life. A man dies and stiffens into something like a wooden dummy at which one glances for a second with furtive curiosity before staggering on.

'John,' Elizabeth said, holding him. 'What's the matter? You're shaking.' Elizabeth recognized the look of a man who had just seen death. She was reminded of David and for a moment saw his face in her mind.

John looked up at her through hollow eyes. 'It's just a bad memory. I get them sometimes. We all do I suppose, it's so damned difficult to shake them off.'

'I know.'

'Do you have them too?'

'Yes, one in particular. The day Fritz began his spring offensive in March '18, the day I was taken prisoner. I was following a friend driving back from a cemetery after a hospital drop. We were the only two; the convoy had left earlier. I stopped and picked up a VAD nurse you know, Voluntary Aid Detachments, who wanted to get back to Albert. Bella had driven right past her close to the hospital gates. She probably didn't see her, but I did. I can see her smile as I tell it to you now. She was very young. We all were, I suppose. We had almost reached Albert, when Fritz started to shell the road. Their push had started. Bella's ambulance was hit almost immediately.'

Elizabeth remembered the explosion and Bella's ambulance losing control, coming to a halt off the road. John recognized in Elizabeth's eyes the agony of that moment - a haunting memory as vivid in every detail to her now as when it happened.

'I could see Bella was dead. Darling Bella; it's difficult to imagine what I went though at that moment, seeing her slumped over the wheel with half her face…' Elizabeth stopped to calm herself. John tightened his grip on her hand and kissed her wet eyes. They lifted and met his. 'I didn't want to leave her, don't you see? I jumped down from my ambulance and with the nurse's help put Bella into the back of my old bus.'

'Elizabeth—'

'Let me finish. The shellfire increased, strafing the road. I'd driven through shellfire earlier and thought; I got through that so I can get through this. The young nurse with me was wonderful. Throughout it all she hardly flinched. She seemed to have no fear, yet I was scared witless. Then shrapnel hit my ambulance which knocked out the engine, bringing the vehicle to a halt further down the road. We made a dash for the nearest ditch as more shells came over. The nurse, I never knew her name, stopped to pick up my bag. There was another explosion. I felt a thump here,' she said pointing to her neck. 'Then it began to hurt. I knew I'd been hit. The nurse was on the ground. She looked up at me with haunting eyes appealing for help.'

Elizabeth became silent again. In her mind she saw the girl's young body lying in the road, her out-stretched hand gripping the strap of the bag. The back of her head was open as an egg, hairy, with thick blood and broken, sploshed grey brains. She began to twitch and then became quite still. Her eyes remained open, staring accusingly at Elizabeth because she was alive. 'She died in front of me. I still see her eyes. They have kept me awake for nights on end.'

He enveloped her in his arms as she began to sob. He stroked her hair until she stopped her tears. The train stopped at a station then passed through another. She looked into his eyes and smiled. He kissed her. His hand began to follow the contours of her body - the curve of her waist, the side of her ribcage, the swelling edge of her breast under her arm. It slid and slithered as if a snake over her shoulders to her head, combing though her luxuriant chestnut hair, which spilt in waves through his greedy fingers. She clung onto him as if a trusting child feeling the comfort of his caresses, for his hand, which although passing the periphery of intimate areas, it had not strayed or lingered beyond to alert her of anything other than a comforting action. She did not stir or object when his lips brushed lightly over her neck and throat; it seemed only to add comfort to the caresses.

Thick eyelashes rose revealing large dark pupils that met his. He whispered that she was beautiful then he kissed her mouth again. He began skilfully fumbling with her clothing. As his confidence grew, his free hand fell below the hem of her dress. He held his breath. It would be now, if at all, her objection would sound, splitting the silence like the crack of a rifle shot in the still night. Yet neither her hand nor her voice prevented him reaching above the tops of her stockings to her soft, warm flesh. He felt her thighs relax, her knees part. She wanted him there, which sent uncontrollable blood swelling his flaccid flesh.

Elizabeth's body surrendered to a sensation so relaxing she did not want to waken from it. She felt wonderful, floating in sensual weightlessness above the thick black clouds of her past. A deep, involuntary sigh escaped her lips, her back arched, pushing against the force that was the source of all these feelings. Her eyes fell open, focussing on John's intense, passionate gaze.

He desperately began pulling at her knickers, knowing she would

144

not resist him; he had taken her beyond her will to stop it now. John felt her lift her bottom in an act of submission, to allow the garment to be released. She laid back on the seat waiting, spreading her thighs as he manoeuvred himself above her. 'Be careful,' she whispered, but her words, with the sudden intake of her breath, were lost in the blast of the whistle as the train entered the tunnel.

Chapter 3

A month after the passionate train journey home, John received a letter from a new public school in Buckingham, announcing that he had been appointed housemaster to begin in the New Year. The school was set in hundreds of acres of landscaped gardens only a mile from his present school. It was perfect for him and his ambitions.

His mind went back to the final interview, remembering the serious faces of the Board melting into smiles as they learned more about the last of their short-listed candidates. Wellington School, Oxford, an impressive war record, a Military Cross on the Somme, a second at Passchendaele, and since the war, Head of Classics at The Royal Latin School, one of the country's oldest grammar schools. John felt instinctively that the Board liked him.

Then the Chairman asked if he was married. He said that he was; he had married a war widow with a child, which went down very well with the Board. He had lied, and in doing so it made him realize how much he wanted the job. On witnessing their smiles and the hearty handshakes as he left the room, John sensed he might have clinched it.

As he reread the Chairman's words, his mind was on Elizabeth. Now she was critical to his future plans. His ambition as housemaster would lead to headmaster. He needed a wife and Elizabeth fitted the bill. She was intelligent, educated at the Sorbonne and Oxford and could speak fluent French, which would be an asset to any school. She was a beautiful woman, an asset to any ambitious man. If Elizabeth refused him, there was always the young widow in Winslow, not quite up to Elizabeth's mark but pretty enough, reasonably bright and she had a young daughter, so she was a reserve and she fitted in with his lie.

As he tucked the letter back into the envelope, he decided to ask Elizabeth to marry him when he saw her that afternoon. He had to be hasty. Next week, she was going away to Sussex to visit her sister and he needed to be married before Christmas, which gave him just over four months to prepare for the wedding in Kent.

The morning gave way to a hot midday. After lunch, Elizabeth strolled in bright sunshine along that part of the lane where the fragrance of the lime trees hung in the air. She felt happy as she watched John chase Catherine, flapping his arms as he growled like a monster with Catherine squealing, finding the top of her register when he caught up with her. Elizabeth laughed too when he picked her up high above his head, sending her daughter into fits of uncontrollable giggles, begging for more when he stopped. He arrived breathless at her side and lowered Catherine to the ground. Elizabeth took his arm and ran a finger along his brow removing a film of perspiration from his forehead. She pressed her body into his and kissed him.

'You seem to be paying Catherine a lot of attention today.'

'She's a lovely girl.'

'Umm, I suspect you are after something. It can't be sex because you're now getting plenty of that, so what can it be?'

He looked into her face which was flushed and her eyes glowed by some inward flame that lighted them. 'Marry me,' he suddenly said.

The proposal came as no surprise to Elizabeth. She was surprised he hadn't asked sooner, because she had expected it from the moment John told her that he was on the shortlist for the job he was after. Boarding schools, she knew, preferred a married housemaster who lived in, so John needed a wife. Since the conversation about his first interview, Elizabeth had given some serious thought to the proposal of marriage she was certain he would make. The more she thought about marrying John the more it seemed to make sense to her. She would enjoy living in the private world of a public school environment and, she may even be able to teach French. She would only be a couple of miles away from her mother and Catherine needed a man's influence and guidance. Catherine liked John, but Elizabeth still questioned her own feelings for him. She liked him well enough; he was bright and they could talk to each other. She was happy enough making love to him and would certainly have children with him, something she now wanted for Catherine. She even felt a particular closeness to him, but not love, not the love she had felt for David. Whether she would be happy was something that only time would tell. Her only concern was for her mother being left alone in that big house with Harry. 'Are you sure?'

'Yes... I am.'

Elizabeth left his embrace and went to Catherine. 'If you want me, then you must take Catherine as your own.'

'That goes without saying.'

'Then yes, I will marry you, John.'

Elizabeth wondered if his face brightened more in relief than in joy, but his actions following her acceptance surprised her. He lifted her into the air in his arms. 'I love you. I love you both,' he said kissing her. 'You know that, don't you?'

'I love you too,' she said because she knew he would want to hear that.

'Do you love me Elizabeth, or am I still sharing your heart with another?'

'John, David has gone from my life. As I have said before, I have to move on. I want another child... children. I want you to be their father.'

He kissed her and squeezed her to him. Catherine looked up at her mother and John in confusion and began tugging her mother's dress demanding to be lifted. Elizabeth ignored her daughter and kissed John again, his hands running over her body. Catherine's demands increased, crying out to her mother in French. Elizabeth withdrew from John's arms and picked up her daughter. She deliberately made it a policy to answer Catherine when she spoke French. This way, she considered, and it seemed to work, Catherine would not lose interest in the language.

'Don't cry my angel. Uncle John and I are going to be married. He is going to be your new Papa.' Elizabeth looked at John and smiled, and at that moment she felt happy. 'Just care for us John and I shall be a good wife to you.'

When they returned home and told Christina of the engagement, she went to her daughter and hugged her. At last, Christina thought, she could now look forward to Elizabeth settling down and having a proper family. Catherine was picked up and almost had the life squeezed from her by her happy grandmother.

*

At breakfast the following Monday, Susan walked into the dining room with a letter and handed it to Elizabeth, then disappeared with Catherine to give her a bath.

'I'll be up in a moment, Susan.'

'Who's written to you?' Christina asked.

'Louisa. Her handwriting hasn't improved. It's still a slurred suggestion of words. Oh Mamma! Listen to this:

> ...I know you will be here in a few days but I have some news that
> just cannot wait until then. I'm pregnant - it was confirmed two
> days ago. I know Mamma will be thrilled so tell her for me. Isn't it
> good news? Bertie told me that Sir Edward congratulated him...'

Elizabeth's voice trailed away as she silently read on to herself.

'Bess, for heaven's sake. You're supposed to be reading it to me.'

'The next bit is hardly worth listening to,' Elizabeth said looking up. 'It's Lou doting over her aristocratic neighbours.'

'Oh hush, Bess. Finish the letter.'

'After the sycophantic bits she says,

> …If my baby's a girl, I have decided to name her Hannah, after Lady Hannah. It is such a nice name, aristocratic, if you know what I mean.
> I can't wait to see you and Catherine next week, but please, for my sake, be nice to Sir Edward if you bump into him…blah, blah, blah. Give my love to Mamma. I shall now write to Jane and Stephanie and give them the good news. I'm so happy. Much love, Lou.'

When she had finished reading it, Elizabeth stared at the letter in thought. 'Why call her Hannah?' she said looking up. 'Why not Catherine, or Isabella; they're such beautiful names and far more aristocratic, if that is what Lou wants.'

'Oh go away, Bess,' Christina laughed. 'We already have a Catherine in the family and Isabella has too many syllables.'

'I'm looking forward to going to Sussex, seeing Lou. Make up for the last time.'

'I hope you will do as Louisa says and be nice to this Sir Edward fellow if you meet him. I know what you're like when your back is up.'

'Meow,' Elizabeth purred. 'Actually, if I remember correctly he is rather handsome. Perhaps this time I will be particularly friendly towards him,' she teased.

Lines appeared on Christina's forehead as she faced her daughter. 'You're engaged to be married now, young lady. I hope you'll remember that.'

*

Elizabeth stepped down from the train at Petworth station in Sussex with Catherine holding her hand, followed by a young man carrying her suitcase. Louisa spotted her sister strolling towards her with a little angel holding her hand, almost running to keep alongside her mother's long, lazy stride.

'Bess.' Louisa kissed her sister. She bent and picked up Catherine, attacking her little face with wet kisses. 'And how is my lovely little niece then?'

149

Catherine wiped her cheek with the back of her hand and said, 'Hello, Aunt Louisa. Are you well?' before looking up at her mother to see if she had said it just as they had rehearsed.

'Very well, thank you. Do you remember your cousin? Danny, say hello to Catherine.'

The two children looked at each other but said nothing. The gentleman holding Elizabeth's suitcase coughed a little to remind Elizabeth of his presence.

'I'm so sorry,' Elizabeth smiled warmly. 'Thank you for your kind assistance.'

'It was very much my pleasure,' he replied. 'I do hope that you and your daughter enjoy your stay in Sussex, Mrs... er...'

'It's Miss, Miss Brennan, and thank you; I'm sure my daughter and I shall.'

He coloured, raised his hat again and turned, leaving a smiling Elizabeth and a blushing Louisa at the ticket barrier with their children.

'Elizabeth Brennan, you're awful. Why do you enjoy shocking people so much? "*It's Miss Brennan, and thank you I'm sure my daughter and I shall.*" There was no need to have said that. Look at you; you're not even wearing a wedding ring. Honestly, what will people think of you?'

'I'm really not very much bothered by that.'

'You're a widow, Bess. There's no shame in that. You could have at least kept your married name and worn your wedding ring.'

'Why?'

'For the sake of decency.'

'Don't be so stuffy, Lou. How are you? That certain condition suits you,' she teased. 'You're looking radiant.'

'I feel it. Here, you take the case and I'll take little Cathy.'

'Her name is Catherine, not Cathy and the porter can take the case.'

'Hark at you, bossy boots Brennan.'

'I'm sorry Lou. I just don't want a diminutive for Catherine's name.'

'Did you hear that Catherine? A diminutive is good enough for Aunt Lou, even for your Mamma Bess, but not for you.'

'It's just that Cathy is someone else. She was very special to *me*... that's all.'

'Yes, well, let's hear about your bloke then.'

'Mamma has obviously written to you.'

'The paper still has scorch marks on it. She said you're now engaged, so where's the ring?'

'I didn't want one. I don't need a label to advertise that I am promised to another.'

Louisa laughed. 'Honestly, I don't think the world is quite ready for you yet.'

They walked up the hill from the station and made their way towards Louisa's home. Louisa said. 'I'm surprised Catherine hasn't got your lovely colour hair. She is very pretty. Lucky Catherine, she's going to inherit your good looks.'

'Honestly Lou, you do go on. Some women might like compliments, I don't.'

'Surely you like to be admired for your beauty.'

'That's absurd. Admire me for my achievements, but not for an accident of birth.'

Louisa offered an affectionate smile. 'What's this fellow of yours like? Mamma said he is scrumptious. Is he so handsome?'

'Yes, I suppose he is. Now John does like to be admired for his good looks. He cannot pass a mirror without being dazzled by his own magnificence.'

Louisa laughed again. 'You do make me laugh. When's the wedding?' Louisa watched her sister shrug. 'You don't seem like a woman madly in love.'

'I'm not. The arrangement suits us both. He says he loves me, but I don't think he does. He needs a wife and I want more children.'

Louisa shook her head. 'You're quite mad, I'm convinced of it.'

*

A few days before the end of her holiday, Elizabeth's mind began to turn towards returning home. She stared out of the window and watched several smart cars pass through the gate. Louisa explained that they would be parents bringing their children to the birthday party.

'Whose birthday party is it?'

'Elizabeth's... Sir Edward and Lady Hannah's daughter. Such a common name, everyone seems to have it,' Louisa teased. 'She is never called Bess though, oh no, no - no diminutive there.'

Elizabeth smiled at her sister imitating a toff's accent. 'It's Catherine's birthday on Monday, Lou.'

'So it is. We could have a special picnic down by the lake. We were on the way there the last time you were here when we bumped into Sir Edward... remember?'

'Oh yes, *poor, poor* Sir Edward.'

'Poor is something he is not and as I remember it, he certainly took a shine to you.'

*

Monday arrived. The two mothers and their children headed towards the lake. When at last they reached the water's edge, Catherine was feeling ready to have her picnic. Louisa had baked a little cake and made some trifles, Elizabeth had prepared the sandwiches, jellies and lemonade. The air rang with the sound of 'Happy Birthday', while Catherine looked suitably coy, then they ate, drank, sang songs and played little games.

'What time are you and Bertie leaving tomorrow, Lou?'

'Early. Why don't you stay on for a few more days if you've nothing else planned?'

'Really? Would you mind? It would be fantastic to spend a few days alone with Catherine. I mean completely alone… just the two of us together.'

'And will John mind you staying on?'

'John has no say in the matter. I'm not his wife yet.'

Louisa laughed and rose to her feet calling the children to her. 'Come along you two; let's go for a little walk. We'll show you the goldfish Catherine, while your Mamma relaxes and thinks of an excuse why she's not returning home.'

Louisa and the children headed across the field towards the great Cypress of Lebanon tree carrying table-like masses of foliage that were home to several noisy rooks. Beyond were the rose-garden and lily pond, full of goldfish - and then the terrace to the Manor. They reached the tennis courts and saw Lady Hannah approaching, her daughter Elizabeth at her side.

Louisa smiled nervously. 'Good afternoon, Lady Hannah. You know my Danny, but not my niece. It's her birthday today so we're having a picnic down by the lake. I hope you don't mind if I show her the goldfish in the lily pond.'

Hannah Wyatt glanced into the big blue eyes and smiled tenderly. 'She is very sweet, Mrs Simpson. What's your name, young lady?'

'Catherine,' she replied shyly. The two girls stood staring at each other - both with large blue eyes and long dark hair; of equal height, a few days between them at birth - a world apart since.

'Must dash, Mrs Simpson. Expecting Sir Edward home very shortly. Do enjoy the rest of your niece's birthday.'

'Lady Hannah, my husband and I are going away for our annual holiday tomorrow. My sister is staying on for a few more days. Would you mind if she uses your grounds? She loves your lake and enjoys walking with Catherine.'

'Of course she may, Mrs Simpson. Good day.'

*

The following day, Elizabeth stood with Catherine waving as the taxi disappeared down the road blowing great blasts of black fumes from the exhaust as it picked up speed. Elizabeth turned to her daughter and immediately began to speak in French, as she always did when they were alone together. They walked towards Louisa's house when a Bentley suddenly swept past them through the gates. The driver, Elizabeth noticed, gave her a long hard look as he passed.

'Excuse me Madam... are you looking for Mr Simpson?'

Elizabeth turned and saw a shy looking girl by the gate. 'Do you work at the Manor?'

'Yes, Madam. I'm a housemaid. My name's Tucker, Madam.'

'Tell me… Tucker, was that Sir Edward Wyatt driving that car?'

The girl nodded. 'I have to go, Madam, I don't want to be late.'

The girl placed a hand on her hat as she ran along the road. Elizabeth watched her go and she turned to Catherine. 'Viens chérie, allons-y pour une promenade.'

'Vais-je voir la dame avec la petite fille encore, Maman?'

*

Sir Edward Wyatt entered the building with a spring in his step. 'Hello,' he said walking towards his wife and kissing her upturned cheek. 'Has Simpson got guests?'

'Mrs Simpson's sister. Her daughter's a pretty little thing.'

'So is the mother,' he grinned. Suddenly looking thoughtful, Edward Wyatt related his encounter with Elizabeth. 'Damned sure I've met her somewhere before. Bloody rude to me she was. Have you met her?'

'No. One sister is enough for me, thank you.'

'I know her face from somewhere, I'm sure of it. The colour of her hair is quite stunning, Rather short but stunning... copper... brightly polished copper.'

Hannah Wyatt went into a sudden dream.

Chapter 4

Lady Hannah Wyatt sat in her private study writing a letter of apology to a friend in Yorkshire, the county from which she had moved after she married Edward. She had been unable to attend her wedding because of a prior engagement she could not break. Hannah removed a few strands of her dark hair from her eyes while she paused in thought. Now all of her friends were married and scattered around the kingdom in various manorial, noble or ancestral homes. Or they had simply disappeared because they failed to keep in touch, or were dead, victims of the great struggle that had claimed so many lives from her unfortunate generation. She looked up and stared out of the window past the cherry trees that lined the driveway, through the lawns to the far distant trees, while her fountain pen rattled between her teeth, a habit when she sat in thought. Edward had left early saying that he would not be home that evening, because he had a late meeting with his minister and would stay over in their London home. He hardly ever seemed to be at home these days. She wondered if he had a mistress - many MPs did; a young secretary flattered by his attentions, a lonely war widow needing a man's love, a predator trying to usurp a wealthy man's wife, there were plenty around, or a bored wife looking for some excitement as she herself was, since the end of the war. Hannah wondered if she should take a lover to fill the hours of her lonely existence. It would be easy enough. Her beauty guaranteed male attention. She had many admirers. Most of whom were wimps who stood panting like puppy dogs in her presence, doing her bidding, fetching and carrying, rather than being a man and trying to seduce her. If only someone would try; she would almost certainly reward him for his efforts just for the hell of it.

She sighed at the thought, taking a lover was not the answer to boredom; one would soon become bored with that. Even the charity work she did and was expected to do, and the endless round of dinners with people who might further her husband's career, did not fill the emptiness of the long summer days and longer winter nights. Maybe she ought to have another baby, although she did not enjoy the pregnancy that brought Elizabeth. It had been a great relief to her when she was born. It was a thought that lingered with her until she began to write again.

Her concentration was broken when her study door suddenly opened and one of the housemaids entered with a duster in her hand.

'Oh!' cried the flustered maid in a curtsey. 'I'm sorry my Lady, I thought the room was empty.'

'Who are you?'

'Tucker, my Lady,' she replied with another quick bob of her body. 'I'm new. I'm standing in for Miller's duties today, my Lady.'

'Is Miller unwell?'

'Yes, my Lady.'

'Very well, Tucker. Come in do, but don't make a noise.' Hannah began to write and the maid began to dust. When only the area around the figure bent at her desk was left undone, Tucker loitered nervously. Hannah looked up at her, 'Yes, Tucker.'

'Should I come back later and finish, my Lady?'

'No. Just give those photographs a wipe then you may go.'

The maid dusted one, and then another and when she picked up the third she wiped the glass slowly, concentrating hard on one of the two faces in the photograph. Hannah's eyes lifted because of the inactivity.

Tucker felt Lady Hannah's gaze and blushed. 'I'm s-sorry, my Lady. I... I didn't mean to be nosy.'

'I'm interested to know what has caught your attention, Tucker.'

'It's your friend, begging your pardon my Lady,' she said with another dip of her body.

'What about my friend, Tucker?'

'She has such a happy smile. I was thinking, it's such a shame they can't make photographs in colour, then you'd see what lovely hair she has; the colour of autumn fern... copper, like, my Lady.'

Hannah Wyatt went cold. 'What did you say?'

Tucker saw the sudden change of expression in Lady Hannah's eyes and backed away, certain she had committed a terrible blunder by talking intimately of one of Lady Hannah's friends. Her mother had warned her never to do that, but lulled into the friendly manner of Lady Hannah; she had forgotten her mother's advice.

'I'm sorry my Lady, I... I...'

'You've described her hair perfectly from a black and white photograph. How can you possibly do that? Answer me girl. How can you know that she has that colour hair?' Hannah snapped, then letting out a heavy impatient sigh when she saw the girl's eyes fill with tears. 'Calm down, Tucker, there's no need to weep. I'm not cross with you. Just tell me... *Tucker*! Come along now, calm down... that's better.

155

Now, what makes you say she has copper hair?'

'I saw her, my Lady. She was outside Mr Simpson's house. I thought she was looking−'

'You are mistaken Tucker, it was probably Mrs Simpson's sister who is staying there,' Hannah said irritably. 'Now leave me Tucker. Quickly now, go.' In her rush to leave, Tucker knocked the writing table and a paperweight fell to the ground. 'What are you staring at now, Tucker?'

When Tucker picked up the paperweight, she said, 'This is exactly the same colour as that lady's eyes. I remember because I've never seen such beautiful eyes…'

Hannah let out a low groan and bent double as if she had received a blow in the solar plexus. A voice rang in her ears, '*It's a paperweight Cathy, the exact colour of my eyes. It's not much, I know, considering what you have spent on me, but each time you look at it, you will be looking into my eyes and know that I'm thinking of you…*'

'It cannot be possible,' Hannah choked. 'She… she died on the Bapaume Road.'

Tucker's hand reached out for Hannah but stopped short of touching her. 'Are you all right, my Lady?'

'Leave me, Tucker. Go... GO!'

Tucker fled the study in such haste she almost knocked the butler off his feet. Jenkins chided her, questioned her then went to his mistress. When he entered the room, Hannah was staring at the picture in her hand.

'My Lady,' he said bowing, noticing that her beautiful features had become ashen as she turned from him. 'Is Tucker unsuitable?'

'Jenkins, have you ever seen Mrs Simpson's guest about the estate?'

'Yes, my Lady.' He remembered first meeting her walking with Mrs Simpson during a short visit four years before. When he had first met her, he had thought how remarkably similar she was to the girl in the picture with Lady Hannah, but a sister of Mrs Simpson would certainly not be friends with the daughter of an earl, so he did not give it another thought. The next time he met Elizabeth was the day the Simpsons left for their holiday. She had grown her hair and was speaking French to her daughter. At first he wondered if it was the same woman, but when she greeted him by name, he knew that it was Mrs Simpson's sister. He asked Elizabeth if she knew Lady Hannah, she shook her head and said she had never met her. 'I believe the lady is named Brennan, my Lady. Mrs Elizabeth Brennan.'

Hannah's knuckles whitened on the chair that supported her. 'Elizabeth Brennan, not Turner? Yes, she would be married, her little girl...'

Jenkins eyed his mistress with some concern, for he had never witnessed her in such an agitated state before. 'I heard Mrs Brennan speaking French to her little girl.'

'She spoke French! Have you been close up to her... spoken to her?'

'I have, my Lady.'

'You have?' Now she said facing him. 'How did she strike you?'

'I would say she was a very different personage from her sister, my Lady.'

'Does Mrs Brennan look anything like the lady in this picture?' Hannah asked handing her butler the photograph.

Jenkins' eyebrows lifted as if in surprise. 'My Lady... I'm certain that it is Mrs Brennan.'

Hannah steadied herself against her writing table, hardly able to breathe. 'Oh Bess! How can this possibly be?'

'My Lady! Let me fetch you some water. You have turned quite pale.'

'A brandy, Jenkins.'

After Jenkins had left, Hannah looked at the photograph again. Tucker was right, Elizabeth had such a happy smile - they were happy then, in Paris, despite the war. In the background, the great dark shadow of the Eiffel Tower rose up to the sky. She remembered it as if it were yesterday. She was no longer Lady Hannah Catherine Somerville, the only daughter of an earl, the grieving twin of a brother killed, but Miss Catherine Neale, ambulance driver, freed from her aristocratic chains, temporarily relieved of her sickening grief.

Hannah sat back in her chair and remembered the last image she had of Elizabeth, waving her goodbye as she left the hospital yard. When the convoy arrived back at Albert, they were instructed to move on to Amiens, twenty miles further away from the front line, because of the heavy German shelling. Everyone was convinced it was the start of the long-expected German offensive. It had been a terrible night in which she could not sleep, even though her eyes had stung and ached with fatigue.

Now, from her study, watching a gardener trimming the edge of the lawn, she remembered the voice of the commandant when she broke

the news to her. 'I have terrible news Catherine, the worst kind…'
Those words broke her spirit and her will to live. Miss Catherine Neale
was released from her duty and she returned to England a week later
suffering from what was described as nervous exhaustion. But it
wasn't that at all, it was a broken heart that made her collapse and be
rushed to hospital in one of her own ambulances by the commandant
herself.

What Catherine didn't know was that the German Red Cross passed
on the news to the British Red Cross that Miss Elizabeth Turner had
been captured on the Bapaume Road during the morning of 21 March
1918. The news arrived at the FANY headquarters two weeks after
Catherine left France. Back in England, Catherine Neale no longer
existed and that news of Elizabeth never reached her.

Hannah was woken from her thoughts by a tap on her door and the
sudden appearance of Jenkins, who informed her that he had seen Mrs
Brennan heading towards the lake with her little girl.

*

Hannah's pace slowed when she reached the trees, but not her heart
for that was thumping inside her breast, as if she had sprinted to the
lake. In the distance sitting under the shade of a Common Alder tree,
she saw the figure of a young woman with a little girl lying beside her.
From the position of Hannah's approach, she was able to walk a lot
closer unseen. When the young woman turned at the sound of a
woodpecker's drumming, Hannah recognized the profile of her dearest
friend. The strength in her legs weakened and, for a moment,
prevented her from advancing further, so she sat and gazed towards the
silent pair. Hannah remembered the disappearing figure of Mrs
Simpson's sister four years ago, which now caused a sudden well of
tears to flood her eyes. Had her horse not picked up a stone, she would
have been with Edward when he stopped to talk to the sisters. How
cruel fate can be. Hannah wiped her eyes, her throat too dry to utter
any sound. Instead, she continued to watch Elizabeth and saw her raise
her knees so she was able to rest her forehead upon them. She
completed her pose by cradling her legs with her arms. It was a
position Hannah had often seen Elizabeth take in France when she was
in deep thought.

Unaware that she was being observed, Elizabeth cradled her legs,
her mind planning her return home the following morning. She
thought of John, his handsome features and his bright smile each time
he met her. She thought of the simple joy of his company and the

passion he felt for her. He would be looking forward to seeing her the moment she returned, wanting her when her mother retired to bed, but something gnawed at her. She should be happy. In many ways she was, but not in the way she had been when she was in Ireland and desperate to return to David. Soon she would be under pressure to set a date for the wedding. The thought suddenly made her body shudder with uncertainty.

She was woken from her thoughts by the sound of what she first thought were screaming children at play, but realized it was more likely to be the peafowl flirting with each other, while strutting about the lawns behind her. She became aware she was not alone and from the corner of her eye she saw a white figure move. She turned to look. The figure stood and began to walk towards her. Elizabeth's lungs became so heavy with sudden emotion she could hardly breathe. It was Hannah who spoke first.

'Bess, my darling, darling Bess.'

Elizabeth tried to rise, but was transfixed and incredulous. She sank back onto the ground with outstretched arms and burst into tears.

Chapter **5**

Elizabeth woke at eight and looked around the bedroom. For a moment she was confused. It was a luxury suite, beautifully furnished and with high ceilings. She groaned, her head ached and her mouth was dry. On her bedside table stood a bottle of Krug Champagne, uncorked and two thirds empty, a glass half full and a note telling her to, 'sleep in as Nanny is looking after Catherine'.

As she regained full consciousness, the recollections of the evening before began to return to her. She had eaten dinner at the Manor, drunk too much champagne and stayed rather than wake Catherine up to return to Louisa's cottage. All the old feelings Elizabeth had felt for Cathy, now Hannah, had come flooding back as they sat and talked into the early hours. It unsettled her. Hannah did not want her to return to Buckingham just yet, but stay a few more weeks and move into the Manor, which was large and comfortable with so many rooms.

Elizabeth trembled as she recognized anew the symptoms of infatuation, and when she saw Hannah's face in her mind, Elizabeth felt a frisson run down her spine. That one lingering kiss by the lake when they embraced had stirred in her something John had never done and reminded her so much of David's lips. What was she to do? John's lips would never be the same again. She climbed out of bed and went to the window. When she pulled open the curtains she was almost blinded by a stream of bright sunlight. She looked towards the great cedar silvered by dew. Today she had planned to return home to Buckingham, but now fate at last had dealt her a good hand. She went back to her bed and allowed her mind to drift back to the conversation the day before.

Sitting by the lake, they had talked for an age about their five-year separation. When they eventually exhausted their memories, Hannah looked tenderly at the little girl curled in sleep. 'And this is your little Catherine. She's very pretty.'

'I named her after you.'

Hannah smiled and squeezed the fingers of Elizabeth's hand. 'I find it amazing that your sister has been our tenant all this time. I once thought I saw you. My heart leapt thinking if only... little knowing it was you. Your sister never spoke of you. Never once said you were a FANY ambulance driver. She only ever spoke of herself and her dreary husband. Why did we keep our lives a secret, Bess? I only learned today that your sister had told my tight-lipped butler Jenkins, that you served in the Corps and that you were awarded a Military Medal... for saving Trisha's life I imagine. We all thought you deserved a VC.'

'The other girls knew I survived. News apparently came though from the Red Cross.'

'I returned to England and lost touch with them. Catherine Neale only existed when I was in France. They wouldn't know about Hannah Somerville or who Hannah Wyatt is now–'

'Your family name is Somerville?'

'Yes.'

'My God... I went to Somerville College. That's unnervingly coincidental.'

'Oxford... yes, I remember Bella telling me that. Poor Bella,' Hannah said. 'Anyway, let me finish, Jenkins said that he never mentioned his conversation with your sister to me because he thought Mrs Simpson was just trying to impress him. He didn't believe she could have a sister who served in the same Corps as me.'

'Why on earth should he think that?'

'Jenkins is a terrible snob; typical of his class.'

Elizabeth laughed. They held onto each other's hands, each in turn squeezing the other's fingers to feel them in their grasp, not daring to loosen their grip, afraid that one might escape the other and be lost forever.

'Our secrets have cost us five long years. To think, Louisa always talked about you. I began to hate you.' Elizabeth smiled and kissed Hannah's hand.

'So... Mrs Brennan, you too are a wife.'

'Brennan is my maiden name and it's *Miss* Brennan, *Lady* Hannah Wyatt.'

'I thought Turner was.'

'That was my married name. My husband was killed on the Somme.'

'Like my brother James was.' Catherine glanced at the sleeping child. 'And Catherine?'

'I was in love with her father. She was the result of that love.'

'Honestly Bess...'

'I wanted her. I wanted a part of him. I suppose in the back of my mind I knew I might lose him as I lost everyone I loved. The sad thing

161

is, David doesn't know about Catherine.' She looked Hannah in the eyes and smiled affectingly.

'So you're a widow? God... we know absolutely nothing about each other.'

'I seem to remember it was your suggestion to keep it to ourselves.'

'What folly that was. By the way you examined the others on our first day I thought you would hate me if you knew my background. I didn't want that. You seemed so sweet to me. I was thrilled when I had to share a room with you.'

'I remember being terrified of you.'

The friends laughed and embraced each other for what might have been the hundredth time. 'I suppose I must learn to call you Hannah?'

'No, Bess. Cathy. It's special to me - to us. Remember Edward? He said that he was certain he had seen you before and of course he had... the photograph of us in Paris, 1917. Do you remember it?'

'My mother has the same picture. Poor Edward, I was rather rude to him.'

'He said.'

'I feel guilty now. When he said that he thought he had seen me before, I presumed he was trying to seduce me.'

'Edward has an eye for a pretty face. He was at school with Guy, a friend, and my brother James. They spent the summer at Mountfields, the family seat in Yorkshire. My father's the Earl of Kepwick.'

'Of course he is.'

'Stop it,' Hannah said, playfully slapping Elizabeth's knee. 'Edward, Guy and James were at school together. James went to Sandhurst with Guy. It was Guy I thought I would one day marry, a crush really. Edward volunteered for the army when war was declared. He was always keen on me. When James and Guy were killed, Edward came up to Mountfields during his leave to comfort me. He came again when I returned from France after we lost you. It was my mother's doing, I know. He asked me to marry him; caught me at a low ebb, I suppose.'

Elizabeth's affectionate gaze brought a soft warm smile to Hannah's lips, which made Elizabeth tremble inside. The urge to kiss her was suddenly so strong it was a relief when her daughter stirred from her sleep.

Elizabeth turned to Hannah and smiled. 'It's very strange but Catherine has your lovely eyes... the very same colour.'

*

After a bath, Elizabeth dressed, wrote a letter to her mother and one to John explaining that she was going to stay on for another couple of weeks. She also added that she would agree with any arrangements he made about the wedding. Later, she descended the stairs admiring the beautiful curved staircase balustrade; the ornate patterns and brass greyhounds gleamed with an early morning polish from one of the many domestic staff, who had busily cleaned the house before any of those 'upstairs' stirred in their beds. Elizabeth almost jumped the final steps and skipped halfway across the black and white squared flagstone floor between the rugs in the main entrance hall, as if she were playing hopscotch.

The smile left her lips when she turned, Jenkins was standing looking bemused. He offered her a slight bow. 'Good morning, Madam.'

'Oh! Mr Jenkins! Good morning,' she said feeling silly. 'Hopscotch… I haven't played it since I was a child. Have you caught any more carp since we last spoke?'

'No Madam. And Madam, you address me as Jenkins, not *Mr* Jenkins.'

'And you may call me *Miss* Brennan, not Madam. Am I not the same person you met in the grounds, where I seem to remember we had rather a pleasant conversation?'

'No Madam, if you forgive me, you are not. *Then*, you were Mrs Simpson's sister. *Now* you are a friend of her Ladyship's and a guest in her house.'

'Don't be such a snob, Mr Jenkins.'

Jenkins coloured. He knew from his previous conversation with Elizabeth that she was an educated woman, although not of the class of person usually invited to the Manor. He imagined her to have been a suffragette, a young woman with opinions, and of course she had been awarded the Croix de Guerre and Military Medal, which was not really a feminine thing at all.

'Would you care to breakfast, Madam?'

'No thank you, Mr Jenkins. I'll make myself some tea. Where's the kitchen?'

Jenkins coloured more. 'If you care to make yourself comfortable in the sitting room Madam, I will fetch you some tea.'

'Poor Mr Jenkins,' Elizabeth smiled. 'I'm teasing you. Forgive me. I just do not agree with all the pomp and subservience that accompanies privilege.'

Jenkins was now bright vermilion. 'Her Ladyship has an engagement until mid-day. She asked me to convey her apologies and will see you at luncheon.'

'Forgive me Jenkins, I have embarrassed you. Sometimes I can be rather insensitive. No tea, thank you. I think I shall go and see my daughter.'

'The children are in the care of Nanny, Madam. Her Ladyship thought they would like to play together.'

'Good. Then I shall pop my head round the door to say hello, then go for a walk.'

'Yes, Madam. Luncheon will be served at one.'

*

The breeze, soft and languorous that came up from the south, was charged with the sweet perfume of jasmine. Elizabeth breathed in deeply when she stepped onto the terrace. The damp, dark earth still seemed to retain within it the rosy pinkness of the sunrise as she began her walk. Everywhere, fine dew shone on the leaves and grass, and glittered silver on spiders' webs. She walked miles across the Downs, through the woods and back to Burton Park towards the lake. Now it was hot. She adjusted the large straw hat on her head to protect her skin from the harsh rays of a hot, mid-August day. Elizabeth stopped under the shade of an old knotted oak whose foliage seemed to fill the sky. She sat down suddenly feeling sick and a little faint.

Later, having recovered from her nausea, she made her way to the lake where the shimmering water winked with silver sunlight between the shadows of the trees. A heron gave a sharp *kaark*, its great grey wings lifting it off the ground, circling the water in a wide arced glide before settling on the other side. She thought of Hannah's offer to live with her at the Manor. Of course, she couldn't accept it. Such opulent privilege was against her social conscience. To stay occasionally, yes, it would be no different from staying at a very smart hotel. To live, no, especially with her sister domiciled only half a mile away in a small cottage. Then there was John, their marriage and his new job.

The sudden desolate, puckered cry of a crow matched Elizabeth's change of mood. She put her face in her hands. 'Oh God, I don't love him. What am I to do?'

That ache, that deep irrational longing for someone, always gnawing at her stomach when gazing into David's face was not there when looking into John's, yet the moment she was reunited with Cathy those feelings came rushing back to her, filling every part of her with an inexplicable sexual longing. A long sigh left her lips as she began to walk to the other side of the lake. She paused and looked around her. The South Downs, from which she had just descended, looked like giant broccoli rising high into the sky. At her feet, the water with its mirror surface invited her to step into it. It was as though nature had created this spot for her alone. Her fingers began to remove buttons from their fastenings. When the dress fell in a heap at her feet, she stood wearing only a pair of cream, silk knickers. She hesitated, looked around her, then removed the silken undergarment and stood naked with the hum of summer buzzing about her in approval.

Elizabeth shared the water, warmed by weeks of blistering sunshine, with a pair of swans and several ducks that disappeared across the lake away from the floating object imitating the tragic figure of Millais' *Ophelia*. After fifteen minutes of bathing in the shaded part of the lake, the sun moved from behind a tree diminishing the shaded area further. She did not want to be caught in its rays so she returned to the bank where her clothes lay on the ground. It was almost luncheon and she would soon see Hannah again. Elizabeth left the lake and walked back towards the Manor. When she reached the line of cherry trees she began to feel faint again and stopped. Leaning against a tree, everything went black as the world began to spin, sending Elizabeth crashing to the ground.

*

For several minutes, Elizabeth watched Hannah through the strands of hair that had fallen across her eyes. She was sitting in a deep chair twirling a finger round a long string of pearls hanging from her neck as she flicked through a magazine, breaking into a smile at something she had read, which brought a smile to Elizabeth's lips when she saw it. Hannah suddenly looked up and caught Elizabeth's retreating eye that was too slow to close. She rose from the chair and sat on the edge of the bed.

'How's my little patient feeling?' she said, softly stroking Elizabeth's brow. Her hand felt cool and comforting.

'What happened, Cathy?'

'You fainted. Gave Jenkins quite a scare.' She combed the hair from Elizabeth's face with her fingers then kissed her cheek. 'You've slept for over an hour.'

'I still feel tired now.'

'It was all that walking in the sun. Our doctor's on his way.'

'Thank you, but there really is no need.'

Hannah went to the bowl of cold water and wet a flannel. Elizabeth watched her every movement and knew she must leave this house and move back to Louisa's cottage. She closed her eyes when the cool flannel was placed on her forehead. 'Try to sleep again Bess, darling. I'll see you after the doctor has been.'

*

Just before midnight Elizabeth was woken by thunder and pouring rain beating against the window pane of her bedroom. She blinked and glanced at her watch. Outside, the rumbles became rattles, one crashing noise after another making her jump. Her mind drifted back to the night she and David became lovers and wondered if he still suffered during storms. Questions filled her mind. Had his memory returned to him? Was he back with his family? Did he ever think of her? Was he thinking of her now or lying in sleep alongside the body of another woman?

Her thoughts turned to Hannah. Her husband had earlier returned from London and Hannah would now be moulded safely against the warmth him in their bed. Elizabeth climbed from her bed, went to the window and pulled open the curtains. A silver blade of light slashed through the dark sky and momentarily brightened up the landscape so she could see the lake in the distance then, as if snuffing out the flame of a candle in a bottomless pit, the dark became so intense she could not see the window frame six inches from her eyes. The growing intensity of the storm reminded her of the German barrage that killed Bella. Another sharp crack made her jump again. The storm was almost directly upon them. Elizabeth began to shake and felt desperately alone. She left her room and went along the corridor to Hannah's bedroom door. She hesitated before gently pushing it open.

As Hannah listened to the storm in half sleep, lightning momentarily illuminated the ghostly image of Elizabeth's naked body standing by the door. The brilliance of light was exchanged for a great explosion of sound that seem to ricochet through the sleeping building now shrouded in deep, fathomless darkness. Hannah sat up when the room lit up again; the image was gone. She did not know whether she had imagined Elizabeth's appearance or wished for it. Edward turned in his sleep, mumbling to his platoon to keep their heads down. She climbed out of bed, glanced at her sleeping husband then made her way along the corridor to Elizabeth's room where she found her friend sitting up in her bed, shaking.

'Bess, what's the matter darling? Is it the storm?'

166

Elizabeth reached towards Hannah and wrapped her arms round her waist, resting her head against her belly. The silk nightdress felt cool against her flushed cheeks. 'It reminded me of that time Bella and I came under attack… coming back from the hospital.'

Hannah sat on the edge of the bed. 'Would you like me to stay with you?'

'Yes.'

Their eyes met. Elizabeth pulled Hannah to her and kissed her lips. Hannah climbed into bed and slid alongside her. The thunder crashed and the rain lashed and while the household slept, the two friends were in Paris again, away from the horrors of the Western Front.

Chapter 6

Elizabeth woke as soft lips and warm breath brushed against her mouth. Her eyes fluttered open when she heard her bedroom door close. The pillow beside her smelt of Hannah's scent. Now her eyes were fully open as she remembered the events of the early morning.

A smile stretched her lips; it disappeared when the image of Hannah's face in her mind was replaced by John's. She experienced an unexpected flush of guilt. Had she betrayed him by making love to Hannah? She reasoned with herself that she had not. Betrayal, surely, was sleeping with another man, the possibility of having another man's child, a cuckoo in the nest. She was not yet married to him; no vow had been taken, only a promise, however tenuous it might have been.

She sighed loudly. Her mind was full of John when she wanted to think of Hannah. Although nature's hand had carved the fine lines of his masculine features quite beautifully, her work began to melt as if wax and mould itself into the beauty of Hannah's bright eyes, her smile, and the smoothness of her soft, firm body. As Hannah's image began to fill Elizabeth's mind again, John's features flickered and dimmed as if in the dying moments of a candle about to burn out.

Making love to Hannah had settled her mind about John. Her stomach knotted in the certain knowledge that it was over between them; that she could no longer marry him and he would be hurt by that. She left her bed to have a wash.

By the time Elizabeth stepped onto the terrace, the dewy morning had given way to the heat of the day. She looked across at the Cypress of Lebanon beyond the rose garden and lily pond, and felt a sudden sensation of complete happiness. After a short walk past the walled garden, with a statue of a dog on the top of the brickwork, to the greenhouses filled with potted plants and then down to the stables, she returned to the house.

Hannah looked up from her newspaper and met Elizabeth's smile. 'Bring some tea and toast Jenkins, then you may go. We'll look after ourselves.'

'Yes, my Lady. I hope you are feeling well this morning, Mrs Brennan?' his eyes widening as Elizabeth slumped into a sofa, in what he considered to be a most unladylike manner.

'Much better, thank you. And Jenkins... it's *Miss* Brennan, not Mrs.'

Jenkins blushed and left the room. Hannah threw her paper aside and approached Elizabeth from behind the sofa. 'You, *Miss* Brennan were a beast with me last night. I have scratches and bruises all over my body. Heaven knows how I would explain them to Edward if he saw them.'

'Cathy,' Elizabeth said, looking up into her eyes. 'Do you love Edward?'

Hannah shrugged. 'Yes, I suppose I do... why do you ask?'

'How can you do what we did then go back to his bed?'

Hannah kissed the top of Elizabeth's head then sat close to her on the sofa taking her friend's hand in hers. 'He's my husband, Bess. I'm the mother of his child. What *we* have is separate from that.'

Elizabeth lifted her eyebrows with the pretext of a smile as she returned Cathy's glance. 'You said you loved me last night. You said it several times.'

'And I do. Bess... you're very good in bed. Have you had other women?'

Elizabeth's eyes couldn't meet the pair now concentrated on her. 'Why do you ask?'

'I'm not jealous, promise.'

'Yes, I have. I like women, but I love you. I have only ever loved you... and David.'

'The father of your child?'

Elizabeth smiled. 'If only I could have you both; life would be perfect.'

Hannah rose from the sofa and walked to the window as Jenkins entered the room with Tucker carrying a tray of tea. 'Good morning Tucker,' Hannah said. 'I'm sorry I shouted at you the other day.'

Elizabeth was pleased that Hannah could find it in herself to say what she had said to a servant, but Jenkins' eyes opened like a startled rabbit. He swallowed; the daughter of an earl apologizing to a maid... whatever next? He blamed the influence of *Miss* Brennan.

Tucker curtsied and glanced towards Jenkins' humourless features. His eyes moved rapidly in the direction of the door. Tucker curtsied again and hurried from the room.

'Will there be anything else, my Lady?'

When Jenkins closed the door behind him, Hannah turned to Elizabeth and said, 'I want to take you to Paris. Make up for us missing our leave there in 1918. We could visit all the old haunts of 1917. Do say you'll go.'

'Of course I'll go. Catherine will love it.'

'I meant the two of us... as we did before.'

The smile left Elizabeth's lips. 'I can't go without Catherine. I've never left her alone before.'

'She'll be well cared for here, I promise, and she has my Elizabeth to play with. They are already great friends. Please say yes.'

'I shall need to think about it.'

'The treat is mine.'

'I am perfectly able to pay for myself, thank you.'

'Now you're cross with me, but the treat is still mine.'

Elizabeth smiled. 'I'm not cross with you. I can never be cross with you.'

'Just one week. Catherine will hardly know you've gone.'

Elizabeth looked up into Hannah's large expectant eyes and nodded, feeling guilty in doing so. It was received with a yelp of delight from her friend.

'Darling, we'll have fun. Listen, have you ever danced the Charleston? It's a new dance from America.' Elizabeth laughed when Hannah sprang to her feet and demonstrated the twisting steps of the dance singing, *Charleston, Charleston*. 'I'll teach you, but not now.'

'Yes! Yes, now,' Elizabeth laughed excitedly. 'I want to learn it.'

'Later. This evening I'm having family over for dinner. You'll meet my mother... she arrived just before you fainted after your walk. She loves your little Catherine, can't take her eyes off her.'

'Is she here now?'

'No, she's gone to London with my odious cousin Henry and his ghastly wife to visit a friend. They'll return this evening. You'll meet Edward of course. He should be home by seven.'

'Oh Lord! I'll never be able to look Edward in the eye. Must I?'

Hannah laughed and encircled Elizabeth's waist with her arms. 'They'll love you, really.'

'Sometimes you can be so naïve, Cathy. Behind your back I shall be regarded a common little upstart. This is not my world. I mean, look at it. I was brought up modestly. My father was a schoolmaster.'

'Heavens Bess, you surround yourself with schoolmasters. No wonder you're so clever.' Hannah lit a cigarette and blew the smoke up into the air from the side of her mouth, tilting her head at an angle, which always amused Elizabeth. 'Now, who can I pair you with this evening? Someone who will not try to seduce you... I know the very fellow, Ralph, he's a sweetie, and you'll be perfectly safe; he's homosexual.'

'How do you know that?'

'Bess, I think you're the one who is naïve.'

*

At seven that evening, Elizabeth stood in front of the mirror and saw her image dressed in an exquisitely beautiful and expensive evening dress given to her by Hannah. The printed silk voile in subtle shades of russet and green was embroidered with sequins and bugle beads, inset and trimmed with gold lace. It fell above the ankle, exposing the cream silk stockings and champagne-coloured shoes. The pearls hanging from her neck matched the buckle of the belt on her hips. She twirled as if a model showing off the latest fashion. A glow of satisfaction brightened her eyes; she had never felt so attractive.

Her smile suddenly disappeared. 'Be very careful little canary,' she whispered to her reflection, 'However bright your feathers, once you begin to sing, those hawks will know you are nothing but a simple sparrow and they will eat you alive.'

When Jenkins opened the door to the drawing room at seven-thirty and announced Elizabeth, the room broke into cold silence. The room seemed a blur, and although Elizabeth was aware of a group of people looking in her direction, she became conscious only of the owl-like stare from Lady Somerville. Their eyes met and held.

Hannah broke into a smile. 'Bess darling, you look absolutely divine. Come and meet my mother.'

'She knows about us, Cathy. I sense it. Look at the way she stares at me,' Elizabeth whispered as she was led across the room.

'You're imagining it,' Hannah replied, squeezing her arm. 'Mamma, this is my dearest, dearest friend, Elizabeth Brennan. Isn't she just simply lovely?'

'Good evening, Mrs Brennan. I hope you have fully recovered. You gave us all quite a fright.'

Elizabeth smiled politely. 'I am quite well, thank you Lady Somerville... and it's *Miss*, not *Mrs* Brennan.'

Lady Somerville's eyes widened as they turned to her daughter. 'Elizabeth is a widow, Mamma. She now prefers to use her maiden name.'

'Does she indeed? And why do you choose to do that, *Miss* Brennan?'

171

'Because I wish to live my life as me... not as my late husband's widow.'

'What about your child? Surely she is entitled to her father's name.'

'My late husband is not the father of my child.'

'Bess, come and meet Edward and Ralph,' Hannah said, pulling Elizabeth away from her mother who had turned vermilion. 'Don't be naughty, Bess. You've shocked my mother and she is such a sweetie. You'll find her a far better friend than an enemy.'

Elizabeth's escort, Lord Ralph Nugent, was the youngest son of a duke and therefore had no responsibility in life other than to keep the family name free of scandal. As a youngest son he was not such an attractive commodity on the marriage market within his own class and therefore he could attend functions without commanding an ambitious mother's attention or her dutiful daughter's tedious gaze, which was a blessing to him. After overhearing what Elizabeth said to the Countess, he decided that he liked her. It was also with some relief that she appeared to have no interest in him other than polite conversation. He noticed however, Hannah would periodically catch Elizabeth's eye and smile an affectionate smile to all those who observed it - except he and the Countess, who sensed it to mean much more.

'When did your friendship with Hannah begin, Miss Brennan?'

'Hannah and I first met at Pirbright. I knew her as Catherine Neale...'

'That was the name of her Nanny.'

Elizabeth smiled. 'It suited her. Our friendship grew and strengthened in Flanders.'

'I have heard of your exploits and congratulate you on your Military Medal and Croix de Guerre. I served in Belgium. Ypres was rather a bloody place. I understand you were there during the third battle?'

'Yes.' Elizabeth took some wine then looked into the young man's face. 'You must forgive me if I seem a little uncomfortable. I really am only here at the insistence of Hannah.'

He smiled, 'Miss Brennan, the dinner is in your honour.'

Her reply was a tender smile. 'Did you know Hannah's friend, Guy?'

'Guy Wakenshaw, yes.'

'Tell me about him and James. What were they like?'

'Decent chaps. I was at school with them, and Edward. We were in the same house. The Four Musketeers.' Guy and James always had their noses stuck in books, poetry mostly, can't stand it myself. No soul, I suppose. Hannah had known Guy since childhood; they were like brother and sister. Then one day... a lingering glance, fluttering hearts which became one.'

'I thought you disliked poetry. You *are* a poet.'

His deep brown eyes warmed when he smiled. 'Edward and Guy became quite chummy. James tended to be a bit of a loner, didn't make friends very easily... bagged a Victoria Cross at Loos... wonderful chap. Why did all the best fellows go west?' he said sadly. A sudden roar of laughter punctuated Ralph's story. He glanced up towards Lord Westerland and whispered to Elizabeth, 'Unlike Hannah's cousin; a complete ass, had a cushy job on the staff... never got mud on his boots. James' death has made Westerland heir to the Kepwick title.'

'Describe him to me.'

'Who... Henry Westerland?'

'No. You've described him perfectly, already,' she said with an impish grin. 'I mean Guy Wakenshaw. Was he engaged to Hannah?'

'Yes. She took his death rather badly,' Ralph's eyes narrowed. 'But not as badly as her brother's. They were twins.'

'Oh my God!' Elizabeth gasped. 'She never said. That's awful. Poor Hannah,' she said, glancing over towards her friend now locked in conversation with her mother. 'I have twin sisters. Although they fight like cat and dog, there is an undeniable bond between them.'

'Hannah's parents returned from Canada and found a letter from Flanders waiting for them, explaining that she had joined the First Aid Nursing Yeomanry... doing her bit for the flag and all that. That is, of course, where you enter the scene.' He saw Elizabeth's smile which needed no interpretation as he watched her eyes wander in Hannah's direction again. 'What you won't know is, she came back from France a wreck and Edward was there to comfort her. She told me that the death of a very close friend had affected her very badly. You were that friend Miss Brennan, now looking anything but ghostly.' The smile on his face suddenly dropped. 'Err... on your guard, Westerland has his eye on you.'

Lord Westerland's booming voice found the ear of all the other guests as he addressed Elizabeth. To her dismay the whole table suddenly fell silent.

'Miss Brennan,' he said, wiping his mouth with his napkin. 'Lady Hannah tells me you're a bit of a blue stocking...'

173

Elizabeth glanced towards a smiling Hannah. 'Your cousin exaggerates.'

'Don't be so modest, Miss Brennan. Perhaps we may benefit from your learned opinion. We were discussing this dreadful music coming over from America...'

'Is it so dreadful?'

Westerland's wife looked across at Elizabeth through cold eyes. 'I find it all in very bad taste. It's mediocrity.'

'What is thought mediocrity today may be considered genius tomorrow, Lady Westerland,' Elizabeth said. 'During his lifetime, Haydn was regarded a genius, but not Mozart. Yet today, together with Haydn, Mozart's music marks the height of the Baroque age in its purity of melody and form, although strictly speaking Mozart's music was in the Rococo period.'

'Well, I don't know about any of that,' Lord Westerland sniffed, deciding he'd heard enough.

Before she spoke, Lady Westerland's nose had a habit of twitching like a rabbit's said, 'And for all his genius Mozart was buried in a pauper's grave.'

Elizabeth did not like Lady Westerland. She imagined her to be spiteful and a snob. 'A pauper's grave, a rich man's grave... what difference does it make to the dead?'

'But surely, Miss Brennan,' Lady Westerland continued in a contemptuous voice, 'the tomb is a mark of a man's achievement in life. Wouldn't you agree?'

'No, I wouldn't. It's more a mark of his conceit,' Elizabeth said sharply. 'Our soldiers were buried in mass graves just as paupers were in Mozart's day. I witnessed dozens of men laid side by side without distinction. You talk of mediocrity, those soldier's lives were taken from them by mediocre staff officers and their mediocre plans, while the architect of their destruction is showered with honours and an earldom.'

The words reverberated round the table like an electric spark, which struck Lady Westerland. She was speechless. Her lip curled as her eyes focused hard on Elizabeth. Jenkins standing close to Edward closed his eyes, while Ralph and Edward lowered theirs. Hannah sat chewing her lip. She had never seen Elizabeth so angry. Lady Somerville eyed Elizabeth with expressionless features and Lord Westerland's face was crimson.

'Miss Brennan,' Lady Westerland said sharply. 'I regard your remarks as very insulting. I'm sure you know very well my husband was on Field Marshall Haig's staff. They were men of standing, men of good breeding. Do you know what good breeding is, *Miss* Brennan?'

'I believe, Lady Westerland,' Elizabeth said in a controlled voice, 'it is how much one thinks of oneself and how little one thinks of others.'

Stifled sniggers from Edward and Ralph could no longer be contained. They were cut short by the fierce glare from Lady Westerland. Elizabeth caught Lady Somerville's gaze and thought she detected humour in her eyes.

'That will teach you a lesson for being such a snob, Augusta,' Hannah said coldly, 'and for being extremely rude to my friend. You haven't her intellect to continue this argument so let's put an end to it now.'

In unison with the intake of Lord and Lady Westerland's breath, Edward tapped his glass and raised it.

'I think this is a very good time to offer a toast to our guest of honour… a young lady who has risen from the ashes, like the phoenix, with fire still in her belly, a fire which has brought warmth and light to my beautiful wife's eyes. I give you Miss Elizabeth Brennan, MM and Croix de Guerre.'

Chapter 7

For some of the journey to Paris Hannah was asleep. Elizabeth could neither sleep nor concentrate on her book; her mind was occupied with the events of the previous morning. Louisa had returned a day earlier than planned and found her house empty as she had expected, yet there was no note from her sister or any other evidence to suggest that she had actually stayed. As she began unpacking, Louisa heard a car pull up, a door close, a woman's laughter, which was unquestionably her sister and then another voice, Lady Hannah's voice, calling Elizabeth back to her. Louisa went to the window and saw Elizabeth step into Lady Hannah's outstretched arms and kiss her. Louisa stood transfixed. For her sister to kiss Lady Hannah on the cheek would be quite unbelievable, they were socially worlds apart, but to kiss her deeply, as a man would a woman he desired, was disgusting to her. When the car began to move away, Louisa watched her sister wave until it was out of sight then turn with the happiest of smiles warming her face. She strolled towards the house carrying a large bunch of flowers in her arms, flowers that had obviously been cut from the gardens.

Louisa stepped back from the window feeling suddenly cold. Tears came to her eyes because she now knew that the rumours about Elizabeth and Katie Crenshaw were true. She had never believed them. It wasn't uncommon for women of Lady Hannah's class to have unnatural feelings for their own sex, but this was not just another woman, it was her younger sister, the mother of her niece. Louisa slumped down onto the bed when she heard her front door open and footsteps pad from one room to another. A receptacle was filled with water. Scissors began to snip at flower stalks. A soft voice hummed *Charleston, Charleston*. Louisa placed her face into her hands, not wanting to go downstairs.

Watching the familiar French landscape passing by, Elizabeth sighed as she remembered climbing the stairs and finding her sister sitting alone in her bedroom. Louisa's demeanour was cold. She backed away from her sister's attempted embrace.

Elizabeth noticed Louisa avoided her eye. 'What's the matter, Lou?'

'Very chummy with Lady Hannah, aren't we?'

176

Elizabeth looked at Louisa then walked over to the window and peered outside. 'You saw us, didn't you?'

'It made my stomach turn.'

'Lou… Hannah is Catherine, my friend from the war—'

'*Friend*! I think she's more than that.'

'I don't expect you to understand—'

'Oh yes I do,' Louisa interrupted again. 'I've heard about women like you. You're one of them, aren't you?'

'If you mean lesbian, then no, I'm not. I've always liked women, you knew that, Lou. You also knew about Katie and me. You said so.'

'I thought you had got over that. You got married. You're getting married again and you have a child.'

'So I like men too. I'm bi-sexual Lou,' Elizabeth shrugged, 'I get the best of both worlds.'

'It's nothing to joke about! Get out of this house. You're disgusting! You make me sick!'

When Elizabeth opened her eyes the trees and wide flat fields had transformed themselves into the suburban sprawl of suburban Paris. In the distance, reaching into the sky, she was warmed by the familiar sight of the Eiffel Tower.

*

Paris lacked the excitement of 1917. In the luxury of their hotel suite, Elizabeth brushed Hannah's hair. She was feeling restless and wanted to leave the city to visit the new war cemeteries being created all over the old Somme battlefield.

'I'd like to pay my respects to my father and brother,' Elizabeth said softly. 'The cemetery in which they are buried has had all the wooden crosses replaced by the new Portland headstones. Sylvie wrote saying she placed flowers on their graves. She's so very thoughtful. We could go and visit her. I should love you to meet her.'

'Did you and Sylvie ever...'

'No. I love Sylvie, but not in that way. We went through a lot together.'

'All right, why not? I'd like to see James' grave again. See if where he is buried is an improvement on the last time I was there.'

'You went back?

'With my father, a year after the war. Poor Pa, he misses James so much. We all do.'

'And your mother, did she visit too?'

'No. She doesn't believe he's dead, poor love. I suppose seeing his

177

grave would confirm it to her. Although I understand, I sometimes feel his presence, particularly since your reappearance in my life.'

'Cathy ... does Edward mind you being away for so long?'

'He can hardly complain. He's rarely ever at home these days.'

'I like Edward,' Elizabeth smiled. 'I wish I didn't then I shouldn't feel so guilty about us.'

'He likes you too. He says he now has three beautiful women in his life - his sister Constance, who you'll meet when we return; me, of course, and now you. We are his three Graces. He did name them but I can't remember them.'

'Aglaia, Euphrosyne and Thalia, daughters of Zeus and Euryoneme,' Elizabeth said brushing the last strands of Hannah's dark brown hair. 'They personified pleasure, beauty and charm…'
Elizabeth placed her chin on the top of Hannah's head and studied their images in the mirror whispering, '*Her beauty made the bright world dim, and everything beside seemed like the fleeting image of a shade*. Percy Shelley must have seen into the future and had a vision of you when he wrote those lines.'

Hannah laughed. 'Darling Elizabeth, you're the sweetest thing.'

*

Cutting through the flat, featureless landscape, the road from Albert to Bapaume is level and arrow-straight, except for the approach to La Boisselle where it dips then rises again past the village. Looking through the window of the taxicab, Elizabeth remembered the time in 1918 when she drove along the very road they travelled now. Then, the road was littered with the debris of war; broken smoking limbers, abandoned burnt-out vehicles, dead horses with wide unseeing eyes and the corpses of young men. Some lay as though in peaceful sleep, others butchered and hideous under a blanket of flies. How different it all looked now. Long soft fingers curled around hers in a grip that told her Hannah knew what was on her mind. Elizabeth turned and looked into her friend's face made more beautiful through the ugliness of her memories. They sat in the cab in silence; there was no need for either to say anything.

Ahead of them, Elizabeth saw a small cemetery by the side of the road and asked the driver to stop beside it. 'I'm sure it was somewhere around here Bella was killed and I was taken prisoner. She could be buried in there.'

They entered the cemetery and walked between the rows of bright white headstones looking at meaningless names carved above

178

regimental badges or crosses. Fresh flowers adorned some of the plots where recent visitors had been. It was an eerie feeling walking among the bones of young men; men she had once seen whistling, cheering and waving their steel helmets at her as they passed in endless columns. For many of those men, she was the last woman they ever saw. She felt a sudden chill embrace her. It was only a matter of chance she was not buried in this cemetery herself.

Elizabeth stopped and caught her breath. The words on the clean Portland stone in front of her read, *Lady Isabella Ann Fitzclarence. First Aid Nursing Yeomanry. Age 23. 21 March 1918.*

Tears ran down Elizabeth's cheeks. 'Cathy,' she whispered, her voice hardly audible, 'look, it's Bella.' Hannah took hold of Elizabeth's arm and looked at the headstone bearing Isabella's name. For a moment they both stood in silence remembering the young woman who was once their friend. 'I can see her now, waving at me, smiling that lovely smile of hers. She didn't have to go to the cemetery that night. I would have taken her dead.'

'I insisted she did, remember.'

'She was so lovely, now look at her…' Elizabeth said wiping her eyes, 'a tablet of stone with her name on it.'

They lingered in front of the stone for a while in silent memory of their friend. When they turned to leave, Elizabeth's eye caught the name on another gravestone. *Nurse Margaret Emma Wheeler. Age 22. Voluntary Aid Detachments. 21 March 1918.*

'So your name was Margaret,' Elizabeth whispered. She turned to Hannah. 'It's because she had my bag in her hand, with all my identification inside, that I was mistaken for her.'

'And all the subsequent trouble that caused.' Hannah placed an arm round Elizabeth's shoulder and kissed her cheek. 'Come on… let's leave here and find my brother.'

Elizabeth placed a hand on Margaret Wheeler's gravestone and shivered, as if she had rested her hand on the Grim Reaper's shoulder. Her eyes lingered on the name carved into the stone and for a moment, saw her own.

Before they left the cemetery, Elizabeth went to where the register was kept and took out the book that listed the dead. She made a note of Margaret Wheeler's address and told Catherine she would go and visit her parents.

'She was so brave. They may find some comfort in knowing that.'

They continued their way in silence along the road towards

Bapaume. The cab turned right into what was once the small village of La Boisselle and right again, along a makeshift piece of road, which the driver said led up to an enormous crater. The cemetery was across a field a hundred yards away.

'Je suis desolé mais je ne peux pas conduire plus loin. Vous devrez marcher.'

Elizabeth explained to Hannah that they couldn't go any further in the taxi. 'We can walk. It's just across there, Cathy. Do you see the cross?'

'There is another road leading to it through the ruins of the village. I remember it when I was here with my father.' Hannah sighed impatiently. 'What's he saying now?'

'He said many people come to visit this crater. It measures approximately three hundred feet across by ninety feet deep. Apparently our engineers blew the mine just before the attack on the first of July, 1916.'

'It was probably my stupid cousin who ordered that.'

Elizabeth smiled. Hannah turned and saw a distant cemetery in which her brother was buried. 'Tell the man to turn round, Bess. We haven't the shoes to walk across there.'

*

When they left Gordon Dump Cemetery and were back in the taxicab, Elizabeth saw the sadness in Hannah's eyes, but no tears. Elizabeth knew Hannah was a woman disciplined in the rules of her class, a victim and accomplice with no respite. Her silence locked her into the system like a cage. She was a prisoner and guardian of her own prison. Elizabeth reached across, kissed a dry cheek and whispered, 'Escape Cathy, escape. Let your tears set you free.'

Hannah just smiled, squeezed Elizabeth's hand and turned to look out of the window fixing her gaze on the horizon.

The sun began to shine brightly when they reached the village of Thiepval. The taxi pulled alongside the Connaught Road Cemetery, which stood on high ground overlooking the valley of the Ancre. Behind the great cross which cast a shadow along a neatly trimmed lawn were planted Japanese cherries, lime and Irish yews. Along the rows of headstones, they passed a boy from Fermanagh, one from Antrim, another from Donegal. Elizabeth stopped, feeling sudden nausea welling up inside her as she looked at the names which developed into the faces of her father and brother. 'Papa... and dearest William.'

When Hannah saw Elizabeth's wet eyes, she asked her if she wanted to be alone. Elizabeth took Hannah's hand and shook her head.

Standing beside the cab, the driver nonchalantly lit a cigarette and exhaled the smoke, which lingered in the air about him. He watched the two ladies and remembered his own son's grave at Verdun where his wife had collapsed in tears. He never returned. The shame of seeing so many crosses was too much for him to bear. The driver's thoughts were disturbed by the sound of someone singing. It was a tune he had heard the British soldiers sing when on the march. He turned and saw one of the gardeners slowly making his way towards the cemetery with an unsteady gait, yet it had the remnants of a military bearing. When the gardener saw the two women in the cemetery he stopped singing and went to the cab driver to leave them in peace. Each man greeted the other with a nod. The gardener dropped his tools and took a cigarette from behind his ear. He turned to the Frenchman and commented how sad it was to see two beautiful women looking so unhappy. When the cabbie shrugged his shoulders the gardener repeated what he had just said.

'Bloody frogs don't understand their own bleeding language,' the gardener muttered to himself. 'You lot were bloody useless in the war,' he said smiling and nodding at the grinning cabbie. 'A bunch of wankers, weren't yer, me old son?'

*

Elizabeth threw an affectionate smile at Hannah. Slowly, they walked towards the seat and sat in the shelter away from the sun. Along the rows of headstones, Elizabeth noticed that the gap between the two where her father and brother were buried was not as uniform as the others. They had deliberately been placed closer together, as a pair in the long line of individual plots. Amid sudden birdsong, they made their way towards the waiting taxi. Elizabeth turned and saw her brother's mischievous grin shine from one headstone and her father's eyes glow from the other. She remembered the last time she had seen him. He had raised his hand, winked and then smiled from the carriage of the train that took him away from her. Now she raised her hand towards his grave, but she did not wink and she could not smile.

The gardener removed his cap as the two young women approached the cab. Elizabeth asked if it was he they should thank for looking after the cemetery so well.

'Err...parlez lentement s'il vous plait, Madame,' he said in a panic.

'You're English?' Elizabeth replied.

''Ow did you know that?'

Elizabeth smiled at his toothless grin. 'I asked if it was you we should thank for doing such a lovely job. The cemeteries are so beautifully cared for.'

'There are a few of us, all ex-servicemen.'

The gardener looked at his pocket watch, said it was time for his grub before he got on with some work and asked if they would like to share the food he had.

'I don't think so, thank you,' said Hannah, her disbelieving eyes focussing on the size of his sandwich. 'Please, take this. As my friend says, you're doing a splendid job.'

'Ta, very generous of you,' he said touching his forelock then separated the bread to see what was inside it. 'I'm so 'ungry I could eat an 'orse.'

'I think you are about to,' Hannah said looking at the meat in disgust.

'Nice one,' the old soldier grinned then, stretching his mouth as wide as he could, bit into his sandwich. Hannah winced.

Elizabeth smiled at the strange fellow. 'Goodbye, Mr...'

'Jacks,' he spluttered, wiping his mouth on the sleeve of his jacket. 'It's Jacks, but you can call me Jacko, everyone does.'

Chapter **8**

On their return to England and Burton Manor, there was a letter waiting for Elizabeth. She glanced at the envelope. The writing showed a hurried, impatient hand. It was from John. Elizabeth opened it with mixed feelings. Hannah's company had erased him from her mind yet she had thought of her little Catherine day and night.

She began to read it half watching the girls, hot with shrieking laughter, being chased by Hannah. Her full attention turned towards her friend; the way her body moved, her laughter, her eyes that periodically threw a glance in her direction. She sighed, knowing she could no longer stay; that she would have to leave her the following day. As the letter progressed from sarcasm to his disappointment in her, she lost interest, stuffed it into her bag and continued to watch the frolicking on the lawn, laughing with the others when Hannah tripped over one of the dogs growling at her feet.

Edward lowered his paper. 'Not bad news I hope, Elizabeth.'

'No,' she replied. 'Will you excuse me, I need to go and lie down for a while.'

'Please stay a moment. I have something to say. It's Hannah. I've never seen her so happy these days. I know it's because of you, you being here. Hannah spoke to me about letting you have a suite of rooms in the west wing of the Manor. With my new job keeping me away so much, I think it's a wonderful idea.'

Unable to meet his eye, Elizabeth looked up into a clear blue sky and followed the flight of a hawk. 'That's kind of you Edward, but I shall not need them. Thank you anyway.'

She hurriedly left him and disappeared into the house and up to her room. Ten minutes later, a knock on the door preceded Hannah's hot, red face. She crossed the room and sat on the bed beside Elizabeth's prostrate body.

'Bess darling, Edward tells me you are feeling out of sorts. What's the matter?'

'I'm pregnant.'

'Bess,' Hannah sighed. 'Do you never protect yourself?'

'I want this baby.'

'Then why are you looking so glum?'

'Because I had made up my mind not to marry John. Now I shall

183

have to.'

'Why do you have to?'

'I cannot have this one born out of wedlock too. It would destroy my mother.'

'Have your baby here. No one will know.'

'And how do I explain it to my family? Tell them the baby's yours and I'm his nanny?'

'Tell them anything otherwise you'll end up in a marriage you'll always regret.'

'Since when did your class ever care whether marriage was anything other than a union of convenience?' Elizabeth snapped. In the silence that followed, she reached for Hannah's hand and pressed it to her lips. 'I'm sorry Cathy, forgive me. We've never once argued. I don't want to now... especially not now.'

'You're leaving, aren't you?'

'Tomorrow... I should have gone weeks ago.'

Hannah walked to the window and looked towards the lake where she was reunited with her friend. 'I have property in Devon. We could take the children and leave. You could have your baby there.'

'That would be irrational and very stupid. Consider the scandal. Your friends and family don't deserve it and Edward would take Elizabeth from you. You'd never see her again. How will your parents feel about it?' Elizabeth went and kissed Hannah's cheek. 'I shall lose nothing by it, you will lose everything.'

'I'll have you, Bess.'

Elizabeth took her into her arms. 'Cathy darling, you know it doesn't make sense.'

'I'm going to lose you, aren't I?'

Elizabeth ran her fingertips down Hannah's cheek and smiled. 'You'll never lose me again, I promise. We'll write... often and I'll visit. You can come to me—'

'No!' Hannah burst into tears. 'The thought of him fucking you makes me feel sick.'

Elizabeth gasped. She had never seen Hannah cry or heard her swear before, even in France where the language they heard was new and appalling. 'It will mean nothing to me. A duty to my husband, that's all. Darling Cathy, please... you'll set me off too.'

*

The following morning, Elizabeth leaned out of the window and blew Hannah a kiss as the train pulled out of the station. When she took her seat, her hand went to the necklace of gold with a diamond pendant that Hannah had given her.

'This was the last present I ever received from my brother James,' Hannah had said. 'It's the most precious thing I have. I want you to have it. Wear it always and think of me.'

Elizabeth caught Catherine's eyes and she smiled at her little girl. 'We're going home, my love.'

'To see the chickens?'

'Yes darling, to see the chickens.'

*

Christina's face was a mixture of relief and confusion as the cab pulled up outside the house, but it changed to exaltation at the sight of a little waving hand. She hurried outside and threw her arms around little Catherine.

'Hello my little darling. Have you missed Grandma? Of course you have you little cherub. Let me kiss you.' After a barrage of kisses, she looked up at Elizabeth with enquiring eyes. 'Bess, what on earth have you been up to?'

'I'll tell you over some tea, Mamma. Has... has Lou written to you?'

'Why, have you two fallen out again?'

'No... no, we haven't. She's looking well.'

Over tea, Elizabeth spoke of her reunion with Hannah, and how Hannah's daughter had enjoyed little Catherine's company so much. 'So all this time, Cathy was Lady Hannah Wyatt, Lou's aristocratic neighbour.'

'What a coincidence. Can you believe the chances of that happening... millions?' Then Christina smiled. 'I bet that put Louisa's nose out of joint.'

'Yes, I think it did.'

When her mother left the room to ask Susan to make more tea, Elizabeth remembered how Louisa had shunned her on her return to England. Bertie answered the door with lowered eyes and red cheeks, making excuses that Louisa was out, yet he kept her standing at the door without inviting her inside. She left the house feeling wretched, knowing her sister was probably watching her departure from a bedroom window. 'Hannah's mother is nice,' Elizabeth said when her mother returned to the drawing room. 'At first, I was certain she disliked me. Gradually she warmed, probably because of Catherine; she couldn't leave her alone. I used to watch her chat to Catherine for hours.'

'Bess, tell me about the cemetery where Papa and William are laid to rest.'

'I can tell you no more than I did in my letter, Mamma,' Elizabeth said, 'Ex-British servicemen look after them. They work for the Imperial War Graves Commission who really is doing a wonderful job. Why don't you go over and see for yourself?'

'I want to. We were going to go in the spring before you... before you left Buckingham. Somehow I never got around to it. I couldn't bear to go without you.'

'Thomas Cook has excursions to the battlefields. Book a trip with them. Go now before the weather turns.'

'I will, but would you come with me, Bess? I'll not go with a lot of strangers.'

'Of course I will, but if we go together then I'd rather we travelled alone.'

'Well, that's settled then.' Christina smiled and tapped her daughter's hand. 'Bess, you haven't mentioned John's name once. I hope everything is all right between you,' she said and then casually added, 'I'll invite him over for supper. I expect you'll be pleased to see him.'

'Yes, of course,' Elizabeth replied, suddenly feeling cold and filled with anxiety.

*

During the silences over supper, John kept looking towards Elizabeth. She returned his smile, but found it difficult to hold his eye. When supper was finished they went for a walk. Her hand felt hot and uncomfortable in his as they strolled across a field. Elizabeth would often find an excuse to let go of his hand to pick a flower, while all the time her mind was filled with thoughts of Hannah as she listened to John complain about her long absence, and how much he had missed her. She kept quiet throughout and when they were out of sight of the house he stopped complaining, pressed her against a tree and kissed her.

'God, I've missed you,' he said running his hands over her body. He kissed her again and before she could prevent it, he pushed his hand between her legs. She felt sudden revulsion.

'No John! Don't... don't do that!'

'What's the matter?'

'I would just rather you didn't do it.'

'I've missed you. I want you, now, against this tree.'

'No John! I don't want to do it.' She looked into his eyes. In them, she saw hurt and confusion. She realized that, since they had become lovers, it was the first time she had refused him. 'I'm sorry, but this is not the place,' she said pushing him away from her. 'Later perhaps, when Mamma has gone to bed.'

'You're fussy all of a sudden,' he said sulkily. 'What's the matter with you? You've practically ignored me all evening.'

'John, there's something I have to tell you.'

He sighed heavily. 'What?'

'I'm...' The word, *pregnant,* seemed to stick in her throat. All she could manage was to meet his eye in the hope that he would guess.

'What?' he said, unfastening a button between the swell of her breasts. He bent and kissed them. She repelled his affections in a rage and cried out for him to stop. 'We're engaged aren't we?' he said forcing his lips on hers.

'Please stop!' she snapped, 'I'm not yours yet, so just leave me alone.'

In another struggle to be free of him she lost her balance and fell. John quickly threw himself above her, his weight pinning her to the ground. When he forced himself into her, she felt nothing other the shame of her past welling up in her eyes. She lay motionless, a corpse for him to do with as he wished. Yet the corpse's eyes filled with tears, and when he groaned, a sound that once excited her, it now reminded her of the same sickly sound she used to hear from her German guards as they finished with her.

When John moved from her, she glared at him while he casually began to search his jacket pocket for his cigarette case. 'You could have joined in. You didn't have to lie there like a dummy.'

'You'll never have me again. Do you hear me? It's over between us!'

'Stop being so melodramatic, Elizabeth. You know you wanted it as much as I did.'

'You arrogant pig. You've just raped me!'

'Rape! That's a laugh.' She slapped his face hard and was hit in return.

'Don't you dare slap me!' His bright red face was so close to hers the spittle from his distorted mouth showered Elizabeth's hand that was covering her stinging cheek. He rose to his feet, his teeth gritted and fists clenched without thought or concern for what he had done.

'You stay away for God knows how long. What kept you there? Not your bloody sister, I bet. There was someone else, wasn't there? You've been fucking someone else. Tell me, tell me you've been–'

'YES! With someone who made me feel clean,' Elizabeth cried, looking up at him through hateful eyes. 'Every day, sometimes we were at it two or three times a day–'

'You tart! You bloody tart.'

She raised her arm to protect herself against another blow which struck her at the side of her head. He then crouched down beside her and looked into a pair of frightened eyes.

'You're no different than the whores I had in France. Worse, at least they gave me a bloody good time.' He walked up and down attempting to light a cigarette then crouched down beside her again. 'No wonder your precious David cleared off. He knew you to be a whore. How many men did you fuck on that farm eh, how many?'

Elizabeth began to weep while John paced up and down, talking more to himself than to the frightened figure on the ground. She heard him say what a lucky escape he had had; that she could find some other mug to bring up her little brat. She would be the last person in the world he would ever marry now, boasting how easily she could be replaced and told her about his other woman. She listened, but said nothing. There was little point in telling him that she was carrying his child. Too much had been said that could never be forgotten.

When he was gone, she rolled onto her back and looked up into a darkening sky at Polaris winking at her. It should not have ended like that - not like that. She thought of Hannah's offer to live with her - how happy they would be together. Elizabeth gazed up at the faint but familiar shapes of Ursa Major and Orion, and wondered if, at that very moment, Hannah was looking up at them too.

Chapter 9

At breakfast the following morning, Christina knew that there was something wrong. Elizabeth was unusually quiet and the attempt that she had made to hide the bruise on her cheek had failed. 'Mamma,' she said. 'I'm no longer going to marry John.'

Christina's face crumpled and she began to fire a barrage of questions at her daughter who sat in silence. Finally, when Christina asked if there was someone else, Elizabeth lowered her eyes. 'I knew it. You've been carrying on with another man, haven't you?'

'Mamma, please do not presume the worst of me.'

'Then what is it? What has happened? You've ruined the best chance of marriage you had. Not every man would take on another man's−' Elizabeth leapt from her chair and began to leave the room. 'Elizabeth, come back here,' Christina cried. 'You'll sit down and explain yourself.'

'Mamma, I am almost twenty-six,' Elizabeth said calmly, 'so please do not speak to me as if I were a child.'

'You are behaving like one! This is still my house and you'll do as I say when you are in it otherwise you can leave.' She gasped as the words left her lips. 'Bess… I didn't mean that.'

'Yes you did Mamma. If that is what you want then I'll start packing.'

'No!' Christina cried, taking her daughter's hand. 'Please Bess, I'm sorry. Sit down. Let's just be calm about this…' Christina's voice trailed away and her chin suddenly began to tremor. She stood and turned from her daughter, her eyes finding refuge through the dining room window. 'I couldn't bear it if you went away again as you did before. Please promise you won't leave me. I shall be so lonely without you and Catherine. I was saying to Susan last week that I hoped you and John would have made this your home.'

'We would have lived at the school, but that's now history.' She looked up and sighed. 'For heaven's sake Mamma, turn round, I can't talk to you with your back to me.'

'I can't...'

Elizabeth heard the wobbly tone of her mother's voice. She rose, feeling a sudden wave of affection towards her. 'There, there, Mamma… it's all over, we're friends again. Hush now. You know how much you mean to me, don't you?' Christina's thin lips made a slight movement, but there was no sound. For a brief moment the two women stood motionless in each other's arms. When they parted, Elizabeth kissed her mother's cheek and walked to the window. She looked towards the sloping landscape filled with the first signs of autumn. 'I grew up loving my Papa thinking that all men were like him, but they're not.'

'Bess darling… you seemed so happy together. What has happened between you?'

Elizabeth turned from the window and faced her mother. 'Sit down, Mamma. I'll get Susan to make some more tea.'

'I've had enough tea, Bess,' she sighed. 'Is it definitely over between you and John?'

'Yes. I don't think he ever loved me, anyway. It would never have worked. I know that now.'

'Then I must tell you something before you hear it from someone else…'

'Don't bother, Mamma. John has already told me about his other woman. I'm only surprised you didn't let me know about her.'

'It might not have been true and you wouldn't have thanked me for telling you.'

'Well, it is. I don't mind. It makes it all the easier for me. He needed a wife, any wife, so he could have his new job. I hope the girl will be happy with him. She will never have him to herself. I suspect he will never be happy with himself. He's simply another victim of the war.'

'I don't understand.'

'No, Mamma. I do not expect you do.'

*

Later, during the afternoon, Elizabeth walked to the lake and sat at the spot where she and David had always sat. For two hours, she weighed up her future. In a few months she would not be able to hide her pregnancy. If she left Buckingham, she would be deserting her mother. If she stayed, her mother would have to face further gossip. Elizabeth knew she had to leave, but go where? She could not accept Hannah's offer to live at the Manor. Life would be intolerable. She would be living in the shadows of the house, creeping from one room to another, unable to look Edward in the eye, and worse; Louisa would know why she was there.

To the sound of squabbling ducks, she left the lake deciding to return to France and stay with Sylvie, at least until she could find a suitable home for herself and Catherine... and her unborn child.

As Elizabeth walked back to the house along a footpath close to the road, she heard the sudden sound of screeching car tyres followed by an eerie silence then a sickening crunch of metal and breaking glass. She quickly made her way round the tall hedge and saw a dying pheasant in the middle of the road, flapping one wing, the other, still, bleeding and broken. She broke its neck then, further along the road, she saw a car resting against a tree with steam gushing from the burst radiator. She gasped aloud when she recognized it.

Slumped across the wheel was George Turner, motionless, with blood oozing from a large wound on his head. The car stank of cigar smoke and the sickly odour of leaking petroleum. She remembered Trisha's ambulance and how it had exploded. Forcing open the door she clutched her father-in-law under each arm and found hidden strength as she pulled him from his seat.

'Wake up Papa, please, help me.' With a Herculean effort, Elizabeth pulled him clear.

Elizabeth felt sick as she dragged his heavy body away from the flames. In her mind she heard shells exploding and saw visions of ambulances enveloped in flames. Another sound brought her sharply back to the present - whommmphhh - as the leaking petroleum burst into a ball of fire. She was suddenly blown off her feet and pitched forward by the blast from George Turner's exploding car.

Elizabeth tried to rise, but a great weight seemed to descend upon her holding her down. She relaxed, defeated by the effort. A machine somewhere on the farm spluttered into life, putt-putt-putt it went as if a distant machine gun. The cries of men echoed in her ears, the fear and loneliness she felt as her ambulance burned, Margaret Wheeler's staring eyes, the bayonet at her throat as two German soldiers pulled her out from the ditch. Little Catherine's voice cried out in her mind. She saw David's face. He smiled at her. Was she dying? She laid her head on the ground and listened to her breathing growing weaker.

*

A week later, Elizabeth returned home from the hospital. She sat in her bedroom and began to write a letter to Hannah. It was never going to be an easy letter to write and indeed she struggled trying to find the words she needed to say. At last, as the early evening light began to fade, she finished it.

My darling Hannah,

You see - I am now using your name because this is a new start between us.

I have lost my baby. I was involved in an accident which caused me to miscarry. Apart from concussion and a few cuts and bruises I seemed to have survived unscathed.

My father-in-law crashed his car trying to avoid a pheasant. They are such stupid birds. He is still very ill. All I can do is keep my fingers crossed. If he survives it will be because of a surgeon's skill rather than divine providence. If he dies then, as with my baby, it was meant to be. My mother visits him regularly. It's her new mission in life, as though it has given her some purpose. Sometimes, I don't think he even knows she is there, but it makes her happy to be of some use.

I am no longer engaged to marry John, so you no longer have to be sickened by any thoughts of us together. He didn't know about the baby and now he never will. He was convinced I was sleeping with someone in Sussex - if he only knew. Anyhow, he said some hateful things and although I believe he said them because he was hurt, the things he said came from his heart and I can never forgive him for saying them. Now I am footloose and fancy-free. There will be no more lovers in my life; I want to live without them. I'm now celibate. I shall devote my life to my darling Catherine.

After the Service of Remembrance next month, my mother and I are going to France for a few days to visit my father and brother's graves. I am taking Catherine with me so she can see where her grandfather and uncle are buried.

Hannah darling, I have made some major decisions. I will no longer be coming down to Sussex as I said I would, at least not for a while. It would be unfair to you, unfair to Edward who loves you, and unfair to me who adores you. I have decided to start a new life. I could see in your eyes when we said goodbye at the station that you knew it was over between us, we both knew that, didn't we? Please do not be upset my love; we could not continue in 'that way' any longer, not without someone getting hurt. Please don't come up here to see me. If you love me, please don't do that. I think we have spent the passion we had for each other - now let us be friends, sisters. You said you always would have liked to have had a sister, let her be me. What I'm struggling to say my love is, I have decided to leave England and live in France - permanently. If I do not go to France I shall come to you in Sussex and that will ruin my determination to leave you alone with your family.

My mother does not know yet that I am going to move across the

Channel. It will hurt her very much I know and I feel awful about it, but I must find a life for Catherine and myself. France is the country of her birth. It is also where I fell in love with you and it is where Robert, Papa and William are now at rest, so you see, it is intrinsically tied up with my life. France draws me back to it and I have not the strength or will to fight it.

Write me hundreds of letters. Visit me, but wait a year. By then, I may be able to face you without throwing myself at your feet.

Hannah, I will always love you.

Take good care of yourself, my dearest, dearest Hannah.

With all my love and kisses.

Your unworthy Bess.

Elizabeth called Catherine. As they walked together along the narrow lane to the post-box, she could smell the decay of summer, their feet crunching through the first few crispy golden brown leaves of autumn. Above them an arrowhead of Canada Geese stretched across a dull, cloudless sky. When they reached the postbox, Catherine begged her mother to lift her so that she may post the letter. As it dropped inside the box, Elizabeth tried to smile at Catherine's excitement. The walk home seemed long and lonely. Catherine, oblivious to the storm raging in her mother's heart, hurried ahead, wanting to reach home in time to help her grandmother and Harry feed the chickens. Elizabeth followed, watching her daughter skipping, singing a French nursery rhyme, stopping only to catch the odd falling leaf. She smiled at the sight of her daughter's raised arms and spinning body - David's precious gift to her.

Catherine rushed ahead to her grandmother. Elizabeth left her daughter with Christina and climbed the stairs to her bedroom. She closed the door behind her, curled up on her bed and closed her eyes. Between her fingers she felt the diamond pendant round her neck. Her pretty features distorted as the tears began to leak from her eyes.

Chapter 10

The weather was mild for November. The sky was clear of cloud and a low sun shone down on a gathering crowd by the new war memorial, outside St Peter and St Paul's church in Buckingham. All watched as the approaching parade marched towards them to the accompaniment of the town band. Elizabeth stood with her mother who was holding Catherine's hand. Beside them were her twin sisters who had come to remember their father and brother.

As the band approached, Elizabeth noticed little swagger in the solemn step of the civilians who were once soldiers. There was no humour, unlike the times she had watched them marching towards the front in Flanders. Then they sang and joked, as if out on a country stroll. Those who were brave enough, or liked to think they were a lady's man, shouted out asking for a date on their return, which encouraged others to do the same until the bark of the Sergeant-Major brought them to order again. Elizabeth remembered waving back at them as she stood beside her ambulance with Hannah. It seemed ludicrous to her now, that the God to whom Elizabeth prayed for their safe return, is the very God the congregation was about to worship in remembering their sacrifice.

When the parade came to a halt, the men dispersed with the others around the memorial. Hanging from the left breast of the men's chests were colourful ribbons above shining medals, trinkets from a grateful government for subjecting them to such horror. Above her right breast, Christina wore the medals of her first husband and her son. Elizabeth wore her own medals. She had given Robert's medals to his parents. A man passing her recognised the Military Medal and the thin green and red striped ribbon of the Croix de Guerre. He stopped and suggested that she removed the medals from the left side and pin them to the right.

'Medals worn on the left are for recipients only,' he said pompously. 'When you wear them on behalf of another, they should be worn on the right.'

An old soldier caught hold of the pompous fellow's arm in a firm grip, pulling him aside and whispered something to him not fit for a young lady's ears. He returned to Elizabeth who was embarrassed by it all.

'Don't you listen to him, my duck. He were only out in France at the end and then nowhere near the line.'

Behind the great walrus moustache and piercing blue eyes, Elizabeth saw a friendly, sympathetic face. Her eyes lowered to the Victoria Cross hanging beside the two medals of the South African War and three from the Great War. It reminded her of another Victoria Cross that she had seen carved into Portland stone. Her mind wandered back to France as she thought of Hannah's late twin brother, James Somerville, the Viscount Deerfield. She tried to imagine what he would look like if he were standing before her now. Would he be as handsome as his sister is beautiful? Would he be the same pompous oaf as Lord Westerland, his cousin? Elizabeth smiled warmly into the weather-beaten face of the old soldier, as he took his place beside her when the service began.

After a few hymns and prayers, the plaintive song of the *Last Post* echoed from a sad, single bugle, which rang round the churchyard. During the two minutes of silence that followed, only the last restless rustling leaves and a distant barking dog could be heard. All eyes were lowered in private thoughts. Elizabeth remembered many other bugle calls in France. She concentrated on those she had lost and found that she could now think of her father without feeling sick with grief. Of Robert, whose life and children she was destined not to share, and of her brother William, fated with his generation never to grow old. She thought of Bella, whose lovely smile would fade from her memory with time and Margaret Wheeler whose staring eyes would remain with her for the rest of her life. She thought of David and hoped that his memory had returned him to his family. She would not think of the other faces, the thousands of other faces, because throughout the King's realm, each of those faces would have someone standing by similar memorials remembering them.

As her mind returned to the present, she felt the heat of someone's gaze burning into her bowed head. Her eyes moved and below the brim of her hat she met John's eyes. Elizabeth thought how handsome he looked in his dark blue suit, the Military Cross gleaming in the low November sun. By his side was his wife. Between them both stood a little girl with her teddy in her hand. Elizabeth lowered her eyes. There was no regret.

After the service, she spoke with the old soldier who took her hand in both of his and said, 'A lot of men owe their lives to you girls Miss Brennan, me included.' Then he placed his hat on his head, raised it and said goodbye.

Other ex-servicemen who passed her raised their hats to her too, their eyes lowering to her Military Medal and the Croix de Guerre. Christina and the twins watched this with pride, for there is a gulf between men who have seen action and those who have not been in the show, as unbridgeable as that between the sober and the drunk. Elizabeth knew this too, for there was something in their eyes that only those who had seen fighting understood. She felt a sudden gush of pride swell up inside her and sting her eyes, because she also knew she was considered one of them by them all. For the first time since her return from the war, she felt one of them and her head lifted. Catherine took Elizabeth's hand and pressed against her legs when she saw a tear glint in her mother's eye.

While Christina stood chatting with Jane and Stephanie, Catherine went with her mother to the memorial cross and lingered there. They read the tributes on the laurels and looked at the rows of names etched into the stone. Elizabeth pointed at the names. 'That is your grandfather, Catherine darling, this one here is your Uncle William and this here is Robert Turner, my late husband. I was at school with this man here, and him, and him and his brother here... and I knew this man and his cousin too.' Elizabeth shook her head. 'We are indeed an unlucky generation.'

'Did my daddy die in the war?'

'No, but he was hurt in the war.'

'Where is he now?'

'He's lost, my love. Your daddy is out there somewhere trying to find us. Listen darling, tomorrow we are going to France. That will be exciting, won't it? Do you remember France?'

Catherine nodded and smiled. 'Oui, Maman.'

'Bon, ma chérie. Il y a tellement de choses intéressantes à voir à Paris. Ensuite, je vais te montrer Amiens et Albert. Ça nous permettra de parler français. Quel dommage qua ta grand-mère ne la parl pas.

Catherine looked over towards her grandmother then back into her mother's smiling face. She put her hand to her mouth, hunched her shoulders and giggled. Elizabeth bent and kissed her pretty, upturned face. 'Je t'aime, Catherine, ma chérie. Je t'aime.'

Chapter 11

Christina gazed beyond the cemetery wall, out across the scarred landscape and back to the gravestones that bore the names of her late husband and son. 'Danny my love,' she whispered, running her fingers across his name as if it were the warm soft skin of his face, the prickly hair of his dark moustache as his lips moved in a smile. Her eyes then settled on the name of her son. The neatly carved letters in the white Portland stone stared back at her with an oval face, blue eyes and a youthful grin. He had not grown a day older in her mind, yet she had aged eight years since he leant out of the carriage waving at her. It seemed as if it were only yesterday that she stood with her daughters on the station platform - her eyes fixed on them both yet only seeing her son.

She remembered the first time she held him, the first word he spoke and the first step he took. She remembered how he cried when she left him on his first day at school, how shy he was when he brought home his first girl, and how young and proud he looked the first time she saw him in uniform. She also remembered the pain she felt on his birthday after he was dead.

Christina, who had chosen to wear black, slowly walked between the rows of headstones towards the shelter with her daughter and granddaughter. She glanced down at other names, names that meant nothing to her only to some other grieving mother. In the shelter she sat on the stone bench, holding two small jars into which she had placed some soil taken from each of the graves. With a trembling hand, she attempted to write her husband and son's names on the labels. Elizabeth took the pen from her mother and completed the task. Christina's eyes lifted to the numerous headstones lined up with meticulous precision, then beyond the cemetery at the scarred landscape half covered with red poppies.

Elizabeth could see the pain in her mother's face as she surveyed the area of the old battlefield where the flower of Ulster had left Ireland's green fields to wilt in the chalky, blood-soaked soil of Picardy. Elizabeth held Catherine close to her body and said nothing.

Catherine looked up at her mother through her father's sapphire eyes. She pouted her little lips, pressed them to her mother's large soft mouth, and kissed her. 'Maman, pourquoi est-ce que—'

'Catherine darling, we only speak French when we're alone, otherwise Grandma will not understand what we're saying.'

'Why is Grandma crying?' Catherine whispered.

'Because she is unhappy seeing the graves of your Uncle William and Grandpa.'

'I don't like it here, Bess,' Christina suddenly said. 'It's horrible. My poor little William stuck out here in a foreign place.'

'Don't upset yourself, Mamma. I know it's hard when you see them together for the first time, it brings home the awful truth of it all, but he is with Papa and his friends. Look… just look at their plots, how beautifully they are kept. He is being cared for. They both are.'

'Yes love, the man has done a wonderful job, but I'm sorry, I can't stay here any longer. I want to go home… back to Buckingham. I want to go home to Harry. It's unfair leaving him with Jane.'

Elizabeth kissed her mother's cheek. 'Mamma, *please* stay a little longer. I should like to visit James Somerville's grave and then I should like you to meet Sylvie.'

'Sylvie... Oh *her*! The one that had you for the three years I didn't.'

'She also had me when I was a prisoner and gave me the strength to carry on. It was Sylvie who took a beating to save me one and it was Sylvie who brought Catherine into this world when the midwife was late arriving. So please Mamma, don't say such a thing to me again.'

Christina brought her handkerchief to her nose. 'I'm sorry, Bess. I'm upset. You stay and visit her. I'll take Catherine home with me.'

'Catherine is staying with me,' Elizabeth said, looking down at her little girl. 'There's no reason to rush back home now that we are here. If you are against meeting Sylvie, then go back to Paris for a couple of days, see the sights and we'll meet up with you there.'

'Let's go back to the hotel, Bess. I want to leave this place. Look at it... you can still see the shell-holes in the ground. God, it makes me feel sick to think what William and your Papa must have suffered.' She looked around her, shivered and suddenly said, 'No, I've made up my mind. I'm returning to England. I'll find my own way back. Someone is bound to speak English.'

'I won't have you travelling alone. If you must go then I'll return with you.'

'There is no need. I am quite capable of making my own way back.'

'No, you're not. I'm going home with you,' Elizabeth said. 'That's an end to it.'

Back at the hotel, Christina washed and packed while Elizabeth went to the restaurant with Catherine. When a waiter arrived, she encouraged her daughter to order her own drink, and smiled at the shy way Catherine spoke to him. When at last Christina joined her at the table, the language reverted to English. As Christina spoke, she felt a woman's eyes burn into her from the adjacent table. The woman, wearing a large black hat, leaned closer and smiled sympathetically.

'Have you been visiting a loved one?'

'My late husband and son,' said Christina, happy to hear another English voice.

'A husband *and* son. Oh dear, what a dreadful business that war was, and what was it all for? We have just seen where our son is buried. It's our first visit.'

The man joined in the conversation. 'The name's Trollope. No relation to the author, I quickly add. Our son was in the Medical Corps, based here in Albert for a bit.'

'He might have known Elizabeth. She was billeted here, driving ambulances.'

The man's face lit up. 'Our boy wrote home about you girls. Said you did a wonderful job. Alas, he was killed when the Germans shelled Albert during the early morning of their March offensive. I expect you girls were well behind the line by then.'

'We thought you were French when you sat at the table,' said Mrs Trollope to Elizabeth. 'And what about you my little angel? I bet you'll break a few hearts when you're older,' she said to Catherine. 'You speak the language so well and so does your little one. Is your husband here with you, Mrs...?'

'Mrs Turner and I am Mrs Wilding,' Christina quickly interrupted. To change the subject she asked Mrs Trollope where in England she lived.

'We're from Kent... Maidstone.'

'We're from Buckingham in the county of that name.'

'When are you returning home?' Mrs Trollope asked.

'This afternoon.'

'Perhaps we can travel together. We're also leaving today.'

Conversation then flowed easily between the three elders while Elizabeth sat in silence, occasionally kissing the head of her sleepy daughter.

'Bess dear, I have an idea,' Christina said, bringing her daughter back from 1918. 'If you wish to stay on and visit your friend, I can travel home with Mr and Mrs Trollope.'

'We shall be happy for the company,' said Mrs Trollope, smiling at Elizabeth. 'Where does your friend live, Mrs Turner?'

'In Amiens... we met during the war.'

'It must have been awful for you, so close to the shelling.'

'I was never anywhere near the shelling, Mrs Trollope.'

Christina glanced at her daughter and gave her a tender smile.

*

The following morning at breakfast, Elizabeth recognized the gangly, bushy-moustached gardener she had met during her previous visit with Hannah. He was trying to explain something to a waitress, but the young woman's smile began to lose its light as his linguistic struggles increased by the second. Finally her patience expired and she left him in a huff. The old soldier shrugged his shoulders and rose from his seat. As he passed Elizabeth's table, he glanced at her and stopped.

'I remember you,' he said. 'It's that lovely hair of yours. A feller can't forget that, begging your pardon. You were with a toff... er... another lady, very posh, like.'

Elizabeth smiled. 'Yes, I was and you are right, she is very posh, Mr Jacks.'

'Gawd, yer remember me name. Well, well, call me Jacko, everyone does. So, yer come back again, eh?'

'This time with my daughter. We're staying for a few more days, aren't we my love?'

'This yer little girl? Pretty little thing, ain't yer mate?'

Catherine looked up at Jacko with a puzzled expression and when he asked her name she replied in a shy low voice, 'Catherine.'

'Catherine is it? That's a nice name, ain't it me precious?'

'Mr Jacks... Jacko, do sit down and have some tea.'

'Ta, I will. It's the first time I've been to this place. It's a bit too posh for me, like. Usually I stay at 'ome and cook me own breakfast, but occasionally, like today, I like something out, bit of a treat like. Only they don't cook an English breakfast. Croissants and jam and they can't make a cup of tea to save their lives. I don't call that a breakfast for a working man.'

Elizabeth smiled. 'Do you not have a wife, Mr Jacks?'

'Not bleeding likely, begging yer pardon Miss. Been a bachelor all me life.'

Elizabeth poured Jacko a cup of tea and passed it to him. 'We're going over to La Boisselle after breakfast.'

'Why there?'

'To pay my respects to my friend's brother, then we're off to Thiepval to see my father and brother before we leave this afternoon,' she replied, startled by the quantity of sugar Jacko spooned into his tea.

'Father and brother you say. Now 'ang about, let me think…' he said, screwing up his eyes in thought, 'Lieutenant and Private Brennan, Royal Irish Rifles.'

'That's right.'

'It's not easy to forget a father and son together bless 'em. Was it you that left the flowers yesterday?'

'Yes, it was. My mother and I.'

'And me, Mummy,' whispered Catherine, regaining her courage to speak.

'Yes darling, you too,' Elizabeth smiled, kissing her daughter's head.

'I've seen another young woman about your age visit those two graves. French, she was.'

'That would be Sylvie, the friend I'm off to see in Amiens this afternoon. Mr Jacks, I hope I will not offend you, but would you accept this?' she said, searching through her purse and handing Jacko a banknote. 'My father and brother's graves always look so beautifully cared for. You do such a wonderful job.'

'No, I can't take it Miss. I'm only doing my bit for the lads who didn't make it back home. That's reward enough for me.'

'You took my friend's money.'

'Yea, well that were different. She were looking down 'er nose at me. Anyway, it ain't me that looks after your kin's graves. It's me mate.'

'Then give it to him.'

''E won't take it. And something else, 'e won't let anyone else do your loved ones' graves, either. That's 'is job, 'e says.'

'Why? Did he know them? Did he serve in their regiment?'

'Dunno. I doubt if 'e served with a Paddy regiment.'

'He sounds a nice fellow.'

'The best.'

'How long have you worked together, Mr Jacks?'

'Since February, 1920. I knew him before that though. We shared a ward in 'ospital like. Against all the odds we became pals, 'im being a gent like. I was cut up a bit, wounded if yer know what I mean. 'E were in the bed beside me. The poor lad used to just sit and stare at you with his big blue eyes, just like yours,' Jacko said winking at Catherine who was looking up at him. 'Apart from his gammy leg 'e's a lot better, and the feller's got 'is voice back. Not 'is memory though, poor bugger, begging yer pardon Miss. Dead posh 'e is. Well, I always knew 'e were a gent, if you know what I mean. You don't have to speak to know that. You can tell, can't yer?' Jacko took another gulp of tea and wiped his mouth with his sleeve. 'All I can say is, I'm glad 'e came to me after 'e 'ad that bust-up with some farmer...'

Jacko's voice became an echo in Elizabeth's mind, his face a blur as the room blackened and closed in on Elizabeth. Her heart raced so quickly she felt sick and could hardly breathe. She took a sip of tea, but her shaking hand made her spill it, annoying a waitress who passed close by.

'You all right, Miss?'

'I'm f-fine... really.' She took another sip of tea and forced a smile. 'Has he... your friend... ever explained why he had a *bust up* with the farmer?'

'Over a woman... didn't like to talk about it. Poor Davie looked more miserable than when I first met him in 'ospital. Been jilted, you see. Took it very 'ard 'e did.'

With all the calmness she could muster, Elizabeth said, 'Been jilted?'

'Yer sure yer're all right, Miss? You look upset.'

'I'm sorry. I have something in my eye,' she said wiping it with her handkerchief. 'You say your friend had been jilted by this woman, Mr Jacks.'

'Well, not exactly, but that's 'ow I see it. The lad loved the girl, was certain she loved 'im back. Davie went ter see the farmer, 'er step-dad like. The farmer slung 'im out. Told 'im that she were marrying some other geezer.'

'And did she marry someone else?'

Jacko shrugged. 'Dunno. Apparently, she were two timing the lad.'

'Your friend believed that?' Elizabeth gasped. 'I'm sorry, Mr Jacks. It's just that... I mean... I can't believe any woman would do that to the man she loved.'

'Yea, well, I dunno, I'm a bachelor like, but as I said, 'e wouldn't talk much about it so I ain't got the 'ole story, like. In fact, 'e wouldn't speak about 'er... except to say she were the best thing that 'ad ever 'appened to 'im. Women eh! Now yer know why I'm still a bachelor.

Anyway, it's 'er loss and my gain.' He stretched and grinned at
Catherine. 'Well I can't sit chin-wagging all morning as much as I'd
like ter. Got ter earn me crust. Now Miss, are yer sure yer all right, cos
yer've come over a bit queer, like.'

'I'm fine, Mr Jacks. I haven't been all that well recently. Seeing my
father and brother's graves always has a bad effect on me.'

'Know what yer mean, Miss. I see a lot of ladies in tears. It's
upsetting, even for an old soljer like me, twenty-five years under the
colours. So if yer sure yer all right, I'm off. Ta for the tea… it were
nice seeing yer again ... and it were very nice to meet you, young
lady,' he said, imitating a posh voice to Catherine, who smiled as she
pressed her cheek into a raised shoulder.

'Is your friend working today?'

'It's 'is day off but 'e lives in *Avenue Georges Clemenceau.*' Jacko
glanced at his pocket watch. ''E'll be 'ome at this hour with
Mauricette and little Audréy, if yer'd like to knock on 'is door. Say I
sent yer, 'e won't mind.'

'Mauricette and Audréy?'

'Yea, Mauricette's nice for a Frenchie. Cooks a decent bit of grub
does Mauricette. Audréy's the daughter, cracking little girl.' He
sniffed and ran his sleeve across his nose. 'Yer'll find 'is 'ouse close to
the railway station, opposite a café called, *Café au Départ.* Number
15. If yer shy about calling, being a lady like, I'll tell 'im where yer're
staying.'

'No! Please don't. I shan't trouble him on his day off.'

'Shame. Still, Jacko gets all the luck. See yer then. Cheerio
sweetheart,' he said, pinching Catherine's cheek.

With a wave, Jacko disappeared from the restaurant and then the
hotel. Elizabeth buried her face into her hands trying to control the
tears beginning to flood her eyes. Catherine put her arms around her
mother's bowed, shaking head. 'What's the matter, Mummy? Why are
you crying?' she said, her own little chin beginning to quiver. 'Did that
funny man make you cry?'

'No darling,' Elizabeth forced a smile. 'He's a nice man. Mummy
has got a headache, that's all.'

*

An hour later, Elizabeth sat drinking coffee as she looked through
the window towards the terraced houses opposite her. She focused her
attention on number 15, while Catherine patiently sat colouring
pictures in a book bought for her by Lady Somerville. Elizabeth's

heart began to beat faster when the door opened and a young woman appeared, holding the hand of a little girl. She was laughing. A man with dark hair combed in the British style followed them out. It was David. He smiled into the woman's eyes when she turned to him. He said something to her and she playfully hit out at him. He recoiled as though the punch had hurt him, and when they both stopped laughing, he bent and picked up the girl, lifted her high into the air and kissed her. David waved them both goodbye; watching, until they turned the corner. For a second, he peered towards the café as though he was thinking of crossing over. Elizabeth quickly moved her head behind the curtain and held her breath. When she took the courage to look again, she saw the door to his house closing behind him.

'Quickly Catherine, we must go.'

Ignoring the sudden protest from Catherine, Elizabeth threw her book and crayons into her bag. She left money on her table to cover the cost of her drinks and hurriedly left the café, with her daughter continuing to complain about their hasty departure. To avoid passing David's door, they walked across to the station and boarded a waiting taxicab, which took them to Thiepval. At that moment she needed to be near her father, to talk to him, feel his love for her rise from his cold bed and warm her the way it used to when she was a child.

'Papa,' she whispered to the name etched into the stone, 'David looked so happy. I could have made him happy, I know I could have.'

'Mummy, why are you whispering?' whispered Catherine.

'I'm talking to my Papa, darling.'

'Can he hear you?'

'I hope so, my love. I really hope so.'

Elizabeth was content that David looked so well and was pleased she had seen him. It was as though she had found the body and could at last bury the dead and complete her mourning. She decided that she too had a life to live and must live it. She walked back to the little shelter where a few days before she had sat with her mother. Catherine began to yawn and rub her eyes.

'Come and sit beside Mummy and have a little nap.' Elizabeth said, looking into the face of her daughter, whose eyes began to flutter then, close. Her fingers loosened on the rag doll in her hand and it fell silently to the ground. 'Yes my precious, sleep. Your Papa doesn't know about you, so I think it is better not to see him and upset him. He has his own life now and we must find ours.' Then as if talking to herself, she said, 'We'll spend a few days with Auntie Sylvie then perhaps go to Ireland and live there. We can't live in France now.'

A light breeze blew across a field strewn with poppies, which sent a rush of colour rippling through the valley. It was so peaceful where the two of them sat. The only sounds to be heard were the rustling leaves from the Irish yews and the regular light breathing of her sleeping child. Although isolated, she felt no fear, no apprehension. Around her were the sleeping souls of her people; her father, brother and the ghosts of Ulstermen. This quiet solemn setting, once choked with death and destruction was now, for her, the safest place in the world. She looked around at the young men's graves and whispered, '*Ay, but to die, and go we know not where; To lie in cold obstruction and to rot*.' Elizabeth shuddered and held Catherine closer to her body. Was that *Hamlet* or *Measure for Measure*? At that moment she could not remember. What did it matter anyway? The words were chilling, whatever the play.

She woke with a start at the sound of the taxi's horn, an impatient driver looking forward to his lunch. Gently, she shook Catherine and together they went to the two headstones that meant so much to her. She bent and kissed them both then told Catherine to do the same.

'Bye, Papa, William,' she whispered. 'I'll come back and see you again, but I'm not sure when.'

Elizabeth took one last look, then walked to the cab and left Thiepval, for her hotel in the small town of Albert.

*

After their lunch, Elizabeth took Catherine for a short walk. 'Are you feeling sleepy again, my darling?' Elizabeth said, seeing her daughter yawn. 'It's all this fresh air. Come on, you can have another little nap.'

They returned to the hotel and, while Catherine slept, Elizabeth wrote a postcard to Hannah. When she finished, she glanced at her watch; just over an hour to go before their train left Albert for Amiens. She sat and opened a book, but could not concentrate on it. Words became a face, sentences eyes and paragraphs memories. She did not hear the first light tap on the door, but she heard the second, which was louder and more determined. She looked over towards Catherine to see if it had disturbed her then rose and went to the door.

'Hello, Elizabeth.'

Her name sounded wonderful on David's lips. At first, she was visibly shocked by his presence, although she knew she should not have been. She looked into his face, the face that had kept her awake at nights for so long. He looked so well. The scar running down his cheek had weathered, no longer so prominent and obvious to the eye. When he moved towards her, she retreated a step.

'David!' It was all her vocal cords had the strength to utter.

'Are you alone?'

'No,' she said awkwardly. 'I have my daughter with me.'

'Yes, Jacko said you had a daughter.'

'Please… come in. She's asleep.'

Elizabeth's eyes lowered to the ground as she stepped aside to allow David to enter the room. He looked towards the little girl lying on the bed. Her hair, the same dark brown as his, crowned closed eyes and pouting, cupid lips.

'Jacko guessed it was you, the girl he discussed... the farmer's step-daughter. You made it rather obvious to him by your emotion,' he said, his eyes still on Catherine. His voice had the same upper-class tone of Edward Wyatt. She smiled to herself and wondered what her mother would make of that. 'I took some lunch over to Jacko. He described you perfectly. Forgive me. I… I had to come and see you, Elizabeth.'

'It was a shock to me… hearing that you were here.'

'Yes, I imagine it was.'

'Thank you for looking after my father and brother's graves. How did you know?'

'I have known for almost three years. It was the name Brennan that attracted my attention, your twin sisters' name. I looked in the cemetery register; there it all was: your address in Buckingham, although not the farm, your mother Christina, daughters Louisa, Elizabeth, Jane and Stephanie.' He cleared his throat and almost whispered the words. 'At first I couldn't believe it… it seemed as if it were an omen, like the time we met by the lake. I prayed you would come here to visit, but time passed and you never did. It felt as if I were serving a prison sentence as I did in the war, not knowing the length of my incarceration, never knowing when the end would come. Then you did come and I missed you.'

'You look well David… happy even.'

He crossed to the window and gazed across the square where he once marched with his men towards the trenches opposite La Boisselle, two evenings before the disastrous attack on the German front line. Images from his past were gradually beginning to flash through his mind as though he were flicking through the pages of a magazine and catching a fleeting glance of faces that he recognized. If only a place name would spring to his mind, somewhere to start looking.

'I am content with what I have and do,' he said at last and turned towards Catherine who rolled over in her sleep. A smile crept to his lips. 'Your daughter is very pretty. I'm surprised she hasn't got your colouring, your lovely hair.'

'She has her father's colouring,' she said, glancing at his profile.

'May I ask what he is like… her father?'

'He is a wonderful man, gentle and kind. I loved… I love him, very much.'

'Good,' he whispered sadly, 'that's how it should be.'

Elizabeth asked about Mauricette at the same instant as he asked if she would like a coffee. They both laughed nervously. She invited him to repeat what he had said.

'I asked if you would like some coffee, unless you would prefer something stronger.'

'I have some cognac here.' She went and took the bottle from her suitcase. 'I'm told it's a very good one, but I haven't any glasses.'

'I'll go and fetch some from the bar downstairs.'

'You'll have to hurry. I have a train to catch.'

'When are you leaving?'

'An hour.'

'So soon!' he exclaimed. Sudden sadness clouded his features. 'Couldn't you catch the next? It leaves this evening.'

'Someone will be waiting.'

'Sylvie?'

Elizabeth smiled. 'You remembered.'

'Forgive me. Of course you must go.'

Their eyes met for a split second, yet it was long enough for his to burn into hers, causing a frisson of excitement to run down her spine. She suddenly felt annoyed with herself - and awkward. Annoyed because inside she had turned to jelly as if she were a lovesick girl in the presence of the man she secretly desired, awkward, because only feet from him slept their daughter, their flesh and blood. Elizabeth would have given her life for him once, yet now, she kept her distance as if he were a stranger to her.

'Perhaps we will just have time for one drink together,' she said, placing the bottle on the chest of drawers, insisting when he said it no longer mattered.

She panicked when he left the room fearing he would not return. She went over to Catherine and stroked her cheek. The child slept, unknowing that the father about whom she had often enquired had just breathed the same air as she. Elizabeth went to the mirror, brushed her hair then anxiously waited for what seemed like a lifetime before the sound of the knock at her door filled her with relief.

David smiled as he entered the room and went to the bottle. He poured some cognac and handed her the drink. There was only an armchair to sit on - she motioned him towards it and sat herself on the edge of the bed. The cognac warmed her stomach. She took another sip, then another - and another.

'David, why didn't you ever try to get in touch with me?' she said in a soft, unsure voice, which lifted his eyes from the floor to meet hers. 'It broke my heart when I returned from Ireland and found you gone.'

Her words made his throat go dry. 'I… I wrote you a letter explaining everything.'

'It was burnt by my stepfather.'

'As a back-up, I gave Mrs Willows a time and rendezvous where we could meet. I waited each day as arranged.'

'My departure from Ireland was delayed a week because of bad weather. Mrs Willows was dead when I returned. She had suffered a heart attack.' Elizabeth could see the shock of the news cloud his eyes as he thought of his old friend and neighbour.

'So that's why she did not return any of my letters,' he said sadly. 'When you never contacted me I thought it was to let me know it was over between us. Your stepfather said you were engaged to marry Jacob Wilson and I was… a temporary distraction.'

'A distraction?' she gasped. 'How could you believe that?' She glanced at Catherine and lowered her voice. 'Is that why you never returned to Buckingham, because you thought I was having fun with you before marrying that great oaf? Do you think me capable of such a thing? Oh David, how could you think that? I loved you, only you.'

He felt wretched at the sound of her words. 'Wilding said he wouldn't give you a penny if I didn't leave the area. I believed him. For your sake, it was better that I left.'

'Please! Say no more.' Her hand shook as she raised her glass to her mouth. 'How could you? Do you think I would marry for *money*?' she cried in a restrained voice, looking down at her daughter again. 'You should have trusted my feelings for you and returned to

Buckingham for me.'

'I did. I was told you had left the area.'

Elizabeth's eyes filled with tears. 'Oh God... you came back.'

'Yes.'

'But why leave... why didn't you just wait?'

'I didn't want to make your life more complicated than it had become.'

'How noble of you,' she snapped. 'So you decided for us both. If you had spoken to me instead of playing the martyr you might not have made your decision so hastily. You have no idea what you did to me, David. No idea what you have done.'

'And your family, didn't they matter?' He said calmly. 'How do you think they felt, Elizabeth? I was nothing. I could give you nothing. They saw our union as a disaster for you. It would have been extremely selfish of me and very unfair to you.'

'Please! Let's not discuss this any further. It's all in the past.' She turned from him unable to face the hurt in his eyes. Each sipped their drink in silence. David stood and offered another drink to Elizabeth. She shook her head. 'So I presume it wasn't Jacob Wilson you married?'

'No, nor did I ever want to. I loathed the man.'

'Do I know your husband?'

'No, you don't know him,' she whispered and glanced at her watch.

He went over to Catherine who stirred in her sleep, looked down into her face and brushed a curl from her forehead with his fingertip. 'I once dreamed that we might...'

She saw him close his eyes when he could not finish the sentence. Elizabeth remained silent. She could not tell him Catherine was his. It was too late for that. Their eyes met again. 'I have to leave very soon.'

'Would you like me to accompany you to the station?'

'It's probably better you didn't.'

He nodded and placed his glass on the chest of drawers. Elizabeth watched him walk to the door. His lame leg had not improved she noticed and guessed it never would. 'Well, goodbye Elizabeth. Thank you for the drink.'

'Please take the bottle now that it has been opened. It was to be a present for my father-in-law. I'll buy him another.'

'Thank you. I'll share it with Jacko. We cannot afford to drink cognac as good as this.' After another silence, he said, 'Will you return to Albert?'

'No.'

'Then I'm happy I came to see you. I should have always regretted missing you a second time. It's a shame we didn't have longer to–'

David did not finish the sentence because Elizabeth went to him holding out a hand, as if in a hurry to say goodbye. In a friendly but formal voice, she heard herself say, 'Thank you again for looking after my father and brother's graves, David. Goodbye, and please take good care of yourself.' Her outstretched hand was taken in his. He caught an involuntary movement of her chin before she managed to control it, but the tear forming in her eye swelled and spilled onto her cheek. He stopped its progress with the edge of his fingertip. Her eyes glistened and the smile which crept to her lips twitched as the muscles in her cheeks tried to hold it. 'I'm being silly.'

He went to the door and opened it, paused and then turned. 'I often wondered why I survived the war when the odds were against me doing so. I tried to reason with myself that I had found the answer when we briefly met in that hospital corridor. Our meeting was timed to the second when my wheelchair stopped beside you. A second either way and…well, who knows? Then I found myself at the farm and you were there. I could hardly believe my prayer to see you again had been answered. I marvelled that, no matter how large or cluttered the world, we were meant to be together. Then the great plan went wrong and what was meant to be was not to be. You brought me back to life, Elizabeth. You made me hope. I was happy, something then I didn't think possible. For that I shall always love you.'

'Oh David! Hold me! Please hold me one last time,' Elizabeth begged and threw herself into his arms. She gripped him to her body and kissed his lips. Then breathing heavily she pushed him away from her and turned from him. 'Go! Go now to your family. Don't make me suffer. Don't destroy what happiness you have found.'

'Elizabeth… what has Jacko told you?'

'Nothing… very little, only where I could find you. I saw you from the café window, with your wife and daughter. You all looked so very happy.'

'You poor girl.'

'I wasn't spying on you, I promise. I simply wanted to see you again.'

'Elizabeth!' he said, taking her arm. 'Mauricette is not my wife. She is my landlord's wife and Audréy is their daughter. They are my friends. I'm teaching Mauricette English in return for less rent.'

Elizabeth caught her breath. Her body almost collapsed with unspeakable relief. She turned and faced him. 'Mauricette is not your wife?'

'No,' he said softly. 'I have no wife. I only ever wanted you.'

'And I haven't a husband, only the memory of one.' He glanced at Catherine. 'She's yours… ours. Look at her she's the spitting image of you, my love. Your eyes, your colour hair, she even has the same birthmark as you on her arm.'

'She's mine?'

'Do you remember when you were unwell... before I went to Ireland? I was going to tell you something when I returned.'

'Vividly. I thought you were going to tell me about your engagement to Jacob.'

'I was going to tell you that I was pregnant. That's why I resigned from teaching. I didn't tell you then because I wanted to surprise you when I returned.'

'Oh my God! What have I done to you?' He took her into his arms and pressed her to his body. 'I deserted you. My God, I deserted you when you needed me most.'

She laid her cheek against his, remembering how close she was to marrying John and having his child. Fate dictated that she lost them both. 'I should have said something to you,' Elizabeth said. 'It was like losing my friend... because we kept secrets. Now I have found her... and you.'

David did not attempt to kiss her or run his hand over her breasts and body as John always did. He only wanted to feel her heart beat against his, her warm breath caressing his ear. His gaze fell across to a little open mouth and closed eyes, whose thick black lashes rested flat against red cheeks warmed by the heat of the room.

'When I discovered you had gone, I couldn't live in Buckingham any longer. I had no wish to be near those who had thrown you out. I went to Amiens and stayed with Sylvie. Catherine was born in Amiens, on the 11th August, 1920. Oh my love, I lived so close to you. I even came to Albert. I would have walked past your home on the way into town. Had I a guardian angel he would have led me to you.'

'He has done so now.'

David went to his daughter. He bent and kissed her cheek. Catherine opened her sleepy eyes and saw a stranger looking down at her. She sat up and grabbed her mother's hand. 'Don't be frightened, darling. It's your Papa. Do you remember me telling you that he was lost? Well, now he has found us.'

Catherine watched through inquisitive young eyes as the man's arm encircled her mummy's waist. She looked up into his face and saw him smile. His hands reached down towards her, a strong grip lifting her from the bed, cradling her close to the heat of his body. She felt his lips on her cheek; her mummy was smiling brightly with tears in her eyes. Catherine had never seen her look so happy. It was all right; there was nothing wrong. She was safe in this man's arms. Catherine turned and gazed into the man's face and instinctively felt she could trust him. She allowed him to kiss her warm cheek again. Her eye caught the scar running down his cheek. She touched it very gently. Then her eyes met his and she said to him in a soft, shy voice…

'Are you *really* my Papa?'

Chapter **12**

A year later

Lady Hannah Wyatt's lips broadened as she caught sight of Elizabeth stepping from the railway carriage at Harrogate. In Elizabeth's arms was her sleeping baby son. Little Catherine followed her mother, holding tightly onto her Aunt Jane's hand. Almost sixteen months had passed, yet when Elizabeth caught Hannah's bright smile, it assured her that the friendship between them was as strong as ever. She handed her baby to Jane and almost jumped into Hannah's outstretched arms. The two women embraced warmly under the curious gazes of others unused to seeing such affection publicly displayed.

'Bess, you look the picture of health,' Hannah said, looking about her, 'but where is your husband? Don't tell me he isn't coming. I've been so looking forward to meeting him.'

'He'll be here in a couple of days. Something came up. He couldn't get away, that's all.' Elizabeth smiled as she placed an arm around Jane's waist. 'Hannah, I should like to introduce you to my sister, Mrs Jane Tidmarsh. She's kindly travelled up with me to help with the children. Jane, may I present, Lady Hannah Wyatt.'

Hannah looked into the dark brown eyes of an attractive young woman and could see a resemblance between the sisters in her smile. 'Hello, Jane. I may call you Jane?'

Jane's wide, full lips parted as she consented and took the gloved hand whose grip was firm in hers. Seeing Jane and Elizabeth together, Hannah realized how unlike Louisa they both looked. The three sisters each had the same ingredients yet they were so differently dispensed. Hannah's mind went back to Louisa, who had never come to say goodbye before she left Sussex and moved back to Buckinghamshire. Now Hannah faced a second sister and sensed that Jane was very much closer to Elizabeth than Louisa.

'I do hope we'll be friends, Jane. I've heard so much about you, I already feel we are.' Her smile lingered on Jane's features before she turned to the baby. 'Now Bess, let me see little Robert. Oh! He's adorable,' she said excitedly. 'I should love to have a son. It would make my father so happy.'

'Is he very ill?'

'Yes,' she replied. Then looking down into Catherine's pretty upturned face she smiled. 'Hello Catherine darling. My word, what a pretty little girl you are.'

Elizabeth smiled. 'She's a miniature of you.'

The chauffeur took the suitcases from the porter and led the way to the car. Jane sat in the front of the gleaming maroon Rolls-Royce and the two friends with the children climbed in the back. As the car left the station, Hannah took Elizabeth's hand.

'You look happy, Bess. When you first wrote and said you were married I was very cross. Why didn't you wait for me to come over and be with you?'

'It happened so quickly and I didn't want David to escape me a second time.'

'I'm very happy for you, really', Hannah said squeezing Elizabeth's hand, 'but… how do you manage?'

'Manage?'

'A gardener cannot earn very much.'

'Why does everything have to come down to money?'

'I've offended you, Bess. Forgive me.'

'You haven't. Our needs are simple. The allowance money I have and that which I earn teaching English, and what David earns, allows us a comfortable life. It also buys some extras such as travelling here to see you. We're not in need of anymore.'

'I shall give you some money to cover the expense of travelling up to Yorkshire.'

'No you will not Hannah Wyatt. Any more mention of it and I *will* be offended.'

Hannah returned the smile and looked at the baby in Elizabeth's arms. With a gentle touch, she stroked his forehead. 'I am pleased to have lost you to someone who loves and cares for you.'

'You have not lost me to anyone. You will always be very dear to me… always. Anyway, how are you Hannah, now you're the wife of a Minister of State?'

'I try not to get involved in Edward's work. One meets so many odious people.'

Elizabeth laughed. 'My mother sent me a newspaper cutting showing a photograph of the new minister's wife. "*Society beauty, Lady Hannah Wyatt, daughter of the Earl of Kepwick,*" it said, and very beautiful you looked too. I was so proud seeing you in the newspaper like that. You're very photogenic Hannah, and you know it, you conceited thing, smiling the way you did. I know that smile.'

Hannah flashed another. 'I've had a few letters from the old gang since that was published, one saying that they heard that you had survived the war. Why don't we have a reunion? I think it would be rather nice to see how the others are doing.'

'As long as it's in France and you are prepared to travel over.'

'I'm sorry I had to cancel my visit last month. What with Pa hanging on by his fingernails, it's been a nightmare. I couldn't just leave my mother on her own... you know how it is. Still, you write such lovely letters and you're here now.'

'How ill is your father?'

Hannah shrugged. 'The doctors aren't hopeful, but he's a tough old bird. I'm staying at Mountfields just in case the worst does happen. That's why I dragged you up to Yorkshire. Edward will be coming up this evening so you'll see him at dinner; along with my ghastly cousin and his awful wife, I'm afraid. They have almost moved into the place. They cannot wait to get their hands on the family silver.'

'Storks may carry us into this world, but vultures will see us out.'

'How very true, Bess darling.'

*

The car slowly made its way through the open, vivid green countryside with sloping fields full of sheep, growing lambs, and cattle with calves all grazing lazily in the spring afternoon. It looked so different from the flat, broken fields of Picardy, where few sheep grazed among the ghosts of men who had died in their hundreds of thousands. Gangrenous grey scars of the battlefield were beginning to heal and now produced a flush of colour. It was an area with dozens of monuments and many cemeteries along small roads between the hamlets and villages, in the middle of fields surrounded by crops and bordering the back of people's gardens. Future generations would stop and walk along the rows of names and shake their heads in disbelief. Others would not stop. They would continue their journey unknowing they had crossed a place where a generation of young men had come to die and where women now go to weep.

'How's Louisa?' Hannah said casually, waking Elizabeth from her thoughts.

'She's well. We had a long sisterly chat. I'm sure you know why. Since I married David and have had another child, she considers me back on the straight and narrow. She blames you, of course.'

'What is she up to these days?'

215

'She now runs the farm with Bertie.'

'Runs a farm! Simpson is a bank clerk, surely?'

'Bertie comes from farming stock. He's taken to it naturally and loves it. Jane's husband has the adjoining farm so he helps out if they need it. They're both very happy. The best news,' Elizabeth said smiling, 'is that my father-in-law is now my stepfather; it was all those visits to the hospital.'

Hannah glanced at Elizabeth and smiled. She took her hand and, for the next few miles, the young women's minds were locked in private thoughts until they arrived at the gates of Mountfields. It was as though they were approaching a Greek temple. Two great columns supported an arch, between which hung the huge black, wrought iron gates, with golden speared tips glinting in the sun. Either side of the columns stood a lodge each housing a single man who worked on the estate. The railings extended left and right, stretching, it seemed, forever. The car entered the estate passing neatly trimmed lawns and gardens that had taken centuries to mature. Then it travelled over an ornate bridge spanning a river that flowed past a huge lake. Beyond the lake stood a huge, magnificent building, which shone yellow in the sunlight. It was too big and too grand for Elizabeth to comprehend. She gasped and turned to Hannah who was totally unaffected by it. 'Hannah! *This* is Mountfields?'

'Yes. It's a barn of a place.'

'And you left it for a wooden hut in Pirbright?'

Hannah laughed. 'And you came to my rescue. You didn't think I would stick it, did you? Be honest. I don't think you even liked me.'

Elizabeth looked at the house and was now even more impressed with Hannah, because she had given up such great comfort to help in the war. She leaned over and kissed Hannah's cheek. 'I *did* like you. I fell in love with you, remember. I prayed you would stick it and you did. I was, and still am, very proud of you.'

Hannah squeezed Elizabeth's hand. 'I felt I was doing something useful for once. I'd lost the man I was going to marry, what was I to do? I was simply rotting in that place.'

The car drew up alongside the wide stone steps leading to the huge oak front door. Lady Somerville greeted them in the grand hall. She looked down at Catherine with a smile, her eyes lingering with affection on the pretty little upturned face. Elizabeth watched the Countess caress Catherine's cheek and was touched by her show of affection. The Countess turned her attention to the baby then to

Elizabeth. She offered a smile.

'Hannah tells me you married Catherine's father.'

'Yes.'

'Good... very good. I've heard the story of how you were both reunited; quite fascinating.' The Countess nodded approvingly and focussed her eyes on Jane.

'May I introduce you to my sister, Mrs Jane Tidmarsh?'

Lady Somerville looked into Jane's face and took in her features. 'How do you do, Mrs Tidmarsh? You have your sister's good looks, but not her sharp tongue, I trust.'

'Robins, there will be an extra place at dinner and make up another room for Mrs Tidmarsh,' Hannah said. Robins bowed and disappeared.

The Countess took another long look at Jane then turned to Elizabeth. 'You must sit beside me at dinner this evening, Mrs Shepherd. We can have a little chat.'

*

After a bath, Elizabeth went to Jane's room and threw herself onto the bed. 'Welcome to how the other half lives.'

'God, I'm feeling sick with nerves about dinner tonight. They're not my sort of people, Bess. I mean, just look at this place, it's a palace. We're not used to this... at least I'm not. You seem to have fitted in very nicely. And this frock, I look awful.'

'Jane you look lovely, you always do. I'll ask Hannah to sit you close to me.'

'Yes, please do that. I like Hannah. She seems very nice, but her mother! Did you see the way she looked at me? As if I had crawled from under what a cow left behind.'

Elizabeth laughed and embraced her sister. 'She's not such a dragon when you get to know her. At first I thought I would hate her, but she seems to have made an effort to be kind to me. Now I like her very much. She adores Catherine. I haven't quite worked out why.'

'She collared me when you went to the nursery, wanting to know about David... damn cheek. She probably thinks he's beneath you being a gardener.' Jane sneered, 'After all Bess, you're almost one of them now.'

Elizabeth frowned. 'No I'm not and never will be! What did you tell her about David?'

'I simply said that it was better to ask you. That I hardly know him.' Jane let out another sigh when she looked down at the dress she had chosen to wear for dinner. 'What time does this awful charade begin?'

'Dinner is at eight, but we're expected to gather beforehand for drinks. It allows the guests a chance to meet each other before we sit at the table... apparently.'

'For heaven's sake don't abandon me.'

Elizabeth kissed Jane's cheek. 'Let's explore the place. We have time.'

'I don't mind. What about Catherine and Robert?'

'Hannah's nanny is looking after them. That's how they do things,' and catching sight of Jane's disapproving eyes, she added, 'Don't worry, next week I shall return to being a French peasant.'

Jane smiled and looked around the sumptuous room. 'I suppose could become rather used to this. Come on then, let's take a look at this palace.'

*

They descended the stairs and walked down a long corridor that led to another. They passed deserted rooms encrusted with ornamentation from another age. Silent rooms where footfalls are absorbed by carpets so heavy, so thick, that one hears no step, as though the very ear were far away from the gilt and the splendour; far from the elaborate frieze with branches and garlands of golden leaves.

At the end of the corridor, Elizabeth followed Jane into a suite of perfect symmetry and unprecedented elegance strewn with deep, sumptuous sofas. They fell into one, exhausted by the magnificence around them. Elizabeth closed her eyes, smiled, and shook her head in disbelief. In France, when some of the girls boasted about the money their fathers had, Hannah never once even hinted at such wealth in her family. Her mind returned to France and she remembered Hannah on her hands and knees scrubbing out the back of her ambulance. She looked up as Elizabeth passed, smiled, puffed out her cheeks and wiped her forehead with the back of her hand...

'I bet you're thinking about David... aren't you?'

'What makes you think that?'

'Because you are displaying the expression of a lovesick, fourteen-year old.'

Elizabeth smiled at Jane. They looked around the room and saw enormous portraits of men in uniform, history unfolding itself from other wars; men whose eyes stared at them wherever they turned as though they had no right to sit in their presence. Through the generations, they followed the young viscounts and earls - a proud

Elizabethan, a pompous Stuart, and an earl of Queen Anne. A stern-looking general serving the German King George, a Regency gentleman, a dandy like his king, then an early Victorian, smart in red with gold braid. Next, a portrait of the last in the present line, who lay unwell in his bed in one of the state bedrooms - there was space for many more, as though the Somerville family knew their dynasty would never end.

The sisters rose from the sofa without saying a word. While Jane walked into an annexed room, Elizabeth went to the window and watched the sun begin to sink into the horizon, taking with it what was left of the warmth of the day. She focussed on a gardener finishing his work. She would sometimes walk with Catherine and Robert to meet David on his way home with Jacko, then, after aperitifs, they would all have dinner together.

Elizabeth felt hungry yet she was not looking forward to dinner. Lord and Lady Westerland and their snobby friends were definitely not her choice of table companions, but she would not let them upset her - never again. No one could upset her now - she was far too happy. 'Jane, where are you?'

A little flushed; Jane appeared from the annexe and motioned to Elizabeth. 'Bess, come through here a moment.'

'We really ought to be getting back.'

'Quickly then. This won't take a minute.'

Elizabeth took Jane's outstretched hand and was led by her sister into the room. She followed the direction of her pointed finger. Her eyes settled on the young aristocratic face, and she almost choked on her intake of breath as she stared open-mouthed at the portrait of her husband.

'It is David, isn't it?'

Elizabeth could say nothing. She had seen it all the time yet had been blind to it. Now it was obvious. Hannah and David were so alike; no wonder she kept seeing one when looking at the other.

Panic overwhelmed her. 'Let's get out of here, Jane. I want to leave. We'll collect the children and—'

'Bess, calm down! You can't just leave! You *must* tell them.'

'No, no. I can't do that. It will ruin everything.'

'Bess, stop shaking, calm down. You have to tell them. They have a right to know. How could you live with yourself if you don't?'

'I need time to think about this. God… I feel sick.' She sat down and looked up into her husband's eyes. 'Oh David,' she whispered, 'what will become of us now?'

She picked up a silver frame from the table and studied the photograph. Hannah was standing between two young men wearing khaki. Her arms were linked through theirs and all three were smiling brightly. One of the men was David, her brother James, the other Elizabeth considered, was Guy. In another photograph, she could see a younger Lady Somerville, a Victorian lady, with her husband and their two young children. Hannah, the little girl sitting with her brother, they were no older than Catherine was now. It might have been Catherine. Is that why the Countess was always so kind, buying her little presents, Elizabeth wondered? Could she imagine the clocks turned back when looking into Catherine's little face, or did she think that her son's child might have looked like Catherine? Could she see a granddaughter in those large blue eyes - and wonder - is it possible?

Elizabeth's head ached. Was it a chance in a million that David came to her mother's farm, one ghost of the war finding another? This was one of those inexplicable coincidences in life, where Elizabeth's path led to Hannah and James's path led to Elizabeth - the crossroads of time bringing them all together.

She wiped her eyes; how happy her life had been for the past fourteen months. How uncomplicated everything was. The simple rustic life destroyed with one glance at a portrait of a young nobleman who was dead to everybody, except the two young women now looking up into his face.

'Bess,' Jane said, taking her hand. 'How are you going to break the news to them?'

Elizabeth dropped onto a chair and placed her face in her hands. She suddenly looked up at Jane. 'Oh my God, Jane! It's all making sense to me now. I think David's memory has returned to him and he isn't letting on.'

'What are you saying?'

'He knows who he is but he doesn't know what to do... about me. Ever since Robert's birth, David has been behaving strangely; he seems restless, even Jacko has mentioned it to me. And he's been asking too many probing questions... until now I have been blind to them. Whenever I look up his eyes are on me, critically, as if he is asking himself whether he has done the right thing marrying me.'

Jane gasped. 'He adores you. Everyone knows that.'

'But if his memory has returned and he knows he is James Somerville, then I could become an embarrassment to him. You said it yourself Jane, we don't fit in.'

'I'm not listening to this–'

'Jane, listen to me. I had to almost fight him to come over here, even for a few days. He really didn't want to come to England. He kept making excuses about work. Now I know why. Can you imagine if he had turned up? Hannah would have died on the spot. God… I feel my whole world is beginning to full apart again. Oh why did I come here… why?' Her voice was almost lost as the dinner gong began to vibrate around the Grand Hall.

*

During dinner, Elizabeth looked around the table at her new family and their friends. Edward was talking with Jane. She seemed comfortable in his company. As she looked, Jane glanced up and smiled. Dearest Jane. There was not only the bond of blood between them, but love, trust and friendship. Seated further along the table, Lady Westerland, who had earlier cut her dead, was looking around the room as if changing the furnishings in her mind. Lord Westerland's cold eyes, which had looked straight through her when she acknowledged him, were now fixed across the room at one of the paintings hanging on the wall. Elizabeth knew she would never like the Westerlands. She felt some satisfaction knowing that Mountfields would no longer be theirs, but went cold when she realised she would one day be the mistress of this house.

Then there was her mother-in-law, the Countess, stately and aloof, chatting to a bishop as if nothing bothered her except the order of life. Behind her cold exterior there was warmth. Elizabeth wondered if the noble lady would ever accept her. Would she try to have the marriage annulled? It was one thing being a friend to her daughter, but quite another thing marrying her son and the heir to all this. The thought of that made her shoulders sink at the enormity of it. She caught Hannah's smile. Dearest Hannah who always wished she had a sister, now she has one. Elizabeth looked into the face of her friend and felt no shame in loving her the way that she had. Hannah returned her smile. It was *that* smile, the smile Elizabeth knew came from the heart. It was her brother's smile. David's smile.

'Mrs Shepherd! You must forgive me; I have been neglecting you. You looked quite pale earlier. Now you seem in another world. Are you feeling unwell? I do hope you will not pass out on us again.'

'I'm fine, thank you. I was miles away.'

'In France I expect, thinking of your husband.'

221

'Actually, I was thinking of Hannah.'

'Ah yes… Hannah,' she said, noticing her daughter's eyes on Elizabeth. 'You two are certainly good friends. One cannot help but see that.'

Elizabeth felt herself blush. 'She is a remarkable woman, Lady Somerville. During the war she just got on with things without ever complaining, however bad the situation. Nothing could dampen her spirit. She certainly was an inspiration to me.'

Lady Somerville took Elizabeth's hand into hers and patted it. In her eyes she showed a sudden look of affection. 'Elizabeth… when Hannah returned from France in 1918, she was unwell. The doctor called it post traumatic stress or some other nonsense. Of course, Hannah was distraught. At night, I would sit by her bed and watch her toss and turn, mumbling a name, your name, in her sleep. During the day she wept. Such tears only come from the heart, Elizabeth. I needed her to overcome her grief and to forget this name, Bess, which continuously choked from her lips. I knew Edward was in love with her, so I invited him to stay and I encouraged a liaison between them. It worked. Now they seem very happy together…'

'I am no threat to their marriage, Lady Somerville.'

'Let her go, Elizabeth. Let her go.'

Elizabeth's hand was still under Lady Somerville's but now the grip was tighter. 'I have no power over Hannah, quite the reverse. We have seen and been through so much and are tied together through it, but *that* knot is cut. I have a husband whom I love and adore, and another child to care for. But I will always love Hannah, always... as a sister.'

'Yes, I'm aware what you've been through together. Hannah has told me. You both have my admiration,' the Countess said, loosening her grip on Elizabeth's hand. 'Elizabeth, when I first met you, I didn't like you. You were a young lady with a propensity to break free from social conventions. As time passed, I began to admire your spirit.' Lady Somerville's mind seemed to disappear into the past and when it returned it brought a smile to her lips. 'Hannah tells me that you care for my son's grave. That's kind of you, and I thank you from my heart, but I do not feel that James occupies that piece of France. I never have,' she said, pausing to take another drink. 'I think my son is out there. For some reason something is preventing him from returning home. Like the loss of a memory for instance, as your husband has lost his. Do you think me mad?'

'What do you see in Catherine that deserves so much of your

222

attention? Does she remind you of Hannah when she was that age?'

The Countess picked up her glass of wine and took a sip. She smiled and looked over towards Hannah who was now chatting with Jane. 'Yes… Catherine does have an uncanny likeness to Hannah when she was a child... and to James too,' she said, with such a piercing look that it almost stabbed Elizabeth in the eyes, 'but it is not Hannah I see when looking into your little girl's eyes, I see James. Mothers see more than others do, Elizabeth. I notice certain mannerisms in Catherine that I used to see in my son; the way she tips her head when she smiles, certain gestures one inherits from one's parents, the things she does that he used to do… do you understand that? There's another thing, quiet uncanny really, Catherine has a birthmark on her arm identical to one James has on his. I mentioned this to Hannah, but she thinks I'm a silly old fool who will not accept that my son is dead.' Elizabeth sat in silence. 'I'd like you to look at something, Elizabeth,' the Countess said.

Elizabeth took the photograph and looked into the eyes of her husband. She could feel Lady Somerville's eyes on her, waiting for a reaction. There was no reaction, because the revelation was no longer a surprise to her. A smile crept to Elizabeth's lips as she studied his features. She loved that face, but not as much as the face she loved now. Then, she did not know that face, the proud young aristocrat who was born to inherit titles and land, to find a wife and beget a son, to perpetuate the name of Somerville. Would he have spoken to her then - or even have looked at her? The face she knew now was of a different man, an ordinary working man. They lived and worked as other families lived and worked. His rough hands were often dirty, his nails broken. She scrubbed his back in the bathtub, washed and ironed his clothes, cooked for him. He made love to her in the fields. He handed her his wages. She went with them to the market, chatting with other women performing the same daily tasks. Now all that would end.

Elizabeth went to her vanity bag and pulled out a photograph that she had packed in her luggage to show Hannah, but in the excitement of meeting her, forgot.

'I saw James's portrait in one of your rooms. For the past hour I have been struggling to find a way to tell you...' Instead of saying more, she handed over the photograph of James holding Catherine's hand.

Hannah looked across at Elizabeth and observed her mother holding her friend's hand as though her life depended on its grasp. The conversation between them seemed so intense there might have been no others in the room. Hannah now gave them her undivided attention. She watched her mother pass what looked like a photograph to Elizabeth. She watched Elizabeth go to her bag and give a photograph to her mother. She watched her mother cover her mouth with her hand to smother a cry, which brought the room to sudden silence and all those round the table were drawn towards the Countess and Elizabeth. The gentlemen rose from their seats as Hannah stood and went to her mother and Jane to her sister.

'Is my aunt unwell?' cried Lord Westerland. 'Shall I fetch a doctor?'

'Please do not fuss,' Lady Somerville said, regaining her composure. 'Elizabeth, Hannah, come with me, we need to speak to your father. If any news will get him out of bed then it will be this.'

Hannah gave Elizabeth an enquiring look as she followed them from the room.

*

The following morning at breakfast, Elizabeth looked tired; she had hardly slept because Hannah and she had talked long into the early hours. When the Countess entered the dining room, Elizabeth asked how the Earl was feeling.

'You have given him the will to live, my dear. He wants to see you again and asks when he can see James.'

'I'll leave for France this morning, Lady Somerville.'

'*Mamma*, Elizabeth. Now you must call me, Mamma.'

'Yes… Mamma,' Elizabeth said, her eyes finding Jane whose smile was quickly hidden behind her napkin.

'Bess, may I go with you?' Hannah asked.

'I'd like nothing more.'

'Elizabeth,' the Countess said, taking a seat beside her. 'I must tell you this. In the past I was always concerned about the women who befriended my son. They had a great deal to gain by marriage to him. In my heart, I was suspicious of every woman's motive for befriending him, but you took him for what he is and not for what he has. For that, you have my love and blessing. Now, I have something for you,' she continued. 'This ring has been handed down for the past four-hundred years by each Countess to the bride of her eldest son on their wedding day. I never thought I would have that pleasure, but now I have. Here, see if it fits you. I know you are legally married to my son Elizabeth,

but perhaps you would consider having another wedding ceremony…
for the family, in the chapel where the Somervilles have married for
the past four-hundred years. There I shall give you the ring, as James'
grandmother gave it to me. Ah Robins!' said Lady Somerville as he
entered the room. 'Have a car brought round for the Viscountess
Deerfield.'

'The Viscountess Deerfield, my Lady?'

'Yes Robins, my daughter-in-law, my son's wife.'

The words made Jane's shoulders shake as she tried to control her
amusement, which only Elizabeth understood.

Chapter **13**

A soldier's return

James Somerville sat on the chalky soil and set his gaze towards the great Lochnager crater. He remembered what a spectacular sight it had been when it exploded on the morning of the Somme battle. He could see in his mind how that part of France reached high into the sky, its descent sending a cloud of dust across no man's land like early morning fog. Moments later he had led his company over the top towards that crater. He among just a few of them survived the day. For five years now he had worked on the bloody soil of 1916, particularly around the area of La Boisselle that had claimed the lives of the men under his command. Somehow, tending their graves had been a healing process for him, a humbling experience, like Christ washing the feet of sinners. Each day he walked the lines of Portland stone as he had once walked the ranks of his men on parade, inspecting each individual plot as he had stood before each individual soul, remembering the fresh young faces of his command. Now, at last, he had come to terms with that day and no longer had nightmares or felt the heavy burden of guilt for surviving it.

James rolled some tobacco into a cigarette and lit it, allowing the smoke to climb and thin into a sky of low cumulus cloud. A smile crept to his lips when he thought of those in England who would disapprove of him rolling tobacco with the expertise of a common labouring man, something he now had been for several years. His eyes wandered towards Gordon Dump Cemetery, in which some poor nameless soul was under that soil, not he, probably one of the many unidentified men from his company. It amused him to wonder which rogue he once knew had been elevated to the peerage.

James Somerville's memory had returned to him as it had left him, in an instant, the very night his son Robert was born. Elizabeth was asleep, exhausted with the effort of bringing Robert into the world. Sylvie appeared from the bedroom and went to him, brushing the hair from his eyes. 'You look tired, David. Go to bed. I will look after Elizabeth.' He was tired yet so deeply happy. Somehow he felt complete. He had replaced himself in the chain of life.

He stood at his wife's bed and looked down into her sleeping face. He worshipped her. He pressed his lips to hers. She did not stir as she normally did when he climbed into bed late at night and kissed her. He bent and kissed her lips again. Still she did not stir. Sylvie saw the look of complete affection in his eyes as he gazed into his wife's peaceful face. She went to him and held him in her arms. 'She needs you too, David. Your absence was misery to her.'

'When you were both prisoners, what did she suffer—'

'That is for her to say, not me.'

'Was it very bad?'

'David, the past is past. Let it remain so.'

They stood in an embrace for a minute then each kissed the other's cheeks and parted. He left the room and leaned against the sideboard with tired, closed eyes. When he opened them they focused on a photograph that Elizabeth had brought back from England after her mother's marriage to George Turner. He had looked at the picture many times, admiring the beauty of Elizabeth's friend and the brilliance of his wife's smile. Now, as he stared into the beautiful face of his sister, it was as if he had just woken from a long sleep and she was sitting by his bedside smiling at him again.

'Hannah.'

At first it seemed incredible to him that the friend Elizabeth once called Cathy and now Hannah, was his twin sister. He staggered from the house. Each step he took turned another page of his life. Each page carried another picture. Each picture revealed more of his past. He dragged himself along the same path that had taken him from Albert to the trenches. He crossed the same field in which his battalion had been destroyed advancing towards the German wire. He found himself standing in a cemetery gazing at a slab of Portland stone with his name on it.

The following week, Elizabeth held Robert in her arms and released her breast from her blouse. Robert hungrily fed on his mother, while his father's eyes lifted towards the photograph of Elizabeth with Hannah. David asked her to tell him about her friend. As he listened, he was shocked to hear that she had married Edward Wyatt and not Guy Wakenshaw. Edward was a decent enough fellow, but he thought that it was Guy Hannah loved. Was Guy dead? Now he would learn which of his friends had not survived the war.

'David darling, what's the matter? You seem miles away these days.'

He was. He was in Yorkshire. How could he just return? Did he want to return? Yes, he loved his family but he now loved Elizabeth more. He had got used to the life he now had. Mountfields and all it represents would be another world to him now. Often he would leave the house to be alone and think of the consequences of informing Elizabeth who he really was. Everything would change, except, he hoped, his wife's love for him, but Elizabeth would not like the change, he knew.

The following day after Robert's feed and while Catherine was having a nap, he met Elizabeth's eyes and asked, 'Would you like to live in luxury, as your friend does?'

Elizabeth laughed, almost in relief rather than amusement. 'Is that why you are looking so glum these days? Do you think that I want what Hannah has and you are unable to provide it for me? I imagine she would give everything she has in return for the happiness I have now.'

'Isn't she happy? Doesn't her husband love her?'

'I rarely saw them together, but I'm sure he does. I love her,' she smiled. 'I love her very much as I'm sure you would too, but you would probably fall in love with her. Everyone does. She's so beautiful.'

He closed his eyes and saw Hannah's face in his mind. Yes, he did love her. She was twenty when he last saw her, now she would be almost thirty. Was it now time to tell Elizabeth that his memory had returned; reveal to her his identity, Hannah's twin brother...

'The diamond pendant you've been wearing, where did you get it?' James asked.

'David, I told you, Hannah gave it to me. It wasn't a man,' she said teasingly. 'It was a present to her from her brother James. She said it's her most treasured possession,' Elizabeth said tucking it out of sight, for she did not like to expose such an expensive jewel, even to the man she loved. 'Because she loved her brother so much it makes the gift more special to me. I accepted it in the spirit it was given, but if she ever wanted it back, I would never refuse to return it to her.' She looked up from her sewing and said, 'What do you think, darling? Should I give it back? Should I have accepted such an expensive and sentimental gift in the first place? Do you think her brother would have approved?'

'I'm sure he would have. Anyway, it's hers to give. It looks well on you.'

Elizabeth met his eyes and smiled at him then began to sew another button on his shirt. After a little silence she said, 'I wonder what my tutor at Somerville would think of me now.'

'Somerville?'

'Oxford, darling. Isn't it strange that it should be Hannah's family name? No connection though. Dr Hodge, my tutor, had high hopes of me being a writer.'

'You are. Your book was published. You earned a decent sum from it too.'

James watched her complete the final few stitches and inspect her work. She noticed a small tear. She eagerly threaded another needle with white cotton and began the delicate work of making another repair.

'My tutor sent me a copy asking me to sign it for her.' Elizabeth smiled at the memory of it. 'She even enclosed the return postage. I'm glad I kept in touch with her.'

James nodded, but said nothing. The room was silent other than the metronomic ticking of the clock. Her lashes lifted and caught his eyes fixed solidly on her.

'Why are you looking at me like that? What are you thinking?'

Tell her who you are. Tell her, tell her now! 'Because I love you...'

Her eyes brightened and she looked happy. 'Are you feeling frisky? Do you want to go upstairs?' When he said nothing, she added, 'I love you too David darling, very much.'

My name is James, James... 'Are you looking forward to your trip?'

'Why don't you come with me next month? Hannah is dying to meet you and you really could do with a break. You work far too hard.'

Hannah's face came to his mind. 'There's a great deal of work to do, what with all the new memorials and additional cemeteries, and we are unearthing corpses all the time. It's such melancholy work.'

'That's why you need a break. If you are making excuses not to go because you think you will feel out of place among Hannah's family, you won't. I swear it. You are as much a gentleman as any of them, whatever your employment. Hannah's mother can be a little intimidating, but I'm sure she'll like you. Actually, she's been encouraging me to bring you over to stay at Mountfields, which is her Yorkshire home. It sounds a little too grand for me. She probably wants to thank you for making an honest woman of me.' Her eyes met his and she smiled. 'I like her. She has shown me kindness and is very affectionate towards our Catherine. Edward can be a bit stuffy, but he probably will not home anyway. Lord Westerland, Hannah's cousin, and his hideous wife, are snobs. I don't think you would like them – *no, he didn't* - and Hannah is… well Hannah. You must promise me not to fall in love with her when you meet her. All men do. I don't want to lose you to my best friend.'

'You will never lose me to anyone.'

'Make that promise once you've met her. She can be a little insensitive at times, but it's simply her upbringing.'

'Her upbringing?'

'Hannah's a toff, darling. She belongs to a different world than ours, or at least mine. You sound as if you would fit in perfectly. As Jacko says, 'Davy is a toff if ever I sees one.' Her playful laugh made James' heart sink. 'Jacko is so funny. I do love him.'

'Are you happy? You look happy.'

'I have never been so happy. This rustic life suits me. Lady Somerville once said she envied my freedom, can you believe that?' She laughed at a memory. 'Did I ever tell you that she once bent and kissed Catherine and the little rascal hugged the noble lady and called her grandma? I was so embarrassed, but Lady Somerville seemed to enjoy it. Her eyes positively lit up.' Elizabeth paused from her sewing and suddenly furrowed her brow. 'It made me realize that Catherine does have another grandmother somewhere and we really ought to make an effort to find her. We've never tried, David. I'm surprised you haven't made the effort. I wish one morning you would wake up and with it, your memory too.'

'The doctors are convinced it will return. They say a shock normally does it as it did to take it away.'

'Then how can I shock you? I'm sure I can.'

'Nothing you could do or tell me would ever shock me.'

'Oh yes... that's what Angel Clare said to Teresa D'Urberville on their wedding night. Thomas Hardy got it right there. Confessions are meant for God through his Earthly agents, not for mere mortals such as husband and wife.'

James smiled. 'So you have secrets?'

'Yes and they will remain secrets.'

He went to her and kissed her, and then he took the diamond pendant in his hand and looked at it. 'Yes, I'm certain Hannah's brother would have given you something like this if he had met you.'

'I doubt it. Men of his class do not give girls of mine gifts like this unless they have an ulterior motive.'

'Why do you say that?' he said returning to his chair.

'I met plenty of toffs at Oxford. They mostly tried it on. I found them rather insufferable in their conceit and pompous disregard for ordinary people. I stayed well clear of them. Although, when I returned to Oxford after the war, I have to say those who had fought in France were changed men.'

'How so?'

'They had been released from their gilded cages and forced to share a trench infested with rats and the class they despised. It must have been a sobering experience for many of them.'

'You're rather harsh on them. Do you see Hannah's brother like that?'

'I didn't know Hannah's brother, darling. He was killed. I'm talking about his kind, the Oxford dandies, the toffs, the Lord Westerlands. It was only by chance Hannah and I met the way we did, otherwise we would never have met. How could we have met, we don't mix in the same circles?'

'You like her though—'

'Like her! I adore her. She accepts me for who I am, but I don't know about her family. I really don't think I'll ever be truly accepted by her family and friends, because my father was a schoolmaster, which in their eyes is nothing. I know this by her cousin's disdain for me... and they're not afraid to show it. Many cover it up behind their smiles. You see darling, they stick to their own kind. The likes of me are to bed, not to wed. We are their playthings.' She looked over to him and put down her sewing. 'Oh darling, what a sad expression.'

'I think you're being unfairly cynical.'

'David you're the father of my children and the love of my life, nothing will ever change that, even if you were Lord Thing-a-me-bob or Sir What's-his-name Smyth. I just don't care for any other life than the one we have now. I love it here.'

'I have to go out,' he said. 'Jacko will need help at Fricourt. There's a new cemetery we're building there.'

'You're cross with me.'

'I'm not. I simply think you judge your friend's class too harshly, particularly as you never met any of the friends Hannah's brother had before the war.'

'I've met Edward, he's decent enough; no, actually, he's nice. I like him and Ralph Nugent, he was a sweetie. Perhaps you're right. Perhaps I am judging them all on the likes of Lord and Lady Westerland and some of the Oxford louts. If James Somerville were alive, I think he may have been one of the 'good guys' as Emma would have said; do you remember Emma, from Oxford? The American—'

'Yes, tall, good-looking and enjoys tennis, and from the way she looked at you I expect you two were once lovers.'

Elizabeth stopped sewing. She was silent for a moment then said, 'We were.' Their eyes met. The world seemed so quiet they might have heard a spider cross the room. With a toss of the head Elizabeth said, 'Is that shocking enough for you to regain your memory?'

'And Hannah?'

'No,' Elizabeth said without shifting her gaze. 'I love her as one would love a sister.' She knew it would do no good to bare her soul completely. After confessing Emma, denying Hannah would have a strong ring of truth about it. One day David would meet her and Elizabeth wanted them to be friends.

He went to her and he kissed her cheek. At the door he turned, 'It's the future I care about Elizabeth, not the past,' he said. He put on his cap and smiled at her before leaving the house.

*

James smoked the last of his cigarette then extinguished what little was left of it. In the distance he saw a Rolls-Royce limousine approaching the cemetery in which he had left Jacko working. They had come for him, as he knew they would when he discovered that Elizabeth was going to Mountfields and not Burton Manor as planned. Once at Mountfields, she would soon discover his identity, and when she did, their life in France would be at an end.

He climbed to his feet; the soldier must now return, but first he would have to play out the last scene of this tragedy. To his audience his memory would return to him gradually; his family and friends would slowly begin to see him begin to remember his past and those in it. He must give no clue that for several months he has known that David Shepherd and James Somerville, the Viscount Deerfield, are the same man. And Elizabeth, what was she feeling right now? He would do everything in his power to prevent his mother moulding her into a Somerville. Elizabeth must not change. Yet, she is a Somerville and all that goes with the name.

He stood and headed in the direction of where the Rolls-Royce had stopped.

*

Elizabeth now had to try and convince Jacko to return to England with them, but in her heart she knew that he would never leave France and the cemeteries that he cared for.

'Bess!' Jacko said walking towards her eyeing the car. 'What on earth are yer doing back? I thought yer were gone for a week?'

'Things have changed, Jacko. Do you remember my friend, Lady Hannah Wyatt?'

'Err... yea, 'ow do, me Lady. Very smart car if yer'll permit me boldness.'

'Mr Jacks, how lovely to see you again,' Hannah said with a beaming smile.

Elizabeth glanced at Hannah and was touched by her friendly manner. 'Jacko, let's sit down. I have something to tell you.'

Elizabeth held his hand in both of hers and explained the whole story to him. When she had finished, Jacko's wrinkled and weathered face showed little emotion.

'I shall miss yer both, and the little ones,' he said sadly. 'Yer all the family I 'ave, so to speak.'

'Please... come back with us Jacko,' Elizabeth said earnestly. 'You'll be well cared for, for the rest of your life.'

He glanced round the cemetery then looked at Hannah. 'I'm not surprised who 'e is, me Lady. The lad's a proper gent... always was.'

'Mr Jacks... Bess is right, you must return with us. James will want that.'

'Fancy Davie being 'is Lordship all this time, eh. See over there,' he said pointing. 'We used to sit and 'is eyes would be glued to that gravestone, the one with Viscount Deerfield's name on it, as if 'e knew the feller. Well, 'e'll get to know 'im a lot better in the next few days, so 'e can do it without me 'anging about looking like a spare wotsit at a wedding - begging your pardon, me Lady. France is where I belong now with all me other mates. These lads might be dead, but I've got to know every one of 'em. Call me mad if yer like, but I talk to them. 'Morning lads,' I says and they say morning back, but only I can 'ear them. I can't leave 'em now, who would look after them as well as me and Davie 'ave always done if we both leave?'

Elizabeth leant towards Jacko, placed an arm round his shoulder and kissed his mouth.

Hannah looked on disapprovingly.

Jacko looked up beyond the road and saw James heading their way. 'Stand by yer beds. This is 'is Lordship coming now.'

Hannah stood. 'James,' she whispered. The tears that now filled her

233

eyes began to roll down her cheeks as she ran towards him.

*

At Mountfields, the preparations for James' return were complete.
Rooms had been aired to accommodate family and James' closest
friends, and the kitchen was busy preparing an elaborate dinner, to be
served once James and Elizabeth had rested. The staff gleamed in their
smartest livery.

From within the house, Christina looked out of a window at the vast
manicured lawns and parkland. She shook her head in disbelief. 'Bess,
my love, if your poor Papa could see this now, he'd turn in his grave,'
she whispered to the ghost of her reflection staring back from the
window pane.

Now Christina was in the home of the young man who had been
thrown out of hers. Jane had telephoned and explained everything. She
and George Turner were on a train later that evening by special
invitation of the Countess. Shortly after they had arrived at
Mountfields, Lady Somerville invited Christina to her private rooms
for tea and endlessly thanked her for giving her son a home on the
farm.

'Elizabeth told me how it was you who took him from the hospital
and cared for him. I must tell you how proud I am to have your
Elizabeth as my daughter-in-law,' she said. 'I see in her eyes the love
she has for my son every time she speaks of him… and the
grandchildren we share are adorable.'

Christina, who still felt some guilt for the way James had been
treated, offered Lady Somerville a weak smile. 'Elizabeth has always
loved your son, Lady Somerville. When he was completely alone in
the world, it was Elizabeth who stood by him and loved him.'

*

When at last it was almost time for the car to arrive, Robins, with
the precision and authority of a Regimental Sergeant-Major, lined up
all the household staff as if a guard of honour up the steps to the house.
They looked as smart as the Grenadier Guards, with whom James had
once served. He then went to the drawing room where the family was
having drinks.

The room went deathly quiet when Robins entered, announcing that
the car was approaching the house. It was arranged that only the Earl
and Countess should greet him on the steps, with their granddaughter
Catherine, and Robert in the arms of a nanny. Then, when James was
in the house, he would make his way to the drawing room to meet the

rest of the family.

From inside the car, James looked about him, his eyes taking in the familiar sights of his past life. He turned to Elizabeth whose absence had once tortured him. Now she seemed tortured herself as she entered his world. He took her hand. 'I love you more than all of this,' he whispered. 'Never forget that, my love.'

Hannah caught the sudden look of happiness in Elizabeth's expression. She turned from her brother and his wife. She too had loved Elizabeth more than all of this and reached for Elizabeth's hand, feeling soft fingers grip hers. The car slowed then stopped outside the great building, alongside the wide steps leading up to the terrace and the huge oak doors. Robins stood at the base of the steps braving the cold wind. He stepped forward and opened the car door, allowing the Viscountess Deerfield to alight first.

'Good afternoon, my Lady,' greeted Robins with a slight bow and what looked like a smile threatening to break his morose features.

Elizabeth smiled. It was a smile Robins already liked. 'Good afternoon, Robins.'

Then out stepped James looking splendid in his uniform. Elizabeth had taken it from his room before she left Mountfields and packed it for his return. 'He left a soldier,' she had said to Lady Somerville, 'and a soldier he will return.'

James straightened himself as he looked up at the building.

'You remember Robins, James darling?'

'How are you, Robins?' He extended his hand, which the older man clasped for only the second time since James' birth. The first was to say goodbye when leaving for the war and now, to welcome him home nearly a decade later.

'Welcome home, my Lord.' Robins said, as though James were returning from a week's shooting in Scotland instead of from the dead.

When Hannah was on her feet, the great front door opened. The Earl was wrapped in a shawl and beside him the Countess holding little Catherine's hand. Behind them both was the nanny with Robert. James took his wife's arm and linked it in his as they climbed the steps followed by Hannah. Robins took up the rear in a ceremonial stride.

Lady Somerville eyed every part and movement of her son. The lame walk, the proud upright manner, the well-shaped head held high and the weathered scar running down the side of his cheek that she had never seen before. Inside she trembled yet to the world she appeared calm. Their eyes met. His smile pierced her heart as it used to when he was a boy. It broke her discipline; she could contain herself no longer. The Countess ignored all the years of training, deportment and dignity, and in one sudden movement rushed towards her son, taking him in a tight embrace.

*

At that very moment across the Channel in France, as Elizabeth entered the great doors at Mountfields, a figure waited as a headstone of white Portland stone was being removed from the ground in the Gordon Dump cemetery. Jacko sucked on his pipe. He watched the two men put another in its place and apply the finishing touches to their work. He read the inscription carved into the gleaming white stone - *An Unknown Soldier of the Great War* and nodded as he took into his care yet another nameless soldier, whom he would call Chum.

The two men picked up the headstone they had just removed and carried it to the horse and cart. Jacko steadied the horse while the men carefully laid it on some sacking. One of the men took a last look at the name before covering it with another sack. *Captain James Somerville, the Viscount Deerfield, VC, MC*. 'What's the story behind this one then, Jacko?'

'They discovered it weren't 'im down there after all. 'E were alive all the time.'

'Trust a bleeding toff to get away with it. So what do you want us to do with this?'

'Take it to my gaff,' Jacko said. 'I'm keeping it so be careful with it.'

'Keeping it? Why, did you know the fellow?'

'Lord Deerfield? No, I didn't mate, but I were best chums with 'is ghost. The best pal any man could ask for.'

The two men looked at each other and grinned. 'You've been out here too long, Jacko. You ought to go back to Blighty like your mate did.'

'He was a strange one, that one,' the other man said. 'It beats me what he was doing here in the first place. I mean, he were a right toff himself. Cracking wife though, Jacko. A right looker. I could have done with a bit of that.'

'You watch yer mouth mate.' Jacko replied and looked up at the darkening clouds.

'You want a lift, Jacko?'

'No mate, I'll walk.'

'Come on Jacko, jump aboard. You'll be caught in a storm. It's

236

going to piss down.'

'It's just a passing storm. I've suffered worse, mate. Jacko can look after 'imself. Always 'as and always will do.'

Jacko sat on the cemetery wall filling his pipe with tobacco and watched the cart slowly disappear over the brow of the hill. He looked up at the leaden clouds that had been piling up all afternoon. Trees and fields stood out under them for a little while, curiously transparent in a vivid golden light: then that vanished and it became almost dark. A storm burst on him, shattering the stillness with lightning and crash upon crash of thunder; trees creaked, bending under a sudden onset of wind, lashing them with heavy rain.

'I've seen worse,' Jacko muttered as he adjusted his cap. 'A bit of rain won't hurt yer.'

He collected his tools and began to make his way back home, singing *Roses are flowering in Picardy*.

End

Lightning Source UK Ltd.
Milton Keynes UK
09 February 2011

167228UK00001B/67/P